The Boy and the Bastard

By Russell Newell

First published by Dog Ear Publishing
4011 Vincennes Rd
Indianapolis, IN 46268
www.dogearpublishing.net

ISBN: 978-1-4575-3670-0

This book is printed on acid-free paper.

Printed in the United States of America

For my dad, who always let me know how
much he loved me.

Table of Contents

Part I

Part II

Part III

What though the radiance which was once so bright
Be now forever taken from my sight,
Though nothing can bring back the hour
Of splendour in the grass, of glory in the flower;
We will grieve not, rather find
Strength in what remains behind;
In the primal sympathy
Which having been must ever be;
In the soothing thoughts that spring
Out of human suffering;
In the faith that looks through death,
In years that bring the philosophic mind.

— William Wordsworth, Intimations of Immortality

CHAPTER 1

The Kingpin

December 24, 1977

"**G**us, you smoked the golden boy!" a young man about 27 years old announced as he burst into Gus's office, a small crowd trailing behind him. "You are the king! Nice work!"

Gus Delaney forced a smile and stood; a silhouette against the window outside of which the skyline of Boston bowed before him. His desk was covered with stacks of economic data of companies that Gus had been studying that day.

"We just got a preview of the latest annual return numbers," another man gushed. "The Elysium Fund crushed the other funds at Fidelity. An annual return of 84%! In a year when the S&P lost double digits! Elysium might have the highest return this year *in the country!*" he said.

They all waited for Gus's response. He sat down again, still smiling a smile that did not reveal his teeth; lips pressed tightly together, his hands crossed on the desk.

His black hair was cropped close, not long and wavy like the style of the day; instead the flat-top of a soldier, with enough hardened gel in it that it looked like you could break the hair off like icicles. He wore a blue pinstriped suit, a crisp white shirt, and brown leather suspenders. Underneath the suit was an athletic, six foot three frame.

The young men who huddled in his office wore their hair long and blow-dried. The suits hanging loosely over their shoulders were plaid, gray and brown, slightly wrinkled. They wore patterned shirts and paisley ties.

"You know already, don't you," the first man, Sean McCormick, said.

Gus nodded and continued to smile. "Yes, Mr. Johnson called me at 7 this morning to tell me," he said. The young men's eyes widened.

"Of course he did," a short man named Michael Palin said. "Why *wouldn't* Ned Johnson call his new star fund manager personally to thank him for making him millions of dollars this year?"

"How did you do it? How did you return 84 percent in this market when everyone else got killed?" McCormick asked.

"You should know by now," Gus said. "Because I'm not scared."

"Scared of what?" Palin asked.

"Anything." Gus looked at them looking at him, waiting for him to give them more.

"Scared to fail," he continued. "All the other guys are scared to fail, and they invest that way. I'm not afraid." Gus tried to gauge their reaction. "Well, I couldn't have done it without all of you," he said finally. "Well, I could have, but it would have been a lot more difficult." He laughed.

"Seriously though, thank you guys for all of your hard work." He opened his desk drawer and took out four small boxes and handed one to each of them. "I got you something for Christmas. It's no big deal. I just wanted you to know how much I appreciate all your long hours and hard work."

"You really didn't have to get us anything," Palin said. He looked at his box.

"It's just something to help spruce up your wardrobe."

Frank Kaplan opened his box first. "Wow, cool!" he said. "This looks like an antique or something." The other three tore their boxes open.

"Really nice," Palin said. Gus had given them each a watch. He examined their faces and knew they didn't realize the value of what he had given them.

"Listen, if you don't like them, let me know and I'll switch them and get you a Rolex."

"What?" Kaplan said. "A Rolex? Aren't those like five-thousand dollars? I'll take the Rolex." He laughed it off like a joke but Gus could see he was serious.

"That's fine, but before you do, I'll tell you that your watch is much more valuable than the Rolex I'd get you, at least in my mind. These are Hamilton Byrd watches. They are extremely rare and are from the Explorer series made in 1930. They are solid 14-karat yellow gold. Only 285 were made, and these are in mint condition. Anybody can get a Rolex. These are much more interesting. Besides, I can't have my team looking like a bunch of slobs, you know what I mean? Now if you don't mind, I've got to wrap up a few things here and then I'm going to leave."

"I'll believe it when I see it," Ed Fannon said. "I'll bet that if we call your office at midnight tonight, you'll still be here going over fundamentals for Intel."

"I'll bet that if we call the office at 7 a.m. tomorrow he'll answer the phone," Palin added.

"Sorry boys, I'm afraid you'd lose your bet this time," Gus said. "I have guests coming tonight. They're staying at my place for the week and I don't plan to be in the office at all." He glanced at the stacks of papers on this desk. "Well, maybe I'll check in at some point this week and make sure you haven't burned the place down."

"Oh ye of little faith," McCormick said. "Who are your guests?" Gus's smile disappeared.

"Nobody. Now get out, merry Christmas, and I'll see you next week." He stood and began to flip through some of the stacks on his desk. He didn't look up again.

They took his cue and left the office abruptly without saying another word. Gus followed, stopping at the doorway of his office. He overheard Kaplan comment to the other guys.

"Thirty-two years old and he's a fund manager at the premier mutual fund company in the world, and his first year running it, he outperforms the market and everyone else. He's the kingpin."

"I've never seen the guy get rattled. No matter what happens, he's always as cool as the other side of Fannon's lonely bed," McCormick said. "You're right. That guy's the *King-Pin*."

Gus chuckled and walked back to his desk. He reached into a drawer and pulled out a faded, dog-eared photograph of two children – a boy and a girl. He studied it. Each was dressed in crisp new clothes. The girl, wearing a plaid skirt and blue sweater, smiled into the camera and held a Peanuts lunch box.

The boy, smaller, unaware or unsympathetic to any camera, looked down seriously at his King Kong lunch box, which he held in both hands in front of him. A speck of dirt or dust dotted the girl's cheek. Gus scratched it off and flipped the photo over and read an inscription that he had read a hundred times: "Lilly and Jack, first day of school, 1976."

He put the photograph back in the drawer. He stretched and yawned and then turned back to the desk, packed a few stacks of papers into his briefcase, locked his office, gave final instructions to his secretary, told her to go home, hopped into his Mercedes 450 SL, and sped home.

CHAPTER 2

Waiting

Gus opened the front door of his house, stepped outside, and peered out into the gloom. Big flakes of snow filled the gray, dark sky and began to cover the grass blades in the yard. He lit a Newport menthol. He was angry that he had started smoking again. The neighborhood was silent but for the sound of a lone car that passed with a soft splash on the wet road. It wasn't the car he was looking for. He pulled the cigarette from his lips and threw it on the ground in disgust.

"Where the hell is she?" he muttered, then shivered and stepped back inside where a Christmas tree wrapped in blinking, colored lights and a crackling fire emanated a warm, cascading glow that countered the gray cold outside.

Gus breathed in the pine scent of the tree and sprayed it with water to moisten the needles. He adjusted the ornaments and gazed at one made of Popsicle sticks stuck together. A photograph of two young children in green pajamas sitting in front of a fireplace was glued to the sticks.

This was the fifth year that Gus had gone up to Johnson's Christmas Tree Farm in Nashua, New Hampshire with his handsaw and cut down a huge Douglas Fir. It was the first year the two children in the photograph hadn't been with him to watch.

Gus wiped a coating of dust from the picture and placed the ornament at eye-level on the front side of the tree. Then he climbed a chair to adjust the star. The tree was too big for his living room and the star bent sideways against the ceiling, but Gus knew the kids would like having a huge tree.

Gus adjusted three stockings hung on the mantle over the fireplace - one big one and two smaller ones. The names Jack and Lilly were written in glued-on silver sparkles on the small ones, in the large block writing of children.

The smell of burning chocolate chip cookies wafted into the living room and jolted Gus from a memory. He rushed to the kitchen and pulled the blackened, hardened cookies out of the oven.

"Crap," he said. He pulled the lid off a pot sitting on top of the stove and broke up hardened, cold mashed potatoes with a spoon. Then he cut into the pork loin sitting in a pan next to the potatoes and put a slice in his mouth. It was dry and tough and cold. He put away the three plates that he had placed on the dining room table, grabbed a can of Schlitz from the fridge and guzzled. Then he stirred a bowl of non-alcoholic eggnog.

When he finished stirring, he poured a glass half full of the eggnog and half full of rum, turned off all the lights, and sat by the window and sipped from his glass. He stared at the swirling snow that twirled and fell and clung to the branches of the young juniper tree in the front yard and listened to the wind, the crackle of the fire, and the pfft of the snow hitting the window.

He put another log on and watched the sparks burst and rise up the chimney. He paced the living room. *She better show up*, he thought. He returned to the window and watched for her car.

Gus sat for 20 minutes in the dark before turning on the lights and the RCA record player. Elvis Presley crooned Blue Christmas. Gus heard a car pull into the driveway. "It's about time!" He opened the front door. It wasn't her. It was his parents, Charlie and Vera Delaney. They had just come from the 6 p.m. Christmas Eve service at St. Andrews.

"Hi Ma, hi Dad."

"Where are the kids? Are they inside?" his mother asked.

"Nope. She hasn't dropped them off yet."

"You're kidding? Where is she?"

"I don't know. She was supposed to bring them at four."

"Was her flight delayed?"

"No, I called. That woman is going to drive me to the goddamn loony bin!"

"Don't let her get to you. Don't give her the satisfaction," Vera said. "You have to get on with your life."

"Yeah, that's easy for you to say. I never see my own kids. She moves and takes them with her to New Jersey and the judge says that's fine and dandy. She has them all year. I get them for two months in the summer and alternate holidays. Now my first Christmas with them and she's not here when she's supposed to be."

Gus finished another can of Schlitz, crushed the can, and threw it in the fireplace, where it shriveled and sparked in the fire.

"That's enough! I wish you wouldn't drink so much," his mother said.

"What are you talking about? It's just one beer."

"That's all you have in the refrigerator – beer."

"Give me a break, Ma. I'm fine. Stop worrying."

"I worry. I'll always worry."

Gus walked into the kitchen. He emerged with another can of beer and a cigarette dangling from his lips. He paced around the living room, looking out the window at the accumulating snow. Vera shook her head. "I thought you were going to quit," she said.

Gus had started smoking to calm his anxiety during the custody hearings, bumming cigarettes from others between proceedings. "It's my New Year's resolution. I still have another week," he mumbled through lips pursed around the cigarette.

Vera emptied presents from a large bag and placed them under the tree.

"What are those?" Gus asked.

"Presents for the kids," she said. Gus picked one up.

"It says 'From Santa'. You can't put these under the tree yet. Santa doesn't come until tonight after the kids are in bed, remember?"

"Then we'll hide the ones from Santa until later."

As Vera unloaded her presents, Charlie turned on the television and watched *It's a Wonderful Life* playing on WLVI Channel 56. The UHF signal was lousy and the picture was as snowy as the sky outside.

Gus returned to the window. "She better not use the weather as an excuse," he said. "That would be just like her to say the drive was treacherous and she had to stay near the airport. She should have called."

"Do you think she was in an accident?" Vera asked.

"The roads aren't too bad yet. The snow isn't sticking," Charlie said, glancing away from the television for a moment. "Don't worry. She'll be here. Sit down and watch TV for a little while, take your mind off it."

"I can't," Gus said. He wondered if the kids were excited to spend Christmas with him. After the divorce, when Victoria dropped them off in June for the first summer without their mother, they both clung to her legs and shrieked that they didn't want to stay with daddy. They cried for two days.

Gus had dreamed about a happy family life. Now it was all gone like the sparks disappearing up the chimney. The life he had planned was blown up and he blamed Victoria for lighting the fuse.

Another car pulled into the driveway. Gus looked at his watch: 8:00 p.m.

"Is that her?" Vera asked, patting down the wrinkles in her dress.

"I can't tell." The headlights then turned off. "No, it's Stacy."

"You invited Stacy?" Vera asked.

"Yeah, why?"

"You know that's going to set Victoria off. Jesus, you want to cause a scene in front of the children?"

Gus thought about it. Was it a good idea to invite his girlfriend? At the end of August, after Victoria picked up Jack and Lilly to take them to New Jersey for the school year, Lilly told Victoria during the car ride all about daddy's girlfriend and how she often slept overnight at the house in daddy's room.

Victoria called him on the phone the minute she arrived home. She yelled into the receiver: "If I ever hear again that that whore has stayed over the house I'll make sure you never see the kids! You disgust me! I worry what kind of environment you are exposing them to. Do you really think it's a good idea to have your whore prancing around in her nightgown in front of my children?"

This galled Gus, because Stacy was a better influence on the children than their own mother. She spent more time with the kids than Queen Victoria ever did. Stacy read to them and dressed Barbie dolls with Lilly and fought battles against the Evil Empire with Jack and his Star Wars figures. The completed 500-piece *Little House on the Prairie* puzzle on the coffee table had been Stacy and Lilly's special project.

Victoria used the kids as pawns in her mission to make Gus miserable. She never read to them. Never played. It was always: "Not now, Lilly, mommy's busy." She yelled at Jack if his shirt was untucked, or if Lilly had a stain on her blouse, or if either had dirty fingernails.

She frowned when the kids ran in the house, and hit them with a wooden spoon if they made loud noises, or whined, or talked back. So fuck Victoria. He wanted Stacy there. He had every right to have his girlfriend at the house Christmas Eve. Victoria would have to get used to it.

"Hi Stacy. Merry Christmas," Vera said as she hugged her. Charlie kissed her on the cheek and asked how she was doing. "Here, let me help you with these," he said, taking a large bag from her. "What do you have here?"

"Oh, just some gifts for the kids," she said. "And this is a bread pudding I baked for you. I'm worried it didn't come out too well. It was my first time making it. I tried the recipe you gave me," she said to Vera.

Gus smiled at Stacy and hugged her. "Thank you," he whispered. "Merry Christmas." Gus fixed her a glass of eggnog and rum and scooped a clump of bread pudding for each of them. Vera and Stacy chatted about the children while Charlie continued watching *It's a Wonderful Life*. Every few minutes he'd chime in about kids being spoiled.

"They have everything today. When we were kids my grandmother gave us an apple for Christmas," he said. "We got one gift from Santa and it was usually a pair of trousers or boots." He gestured to the pile of presents under the tree and then looked at Gus. "Don't put yourself in the poor house because you're in a pissing match with Victoria. You'll ruin the kids with all the crap you're giving them."

"Don't worry about it," Gus snapped. "I can afford it." Charlie rolled his eyes and turned back to the movie.

Vera and Stacy ignored them and continued talking. Gus frowned and walked to the side porch off the kitchen to get another log for the fire. The huge-flaked snow continued falling. As he loaded the logs in the crook of his arm, a car crept along the road in front of the house. It stopped. Gus strained his eyes to see if it was Victoria. He didn't know what kind of car she had rented.

The car in the street looked like a station wagon. It idled in front of the house for a few minutes. Gus dropped the logs and walked down the lawn toward the car. He felt a rush of excitement as he waited for the doors to open and the kids to run out to greet him. Instead, the car sped down the road as soon as Gus had taken a few steps.

He shivered and shook the snow off his head and shoulders. He piled the logs back on his arm and trudged inside.

Gus dropped the logs in the wooden box next to the fireplace, threw one on the fire, and wiped the dirt from his shirt. The sparks crackled and some embers spurted out onto the carpet.

"I hate her," he snapped. He kicked the wooden box. Stacy put her arm on his shoulder.

"Don't worry, she'll be here and you'll have plenty of time with the kids. You have them all week remember," she said. "I'll get you a drink. What do you want?"

"Some eggnog would be good. With rum."

"Cause that's just want you need right now," Vera said. "I might as well talk to the wall as talk to you. That'll be great, you staggering around when Victoria arrives. Real smart. That should help you when you go back to court."

"What do I care, she's not coming," Gus said. "Might as well try to enjoy myself." He hurled a tube of wrapping paper into the Christmas tree. The tree shook and the ornaments jiggled. A few of them crashed to the floor.

Stacy froze for a moment at the entrance to the kitchen. She collected herself, and without turning around, continued walking into the kitchen. She returned a few minutes later with a tall mug of eggnog. "One won't hurt," she said and smiled weakly to Vera.

"Yeah, one wouldn't hurt if it wasn't preceded by six beers," Vera snapped. Her face crinkled in a scowl. Then she turned toward the television and focused on '*It's a Wonderful Life.*"

"Maybe I should pull a George Bailey and jump in the river," Gus said. "Then you wouldn't have to worry about me drinking so much." Vera shook her head from side to side but didn't say anything and never averted her eyes from the TV set. "I know who I wish would jump in the river," he added as he walked to the window and peered again at the falling snow.

CHAPTER 3

Victoria

At 8:15 pm, a wood-paneled Oldsmobile station wagon pulled into the driveway. The car door opened and a tall, shapely woman wearing a rabbit fur coat and a matching pillbox hat stepped out into the cold, wet air. She squinted and looked around at the yard and then began to walk up the driveway. Victoria.

Gus ran out to greet the kids. "Nice tacky lights you put up," she said, gesturing at the blinking red, blue, green, and yellow lights strung over all the shrubs and trees in the front yard. "Real classy."

"I couldn't give a shit what you think. Where the hell have you been?"

"Don't start with me. My flight was delayed and the roads are awful…and the kids wanted to see Tricia and Jacob, so I stopped by Donna's."

"You mean I've been waiting four hours because you decided to stop at your friend's house for a chat? You were supposed to be here at four – and don't give me any crap about the roads. My parents drove on them and said they're fine. And I called the airline and they said your flight was on time." Gus stormed past her to the car to get the kids.

"Don't wake them, they're sleeping," she yelled, moving toward him. "They've had a long day and they're tired."

"They wouldn't be so tired if you had brought them here at four like you were supposed to. I'll wake them up if I goddamn feel like it!" Gus ripped the door open and gently shook Lilly's shoulder. "Hi sweetie. I missed you so much."

Lilly rubbed her eyes and looked around with a glazed expression. "Hi daddy," she murmured through a yawn. "Did Santa Claus come yet?"

"No, not yet honey," he answered. "Santa will come later when you are tucked into bed. Give me a kiss." Lilly hesitated and then shyly moved toward Gus and pecked him on his mouth. Gus engulfed her in a bear hug.

"Oh, I missed my little Lilly!" he said. Lilly squirmed.

"Daddy, you're hurting me."

"Oh!" Gus laughed and his eyes became moist. "I'm sorry. I just missed you so much. Look, there's Grandma," he said, pointing to the top of the driveway where Vera stood while snowflakes collected on her head and turned her brown hair white. "Go see Grandma and she'll take you inside to see the Christmas tree while I get Jack."

Lilly pulled her Raggedy Ann doll from the car and ran up the driveway to Vera. Gus gently hoisted Jack onto his chest with one hand and grabbed the children's suitcases with the other. Jack opened his eyes briefly and then closed them and nestled his face against Gus's shoulder. He clung to his favorite blanket, which Vera had made for him when he was born and from which he never parted. "Okay, I think I've got everything," Gus said to Victoria. "You can go now."

"Always the gentleman. Excuse me; I'm going to use the bathroom and wish the kids a Merry Christmas."

"You should have wished them Merry Christmas four hours ago when you should have been here. You can use Donna's bathroom. See you next week." Gus turned and walked up to the front door.

"Don't be an asshole!" Victoria shouted after him. "I can be an asshole too if you want to play that way."

"No kidding. That would be a change," Gus said and continued walking. Jack woke up. Disoriented, cold, and wet, he began to cry and yell for his mother. He squirmed and kicked to break free from Gus. "Mommy!" he wailed.

Gus shook him lightly up and down. "Hey buddy. It's okay. Daddy's here. Let's go in and eat some cookies and drink some chocolate milk and get ready for Santa." He turned to Victoria. "Goddamn...you can't just leave well enough alone. You always have to fuck it up for me!" Jack cried harder and yelled louder.

"That's a nice way to talk to me in front of your son. Way to set a good example." Victoria reached for Jack but Gus turned and held him out of her reach. Jack kicked and wriggled and screamed...a full-scale tantrum.

"Give him to me, you idiot!" Victoria yelled. "He obviously wants his mother." Then she softened her voice when Gus placed Jack in her outstretched arms and said, "Come here darling. It's ok, Mommy's here. Don't you worry. Is Daddy being mean to you?" Jack's sobs subsided to quiet whimpering.

"Come on Jack, Mommy's coming in too," Gus said. "She's going to have a cookie with you and then you've got to go to bed because Santa's coming tonight. He won't come if you're not asleep in bed." Jack nodded his head and tears streamed down his cheeks. His lip quivered.

Gus picked up the bags, which he had dropped on the driveway, and walked into the house.

"What was going on out there?" Charlie asked. Victoria trailed Gus with Jack clinging to her. She tried to put him down on the floor but he wouldn't let go.

"Come on Jack, Mommy's tired," she said. Jack whined but Victoria pulled him off her leg and snapped, "Enough!" and he stopped.

"Nothing," Gus said, answering his father.

"Well there was an awful lot of screaming and yelling for nothing going on," Charlie said

"Just the usual, Victoria being her typical bitch self."

"That's enough Gus," Vera said. "Hi Victoria. Merry Christmas," she said as she hugged her awkwardly and kissed the air. "How are your parents?"

Victoria smiled her forced smile that was more sneer – no teeth, just lips that curled up a little in the corners. Her eyes did not meet Vera's but surveyed the room, and then glazed over in a manner that made it clear she didn't give a shit. "They're great. Everyone's doing fine. I'm just going to use the powder room and say goodnight to the kids and then I have to go."

"I don't have a powder room. I have a bathroom, but last I checked, no powder room," Gus said.

Victoria said fuck you with her eyes and slammed the door to the bathroom. "What the hell happened out there?" Charlie asked again in a low voice.

"Like I said, just the usual. I'm tired of the same old games she plays."

Stacy had disappeared to the kitchen as soon as Victoria walked into the house. Vera occupied herself by listening to Lilly read *How the Grinch Stole Christmas*.

While Lilly read to her grandmother, Jack looked for presents under the tree with his name on them. When he found one, he shook it and looked for creases in the wrapping paper that he might be able to fold back just enough to glimpse what the gift was.

He found Stacy's gift just as Victoria returned from the bathroom. He shook it, saw his mom, and said, "Look mommy, this one's from Stacy."

"Yeah, I bet it's a girlie sweater or yucky clothes," Victoria said, looking with disdain at the gift. Stacy overheard her and came out of the kitchen to confront her adversary.

"Hey Jack! I missed you!" Stacy said as she bounded over to give him a hug and kiss. Gus observed Jack to see how he would respond and whether or not he might be shy with Stacy, but a big smile broke out on his face and he jumped up to hug her. He then asked her what she had gotten him.

"I think you'll like it," she said, kneeling down to look Jack in the eye. "Don't worry – I didn't get you clothes." She smiled and winked at him.

Gus glanced at Victoria to see how she would react to this. Her mouth creased into a frown. "I think you ought to get going now," he said. It's getting late and it's still snowing pretty hard. You might want to leave before it starts to stick to the roads."

"Glad you're so concerned about me. Don't worry, I'll leave when I know the kids will be okay without me." She crouched down to talk to Jack in the same way Stacy had. Gus rolled his eyes. "Jack," she said, "Mommy's leaving now. Are you going be alright here at Daddy's this week?"

Jack fidgeted with Stacy's present, turning it over and over, shaking it. He did not pay any attention to his mother. "Jack," Victoria said a little louder, "did you hear me? I'm leaving and I won't be back until next week. Will you be okay here with Daddy?"

"Yes," Jack said, never looking up from the present.

"Okay then. Give mommy a hug." She pulled Jack over to her and kissed the air next to his cheek. "And tuck in your shirt, Jack. Just because you're at Daddy's doesn't mean you can look like a slob." Then she turned to Lilly. "Lilly, are you going to be good for Daddy?"

"Yes Mommy. I'll be good," Lilly said.

"Good girl. You call me in the morning at Donna's house and let me know what Santa brought you, ok?"

"I will." Lilly hugged her mother and walked back to the couch.

Victoria then scowled in Stacy's direction. "I hope she's not spending the night. I don't think that would be appropriate for the kids."

"Don't worry about it," Gus said.

"Does that mean she's not staying here tonight?"

"That means it's none of your business."

"We'll see what my lawyer says about that," she said, and she slammed the door and walked out into the swirling wind and snow.

Gus's arms tingled and his neck muscles tightened. He didn't say a word but walked into the kitchen. He poured a glass of eggnog, took a gulp, and threw it across the room. It smashed against the wall and glass shards scattered around the kitchen. Vera, Charlie, Stacy, and the kids rushed in as the brown liquid trickled down the wall. A sheepish grin crept onto Gus's face.

"Daddy, what happened?" Lilly asked.

"Sorry, I just knocked my glass off the counter by accident and it broke. Just go back into the living room and I'll be right there after I clean it up." He saw his mother look at the wall, with the new brown wet mark and the glass-sized gash in it. She shook her head and the look on her face needed no interpretation. She put her arms around the kids and brought them to the living room.

Gus was sweeping glass out of the cracks in the linoleum floor when he heard someone knocking at the door. It was Victoria. Gus slammed the broom down on the kitchen floor and rushed to the door.

He stepped outside and closed the door behind him to try to shield the kids from their conversation. "Why are you back here?" he roared.

"The roads are really bad. I'm skidding all over," she said. "I can't drive to Donna's in this weather."

"Well you're sure as hell not staying here!" Gus yelled, louder than he meant to. "Donna lives in Woburn – what's that, about 20 minutes from here?"

"Not in this weather! It would take about two hours."

"Then you better hurry up and get on the road."

"Hey asshole, I told you I can't drive on these roads."

"Yes you can – once you get on the highway you'll be fine. They'll have sanded the highway."

"You drive me then," Victoria said, and she stood there with her hands on her hips.

Gus thought for a second. He couldn't believe this was happening. This was supposed to be his time alone with the kids. He had planned the whole night out in his head.

For weeks he envisioned every detail – how they would roast marshmallows in the fire; how they would wolf down the eggnog and cookies he made for them; how they would sit together on the couch, their little heads resting on his chest or shoulder, all three of them sharing the quilt his grandmother had made him when he was a boy, while he read *Twas the Night Before Christmas* and the *Berenstain Bears' Christmas*.

Now she was ruining his time with them, his first Christmas with them since the divorce. "There's no way I'm driving you – absolutely not. You can't show up here four hours late and then think I'm going to spend four hours driving to Woburn and back because you're not comfortable driving in the snow."

Victoria started crying. "Fine!" she sobbed. "I'll just go out on the roads and kill myself in an accident, and then your kids will have no mother," she yelled loud enough for everyone inside the house to hear. "You selfish bastard!" Then she pushed her way through the doorway and, wiping tears from her eyes, said to the kids, "I guess Daddy wants Mommy to die in a car crash. Merry Christmas."

"That would sure make my life easier," Gus mumbled to himself, too loudly.

"Fuck you!" Victoria shouted. Then she turned, stomped out, and slammed the screen door into Gus.

"That went well, don't you think?" Gus said. Lilly and Jack began to cry.

"Daddy, please let Mommy stay here," Lilly shrieked. "I don't want her to get in a car accident!"

"Mommy's not going to get in a car accident, sweetie. She's just being dramatic. The roads aren't that bad. Ask Grampa – right Grampa? They were fine when you drove on them tonight, right?"

"Listen, why don't you call the Holiday Inn downtown and see if they have any rooms for tonight," Charlie said. "If they do, I'll drive her there. The roads might be icy – it's been snowing steadily since we were on them."

"Dad, you shouldn't have to drive her. Let her drive herself. It's her own damn fault."

"I don't mind. Run out there before she leaves and tell her I'll take her to the Holiday Inn…actually, you stay here. Let me go talk to her."

Gus clenched his fists and his body tightened. That snake had done it again. She did it every time – made him look like the bad guy, turned his kids against him. No matter what he did, she always won; she always made him look like an ass in front of his kids.

He wished she would get killed in a car crash. This was a horrible thing to wish, he knew, but he did wish it. She made his life miserable. He wondered, for the thousandth time, what he had seen in her. Why didn't he see how she really was before he got her pregnant with Lilly?

The Holiday Inn had rooms available. Thank God, Gus thought; Victoria could stay there and drive to Donna's in the morning. She didn't have a choice. She could *not* stay at his house. She would *not* ruin his Christmas – his time with his kids.

"Alright, she said she would stay at the Holiday Inn if I drove her," Charlie said.

"Good," Gus said. He walked to Victoria's car, where she sat mouthing words angrily, crying, and pounding the steering wheel.

"Listen, we got you a room at the Holiday Inn. It's only a couple of miles – right across the street from the mall. My dad will drive you and I'll follow you in my car to make sure you get there without any problems. Then you can drive to Donna's in the morning. And one more thing: don't get any bright ideas to stop by and visit the kids tomorrow morning. I don't want to see you anywhere near the house."

Gus could see the anger building in her. She clenched the steering wheel and he thought she might lash out and grab him and try to rip the flesh off his face.

"This is going to change," she sputtered. "You're going to regret this. I'm going to talk to my lawyer tomorrow and you'll never see your kids again."

"Great, I'm sure your lawyer will love hearing from you on Christmas Day. Let me know how it works out."

"Fuck you. I'm tired. Just get your dad and get me to the hotel." Charlie plopped into the driver's seat of Victoria's car and drove her to the Holiday Inn. Gus followed behind.

The Holiday Inn parking lot was nearly empty. The snowfall had lightened but the parking lot had not been plowed in some time. Charlie parked and Victoria got out and slammed the door of her car. She did not acknowledge Charlie or Gus except to snatch the keys from Charlie. Then, without looking at them, she pulled a suitcase and small duffle bag out of the trunk and stomped into the hotel lobby.

When she disappeared inside the hotel, Charlie, now sitting in the driver's seat of Gus's car, turned to Gus and said, "Seems kind of mean-hearted to make her spend Christmas all alone in a Holiday Inn."

"Don't start dad. With the crap she's put me through I wouldn't care if she slept in the car tonight. She did it to herself – she should have gotten here on time."

"Yes, I suppose that's true," Charlie answered, staring out his window at the red and green blinking Christmas lights strung across the bushes at the hotel's entranceway.

Suddenly, a man appeared and knocked on the passenger side window and gestured for Gus to roll it down. "Yes?" Gus said, not trying to hide his agitation.

"Hey buddy, can you give us a jump?" the man asked. "Our battery died."

"Sorry, I don't have jumper cables," Gus said, and he motioned to Charlie to drive.

"I've got them," the man said. He jogged alongside the car. Charlie stopped. "Please, if you could just pull up to my car, I can hook them up. It'll just take a second."

"I'm kind of in a rush," Gus said. He wanted to spend time with Jack and Lilly before they went to bed. He had a lot of catching up to do. "Can't the hotel help you?"

Charlie placed his hand on Gus's arm. "Why don't we just help him? It won't take long." He stopped the car.

"Okay, we'll help you," Gus said. "Where's the car?"

"Thanks. I really appreciate it. It's the brown Pinto over there." He pointed to a far corner of the parking lot at the side of the Holiday Inn, darkened because of a broken streetlight, where a woman stood next to a station wagon with its hood popped open. She waved.

"I don't like this," Gus said to Charlie while the man ran to the car and opened the hatchback. He took out jumper cables and hooked them up under the open hood of the car. Charlie pulled up alongside them and Gus got out and opened his hood.

"So, just visiting, or are you from around here?" Gus asked the guy as they waited for the battery to charge.

"Just up to spend Christmas with my sister's family," he said. "Drove up this morning from the Cape. We were about to head back to her house and the car was dead."

Gus noticed that he spoke in a strange British or Irish accent. "The Cape? You mean people actually live there during the winter?" he asked. His parents used to rent a cottage in Falmouth near Old Silver Beach for two weeks in August when he was a young boy. Most of the people he met during those summers were also summer people, and he had never known someone who lived there year-round.

"Yes. We like the quiet of the winters. In fact, I wish the summers were more like the winters. Too many people in the summer," he said.

"Try now. It should be charged," Gus said, anxious to get home. The man turned the key and the engine sputtered, then caught, and roared as he pressed the gas pedal.

"Much obliged sir. I really appreciate your help," the man said, and Gus and his father drove away.

CHAPTER 4

Presents

When Gus and Charlie arrived back home, the kids were sleeping on the couch. "They were watching the movie and they conked out," Vera said. "What movie?"

"*Miracle on 34th Street*. It's showing on Channel 38. I shut it off when they fell asleep. They're exhausted." Vera picked up the blanket that had fallen to the floor and covered Jack with it again. "What took you so long? Were the roads bad?"

"Yes, actually, they were pretty bad." Charlie said.

Gus walked over to the couch and crouched beside it, next to Lilly and Jack. They both looked so peaceful. He studied Lilly's face. Aside from her deep chestnut hair, she had her mother's features – high cheekbones, dimples, pouty lips, and porcelain skin dotted with light freckles. He prayed she wouldn't develop her mother's personality.

She had changed since he last saw her. It had been only three months, but she seemed to have grown. She was skinnier, taller. Jack had changed too. His hair was longer and he was also a bit thinner. Gus saw himself in Jack's facial features – Jack was his father's son, no doubt about it.

As Gus stroked Lilly's hair he thought about the past seven years and how far his life had veered off the course he had charted. He pounded his fist on the coffee table and his eyes welled up and then tears rolled down his face.

"Honey, what's the matter?" his mom asked, putting her hand on his shoulder.

"It's just that this is how it's going to be for the rest of my life. She'll always stick it to me and I won't ever be able to spend time with my kids without her controlling it. I don't even think they want to be here," he said, wiping the tears from his eyes.

"Of course they do," Vera said. She held his face in her hands and hugged him. "You're a great dad and those kids love you and of course they want to spend time with you."

"She's going to win, I know it, and then what do I do?" Not only was Victoria trying to gain custody of the kids full time, but she was also pushing to double the

---

monthly child care payments. She decided $1,000 a month in child support was not enough.

"Don't think that way," Vera said. "Don't worry so much about Victoria. Just be the best dad you can be, and it will all work out."

Gus smiled weakly and kissed each child again. "Look how beautiful and peaceful they are," he said to his mother.

"They are, but they're also exhausted. You should put them to bed," she said. "You'll have plenty of time with them tomorrow."

Gus wanted to spend time with the kids that night, but he knew his mother was right. He shook each of them gently by the shoulder. "It's time for bed," he whispered. The children sat up on the couch, eyes blinking, as if trying to peer through a cloud. They didn't immediately seem to know where they were. They moaned.

"I don't want to go to bed," Jack groaned.

"You have to or Santa won't come," Gus said. Jack remembered what night it was and nodded his head.

"We have to leave milk and cookies for Santa and the reindeer," Jack said.

"Oh yeah, I almost forgot. Good boy. Santa will be glad you remembered." Gus, Lilly, and Jack walked to the kitchen where Stacy had taken out a tray painted with a winter scene – a country house with spruce trees wrapped in rainbow-colored lights dotting the yard. A bright Christmas tree gleamed in the window, bathing the inside of the house in a warm, yellow light. A snowman stood sentry in the front lawn looking over a pond on which some children skated and a smiling couple pulled a boy and a puppy on a sled.

Gus studied the scene for a moment. "Lilly, do you like this tray?" he asked after a minute. "We can put the milk and cookies on it."

Lilly took the tray and looked at the picture. "This is good," she said.

They laid out the cookies on the tray and Lilly poured milk into a tall glass. They placed the tray on the coffee table in the living room and Gus brought the kids to their bedrooms to help them put on their pajamas.

The house was a split-level three-bedroom ranch built in 1968. Gus's room was at the end of a long hallway, the center room.

Lilly's room, on the right facing the front of the house, had ivory wallpaper with small pink roses and a rectangular white throw rug. A quilt with pink, blue, and yellow flowers that her grandmother had made covered her bed. A poster of the Fonz hung over it.

Jack's room, facing the backyard, was covered with sports posters and pennants. One wall had three posters lined in a row – one with Dave Cowens shooting a basketball, one with Bobby Orr carrying a hockey puck, and one with Carl Yazstremski swinging a baseball bat. Underneath the posters, pennants for the Boston Red Sox, Bruins, Celtics, New England Patriots, and Providence College, Gus's alma mater, hung neatly.

Jack's bedspread was Star Wars, with matching sheets underneath. An oval braided blue and brown area rug covered the wood floor. Outside Jack's windows, thick woods bordered the yard, and to the left, the lawn sloped into a great swamp.

Gus tucked Lilly and Jack into their beds and kissed them goodnight. He lingered for a long time in Jack's room, watching him sleep. He wondered what his children's futures held and how much of it Victoria would allow him to take part in. "Good night my little angel. Sweet dreams," he whispered as he brushed back the hair on his forehead.

While Gus's parents readied the pullout bed in the living room, Gus trudged down to the basement, which had lush, maroon shag carpet and black leather couches. He carried a glass of eggnog and rum with him. He unlocked a utility closet underneath the stairs and dragged out two large boxes. Each box contained a bike, or more accurately, the parts for a bike.

In one box was a silver Huffy Survivor BMX bike, and in the other was a pink Schwinn Predator with a white banana seat with pink and green flowers and a matching white, flowered basket hanging from the handlebars. These were the two big gifts the kids were getting.

He opened the box with the Huffy, pulled out a booklet – the instructions – and sighed as he read. His head hurt. He laid out the parts on the floor and began to put together the bike. After twenty-five minutes, the Huffy Survivor halfway completed and sprockets, gears, chains, and screws scattered across the carpet, Stacy came down with a mug of steaming cocoa. "They're really going to love these," she said, looking at the picture of Lilly's bike on the box.

"I hope so. I can't wait to see the look on their faces, especially Jack. He's wanted one ever since he learned to ride a bike last summer. This will be so much better than that piece of crap he's been riding."

Stacy placed the mug on the coffee table. "Let me help," she said. She began to open the box that contained Lilly's bike.

"I don't know what I'm doing. Jack's going to sit on the bike and push the pedal and the wheels will fall off," he said. Stacy laughed. Gus paused for a moment and watched her try to tighten a bolt on the bike. She was wearing sweatpants and a tank top that revealed her lean, muscular arms. The muscles rippled with the strain of turning the wrench.

He moved behind her and placed his hand over hers and turned the bolt with her. Her arm glistened with sweat alongside Gus's. Gus's arm tingled with goosebumps. She turned toward him and said, "What are you –" but Gus pulled her into him before she could finish and pressed his lips hard against hers.

"I want you," he whispered. "Right now." He placed his hand on her thigh.

"What? Are you serious? I really think we should get these bikes done and get some sleep. You know the kids will be up at the crack of dawn," she said, pulling Gus's hand off her thigh. "Besides, I don't feel right with your kids and your parents here – what if one of them comes down or hears us?"

"They won't," Gus said.

"You don't know that…no, we can't – not tonight," Stacy said, again pushing away Gus, who had kissed her neck.

"Come on," he pleaded. "When I was a kid we were always allowed to open one gift on Christmas Eve."

"Well, I got you a nice wallet; I'll go get it and I'll let you open that."

"No, we got to choose which present we wanted to open. No offense, but I think I can wait until tomorrow to open the wallet. I want to unwrap something else tonight." He pulled the string loose on the waistband of her sweatpants.

Stacy smiled but pushed him away. Gus persisted. He kissed her neck with soft, wet lips. "That tickles!" she giggled. Gus then kissed the hollow part on her throat at the base of her neck. She moaned softly and her body tensed. He increased the pressure of his lips and continued to kiss this part of her neck.

Her body shuddered and she pushed Gus away again, but this time Gus knew she pushed him away because she soon would not be able to say no. He pulled her back and kissed her earlobe. A deep sigh slipped from her mouth and her breathing became heavier. Gus unclasped her bra and took off her shirt.

She did not push him away this time. She whispered, "We shouldn't do this," as Gus ripped off his shirt and pants and pulled off her sweatpants with an urgency she did not expect but found exhilarating. He kissed her forehead gently and eased inside of her.

As they lay on the carpet sweating and panting in the dimly lit basement next to bike parts, Gus stared into Stacy's eyes for some time. She broke her gaze and got up and resumed putting together her bike. "You're amazing," he said after they finished assembling the bikes. "I don't know what I'd do without you." He paused. "I love you."

She averted her eyes from his and blushed and Gus was afraid that she couldn't possibly feel the same way about him with all the baggage he carried. When she turned her eyes toward him again, they were moist. She whispered, "Merry Christmas." Gus sat on the couch staring at a painting on the wall of a meadow and river in springtime. "What's wrong?" Stacy asked.

"Nothing, nothing. I'm just tired." Gus snapped back to their task and carried Santa's presents upstairs and placed them under the tree, trying not to wake his sleeping parents. He carried the bikes up and hid them, one behind the couch and the other behind the Lazy Boy chair.

He looked at the clock. It was 2:20 a.m. He drank the milk and ate two of the cookies they'd left for Santa. Then he pulled some blankets and a pillow from the hall closet. "I probably should sleep on the couch in the basement," he said. He hoped Stacy would talk him out of it and convince him he should sleep in his own bed with her, but she didn't.

He kissed her goodnight and went to the basement. He was exhausted, but he couldn't sleep. Why hadn't she said "I love you" back? She had said she loved him many times in the past. Gus worried that she was beginning to tire of the miserable situation in which she had become entangled.

It frustrated him that he hadn't found success in his relationships the same way he had in other aspects of his life. His marriage was the one thing at which he had failed – and failed miserably – despite all his efforts to save it.

Gus had been a basketball star in high school and at Providence College not because he was the most gifted athlete, but because he outworked everyone – spending hours doing dribbling and shooting drills to develop his skills. It was the same with school and at Fidelity. Gus had scored highest in his class on the Series 7 broker exam because when his co-workers were getting beers at the Bell in Hand after class, he went home and took practice exams that he had designed for himself. Then he'd practice options trades for hours.

And it was the same after the test. He wanted to be the best trader at Fidelity, so he worked overtime every chance he got, learned the market intimately, got accepted to Wharton, studied hard, became first in his class, and then returned to Fidelity to be an analyst. He then became the youngest analyst in the country to run a mutual fund.

He had wanted to be as good a husband and dad as he was an analyst. He had thought if he just worked hard enough at it, he could save his marriage and preserve his family…but it didn't pan out that way. He hoped he could get it right with Stacy. He vowed to work harder. All these thoughts swirled around Gus's brain until, at 4:30 a.m., he finally fell asleep.

CHAPTER 5

Hangover

"Daddy, daddy, wake up! Santa came!" Gus felt someone tugging on his arm. He couldn't see – everything was dark, and he was unsure of where he was or what day it was. His thoughts still groggy, he closed his eyes again and rolled over, thinking he was dreaming.

"Daddy!" the voice yelled again, louder this time. It was Jack.

"What time is it Jack?"

"I don't know…Santa came! He left presents!" Jack could hardly get the words out quick enough. Gus sat up on the couch, rubbed his eyes and looked out the window at the darkness. He remembered where he was.

"Jack, it's still dark out. Why don't you go back to bed and sleep for a few more hours and wait until everyone gets up."

"Everyone <u>is</u> up! We're all waiting for you."

"Great, " Gus said, aggravated that the kids had gotten up so early. He was disgusted with himself for feeling that way. This was the moment he had been waiting for – the moment he had been thinking about and exited about for months. Now his head throbbed and he was exhausted.

"Okay. Run upstairs and I'll be right up. Just give me a minute."

"Alright, but hurry daddy."

Gus lay back down on the couch and stared at the ceiling. "Shit," he moaned.

"Gus, are you coming up? The kids are waiting!" a voice shouted from the top of the stairs. It was his mother. He had fallen back asleep. He noticed that a dim light now penetrated the windows.

"Goddamn," Gus mumbled. He stood and stretched. His mouth felt like it had eaten a beach full of sand the night before.

He walked upstairs and poured himself a cup of coffee. The smell of cooking bacon made him gag and he tasted vomit in his throat. He swallowed hard, grabbed onto the kitchen counter to stop the room from spinning, and then ran over to the trash bin, stuck his head in, and vomited until his throat was raw.

"I told you not to drink those eggnog and rums," his mother said. Gus felt too sick to argue. He gave her a look and guzzled a glass of orange juice.

He sank into a chair holding a cup of coffee. "Look Daddy! A Holly Hobby Easy Bake Oven!" Lilly squealed, pushing the pie mix to his nose so he could smell it.

"That's great sweetie." He had no energy.

"I got the Millennium Falcon!" Jack yelled, his eyes beaming.

"I got a princess nightgown!" and on and on it went. Gus wished he could have a moment – just fifteen minutes – to nap on the chair, but the kids wanted him to see every present and play with their new toys with them. Gus just couldn't, and it killed him.

"Here Daddy. This one's for you," Jack said. He handed Gus a present the size and shape of a shoe box. Gus shook it.

"Who is it from?" he asked.

"Me," Jack answered.

"Did you wrap it too?" Jack blushed and shook his head no.

"Stacy did it." Gus unwrapped the present and opened the box. A pair of Adidas running shoes – white leather with three green stripes.

"I love them," Gus said. "How did you know I wanted these? These are my favorite!" Jack blushed again and giggled and again pointed at Stacy.

"Oh, no, Jack picked those out all by himself this summer," she said. "Don't you remember, Jack? He knew you'd like those."

"I do. I love them," Gus said.

"Open mine! Open mine!" Lilly yelled, nearly tripping over the Lite Brite set sitting on the floor.

"Okay – whoa! Don't worry, I'll open it," Gus said. He tore open the rectangular box. "Oh boy, a new shirt and tie – Christian Dior!" He held them up to his chest. "Thank you Lilly. I can't wait to wear this to work next week." He hugged her. He mouthed thank you to Stacy. She must have taken them shopping sometime in the summer.

Each child opened and examined his gifts and placed them in a pile. Gus watched Lilly and Jack steal glances to see what the other had opened and then tear into whatever wrapped box their grandmother or Stacy handed them.

This went on for about forty-five minutes, and except for when the box they opened contained clothes and they put it aside in their pile without looking at it, they beamed each time they opened a present.

"Is that everything?" Gus asked

"Yes, I think so," Lilly said.

"You sure?"

Jack began throwing wrapping paper around furiously, trying to unearth some present he may not have seen. Lilly looked under the tree to see if there was some hidden treasure buried there. Gus smiled, delighted with his game. He had saved the best presents for last and two cups of Maxwell House had revived him enough that he could now function.

"What's that behind the couch?" he asked. Barely peeking out from behind the couch was what looked like a wheel. Lilly and Jack raced to the couch.

"A bike!" Jack squealed, hardly able to contain his excitement as he pulled out the Huffy. He read a card attached to the handlebars: "To Jack, from Santa." He sat on the seat and balanced with his tiptoes. It was a little big for him, but he'd grow into it by summer.

Lilly looked as if she was about to cry. "How come Jack got a bike and I didn't?" Her eyes welled. "I asked for a bike too."

"Well there must be another one here for you," Gus said. "Oh, what's that behind the chair?" He pointed to the Lazy Boy in the corner of the living room, on which his father sat sipping coffee and examining Jack's Millennium Falcon ship. Lilly raced to the chair, nearly knocking Charlie over.

"I got a bike too!" she yelled as she pulled out her big-girl Schwinn pink and purple 3-speed. "Oh, I love it!" she said. "Can I try it? Please?"

"How about later today when it warms up a little?" Gus suggested. "Let the plows clean the roads. Why don't we have breakfast and do this puzzle and then we'll go out to try both bikes?" he said, pulling out a *Little House on the Prairie* puzzle.

"Why can't we go now?" Jack whined. "I want to try my new bike."

"Because it's only 8:00 o'clock in the morning and we need to let it warm up outside…and I need to rest for a few minutes. You little turds woke me up too early," he said and he laughed and mussed up their hair. He saw they were crushed. "Don't worry, you'll get to ride your bikes today."

It was a shame that the gifts the kids were most excited about – the bikes – were gifts to be used in the summer, which seemed far away. Gus watched Jack examine his Huffy. Lilly and Stacy put aside Lite Brite and worked on the *Little House* puzzle.

Jack then set up his Star Wars figures in a battle scene and explained to his grandfather who the good guys were. "This is Greedo and this is Boba Fett," he said. "They're bounty hunters trying to capture Han Solo and take him to Jabba the Hut. They're bad guys."

Vera sat in the chair next to Gus and sipped tea. "I think they like everything they got," she said. She paused and looked into her mug. "Aren't you taking the kids to church today? They really should go on Christmas day. Don't you go anymore?"

The priest at the Catholic church, Father Dwyer, was an old, stern man who smelled like talcum powder and body odor. Gus spoke to him when Victoria left with the kids. He sought guidance, but Father Dwyer was not sympathetic. Divorce was a sin in the eyes of God. "Too many young couples discard their vows almost as easily as they discard their clothes and that damages the children," he said.

Gus didn't care much for Father Dwyer after that. What the hell did he know about marriage and kids anyway? He might try to spend a month with Victoria and see if he was against divorce then.

"I don't know," Gus said to Vera. "I should, but I don't really like the priest at Saint Andrews."

"Why don't you like him?" Vera asked.

"Because he's patronizing. He's the one who refused to let me and Victoria get married in the church, remember?"

"Oh yes…but maybe he had something there," Vera said and she smiled. Gus laughed.

"Yeah, you're probably right. I should have listened to him and then maybe I wouldn't have screwed up so badly. Or maybe I should have joined the priesthood myself and prevented my problems before they began."

"When you were a boy we all thought you would become a priest," she said. She smiled and gazed past him at the blank wall. "Remember how you used to pray before eating M&M's to thank God for the blessing of the meal you were about to eat? And you would stay after church to talk to Father Driscoll about God."

"Yeah, I remember," Gus said. He had been an altar boy. "That was a long time ago."

"Yes it was," Vera said. She paused and looked at the kids. "How can you say you screwed up when you look over at those two beautiful children?" Vera nodded in the direction of Jack and Lilly. Gus looked at them again – Lilly yelping with delight at finding the puzzle pieces to complete Laura Ingall's hand, and Jack teaching his grandfather about the Star Wars characters and their ships.

"I know. You're right," Gus said. "I don't know what I'd ever do without them. My life would be nothing."

Vera patted his hand. "Everything happens for a reason and God won't ever give you more than you can handle. Remember that."

"Yes, I know."

She glanced at her watch. "Well, we should head over to Lauren's now. The kids will be waiting for us."

Lauren was Gus's sister. Vera and Charlie were going to her house for dinner. She and her husband Tom lived in Nashua, New Hampshire and had three kids – two girls, Tricia and Kelly, and a boy, James. Tricia was twelve and Kelly was ten. James was Jack's age – seven.

"Grampa, should we get going to Lauren's now?" Vera asked Charlie. "She said she's serving dinner at 1 p.m."

"We probably should." Charlie and Vera kissed the kids. "I love you so much!" Vera said to them. "I can't wait to see you this week." She was taking them to Edaville Railroad's Christmas Festival of Lights. She hugged and kissed Stacy and Gus goodbye.

"You be good now," Vera said to Gus. "Get a good night's sleep tonight so you'll be able to play with the kids tomorrow." Then she turned to Stacy. "Keep an eye on him," she said, looking in Gus's direction. "Thank you for helping so much with the kids. They adore you." Stacy thanked her. Gus walked to the car with his parents and helped them carry their bags.

"She's a nice girl," Charlie said. "You should hang on to her."

"Yes," Vera said. "Be good to her." And before she stepped into the passenger seat of the car she grabbed Gus's shoulders, "And remember what I said. God will never give you more than you can handle."

Gus watched the Oldsmobile Cutlass back out of the driveway, drive down the street, and turn the corner out of sight. He shivered. The sky was overcast and it was cold. Too cold for riding bikes. He walked back into the house and sat next to Lilly on the couch.

"Did you have a nice Christmas?" he asked her.

"Yes," she said without looking up from the puzzle.

"Which is your favorite present?"

"Hmmm." She thought for a moment. "Let me think…"

After a few minutes she said, "I think my favorite is my bike. And then my Holly Hobby Easy Bake Oven."

"Oh, I almost forgot! Daddy I made something for you," Jack said.

"Me too!" Lilly chimed in. "We made you presents at school."

Lilly reached into a gym bag and pulled out something made of yarn and two sticks tied together. The yarn was wound around the sticks in the shape of a diamond in blue and gold. "It's a star," she said.

Jack gave Gus a wreath made of small round cloth balls filled with spices – cinnamon, and nutmeg. "Smell it Daddy. It smells like Christmas," Jack said.

Each child had also made a Christmas card. Lilly's had an angel on the front cover. Inside she had drawn Santa Claus and Rudolph the Red-Nosed Reindeer. The message inside said: *Merry Christmas Daddy. I love you. Love Lilly.*

Then he opened Jack's hand-drawn card. On the cover was a drawing of a Christmas tree. Inside was a picture of a young boy. Next to the boy was a larger stick figure, with "Daddy" written next to it.

There was another Christmas tree drawn on the inside of the card. On the facing page it read, in Jack's block handwriting: *Merry Christmas. You are the best dad in the whole world. Love Jack.*

Gus's throat tightened and he tried to swallow the lump rising in it.

"Daddy, why are you crying?" Jack asked. "Is my drawing bad?" Gus pulled him close and then pulled Lilly in too.

"These are the best presents I have ever gotten," he said. He held his two children tightly for a few minutes. He didn't want to let go.

Gus took each of them by the shoulder and looked into their eyes – eyes that didn't understand the emotions coursing through him. "I hope you know that I love you both very much and that no matter what may happen, I will always love you – no matter where you are or how old you get. Do you know that?"

They both nodded yes. Gus rubbed his eyes and blew his nose. "Hey – do you want to build a fort downstairs before dinner?" he asked.

"Yay!" they both yelled at once.

Gus grabbed all the cushions off the living room couch and threw them down the stairs leading to the basement where Jack and Lilly collected them. Then he pulled all the spare comforters and blankets from the hall closet. Stacy poked her head out of the kitchen and looked at him as he carried an armful of blankets and threw them down the stairs. She shook her head.

"Honestly," she said. "Who's the kid here?" Then she laughed her loud guffaw laugh. "You kids have fun down there."

This small gesture was a perfect example of the difference between Stacy and Victoria. Whenever Gus built forts with the kids using household furniture and blankets, quilts, and pillows from all the beds and closets, he caused huge arguments with Victoria. She'd stand with her hands on her hips and say the same thing Stacy had just said – "Who is the child and who is the adult?" – but without the smile or the laugh.

Gus stripped the beds of their blankets and brought those downstairs too and thought how nice it was that he could build a massive fort taking up half the basement without getting in a brawl.

He moved the couches and turned the coffee table on its side. He built passages using blankets as roofs and walls. He connected secret rooms using play tunnels. When he finished, the kids had a dark and mysterious fortress with crawl spaces and secret doors and hideouts.

Jack collected his Star Wars figures in one of the secret rooms and Lilly brought all her dolls into another. Gus pretended he was a monster, lurking outside the fortress. He crawled around and chased them through the fort. They squealed and giggled when he popped out from behind a blanket or corner and roared.

They ran and he chased them. "Bang! Bang!" Jack said. "Han Solo shot you with his laser gun." Gus played dead and lay motionless on the ground. Lilly and Jack crept up to him. Lilly flicked his ear. Suddenly, Gus sprang up and roared and captured Lilly.

"I've got the princess. Somebody better save her or it's curtains!"

"I'll save you, Princess!" Jack yelled. "I'll kill the monster with my light saber."

"Kill?" Gus asked. "Heavens to Murgatroid! What about just capture…or wound…or spank and say, 'Bad boy'?" he said in his best Snagglepuss voice. "Exit, stage left!"

Jack laughed. "Take that!"

"Oh, I'm wounded!" Gus yelled. "But I'm still alive." Then he pulled Jack by the leg and dragged him over. Jack and Lilly screeched and laughed. Gus pulled them into him and rolled around.

"The monster's out of control!" He thrashed about. "I'm going crazy because my wound is so painful!" The fort crashed down – pillows and blankets fell on top of them and Gus and his two little children wrestled around in them. Then they began throwing cushions and pillows and stuffed dolls at each other. Gus ran toward them holding a couch cushion in front of him like a shield. He rammed into them and knocked them over into a pile of pillows and blankets.

They wrestled again for a few minutes. Then the kids started whacking him. "Hey! Go easy!" he said. They all laughed and lay in the blankets together for a long time, worn out. "This is the best Christmas ever," Gus said.

"Dinner's ready!" Stacy yelled from the top of the stairs.

"Last one there is a rotten egg!" Gus said. All three of them raced up the stairs and jumped into their seats at the dining room table.

"Let's try out those bikes after dinner. What do you think?"

"Yes!" both of them yelled.

Stacy served the steaming plates of food. She sat down next to Gus and leaned over. "Victoria called while you were downstairs," she whispered. "I told her you were all sleeping. She said she'd call in about an hour. She was nasty to me. She said you were supposed to have the kids call her this morning."

"Well, they have phones at the Holiday Inn and at Donna's, don't they?" he whispered back. "Why didn't she call herself?"

"I know, but you should probably have them call her and get it over with."

"Yeah, you're right. I'll have them call her after dinner."

They wolfed down the meat, mashed potatoes, peas and carrots. After dinner they each had a slice of apple pie that Vera had made and a scoop of vanilla ice cream. Stacy helped the kids clear the table and put the dishes in the dishwasher.

Gus took the overflowing kitchen trash bag out to the trash barrel on the side porch. He stepped outside and looked down the street. It was dirty and wet from the sand and salt the snowplows spread the night before. The bikes would get ruined. He pulled out a cigarette and let it sit in his mouth a few moments before he lit it. The sky was overcast and had a grayish purple tint that usually meant snow was coming. It was 3:15 p.m. and it would soon be too dark to ride bikes.

Gus walked back inside. "We better try those bikes now before it gets too dark. You can ride more tomorrow."

"What about Victoria?" Stacy asked. "Aren't you going to call her?"

"She can wait. She made me wait. We'll only be about a half hour."

CHAPTER 6

The Last Bike Ride

"Can I show Bobby my bike?" Jack asked. Bobby was Jack's best friend. He lived four houses down on Kingsbury Lane. They had been friends since they were infants, when Victoria and Bobby's mother Ellen met while pushing Jack and Bobby in carriages one summer day.

They became inseparable not long after, often running through the woods, throwing water balloons from their fort high up in a large pine tree behind Bobby's house, riding bikes, playing with their Star Wars and Adventure People toys, and sledding down the hill in back of the Mahoney's house. They attended Faulkner Kindergarten together, and they were in the same first grade classroom - Miss Monaco's – at Hajjar Elementary School.

Bobby was two months older and tall for his age – a whole head taller than Jack. Jack idolized him. Whatever Bobby did, Jack did too. Bobby had gotten a bike for his birthday in June the previous summer, and ever since, that's all Jack talked about. He wanted the same bike, a Huffy Survivor.

Jack already had a bike, a Schwinn Sting Ray with a banana seat and long handlebars shaped in a 'U'. It was yellow with a black seat. He didn't like it because the chain kept falling off.

Bobby and Jack had biked around the neighborhood all last summer. They were allowed to go anywhere except for a dead-end street where a dirt trail twisted along the railroad tracks and led to a place called Whale Rock. Whale Rock was a large boulder the size of an elephant that sat deep in the woods.

Whale Rock was where the high school kids hung out in the summer and after school. Each side of Whale Rock went straight up and it was difficult to climb. One side had a small foothold where a young aspen tree grew. Pushing off the aspen tree and using the foothold was the only way to climb to the top. Once you reached the top, it was flat and wide. Teenagers often built fires there. They also smoked cigarettes and pot and drank beer.

The rock was partially hidden behind a cluster of spruce trees. These trees bordered a meadow. A ditch ran along the path and the train tracks for about two hundred yards. It ended at the meadow. Because of the teenagers, and because a drunk Korean War veteran named Ross lived in an old shack made of scrap lumber in the woods near the rock, Jack and Bobby and their friends were not allowed to go near there.

Sometimes Bobby talked Jack into biking down the trail. They would veer off the path and walk their bikes in the ditch so no one would see them. One day they hid in the ditch and spied on a group of high school kids. Jack could see they were using tweezers to hold a cigarette. Someone had told him that when they used tweezers that meant they were smoking pot.

He was nervous and wanted to leave, but Bobby snuck up closer and hid behind a holly bush ten feet away. He made bird noises and threw acorns at the teens. He motioned to Jack to come up to the bush and spy with him, and told him to stop being a chicken. But Jack stayed behind in the ditch near his bike in case the teenagers discovered Bobby and chased them.

They did. Bobby was a better rider than Jack and he zoomed past him. "Hurry up! Don't let them catch you!" he yelled. Jack peddled as hard as he could, but they caught up to him and knocked him off his bike.

He began to cry and the boys called him a baby and words he didn't know. The girls told the boys to leave him alone. "Look at him, he's shaking. You're making him cry," one said. "Leave him alone!" The boys pushed him down to the ground and told him that if they ever caught him near Whale Rock again, they'd tie him to a tree by his underwear.

They caught Bobby too, but he didn't cry. He made a joke and acted like a wise guy. They didn't like that and they gave him a wedgie and threw his bike up on top of Whale Rock. He tried to climb the rock to get it, screaming. They kept pushing and kicking him off the rock and stepping on his fingers. He tried to grab them and pull them down.

Then Bobby *did* pull a kid off the rock and the kid fell hard to the ground. He got up and beat Bobby until his nose wouldn't stop bleeding and his face was covered with blood. The kid also tore Bobby's shirt. Jack tried to pull the kid off Bobby but the other teenagers grabbed him and threw him to the ground and told him if he moved they'd break his arm.

When Bobby got home he had to tell his mother that they were at Whale Rock and that the kids there took his bike and he tried to get it back and they beat him up. Bobby's mom stuffed cotton balls in his nose to soak up the trickling blood and cleaned his face. She asked him what he was doing at Whale Rock when he knew he wasn't allowed there.

Then she phoned Victoria to tell her that Jack and Bobby had been at Whale Rock and Bobby had been beaten up. Victoria yelled at Jack when he got home.

"I don't ever want to hear that you went to Whale Rock again," she said. She made him go to his room, where he sat on the bed and wished he was brave like Bobby.

Jack cried when he heard he was moving to New Jersey with his mother. "But all my friends are here," he said. "I don't want to move."

The development in which Gus lived was a quiet, leafy residential area shaped like an oval, with four streets crossing it. Many couples with young families lived there, including the O'Connors, with Bobby and Betsy. Jack had three other friends his age in the neighborhood – Seth Boylan on Burnham Road, Greg Bunn next door on the corner, on the other side of the swamp, and Michael Mahoney two blocks down on Carmel Drive. Bobby was his best friend.

The exception to all the families was the old Schroot couple next door. They were quiet, reserved people, each in their mid-sixties, who kept to themselves and maintained an immaculate lawn and large, orderly garden.

"You want to show Bobby your bike?" Gus asked. "Sure, let's ride down and see what Bobby and Betsy got for Christmas." Betsy was Bobby's older sister. She was two years older than Lilly.

"Let's see how it rides," Gus said. Jack walked the bike down the driveway, carefully avoiding the patches of ice and snow. He straddled the seat and rocketed off like a bully was chasing him from Whale Rock. Lilly hopped on her bike and took off after him. "I bet I'll beat you to Bobby's!" she yelled.

Gus ran after them. "Slow down! Wait a minute!" Just then Stacy came out the front door. She shouted something to him and he stopped running. "Hold on!" he yelled to the kids. Then he turned to Stacy. "What?" She was yelling that Victoria was on the line and wanted to talk to him immediately.

"Tell her I'll call her back in a few minutes," he shouted.

"I think you should talk to her. She sounds angry."

"She always sounds angry."

"She said if you don't come to the phone she's going to call her lawyer."

"Oh for God's sake! I wish she'd leave me alone," he said. "Hold on, I'll be right up." He turned toward the kids, who had biked back to him. "You guys don't go anywhere. Stay right out front for a minute." He ran into the house.

"Listen, I haven't had a chance to call you yet. The kids are trying their new bikes right now and I'll have them call you as soon as they get in," he said before Victoria had a chance to say anything.

"I told you last night to have them call me first thing in the morning," she whined into the phone. "And why are they out biking now? It's already getting dark."

Gus paced back and forth from the kitchen to the dining room to the living room, walking until the cord stretched as far as it could and then walking back. "First, it's not dark out yet," he said. "Second, it's my time with them now. This is my Christmas – not yours. I haven't seen them in three months, you show up four hours late last night and you're mad at me for not calling you at your appointed hour? Give me a break."

Victoria told him it was a simple five-minute call – that's all she asked for, not much to ask. She told him she wanted to make sure they were okay there without their mom.

"I'm not a goddamn stranger, I'm their fucking father – though you're doing your best to try to make me a stranger," he said. She demanded to talk to the kids that instant. Gus told her again he'd have them call her when they finished riding their bikes, which would be in about fifteen minutes, because, as she had pointed out, it would be getting dark soon.

"Listen," she said. "I want to talk to them *now*. I can make this difficult if that's how you want to play."

"Oh please," he said. "You couldn't possibly make it any more difficult than you have already."

"Put Lilly on the phone right now or I'm going to talk to my lawyer tomorrow and make sure the judge knows about this when we're in court."

Gus tried to think about how she'd use this in court. Among all the rules written in their custody settlement, he couldn't remember anything written about scheduled phone calls at specific times. She often didn't let Gus talk to the kids when he called. In fact, Gus thought Lilly and Jack must have been training for the Olympics because every time he called she told him they were at swimming or skating or gymnastics lessons.

He started to say something then stopped. He looked at Stacy, who was watching him, and shook his head. "Fine, hold on," he said into the receiver. He threw the phone against the dining room wall and walked out the front door.

"Lilly!" he yelled. "Come in for a minute. Mommy's on the phone. She wants to talk to you."

"No, I want to ride my bike," she said. She looked as if Gus had told her she had to return the bike.

"Yes. Mommy wants to hear what Santa got you. Tell her about your bike." Lilly peddled up the driveway and gently laid her bike against some juniper shrubs along the walkway to the front door.

"You too, Jack," he shouted. "She'll want to talk to you after."

Stacy stood holding the phone. "Hello?" Gus said. Victoria began screaming at him.

"Don't you keep me waiting like this!"

"Calm down. Hold on, here's Lilly." He listened for a moment and then walked out the front door to call for Jack to come in.

"Jack! Come in and talk to Mommy!" Jack wasn't out front. "Where the hell did he go now?" Gus muttered. He looked up and down the street. Nothing. He called him again: "Jack!"

CHAPTER 7

Missing

Gus guessed that Jack rode to Bobby's to show him his new bike. He ran back up the driveway to the house. "If she asks for Jack, tell her he went to Bobby's and I went to get him and we'll be right back," he said to Stacy. Then he ran to Bobby's to get Jack and drag him back so he wouldn't have to listen to Victoria. Ellen O'Connor opened the door.

"Hi Gus. How was your Christmas?" she said.

"Oh pretty good. I just came to get Jack."

Ellen O'Connor looked at him with a puzzled look. "I haven't seen Jack," she said. "I think Bobby's downstairs playing with his Star Wars."

"Jack was riding his new bike here to show Bobby. He would've gotten here only a few minutes ago."

"Oh. Let me get Bobby and see if he's seen him. She gestured for Gus to come in. He waited on the landing while Ellen O'Connor descended the stairs and called to Bobby.

"Bobby, is Jack down there with you?" she said. Gus then realized he hadn't seen the bike in the O'Connor's driveway.

Gus heard Bobby say no.

"Have you seen him or do you know where he is?" Ellen asked. "His dad is here looking for him."

"No, I haven't talked to him today," Bobby said.

Ellen came back up the stairs. "No, he hasn't seen him. Are you sure he didn't go to Greg's or Michael's?"

"I don't know," Gus said. "He said he wanted to come here to show Bobby his bike."

"Here…come in and I'll call Abby and Sarah and see if he's over one of their houses." She called Greg and Michael's moms while Gus stood in the kitchen doorway. "Yes, Gus has the kids this Christmas, remember? Uh, huh. Ok. Oh good. I'll tell him," she said and hung up. "Abby hasn't seen him but she said Greg is over Michael's and they were playing outside in the yard. He's probably over there with them. Let me call Sarah and see—"

"That's okay, I'll run over, thanks," Gus said. He thrust the door open, bounded down the front steps, and jogged to Michael Mahoney's house, all the while looking for Jack biking on the street or talking to a neighbor in a yard. Shadows crept across the road between the street lamps that were now on. Michael Mahoney's house was about a quarter of a mile away, on Carmel Drive. When Gus arrived he was breathing hard.

He didn't see the boys outside or Jack's bike. He knocked on the door and Elizabeth Mahoney, Michael's younger sister, answered. "Is Jack over here," he asked. She said she didn't think so but she would check with her mom and she disappeared up the stairs. After a minute, Sarah Mahoney, her mother, came to the door.

"I haven't seen Jack," she said. Greg was here and they were playing outside but I don't think Jack was with them. Greg left about five minutes ago – you didn't see him?"

Gus told her he had not.

"He's not over Bobby's?" she asked.

"No, I just came from there."

"Oh. What about Seth Boylan's?" she said.

"I don't know. I don't know," Gus said, absentmindedly fidgeting with his jacket zipper.

Sarah Mahoney offered some other possible places Jack might have gone. "Maybe the Schroots invited him in–" but Gus didn't wait for her to finish. He burst out the door, yelling:

"I'm just gonna check the neighborhood. He must still be riding around." She called after him and said to let her know when he found Jack.

Gus noticed it had gotten darker during the five minutes he spent inside the Mahoney's. He scanned the street. No sign of Jack. He ran to Seth Boylan's house. His father answered the door. "Hi Gus. How was your Christmas?"

"It was okay. Is Jack here, or have you seen him?"

"I haven't seen him Gus. Did you try Bobby's house?"

"Yes, he's not there."

"How about—"

"I've checked at the Mahoney's and with the Bunn's. I don't know where else he'd go," Gus said. He began to tighten like a coiled spring, ready to explode; nervous energy mixed with exhaustion.

He ran back to his house. Lilly was still on the phone with her mother. "Did Jack come back?" he asked.

"No, I haven't seen him," Stacy said. "But Victoria keeps asking to talk to him. She won't hang up until she talks to Jack."

Gus snatched the phone from Lilly. "We'll call you right back, we're in the middle of something," he said and slammed the phone down on the receiver.

"I'll call her back when I find Jack," he said to Stacy. "Can you stay here in case he comes back?" He grabbed a bell he used to use to signal the kids to come in for dinner. It was an old wooden-handled brass bell and its clanging could be heard for blocks away. "Jack!" he yelled. Then he rushed back outside, calling Jack's name and ringing the bell.

"Dammit. Where the hell did he go?" His head throbbed.

He ran to the Schroots' door. He knocked. Bud Schroot answered. "Hi Gus, Merry Christmas," he said.

"Hi Bud. I can't find Jack and I was wondering if you might have seen him. He was riding his bike and now I can't find him."

"No, I haven't seen him."

Gus saw Eleanor Schroot peering from the balcony, trying to see who was at the door. Bud Schroot turned to her.

"Honey, you haven't seen Jack out riding the bike have you?"

"No, why?"

"Gus can't find him—how long has he been gone?"

"About forty-five minutes."

"Maybe he went down the trails to test the bike" Bud said. "Probably doesn't realize you're looking for him."

"He knows he's not supposed to be out after dark."

"You know boys," Bud said.

"If you can, please keep your eye out for him on the street and if you see him, tell him to go home and that I'm looking for him. I'm going to check around the neighborhood."

Bud Schroot grabbed his jacket from its hook and put it on. "I'll walk around too and see if I can find him," he said.

"Oh, thank you, thank you. I appreciate it. I'm going to head up Carriage Street; if you want to go the other side, by Burnham, that would be great."

Gus ran up Kingsbury Lane and down Carriage. Three quarters down Carriage, he saw a few kids playing in one of the yards. He didn't know them. "Do any of you know Jack Delaney?" he asked.

They shook their heads no. Then one kid said, "Oh yeah, I think so. Is he the small blond kid?"

"Yes," Gus said. "Did you see him riding his bike?" The kid said he hadn't seen him, but one of the other kids thought he remembered a boy riding his bike earlier; he didn't know who it was.

"Where was he going? What did he look like?" Gus asked.

"I couldn't really see him that well, but he looked like an older kid."
"How old, older than seven?" The boy said that he thought the kid on the bike looked older than seven but he wasn't sure.

"When did you see him?"

"A couple hours ago, I think," the boy said.

Gus knew that Jack wouldn't have been out a couple hours ago but the kids didn't seem too certain of the time or too reliable with details.

"Which way was he going?" he asked.

"He was going that way," the boy said and he pointed down Carriage Road in the direction of the dead end where the path that led to Whale Rock began. "He went down the dead end. I didn't see him come back." Gus knew about Whale Rock. He had gone there once with an old girlfriend to have a picnic, only to arrive to find two teenage couples already on the rock. So he picnicked on the edge of the meadow under an oak tree instead.

Was Jack the boy on the bike that the kid had seen? Did he go down to Whale Rock to try his bike on the trails? Gus sprinted toward the trail. His lungs felt like someone had lit them on fire.

The streets were now silent except for a dog that barked somewhere in the neighborhood – a high, piercing bark echoing in the cold dusk. The frigid air hurt his throat and he was having trouble breathing. He was out of shape. It had not been warm earlier, but it was colder now and Gus's breath blew like smoke from a cigarette.

He ran down the path. There was no moon and he almost had to feel his way along – it was as if he was running with a blanket over his head. The snow crunched under his feet. He didn't think Jack would bike down the icy path in the inky woods to Whale Rock – Jack was scared of the dark and woods at night. But something compelled Gus to check anyway.

If Jack had met someone he knew or saw kids entering the path on their way to Whale Rock, he might have followed them. But what kids would be going to Whale Rock on Christmas night? Only kids much older and probably up to no good. Certainly not seven-year old kids.

Gus ran faster. He stumbled in a hole and sprained his ankle and tumbled to the ground. He got up and staggered along the path as fast as he could. His ankle began to throb. He arrived at Whale Rock. He didn't see anyone there. He didn't really expect to. It was dark and quiet except for the wind moaning.

He began to limp back. His mind raced as he tried to figure out what to do next. Then he saw a faint light. He squinted and peered past the ditch. There, hidden among a cluster of pine trees, was a wooden shack made of scrap lumber. The light came from the shack. Gus knew that Ross, the Korean War veteran who walked around town all day and stumbled drunk around the Billerica Mall at night, begging for money and food, lived somewhere out here. This must be his place, he thought.

Gus limped to the shack. Newspaper was stuffed into holes in the walls where the wood didn't cover completely. There was one small window with a sheet of plastic across it to block the wind. Outside the front door, a hatchet rested on a stump next to a small pile of cut firewood. About two dozen cigarette butts lay scattered in the snow-dirt outside the door. A wisp of smoke billowed from a pipe sticking out of the roof.

Gus knocked on the door. Only then did he become nervous and wonder exactly what he was going to say. Most people said Ross had mental problems – that he was crazy or schizophrenic. At the least, he was usually drunk and ornery.

He was the town bum. Everyone knew him and accepted in some perverse way that he was a member of the community. He had never hurt a flea – as far as anyone knew. There were rumors that he snapped during the war and went AWOL, but nobody really knew anything about him. Gus thought maybe he had been walking – he often walked the streets of the neighborhood at night with his cocker spaniel Bonnie – and had seen Jack.

Gus knocked again. He heard cans rattle and muffled curses. "Who's there?" a thick voice bellowed from the other side of the door.

"My name is Gus Delaney. I live down the street. I'm looking for my boy. He was riding—"

"He's not here so get the fuck away," Ross said through the doorway.

"Please, I just want to know if you've seen any kids or heard anyone at Whale Rock tonight," Gus said. The door remained closed.

"I told you, I haven't seen your kid so get the fuck away from me."

Gus couldn't leave until Ross opened the door. He had to see inside. He didn't really expect to see Jack in there, but something compelled him to make sure. He tried to push this thought from his mind but he was beginning to think that maybe someone had taken Jack. Jack was not the type of kid to ride around on his bike alone in the dark.

"Do you mind coming out for a second?" Gus asked.

"Listen buddy," Ross said through the door. "I don't know who you are or where your boy is, but you're asking for trouble."

Gus pounded on the door. He kicked and punched it and screamed in desperation, "Open the goddamn door for a minute and talk to me! Is that too fucking much to ask?"

Suddenly, the door swung open and Ross burst out. He jabbed the end of a rifle barrel so hard into Gus's chest that it knocked him down. Ross jammed his boot into Gus's stomach and pointed the gun at his head.

"Don't shoot!" Gus cried. "I'm sorry. I just can't find my son and I thought he might have come here or you might have seen him."

"I told you, I haven't seen your boy." Ross lifted the gun in the air, pointing it toward the treetops. "Now get the hell out of here and leave me alone."

Gus staggered to his feet and limped down the path, fingering the welt on his chest from the rifle butt. His backside was soaked from lying in the snow, and the wetness made him cold. It began to snow, slowly at first, and then more steadily. His head hurt. His chest ached. His ankle was swollen.

He prayed, asking God that when he got home Jack would be there. He promised he would go to church again. He wasn't sure what he'd do if Jack wasn't at the house. He didn't want to think about it.

When he reached the driveway, Stacy opened the door and stood on the steps. Gus knew instantly from the anxious look etched on her face that Jack hadn't come home.

"Oh Gus! Where is he? I'm really worried," she said.

"I don't know." She noticed his limping.

"Where have you been? What happened?" Gus's body nearly went into spasms from cold and worry. "You're soaked! Come inside and get out of those clothes." She pulled him inside and yanked off his shirt. "What happened to your chest?" she said, pointing to the swollen, reddish-purple welt.

"Nothing."

"What do you mean nothing! You have a welt the size of a golf ball!"

"I don't want to talk about it right now," Gus said. Stacy didn't force the issue. She gave him a dry tee shirt and a wool sweater and then covered him with a blanket.

"Bud Schroot came over," she said. "He said he walked up and down the streets and he didn't see him. Ellen O'Connor called, and Sarah Mahoney. They asked if he came home yet." Stacy noticed that Gus was staring blankly into the fire. She didn't know if he was listening to her. He seemed somewhere far away.

For a moment, she saw a look in his eyes she had never seen before. She had seen anger and frustration and worry on his face, but never the fear that shone in his eyes now. They were lifeless, like a dead fish's eyes. Then he snapped back. "Where's Lilly?" he asked.

"She's in her bedroom. She's nervous about Jack."

Gus stumbled down the hall. Pain shot through his ankle every step. He knocked on the door and went into Lilly's room. She was lying in bed with her blanket and Raggedy Ann doll. She sprang up. "Did you find Jack?"

Gus picked her up and pulled her to him. His body shuddered as he convulsed with silent sobs. He tried to hide his tears from his little girl; he tried not to get her worried, but he knew he wasn't hiding it at all. He couldn't control his shaking.

"What's wrong Daddy? Where's Jack?" she asked. Her voice had a slight catch in it – a quiver, and Gus knew she was scared.

"I don't know," he said, trying to compose himself and project calm, "but we're going to find him." He wiped his eyes and looked at her. "Did Jack say anything to you about wanting to bike anywhere?" She shook her head no.

"He didn't tell you he was going to go to anyone's house or visit anyone or bike anywhere – the trails down by Whale Rock?"

"No, only Bobby's but then you told us to wait out front," she said.

"All right. I'm going to go back outside and look for him. You stay here with Stacy and watch for him, okay?" He hugged her tightly and kissed her on her forehead. "I love you."

"I love you too," she said. She paused for a second. "I'm scared."

"Don't worry honey. I'm going to find Jack and we'll ride bikes tomorrow and we'll all build another fort together."

"But it's dark out and Jack is scared of the dark."

PART II

CHAPTER 8

Stolen

The brown Pinto station wagon slipped down Route 3 south past Plymouth, following the caravan of cars – red tail lights flaming – zooming home from Christmas travels. A woman wearing a worn black robe sat in the passenger seat. She spoke in a soft voice to the driver of the car, a man bundled in an old brown corduroy coat, a red and black flannel shirt and corduroy pants, with a tweed hat pulled just above his eyes. A thick, tangled squirrel's nest beard hid the rest of his face. He looked like he might have crawled out from a cardboard box under a bridge.

"Do you think Abraham will be pleased?" the woman asked.

The man looked in the rear-view mirror. He had looked in the mirror every few minutes since they began driving an hour ago. Below the flashing white lights reflecting off the back window, cowering in the shadows in the back seat, a small boy whimpered. Every so often a car passed and the beam of its head-lights flashed and a harsh light moved across the boy's face and revealed that it was wet with tears.

"Yes, he'll be pleased," the man said after a few minutes' silence. The boy gazed out the window at the dull, dark sky. Lights flashing and then dark again. Shadows creeping across his face and then yellow light and the whoosh of cars passing. He listened to the man and woman in the front seat talking about him.

They crossed a huge bridge. The boy could see the water far below. They had driven nearly the entire way without the man or woman addressing or acknowledging the boy directly. Finally, the woman turned around in her seat and spoke. "You're going to live with us from now on." The boy looked at her. He could only see a dim outline of her face, which was hidden in the night's shadow.

"We're your family now," she continued. We're going to your new home." The boy looked away from her and faced the window. He began to cry.

"You mustn't cry Augustine," she said. "Crying is weak and those who cry will suffer eternal damnation in the fires of hell. You don't understand this, but we are saving you from being damned to hell and cast aside by God. We are rescuing you from great suffering." She paused and considered him. She reached out to place her hand on his knee. The boy recoiled and moved out of her reach, closer to the door.

"My name is Jack!" he cried. "I want my daddy!" His body convulsed in sobs. The woman glanced at the man. He nodded his head to encourage her to continue.

"Jack is your old name, your damned name," she said. "Augustine is your new name, your redeemed name, and you will accept it as your name from now on." She looked at the man, started to speak again, and then stopped and stared out the front window. Jack noticed they had pulled off the highway.

The lights from passing cars became less frequent as they drove down a quiet, dark road lined by bare elms and maples and scrub pine. When cars passed, their flashing lights reminded Jack of that afternoon: Lilly crawling through the blanket tunnels shining a flashlight trying to find him hiding in a secret chamber of the fort his dad had made.

"You must forget your father," the woman, turning again to face Jack, continued in her soft voice. "Your father is an evil person and he is going to hell. We took you from him so you won't go to hell too. We're taking you to a place where you will be saved…where you will find salvation and learn true happiness. It's for the best."

Jack wanted to tell her that he didn't want to go…that his daddy was not evil and not going to hell. But he was scared. He stared blankly out the car window, tears rolling down his face, and hoped his dad would find him and take him back home.

Jack strained to see where he was as the car twisted around the narrow curves, but all he could see were the vague outlines of the murky pine trees on both sides of the road. The woman turned to him. "You are going to meet Abraham. He is the prophet and the one who is going to save you and show you the truth and the light. He saved all of us." The woman also told Jack he would meet his new brothers and sisters. He would forget his old family and his old life, his dark life.

"We know all about you, Augustine," she said. "Your mother told us everything." The car stopped in front of a gate between two pillars. The man got out, turned a latch and swung the gate open. He drove through and then got out again and closed the gate behind him. The car lurched down the narrow, bumpy, winding driveway.

Black trees – thick woods – bordered each side of the car; pine branches hung close enough that they whacked against the roof. Jack searched the woman's shadowy face for some answer to how his mother was involved, what she had told them, why this had happened.

Jack played the scene over in his mind, trying to remember, trying to find the reason why these people had taken him, searching for a connection and some hope that he would eventually be returned home.

He remembered the man and woman pulled up next to him in the old car and told him they were friends with his mom – his mom was Victoria Delaney, right? – and that she had asked them to get Jack, that it was urgent. Jack stopped his bike right away when the woman with the kind voice called his name. She beckoned him over to the car window. She had an important message from his mother.

"We need to take you to her right now," the woman said. "She's at the Holiday Inn up the street." Jack hesitated. He knew his mother was at the Holiday Inn. He remembered turning to see if his daddy was outside, but instead he saw the waist of the large man with the scraggly beard; he had snuck up behind him.

In a flash the man put his gloved hand over Jack's mouth and ripped him off the bike. Jack remembered that the glove smelled like sweat. Then the man threw him into the back seat of the car. The woman told him that if he made a noise or yelled or tried to get away, the man would kill his mother and father and his sister Lilly. Then Jack watched the man throw his bike down the embankment that led to the swamp, into a cluster of bushes.

The woman had jumped into the back seat with him. She had held her hand over his mouth. It also smelled like sweat. "Don't move," she had said.

"Yes, we spoke to your mother," the woman continued now. Jack saw the silhouette of a huge house looming in a clearing, a hulking shadow under the moonlight. The car came to a stop in front of it.

The house had a steeply pitched roof with a towering gable in the center. Monstrous icicles dangled from the trim and a weak, flickering light shone from the window high up on the gable; the lone light in the lone window that Jack could see. Thick bushes hid the lower windows and creaky wooden stairs led to a porch that stretched the length of the house.

"She told us enough to know that this is the best thing for you," the woman said as she opened the car door. "You are impure, sinful. You need to learn the path to enlightenment."

What did his mom tell them? Jack wondered.

"Don't be afraid," the woman said. "You will learn to like it here." Jack shivered in the biting wind as the woman led him up the walkway to the heavy wooden front door. She gripped his hand hard. The man had disappeared.

Inside, the house smelled like dry wood. There were no Christmas decorations. The flame of a candle flickered when they closed the door and caused their shadows to bob, as if on waves, along the wall. The house was cold and Jack thought about how warm and nice his father's house was with the fire roaring in the living room.

The woman stood in the foyer with her hand on Jack's shoulder. To the right, Jack could see a large room, wood-paneled and somber. A red-hued Oriental rug lay sprawled across the wood floor and bookshelves bulging with leather-bound books lined the far wall. A fireplace was also at the far end of the room. No fire burned.

Some paintings – portraits in oil of people dressed in frills and lace – and a tapestry showing two muscular arms with the fingers pointing at each other adorned the other walls. A few more candles flickered on a round table in front of a big, brown leather couch.

The man appeared and signaled to the woman. She grabbed Jack's hand. "Come with me," she said. She brought him into a large kitchen and opened a door that Jack hoped would be a pantry filled with snacks. But when she pulled a dangling string a dim light bulb glowed and revealed a steep stairway descending into a basement.

They creaked down the stairs. At the last stair, they came to a cement floor, and then they crept along a passageway. Shelving on both sides held boxes and tools and stacks of yellowed newspapers and bags of fertilizer, lawn seed, buckets, and rolled up rugs. They came to a door.

The woman opened it and they entered someone's living quarters. They passed a bathroom with a bar of soap and tube of toothpaste on the sink. There was a small kitchen with a linoleum-tiled floor and an old Frigidaire ice box. A small table with three chairs was pushed up against the wall. On it rested a stick of butter and a plate with a loaf of baked bread.

The woman walked to a door with a window and Jack could see it led outside. She checked the lock. Then she opened a second door. A bedroom. "You wait here," she said, pointing to the room. Jack walked in and she closed the door behind him. He heard the click of the lock.

There were two beds, both made, the white blankets pulled tightly over the pillows, not a wrinkle anywhere. There was a window through which Jack could see the blue-gray outlines of tree branches whipping in the wind at the edge of a forest. On a night-stand between the beds was an oil lamp, and a clock ticked quickly – tick, tick, tick – like a bomb, and it mingled with the wailing wind outside. The walls were bare.

Jack shivered in the frigid, mildewy, musty room. He pulled down the blanket on one of the beds and burrowed underneath it. Where was he? Who were these people and would he see his mother and father and Lilly again? He dreamed about his bright house and his bedroom and his warm, soft bed and his blanket and the crackling fire and the Christmas tree and Elios Pizza and his Star Wars toys and his bike.

He wondered if his father was looking for him and what Lilly was doing. He wondered where his mother was and if she would come here to get him later tonight. He hoped she would. He thought of Bobby and wondered if he were here would he be brave and make wisecracks and not let these people scare him, just like with the older boys at Whale Rock?

He knew Bobby would be brave and he cried because he could not be brave like Bobby because he was scared. His teeth clattered. He wished Bobby were with him.

After awhile he heard a noise outside. He got up and pressed his face against the window pane to see what he could see. Suddenly the bedroom door opened. It was the woman. "There is nothing to see out there. Just woods and the bay," she said. "Come with me."

She led him back up the stairs, through the kitchen, past the front entrance, through the room he had seen when he first arrived, down a long corridor, up a staircase, then up another staircase hidden behind a door, this one steeper and winding in a circle. It led to a bedroom. There were many candles lit and the room smelled of spice. There was a large, pointed window on the front wall. This must have been the window near the top of the house that Jack had seen.

The room was different than the other rooms. A king-sized bed, richly covered in a maroon silk bedspread, dominated. Jack stood on thick, golden shag wall-to-wall carpet. A portrait of a man, halo gleaming around his head, hung on the wall over the bed. It looked like Jesus, but it was not Jesus. Jack blinked at himself in the large mirror on the wall above a dresser. A door next to it opened and a man appeared wearing a white robe. It was the man in the portrait.

CHAPTER 9

The Search

Gus stepped outside and stood in the driveway. He was unsure what to do next. Should he go door to door around the neighborhood and ask if anyone saw Jack? Should he call the police? He got in his car and drove slowly up and down the streets of the neighborhood. He didn't see anyone outside, let alone Jack.

Then he drove up Carriage Road, up a hill leading to High Street. High Street was a busier street that led to the Concord River and the old mills. This night it was quiet. He drove a couple of miles without finding Jack.

A horrible thought then occurred to him: what if Jack had been hit by a car? Maybe he was at the hospital the whole time. Or worse, maybe he was on the side of the road somewhere, hurt, and couldn't get home.

Gus turned back in the direction of his house. The car crept down the road and Gus looked along the snow banks for either Jack or Jack's bike. A car came up close behind him and flashed its brights. Gus looked in the rearview mirror. The car honked. Gus extended his middle finger in front of the rearview mirror.

The car sped onto the other side of the road and roared by him, blowing the horn as he sped past. "Asshole!" Gus yelled. He gripped the steering wheel tightly and continued driving slowly toward home.

He rushed into the house and was about to ask Stacy if she had heard from Jack or anyone else, but the look on her face told him he didn't need to. "I'm going to call the hospital," he said. "I'm worried that maybe a car hit him. Why else would he not have come home?"

"Hi, my name is Gus Delaney. I was wondering if any boys about seven years old have been taken to the emergency room tonight," he said.

"What's the name?" the dispatcher who answered the phone asked.

"Jack. Jack Delaney."

"I just came on my shift, so let me check. It'll be a minute," she said and then she was gone. After what seemed to Gus to be at least ten minutes, she came back.

"Yes, a boy came in about an hour ago, fell on some ice and got a concussion and a pretty good gash on his head." As soon as Gus heard this, his tensed body exhaled all the strain that had built up. At least he knew where Jack was and that he was okay. The relief only lasted a second.

"What did you say your boy's name is?" the dispatcher asked.

"Jack."

"No, I'm sorry but his name is not Jack. Have you checked with the police?"

"No I haven't," Gus answered.

"That would be your best bet," she said. "You really should report it to them…see if they have any information."

Gus thanked her and hung up. He had gripped the phone so tightly that his hand hurt. He looked over to see Stacy watching him from the living room couch. He paced the living room, stopping every few minutes at the front window to gaze at the dark, cold street. Then he went to the phone and called the police.

The officer who answered the phone was gruff and spoke with a thick Boston accent. "Billerica Police, Officer Flynn," he said when he answered.

"Hi, my name is Gus Delaney. My son was riding his bike a couple of hours ago in front of the house and he disappeared. I can't find him."

"What do you mean he disappeared?" Officer Flynn said. Gus was taken aback by his tone.

"Just what I said. He was outside riding the bike he got for Christmas and I had to step inside the house for a minute and when I came out he wasn't there."

"And how long ago was this?" Flynn asked. Gus was angry that he had to repeat himself.

"Like I said, a couple of hours ago."

"Can you be more specific?"

"Well, the last I saw him was about 3:30 this afternoon. It's a little past 7 now."

"Have you checked with the neighbors or any of his friends?"

"Of course. None of them have seen him."

"Have you checked the streets around the neighborhood?" Flynn asked.

"Yes!" Gus yelled, exasperated. "Of course I checked around the neighborhood. That's what I've been doing the last three hours. There's no sign of him anywhere."

"Calm down sir. You don't have to take that tone with me," Flynn said.

"Excuse me?" Gus said. "My son is missing and you're telling me to calm down?"

"Yes. Listen, I'm just trying to help," Flynn said in an agitated voice.

Gus's patience had already been tested too far. "You'd be more helpful if you stopped asking me stupid questions," he said.

There was a short pause. Then Officer Flynn continued asking questions in the same methodical pace, ignoring Gus's comment.
"Sir, what is your name and what is your address?"

"Gus Delaney, and I live at 4 Kingsbury Lane."

"And how old is your child…did you say it was a boy?"

"Yes, my boy. His name is Jack and he's seven years old," Gus said. "Have there been any car accidents reported?"

"Car accidents?"

"Yes. I'm worried that maybe he got hit by a car and got hurt and that's why he hasn't come home."

"No, there haven't been any accidents reported," Flynn said. There was another short pause. "Is that where – Kingsbury Lane – Jack was when he disappeared?"

"Yes. Like I said, he was out front riding his bike and I had to go into the house for a minute and when I came back out he was gone. Are you going to send a car out to look for him?"

"Hold on. I'll get to that. First, I have to ask some more questions," Flynn said. "Who else lives at the house?"

"Just me. Jack and his sister live with their mother during the year. I have them in the summer. They are staying with me for Christmas vacation."

There was a long pause. "So you're divorced?"

"Yes, I'm divorced."

"And where does their mother live?"

"Do we really have to go through all these questions right now? I just want someone to come over here and help me find my son," Gus said.

"Does Jack have a history of running away?"

Gus resented the question. "No, he has never run away, nor has he ever threatened to run away or wanted to run away," he said, his voice rising with anger.

Flynn picked up on Gus's anger and he seemed to want to push it. "Has the divorce affected Jack in a way that might make him run away? Have you and your wife fought in front of him – was there an argument recently that might have affected him negatively?"

Gus's mind buzzed with thoughts of the previous night. Yes, they fought all the time, and Jack often saw them fighting. But Jack didn't run away, of that Gus was certain. "I told you, he didn't run away!"

"Again Mr. Delaney, I want to ask you to calm down," Flynn said. "I know you're upset, and the reason I'm asking you these questions is to try to determine what happened to your boy. We'll send someone down there shortly. Now please try to answer the questions. Did anything happen recently that might have contributed to a stressful environment in the household?"

"No," Gus said curtly. He paced back and forth in the kitchen. He was wasting precious time answering questions on the phone about his family life instead of out looking for Jack.

"Who else was in the house with you when he disappeared?"

"Me, my girlfriend, and my daughter."

"And where is the boy's mother?"

"She's at her friend's house in Woburn. She dropped Jack and his sister off last night."

"Have you spoken to her? Does she know her son is missing?" Flynn said this in a way that made Gus uncomfortable. The whole tone of the questioning made Gus feel as though Flynn was accusing him of something. Gus had expected a different response from the police.

"I haven't spoken to her yet," he said. "She's the reason I had to leave him in the first place. She called on the phone and insisted that I speak to her right then. I've been looking for my son and that's all I've been doing since he's been missing, and if you don't mind, if you're going to continue to ask me questions about my marriage and not send someone over here, I'd like to get off the phone and go look for him again."

Flynn asked him to hold on one minute. Gus heard him talking to someone in the background. He noticed Stacy standing at the front door looking through the glass paneled windows into the darkness. She turned and looked at him. Tears rolled down her cheeks. Gus heard Flynn get back on the phone.

"Mr. Delaney? Are you there?"

"Yes, I'm here."

"We're going to send a car down there to talk to you as soon as we can. Our officer on duty is responding to another call right now and as soon as he finishes, he'll come by," Flynn said. "In the meantime, I suggest you call your wife – or your ex-wife – and let her know what's going on. Is it possible that she picked up your son and didn't tell you?"

Is this guy a moron, or is he just not paying attention? Gus wondered. "No, I was on the phone with her when he disappeared, like I told you. She wasn't in the area."

"Okay then," Flynn said. "I'll send over an officer as soon as possible. We'll call you if we hear anything in the meantime." Flynn hung up. Gus slammed the phone down.

CHAPTER 10

Panic

"He's insinuating that Jack ran away," Gus said. "Just get a goddamn car down here to help me find my son! I don't need to answer a hundred questions." Gus put his coat on.

"What else did he say?" Stacy asked. "What are you doing?" Gus was on his knees looking in the coat closet by the front door. He didn't answer and all Stacy could hear was his muffled voice yelling "goddamn" and something about his boots. Gloves and shoes and scarves began flying over his shoulder as he burrowed deeper in the closet.

"Gus, what are you looking for?"

"My Timberland boots. Do you know where I left them?"

"Yes, they are on the porch by the kitchen door…where are you going?" Gus told her that he was going to check around the swamp and trails in the woods behind the back yard. The creeks were swollen four or five times their normal size and maybe Jack had gone to explore and had gotten lost or slipped and fell and broke his foot or something. The kids were always running through the damn swamp and the woods.

"I heard you mention Victoria on the phone," Stacy said as she picked up the shoes and gloves and hats that Gus had thrown about the living room. "What did the police say about her?"

"Nothing," Gus said.

"Shouldn't you call her?"

Gus hesitated for a moment, frozen in thought. He didn't want to deal with her yet.

Stacy looked down at the ground and then looked up at him. "What if she's involved?" she asked.

"Why would she do something like this? And how could she have? It doesn't make any sense," Gus said. "Besides, she was on the phone with me wanting to talk to him…there's no way." He paused and looked blankly at the ground. He was surprised Victoria hadn't called back. "I'll be back," he said. Then Gus turned and walked out the front door. He slammed it behind him.

He walked through the snow, which was about six inches deep with a frozen crust covering the top of it, toward the swamp. He shined a flashlight on the ground in front of him, creating a little circle of light that allowed him to see where he was stepping. But he couldn't see anything beyond the weak beam created by the flashlight. He slid down a hill and knocked against a bush covered in snow. The snow spilled down his neck and back and fell into his boots.

At the bottom of the hill the swamp began. This is where Jack and Lilly came to find frogs in the summer and skate on the ice in the winter. It was frozen.

Gus shined the light slowly back and forth across the width of the swamp. The snow and ice and tree branches flickered pale and cold blue. He swept the light along the ground, looking for any footprints or broken ice.

The swamp meandered a good mile behind the house, then merged with the woods that stretched about another mile. Jack and Bobby and the other boys lived in the woods during the summer. And before Victoria took the kids away, they spent many hours during the winter exploring the winter wonderland that the woods became when snow and ice clung to the branches of trees, the weight lowering the limbs to the ground to create hidden caves.

Suddenly Gus remembered that the boys had a fort – a hideout in a thicket that Seth Boylan's older brother had helped them build with scrap lumber they collected from neighbors. Maybe Jack was there.

Gus walked down the path along the edge of the swamp. He called Jack's name. The only thing that answered him was silence. No gurgling water from the creek. No birds calling. No crickets chirping. The woods and swamp were dark and dead and cold. Gus felt sick deep in his stomach.

The narrow path curled and twisted alongside the creek. Cattails swayed on both sides of the path, nearly obscuring it. When he got to the marsh, he veered off the trail and went to the right and then walked up a hill. Next to a massive pine tree, the fort creaked and groaned in the frosty wind. There was a padlock on the door.

Gus pulled on it, but it was locked. He couldn't move his hands well in the cold. His fingers were frozen numb. He looked around for a rock or something to break the padlock with, but snow covered everything. "Jack!" he yelled. "Are you in there?" He knew it was a stupid question. He knew Jack wasn't in there. No one answered.

He punched the door over and over again. He punched it until his knuckles bled. Then he collapsed and sat on the ground and buried his head in his arms and sobbed in the dark. "Oh Jack...where are you? Where are you?" he cried as he leaned against the fort and looked up at the sky and the black leaf-less branches swaying in a blustery gale. His body shook. He sat for a long time paralyzed, sobbing in the snow.

When he got back to the house, two police cars, blue lights blazing, lit up his driveway. Finally, some help, he thought. Two cops stood in the living room. One wrote on a pad; the other asked Stacy something about the custody battle between Gus and Victoria. Gus didn't catch the whole question – both the notetaker and the inquisitor stopped when he entered the house.

"Mr. Delaney?" the older, heavier one asked.

"Yes, I'm Gus Delaney."

"I'm glad you're finally here," the cop continued. "I'm Lieutenant Goddard with the Billerica Police and I have a few questions for you."

CHAPTER 11

An Investigation

Lieutenant Goddard was an enormous man, with a belly that hung far over his belt like when a cake rises and overtakes the pan and oozes over the side. Officer Baker stood behind him and walked around the living room, examining things. He picked up Jack's Millennium Falcon ship and turned it over in his hand. Gus watched him intently as he listened to Lieutenant Goddard's questions. Stacy sat on the couch and listened.

"Mr. Delaney, can you tell me when you last saw Jack?" he asked.

"I told all that to some guy Flynn already over the phone." Lieutenant Goddard stood with his pen in position to write in the pad. He waited. "Like I've told you all about four times already," Gus continued, "Jack was out front riding his bike and I ran into the house to take a phone call from his mother. I was only inside for about 5 minutes and when I came out he was gone."

"And about what time was this," Goddard asked as he wrote.

"About 4 o'clock."

"And you reported Jack missing at—" he flipped the pages of his notebook back. "7:05. Can you tell me why you waited so long to report him missing and everywhere you have been between 4 p.m. and now?"

Gus stared at him, mouth gaping. "I don't understand what you're trying to say…are you accusing me of something?"

Lieutenant Goddard paused from his writing. "No Mr. Delaney. I'm just trying to get all the information to help us find your son. The sooner you answer my questions, the better the chances we will find Jack."

Gus began to sweat, and a trickle rolled down his forehead. "Listen, I answered all these questions already," he said, his voice rising in volume as he spoke. "I've spent the past three hours running around the fucking neighborhood, talking to all the neighbors. I don't appreciate you talking to me like I did something to my boy, asking me the same questions over and over as if you're trying to catch me in a lie or something."

By this time Gus was yelling. "If you're not going to get some people out looking for him, then you can just get the hell out of my house!"

"Mr. Delaney," Lieutenant Goddard said through his teeth. "If you speak to me in that tone again, I'm going to have to bring you down to the station."

"What, it's against the law to yell at a cop who isn't doing his job?" Gus yelled.

"Frankly, Mr. Delaney, your domestic history is such that I wouldn't be doing my job if I didn't ask you these questions. I don't think I need to remind you that you have a history of domestic incidents that have required us to come to the house." He looked at Stacy and then back to Gus.

"What are you talking about, *incidents*? One time Victoria called 911 during an argument and she later said she shouldn't have. I wouldn't call that a 'history of incidents.'"

"Be that as it may, in situations where the parents are divorced and there is a pending custody case, often one of the parents runs away with the children."

"Well that is clearly not the situation here, is it," Gus said. "Jack's sister is right there in her room. I'm not running away anywhere. I'm just trying to enjoy Christmas with my kids and now one of them is missing and I'd gladly give my life if he walked through that door safe right now."

Goddard continued. "Mr. Delaney, can you tell us where your wife is? Does she know her son is missing?"

"No, I don't know where she is."

"I think it is time you notify her," Officer Baker chimed in, speaking for the first time.

"Yes, I was going to call her but I've been a bit occupied answering your questions…again."

"Why don't you call her now while Officer Baker and I look around. Do you mind if we look around?" Lieutenant Goddard asked.

"Looks like you already are," Gus said, glancing toward the hallway leading to the bedrooms, where Officer Baker had disappeared.

"Great, thank you Mr. Delaney." Goddard began to walk toward the hallway. "Which room is Jack's?"

Gus followed him. "I'll show you – it's down the end on the left."

"I'm alright," Goddard said. "I'll be able to find it. Why don't you call the mother."

"I'll show you the room," Gus said tersely and he walked past Lieutenant Goddard to Jack's room.

He stood in the doorway as the two policemen examined Jack's room. Goddard flipped through the coloring books on Jack's desk and opened the desk drawers and rifled through its contents. Officer Baker checked the windows. He looked to see if they had been opened and he dusted for fingerprints. He placed

Jack's drawing pad, some loose papers on which Jack had written, and a few activity books in a transparent bag.

They looked under his bed and in his closet. "Do you have a photograph of the boy?" Goddard asked. Gus got him Jack's school photo from Miss Monaco's first grade class at Hajjar Elementary School the year before.

Goddard looked at the photo and then glanced out the window. It was dark; Gus didn't know what he was looking at because he surely couldn't see anything in the tar-black night. Goddard turned to him and put his pen to his notepad. "Mr. Delaney, what did you say you did for a living?" he asked.

"I didn't."

Goddard sighed. He looked at Baker. "Okay. Do you mind telling us what you do for work?"

"I'm a fund manager at Fidelity Investments."

"So you must do pretty well?" Goddard interrupted. "Probably make six figures, right?"

"Why is this important?"

"Did you receive any type of ransom note, or do you think you might get one? Do you have any enemies at work?"

"No I didn't get any ransom note or I would have told you about it already. You think someone I work with might be involved?"

Goddard and Baker were both scribbling in their notepads. Goddard looked up. "Maybe someone is jealous. Maybe you're a bit cocky and like to talk about your success." He paused to study Gus's reaction.

Gus thought for a moment about the people who worked with him. He didn't have any enemies, as far as he knew. And nobody at work even knew Gus had kids. He didn't share his personal life with any of them.

"No," Gus said. "I don't think anyone at my work has anything to do with this."

Gus paced around the room as they scribbled in their pads. He saw Jack's blanket crumpled beside the pillow on his bed. He walked over to it and put it up to his nose. He inhaled deeply. Jacks' smell was on it. Tears rolled down his eyes. Jack had never been parted from it.

Goddard turned to him and noticed he was upset. "What's that?"

"This is Jack's blanket. He carried it everywhere with him. I don't think he has ever been without his blanket since he was a baby."

Goddard walked over to Gus and peered at the blanket. In a dispassionate voice he told Baker to put the blanket in his evidence bag and then he began to write something in his notepad. Baker walked over and reached for the blanket.

"Why the fuck do you need Jack's blanket?" Gus yelled. "How on earth is this evidence?"

Goddard sighed. "Mr. Delaney, I'd appreciate if you would just let us do our job. Clearly you don't know the first thing about investigating a crime scene—"

"A crime scene? How is Jack's room a crime scene when he was outside riding his bike? How is it that Jack's blanket is evidence when it was sitting on his bed while Jack was outside? No, Lieutenant Goddard, I'm not familiar with crime scenes, so why don't you enlighten me."

Goddard sighed again. "Mr. Delaney, all we know is a child is missing. Like we said before, we have to look into every possibility. Are we just to go on your word that Jack was taken while he was out biking? What if you made up the whole story to cover up something else that happened? What if someone had tried to take Jack at another time and had broken into his room? There are any number of things that could have happened." Gus squeezed his fingers around the blanket.

"You can't be serious. You think I'd make up a story about my son being missing and then call you to report it?" he yelled. "That's the most ridiculous thing I've ever heard!"

"I've been doing this for twenty years, Mr. Delaney. I've seen just about everything. We need to take the blanket into evidence. There could be blood on it. There could be hair. There could be semen...any number of things we'll want to look for at the lab."

"I don't believe this," Gus said.

"Okay, calm down." Goddard said. "This is the procedure for all cases. We're not trying to pick on you."

"Could've fooled me," Gus said.

"We need the blanket. You understand?" Gus didn't say anything. "Or do you want me to arrest you for impeding an investigation and we'll get a warrant and come back here without you to do our investigation?"

"Arrest me?" Gus said, his voice bristling with rage. Goddard moved his jacket back and flashed handcuffs on his belt and puffed his chest and moved closer to Gus. "Yeah, I understand," Gus growled. "But I want this back as soon as you are done with it."

"No problem Mr. Delaney." Goddard looked at Baker and nodded for him to take the blanket. Baker put it in the plastic bag along with the coloring books and drawing pads.

"All right now. Where's the boy's sister?" Goddard said.

"She's in her room."

"We're going to have to ask her a few questions, if that's all right." Gus thought for a moment.

"Sure, I guess," he said. He tapped on the door. He heard a weak "hello?" issue from the room.

"Hi honey, can I come in?" Gus said. There was a short silence.

"Okay," Lilly said softly.

Gus began to enter the room with Lieutenant Goddard and Officer Baker. Goddard stopped and gestured for Baker to go to the living room with Stacy.

Lilly sat on the bed putting colored pegs into her Lite Brite. "Lilly, this is Officer Goddard," Gus said. "He's here to help us find Jack and he wants to ask you a few questions. Is that okay?" Lilly nodded yes and looked up at the burly lieutenant.

Goddard pulled up her desk chair by the bed and sat in it. He looked ridiculous in the little chair as his fat rolled over the sides of the seat. Gus worried that his girth would overwhelm the chair and it would collapse underneath him.

"Mr. Delaney," he said. "I need to talk to Lilly alone for a few moments. I'm going to have to ask you to leave the room while I interview her."

Gus put his arm around Lilly. "I'm not sure I understand," he said, though he understood perfectly what was going on. "Why can't I stay with my daughter? She's had a rough day and I don't think it would be a good idea—"

"Mr. Delaney, please," Goddard said. "It's only for a few minutes. I told you I've been doing this for a long time. Now are you going to let me do my job so I can help you find your son?" Gus didn't answer. "Please, if you wouldn't mind stepping out for a few moments, I'd appreciate it."

Gus hesitated. He turned to Lilly. "Are you going to be okay if daddy leaves the room for a few moments and Officer Goddard asks you a few questions?" She wrapped her arms around his neck tightly. She didn't want him to leave.

Goddard leaned in. "Don't worry sweetie, everything is going to be okay," he said in a kind voice. "I've just got to ask you a few questions and your answers might help us find your brother. Is that okay? Your daddy can wait just outside the door and I'll bring him in right when we're done. Okay?" She nodded okay.

"Great, he said. "Daddy, can you go just outside there for a few minutes while I talk to Lilly?"

"I'll be right here if you need me honey," Gus said.

Gus stood outside the door and tried to listen. He noticed Officer Baker watching him from the living room. His lips curled in a frown. *Fuck him*, Gus thought. *I told Lilly I'd wait outside the door and I'm going to stay here until he's done.* He couldn't hear anything. He waited a long time. He looked at his watch and walked over to Baker.

"He's been in there for a half hour," he said, pointing at his watch. "He said he'd only be a few minutes."

"Don't worry, Mr. Delaney. She's fine. He's very good with kids."

"Well what's taking so long? What's he asking her?"

"Oh, just questions that might help us shed light on what may have happened to Jack," Baker said.

"Questions like *what?*" Gus said.

"Oh, questions like did she see anyone suspicious or someone she didn't recognize when she was outside, did Jack tell her he was going anywhere, or going to see anyone, things like that."

"I've already asked her those questions!" Gus snapped. "And if that's what he's asking her, why did I have to leave the room?"

Baker shifted in his seat and chewed his thumbnail. "Well, he might want to ask her some family questions that might be awkward for her to answer in front of you," he said.

"Family questions!" Gus yelled. "Why does he need to ask her family questions? Because Jack's mother and I are divorced doesn't mean he ran away – he didn't run away, I can guarantee you that – nor does it mean I developed some master plan to hide Jack from his mother!"

"We're not saying that," Baker said. He looked at Stacy and then back to Gus. "But I'm going to be honest with you, in the majority of missing children cases when the parents are divorced and there are custody disputes, one or the other of the parents is involved." Gus began to speak, but Baker quickly interjected. "Again, we're not saying that is the case here, but we have to look at every possibility."

Gus turned around and went to the kitchen. He decided to call Victoria and let her know what was going on. It was the call he'd been dreading, but he had to, because Baker planted a tiny seed in the corner of his mind that maybe she knew something about Jack's disappearance. Baker was right; he had to be open to all possibilities.

CHAPTER 12

Where's Victoria?

G us first tried Donna's house. The phone rang a long time before someone picked up. "Hello?" It was Donna.

"Hi Donna, it's Gus. Is Victoria there?"

"No, I haven't heard from her since last night. She told me she was staying at the Holiday Inn."

"Are you sure she didn't say anything about coming over here…or coming to get Jack or anything like that?"

"Yes, why?"

"You're positive? Please tell me, it's important."

"Yes, I told you. What's going on Gus?"

"Do you know if she was leaving today or was she supposed to stay with you for a couple of days?"

"She was going to fly back today because Roger's mother is cooking a big Christmas dinner tonight and she wanted to get back for that. Gus, you're not telling me something. What's going on? I can tell something's wrong by your voice," Donna said. Roger was Victoria's boyfriend. Gus didn't know if Donna was telling the truth about not hearing from Victoria all day. He had to tell her about Jack.

"Donna, Jack's missing. He's been missing for about four hours. The police are here and I need to find Victoria to let her know what's going on."

"What? Jack's missing? What happened?" she asked.

"Listen, I don't have time to talk. Just have Victoria call me if you talk to her. I gotta go. Bye," he said and hung up. There. Gus was sure Donna knew exactly where Victoria was. She usually lied to him about her or only gave him half the information. He dialed another number. It rang and rang and nobody picked up. "Dammit!" he yelled.

"What happened?" Stacy asked. She stood from the couch and walked over to him and put her hand on his shoulder. "What did Donna say?"

"Donna says she hasn't spoken to her today, but that she was supposed to stop by her house before flying back to New Jersey. She said she was flying back this afternoon to make it to Roger's mother's house for a dinner tonight. I just tried to reach her at her house but there's no answer. I don't have Roger's number, and I have no idea how I would get in touch with his mother."

Gus glanced towards Lilly's room. The door was closed. Goddard was still in there. Then he looked at Baker. "He's had enough time." He marched over to Lilly's room. Baker jumped off the couch where he had been reviewing his notes and shouted after him.

"Mr. Delaney! Wait! You can't go in there!"

"Like hell I can't!" Gus said. "It's my house; I'll go wherever I want whenever I want." He knocked on the door and entered the room. Lieutenant Goddard was still seated in the child's chair talking to Lilly, who was seated on the bed. He looked over at Gus and then at Baker, who had come in behind Gus. His facial expression to Baker said, "What the fuck?" Then he turned back to Lilly and smiled.

"Okay, Lilly, you've been very helpful," he said. "Thank you for talking with me, and don't worry. We're going to do everything we can to find your brother, okay?" She nodded. Goddard slowly rose from the chair and stretched his legs and back. "Thank you Mr. Delaney," he said as he walked past him toward the living room.

Gus followed him out. "Well, what did she say?" he asked.

"Well, what I can tell you," Goddard said, "is she says she didn't notice anyone suspicious outside – in fact, she doesn't remember seeing anyone at all outside when they were on the bikes. She also doesn't remember Jack saying he wanted to bike anywhere or visit anyone, except his friend Bobby…you've checked over Bobby's house and all his other friends in the neighborhood, is that right?"

"Yes, I've checked with everyone I could think of. What else did Lilly say?"

"Oh, we just talked about anyone else Jack may have come into contact with, if there was anyone she could think of who might want to do harm to Jack or your family, your family situation, Jack's—"

"What about our family situation," Gus asked.

"Mr. Delaney, I don't know how many times we're going to go over this, but the fact that you and your wife—" he glanced over at Stacy – "ex-wife are in a custody fight has to be looked at just as we will look at every single other possibility." Goddard was clearly uncomfortable and aggravated that he had to have this discussion again. "Look, we want to find your son as much as you do, and we're going to do everything we can to help you."

Gus had heard enough. "Sir, with all due respect, you cannot possibly want to find my son as much as I do, so don't insult me by saying that anyone wants to find Jack as much as I do."

Goddard didn't say anything. He ambled over to the front door. "I'm going to talk to some of the neighbors and then I'll come back. Can you point out the…" He flipped through his notepad. "Which house is Bobby's?" Gus told him and also told him which houses were the Boylan's the Bunn's and Mahoney's. Goddard opened the door. Then he stopped and turned around.

"Mr. Delaney, have you spoken to Jack's mother yet?"

"I tried to reach her but I can't find her."

"We need to talk to her. Keep trying."

Goddard and Baker walked down the driveway to talk to the neighbors. Gus wondered suddenly if maybe his parents had picked up Jack mistakenly. He dialed their phone number. As the phone rang, he tried to remember his conversation with them the day before. Did they make arrangements to get Jack? He was pretty hammered and maybe he forgot. The phone rang. Someone picked up. "Hello?" It was his mother.

"Hi mom. Is Jack with you?"

"No, why would he be with me?" Vera asked.

"Mom, Jack's missing." Gus's voice cracked. "He was riding his bike in front of the house and I had to run in to talk to Victoria on the phone. I was only in the house for five minutes and now I can't find him anywhere!"

"Oh my God! Did you check with all the neighbors?"

"Yes, I checked with everyone and nobody has seen him. The police were here. They're talking to the neighbors now."

"Where is Lilly," Vera asked.

"Lilly is here. She's in her room."

"Your father and I will be right there," she said. "I'm sure he'll turn up. You'll find him Gus. You will."

Gus didn't want to tell her how scared he was. He had to be strong for Lilly. He had to be strong for everyone, including himself.

"Okay. We'll be right there," Vera said again. "I love you." Her voice faltered and she hung up.

Gus dialed his sister Lauren's number. His nephew James answered the phone. "Hi James. It's Uncle Gus. Is mommy there?" James went get his mother.

"Well, well, well. Merry Christmas evening to you," she said in a cheery, wine-infused voice. "What are you up to big brother?"

"Lauren, Jack is missing." Gus repeated what he had told his mother. Lauren asked the same questions Vera and everyone else had asked. Then she asked,

"What do you want me to do? Do you want me to come over? We can come over right now with the kids. Can they sleep with Lilly?"

"It's up to you," Gus said. "I'm not sure what you can do at this hour…actually, it might be good for Lilly to have her cousins around."

"Yes, we're coming over," Lauren said. "You're going to find him Gus. He's going to be all right. I love you," she said.

"I love you too." Gus hung up the phone. He dialed Victoria's number again, and again there was no answer, so he walked outside. Cold air bit his ears. He looked up and down. Tried to remember right before Jack disappeared. *He was only inside five minutes.*

He reconstructed the scene: Jack and Lilly riding down Kingsbury Lane in front of the Schroots, toward Bobby's. No cars passed, did they? He didn't remember seeing any cars. Anyone walking? There was nobody walking at that time. The Schroots were not in the yard. Too cold.

Then she had called. He ran in, called the kids. Didn't he call them in to talk to their mother? Lilly came. Why didn't Jack come? Where did he go? Gus was only on the phone for five minutes. Less. Then he went outside to get Jack. Gone. It was light then. Now the sky was black ink. No stars, no moon.

He walked back into the house. He called his other sister Ellen. She lived in Plymouth. She was married but had no kids yet. "Ellen, Jack is missing." Ellen said she would come first thing in the morning. Too late tonight, nothing she could do.

There was a light knock at the door. Gus's heart raced and he ran to the living room to answer it. His heart then dropped when he opened the door only to see the Schroots. "Oh Gus," Eleanor Schroot said. "You haven't found him yet?"

"No Mrs. Schroot," Gus answered. "We haven't found him." He paced around the living room. Mrs. Schroot looked at him nervously, like a mother worried about her son. Then she walked up to him and clasped her hands in his.

"Is there anything we can do?" she asked.

"Yes," Gus said. "Please pray. I know you are religious. Ask God to bring my boy back to me." She told him that she had been praying ever since Bud told her that Jack had gone missing. She said that she would keep praying until he was   found.

"Are you hungry?" she asked. "I've got some turkey breast left over. I can heat it up with some stuffing and mashed potatoes."

"No thank you, Mrs. Schroot. That is really nice of you but please don't go to all that trouble."

"It's no trouble at all," she said. "There now, it's decided. Don't you worry – I'm just going to heat up a few things and I'll be right back." Gus told her he wasn't hungry, but he *was* hungry, so he didn't protest too much. It was now nearing 9 p.m.

"I'm going to take the car and drive around the neighborhood," Bud said. "He'll turn up. We'll find him. Have faith in God to bring him home." Gus thanked Bud as he left.

"I'm going to check the woods again," Gus said. Stacy looked at him, her eyes welling.

"Gus, Jack knows those woods better than anyone else on the planet. Do you really think he could get lost out there?"

"I don't know. Maybe he got hurt and is lying out there, cold, scared, waiting and hoping someone will find him. I don't know what else to do." He began to walk out the door, only to see Goddard and Baker walking up his driveway.

"Any news?" Goddard asked. "Did you talk to the mother?"

"No, I haven't been able to reach her. Her friend told me she's at her boyfriend's mother's house for dinner. I'm sorry to report that she hasn't given me her boyfriend's mother's number."

Goddard frowned and shook his head. "Glad you think this is funny," he said.

Gus stepped forward two feet in front of Goddard and stared down at him. "I'm not laughing. Just find my son."

"Step back Mr. Delaney," Goddard said. Gus didn't move. Goddard looked at Baker and then up at Gus. "Okay, what's her number?"

"Whose number?" Gus asked

"Your wife – ex-wife's?" Gus gave Victoria's number to him and he wrote it down.

"And how about this friend? Who is she?" Goddard asked.

Gus stepped back. "She lives in Woburn. Victoria and the kids visited her Christmas Eve before coming to my house.

Goddard scribbled all this down on his notepad. "And you said she lives where?"

"Who, Donna?"

"No, Victoria," Goddard said, flipping through his notes.

"New Jersey. Denville, New Jersey"

"Yes, New Jersey." Goddard wrote it down again. "And what about her parents, have you spoken to them? Brothers or sisters? Does she have any?"

"No, I haven't spoken to her parents," Gus said. "She has one brother. I haven't spoken to him either."

"Well don't you think they might know where their daughter is? Did it ever occur to you that they might have her boyfriend's mother's phone number?" Gus didn't like his sarcastic tone.

"Look, I just told my own parents a few minutes ago. And no, it didn't occur to me because her parents are in Florida and Victoria is not particularly close to them. Donna would be more likely to know where Victoria is."

"I'm going to need all of their numbers," Goddard said. "Do you have them?" Gus gave the phone numbers to Goddard, who wrote them in his pad. "And your mother and father..." He looked at his notepad, searching. "And you said you had two sisters? Can you give me their addresses and phone numbers?"

"Yes, but they are on their way here right now."

"Good, good. I want to talk to them. May I use your phone?" he asked. He picked up the phone and dialed a number from his pad. Baker stood by and remained silent, as he had since they came back from their meetings with the neighbors. Goddard stood with the phone to his ear and watched Gus as he waited for someone to pick up. Nobody did and he hung up.

He dialed another number. "Hi, is this Donna Butler?" he asked. He introduced himself and asked her if she knew Victoria Delaney and if she knew where she was. Gus listened.

"Uh huh. Yes. Yes. Yes, that's correct. Mmm hmm. No. Yes." After a few minutes of this he said, "Thank you Ms. Butler. I'm going to send someone over there to ask you a few more questions." Pause. "Yes, tonight. I know it's late, but we won't take long."

Goddard hung up and dialed another number from his pad. He looked from Gus to Baker and back to Gus while he waited for someone to pick up. "Hello. Is this Julia Davis?" he asked. "Sorry to disturb you so late, ma'am, but we're trying to find a Victoria Delaney. Is she your daughter?" He paused, listened.

"Well, ma'am, her son Jack has been reported missing and we're trying to locate her."

After a few seconds: "We don't know that yet, ma'am. No I can't tell you that. It's still too early to know. We're with Mr. Delaney now. He reported that Jack was missing, ma'am." Pause. "Lilly is here. No, I'm calling from Mr. Delaney's house. Yes he's here." Goddard held the phone and indicated for Gus to take it.

Gus took the phone and Julia Davis tore into him. "What have you done with Jack!" she screamed. "Where is he? What did you do?"

"Maybe you should ask your daughter those questions," Gus shot back. "So help me God, if she has something to do with this I'll kill her," he said. He noticed Goddard writing something on his pad and he realized he shouldn't have said that. Gus explained everything to her as calmly as he could, while Goddard and Baker sat at the kitchen table and jotted in their notepads.

"That's why she took the kids from you, because you, you drunken fool, couldn't be trusted to take care of them. I'm going to ask the police to file a child endangerment charge against you!" Julia Davis said.

She then told him that she didn't know Roger's number or where his mother lived. Victoria hadn't mentioned going there to her. Goddard indicated that he wanted to talk to her again. So Gus told her to hold on and gave him the phone.

Goddard got her address and told her that he was going to send someone to her house in the morning to ask her a few questions. Gus heard a helicopter overhead, thumping over the woods and swamp. The sound grew louder. Gus looked out the back window and saw it hovering over the backyard at the edge of the woods.

It darted back and forth, a searchlight sweeping the ground below in a bright circle of light. *Finally*, Gus thought, they are doing something productive, searching for his boy, talking to other people and not just asking him the same questions over and over.

Goddard walked into the living room and looked out the window at the street. After a minute he turned to Gus. "You said your parents are coming?" Gus nodded.

"Good, we're going to need to question them all asap."

"Yes, you said that," Gus said. Goddard gave him an aggravated look. The helicopter continued to thump somewhere above the swamp. Thump, thump, thump, thump.

CHAPTER 13

Persons of Interest

"Let's run a BOLO on him," Goddard said to Baker.

"A what?" Gus asked.

"BOLO – be on the lookout for. We'll send it out and the guys on patrol will know to look for Jack."

"You're just gonna do this now?" Gus asked, looking at his watch. "It's after 9. Why didn't it go out 2 hours ago?" Goddard gave him a dirty look and didn't answer. Gus tried to stay in control of his emotions, but his body felt like a guitar string that was being tuned tighter and tighter, turned and turned beyond its limits until it might snap.

He tried to keep his anger at the police in check. He needed their help. But what he really needed right now was someone who knew what they were doing; someone who knew what to do in situations like this, whose sole focus was investigating missing children. It was clear these guys didn't have experience in these cases. They didn't have a clue.

"Does the Billerica Police have a guy who specializes in cases like this where a child is missing? A detective or investigator?"

Goddard looked at Baker and grunted. Then he spoke to Gus. "There's a guy in Lowell who is an expert in child abductions – guy named Boyd. But he's gone into private practice. You'd have to hire him, but hey, you've got money." He looked at Baker, then back to Gus. "But let me assure you, though you might not recognize it, we're doing everything we can to find Jack."

This was bullshit. Gus was tired of this clown talking to him as if he were a child. "Do you have this Boyd's number?"

"You can call the station and someone there should have it. He's also in the Yellow Pages, I believe." Gus went to the kitchen, found Boyd in the phone book – private investigator, twenty years – and began to dial his number. He had no confidence in the Billerica Police to find Jack.

Just as he dialed the last number, he heard someone at the front door call his name. His mother! He hung up the phone and rushed out of the kitchen. "Gus! Oh Gus!" his mother cried and she ran to him sobbing. She held him tightly and Gus noticed she was shaking. His father came up behind her, followed by his sister

Lauren, her husband Tom and her three kids – Tricia, Kelly, and James. They all stumbled to him and embraced as a large mass, swaying, shaking, and crying.

They bombarded him with questions that they had already asked over the phone. Stacy and Lilly appeared from the bedroom and Lilly's cousins hugged her and they all cried together. Gus was glad they were all there. He didn't have time to give Lilly enough attention; her cousins and aunt and grandmother could console her and tell her that everything was going to be all right.

Goddard injected himself into this scene. "Mr. and Mrs. Delaney?" he asked. "Are you the grandparents of the missing boy? We'd like to ask you a few questions if you don't mind." Then he turned to Lauren. "Are you the sister? We're going to want to talk to you as well." He asked them all to sit in the living room. He stood and unfolded his pad. Stacy brought Lilly and her cousins into Lilly's room.

Goddard and Baker began talking to Gus's parents and sister. "I'm going to drive around again," Gus said, "and see if he is out there." He knew he wasn't out there. He and Bud Schroot had walked the neighborhood at least six times in the last two hours. But he had to do something, anything.

He'd go mad if he stayed at the house. It was likely that Jack was far away, and as much as he tried to push out of his mind the thought that Jack had been kidnapped, a thought that made him physically sick, it kept creeping back into his brain and working its way down to his gut.

Gus opened the front door to leave and saw a group of neighbors walking up his driveway. The men. Paul Bunn, Henry O'Connor, Sean Boylan, and a few others. They had heard that Gus hadn't found Jack and they wanted to help. They each carried a plate of food or thermos of coffee.

"Hi Gus. How are you holding up?" Paul Bunn said awkwardly.

"Not well, Paul. Not well at all."

"Eleanor wanted to come too, but she's staying with the kids in case there's—" he cut himself off. Gus knew what he was going to say and placed his hand on his shoulders, a gesture to indicate he understood. The mothers didn't want to leave their kids alone at home in case the same boogeyman who came into the neighborhood and took Jack might still be lurking and try to take their kids too.

"What can we do," Sean Boylan asked. Gus saw a few other neighbors walking toward the house. They had all heard. Gus asked if they could call other neighbors and friends in town and ask them to look for Jack. He had looked in the swamp and woods, but he couldn't cover it all alone. Maybe Jack was out there somewhere, so he asked them to walk through and look again.

The phone rang. "Excuse me," Gus said to them. He ran to get the phone, snatched it off the hook. His heart sank. It was his Uncle Ted. Charlie had called him and told him, he said. He lived in Salem, MA, forty minutes away, but said he and Gus's aunt Sheila were coming to help him look. Gus had hoped it was Victoria calling to say she had Jack and that he was okay. Gus thought every time the phone rang it was someone calling to say that they had found Jack and he was safe.

He was on the phone with his uncle for a few minutes, explaining what happened, when Stacy appeared in the kitchen. "Gus, there's a news truck outside and a guy with a television camera in the driveway."

"Uncle Ted, I have to go." Gus rushed to the front door and saw Channel 4 News interviewing Goddard. He overheard the reporter ask if they thought this was an abduction. Goddard stood, hands on hips.

"At this point," he said, "yes, it looks like an abduction." Then the reporter asked if they had any suspects. Goddard told them there were no suspects but they had a few persons of interest.

Persons of interest? Goddard hadn't mentioned any persons of interest to Gus. He walked up to Goddard. "Would you excuse us a minute?" he said to the reporter. He pulled Goddard aside.

Goddard wasn't used to anyone pulling him anywhere. "I was in the middle of an interview," he said. "Please don't do that again."

"I'm sorry, but I'm just wondering why you've told that reporter, who has nothing to do with any of this, who has never met Jack…more than you've told me."

Goddard stared at Gus with blank eyes. "What are you talking about?"

"You told that reporter there are persons of interest in the case. Who? Who?" Gus pressed. "You haven't told me you have persons of interest."

"Listen," Goddard said. "I'm going to tell you this for the last time. My job is to find out what happened to Jack. I cannot discount anything, and I have to consider everything. I haven't talked to you about persons of interest, frankly Mr. Delaney, because you are one of them." And with that he turned and walked back to the reporter.

CHAPTER 14

A Discovery

Gus trudged back into the house. As he paced around the living room, there was a knock at the door. It was the news reporter, Gloria Winslow, and a television cameraman. "Mr. Delaney," she said. "Do you mind if we talk to you?" Gus let her in and she asked him a series of questions: describe what happened, how old was Jack, did he think Jack wandered somewhere and got lost or did he agree with Lieutenant Goddard that Jack had been kidnapped?

"I don't know," Gus said. He squinted in the bright light from the camera that shined in his face. The only thing he knew was that Jack was alive – that he was still out there. He didn't know why he knew this, but he felt it deep in his gut.

He wanted to ask her if she was almost done. He was getting tired of these questions. But he couldn't because he was on camera. He knew that it was good if this was on the news – more people seeing the photo of Jack, more people aware that a little boy was missing. Put some heat on.

The reporter then asked him if there was a ransom note, or if he thought someone might have taken Jack to try to get money from him.

"I don't know," Gus repeated. "But whatever they want, I'm willing to negotiate. I just want my son back." Then he looked directly into the camera. "If someone has my son, please bring him back. Whatever you want, you can have." His voice caught and he fought to maintain composure. "Please! He is everything to me! I just want my little boy back."

He fought tears back and continued the interview. "Are you planning to offer any reward?" the reporter asked.

"A reward?"

"Yes, a reward for information that leads to the whereabouts of your son."

Gus blinked in the harsh light from the television camera. He hadn't thought of offering a reward. "Yes," he said. "I'm offering $5,000 to anyone who provides information that leads to us finding Jack. No questions asked," he added. Then he told her he had to make a call and he walked abruptly away toward his bedroom.

As he walked, he heard her say in her reporter voice: "And that's the father of seven year old Jack Delaney, who disappeared nearly six hours ago. Police suspect he was abducted. Police are also searching for the boy's mother, Victoria Delaney, who has not been seen since—" Gus slammed his bedroom door behind him.

He bounced around the bedroom like a bee in a bottle, back and forth, bed to bureau, bureau to window and back. He wanted to do something, anything. What could he do? He could walk through the woods again, walk the streets of the neighborhood.

He ran through the conversations he had with Victoria the previous day. Did she say anything to indicate she might take Jack? No. It was impossible. The hotel – maybe the Holiday Inn clerks could tell him something. He picked up the phone on the night table next to the bed and dialed the number.

"Hi. My name is Gus Delaney and I'm just checking to see if a guest checked out," he said. "Her name is Victoria Delaney."

"Yes sir, she checked out this morning," the front desk clerk said.

"So she checked out this morning and didn't come back?"

"Yes sir."

"Was she with anyone?" There was a pause on the other end of the line.

"I'm not sure sir. Hold on a minute please." Gus heard talking in the background for a few seconds and then the clerk came back. "May I ask why you are asking?"

"Well, her son is missing and I'm trying to contact her."

"Oh, I see. Can you hold on for a minute?" He heard more muffled talking in the background. After a minute another clerk picked up the phone.

"Hi sir. May I ask to whom I'm speaking?"

"Gus Delaney."

"Thank you Mr. Delaney. And the woman who stayed here last night is your wife?"

"Ex-wife."

"Okay. Yes. Um…she checked out this morning at about 11 a.m. You say her son is missing?" Gus heard a knock at the front door.

"Hold on a minute," Gus said and he glanced out the window toward the front door. Eleanor and Bud Schroot stood on the step, she carrying a plate of sandwiches, he carrying Tupperware containers of roast chicken, mashed potatoes, and an apple pie. Stacy let them in.

"Yes, sorry, hello?" Gus resumed. "Yes, her son – our son – is missing. I've reported it to the police but I can't locate her and I'm trying to find out if she left with anyone, or if someone picked her up so I can find her and tell her."

"The clerk who worked this morning said he didn't see anyone with her when she checked out," the clerk said. He paused for a moment. "But I worked last night and I remember she was at the bar talking to a couple who were having dinner there."

This was something, Gus thought. She might have befriended this couple and told them things. "Oh, that is helpful," he said. "Do you know if the couple stayed at the hotel too?"

"Let me check," the clerk said. Gus heard more talking in the background. "Yes, they were guests of the hotel last night as well, but they also checked out this morning."

Gus asked if the couple left any contact information or if the clerks knew how he could get in touch with them. "I'm sorry sir, but...oh wait," the clerk said. "No, I'm sorry. We don't have any information. They left the information card blank."

"You don't have anything? Not even their names?"

"Oh yes," the clerk said. "We have that but no way of contacting them. They didn't leave an address or phone number. But the names are Mr. and Mrs. John Smith."

"Great," Gus mumbled. "Couldn't find a more common name?"

"What's that?" the clerk asked.

"Nothing, just talking to myself. Mr. and Mrs. Smith. No phone number, no license plate number or anything like that?"

"No sir. I'm sorry."

"How did they pay?"

"They paid cash sir." Of course, Gus thought. He remembered then for some reason the couple whose car he jumped. He wondered if this couple could have been the same couple Victoria talked to at the bar.

"Do you remember what the couple looked like?" he asked.

"Yes. The man was a big guy with a long beard. The woman had straight black hair. She was dressed in black too. Actually, I forgot, but I think they were from England because they had accents. They spoke with the woman – your ex-wife – for a long time."

It was the same couple from the parking lot. Beard, accent. It was them. "Do you know what they were talking about?" he asked.

"No, I'm sorry, I don't," the clerk said.

"Okay. Thank you. Please call if you hear or remember anything else." Gus hung up and walked to the living room to find Charlie. "Dad, do you remember the couple whose car we jumped?"

"Yes, why?"

"The clerk said Victoria was talking to a couple at the bar for a few hours. He described what they looked like and I'm sure she was talking to the guy and woman whose car we jumped."

"Yeah, and?"

"I don't know. They just seemed shady to me. Didn't you think there was something not right about them?"

Charlie scratched his groin. "I don't know. Nothing really stood out. The guy was big, burly and he had a long beard, but other than that, I don't remember much."

"I wish I could find them, but they didn't leave any information – no phone number, address, or anything. Strange. Aren't they required to leave all that?" Gus asked. Charlie shook his head slowly, his eyes unfocused, staring into space, seemingly deep in thought.

Vera, sitting on the edge of the couch, listened to Gus's questions to Charlie. "Do you think those people have something to do with Jack?" she asked.

Gus had also drifted into thought. He turned his head toward her a few seconds after her question. "What was that?" he asked.

"Do you think these people might have something to do with Jack?" she asked more loudly.

"I don't know. I don't know anything." His voice drifted. "I just want my boy back." Vera hugged him.

"I know. I know," she said.

Stacy had disappeared into the kitchen. She emerged with a plate of Mrs. Schroot's chicken and mashed potatoes. "Gus, you should eat something," she said. "You haven't eaten a thing all night."

"I don't have time right now," he said.

"Gus, listen to Stacy. You should eat. You're going to need your strength. Please," Vera pleaded. Gus grabbed the plate from Stacy, sat at the coffee table, and devoured the food. Even with the use of silverware, he looked like a dog tearing into a bowl of dog food, snout flying, jaw working, nearly biting his master's hand before he can remove it from the bowl.

"Thank you," he mumbled, mouth full of food. Then he shook his head.

"Something's not right," he continued. "I think those people at the hotel might be involved somehow." Gus began to hope that Victoria was involved. This provided him the last bit of balm to his tattered nerves. At least if she had him, he was safe, and that is all that mattered to Gus right now.

By now, people from all over town were coming to the house, asking if they could help. Neighbors, friends, parents of Jack and Lilly's friends, Gus's family, Stacy's parents, and people Gus had never met before – all bringing food and flashlights and offering to help search for Jack.

A crowd of neighbors – maybe fifty, carrying fifty flashlights – had joined together to walk through the swamp and woods. They had formed a human chain to cover every foot, every inch, flashlights lighting up a patch of ground in front of them in the hope that one light would shine on a little boy still alive.

Gus had given a photograph of Jack – his school portrait from last spring – to a man who said he worked at a photo service and could make posters first thing in the morning. The man asked Gus what he wanted printed on the posters in addition to the photograph.

Gus pulled off a paper towel and scribbled on it: Missing Boy: Jack Delaney. He wrote Jack's age, height, weight, hair color, what he had been wearing. Then at the bottom he wrote: $5,000 REWARD for information leading to the where-abouts of Jack. He added his phone number and address and handed the paper towel to the man. "Thank you for doing this," he said.
Gus shook his hand and the man disappeared through the front door. When the man opened the door, Gus heard yelling in the street. He followed the poster guy out the door and listened.

The noise was coming from the right side of the yard not far from the street – the swamp. A bunch of men were yelling something but Gus couldn't make it out. Then he heard something: "We found…" He didn't hear the rest as he bolted down the steps so fast he tripped and fell flat on his face in the snow.

He jumped up and sprinted toward them. His heart beat like mad. "Jack!" he yelled. "Did you find Jack?" He got to the edge of the hill and saw the men pulling something out of the bushes next to the swamp.

"Is that Jack?" He couldn't hear what they were saying. A rush of blood came to his head and made him dizzy and he felt like he was in one of those dreams where you fall and fall through the air and wait to smash to the ground.

"It's a bike. We found a bike," Mike Boylan said. "Is this Jack's bike?" The bike came into view as they pulled it out of the bushes and rolled it up the hill. Gus stumbled over to it. It was Jack's. He squinted down the hill from which the bike had come, trying to see into the bushes. Five men were there, moving their flashlights back and forth quickly.

Jack must have gone off the road and crashed his bike down the hill. *Where is he?* He must have hit his head and got knocked out. *Where is he?* Why weren't they finding him down there? Gus staggered down the hill and joined the other men.

"Where is he?" Gus asked.

"I don't see him," Bill O'Connor said.

"Why can't we see him?" Gus said frantically. "He's got to be here!" He grabbed a flashlight from a man's hand and fell to his knees. He crawled in the snow and mud under the bush and pointed the flashlight ahead of him, searching for his boy. He had to be here. Why wasn't he here with his bike?

"He's not here Gus," Mike Boylan said. "We've searched all around where we found his bike—" Gus cut him off.

"Where did you find it? Where was it exactly?"

"Right there. Right against that bush where you're looking," Boylan said.

Gus thrashed around under the bush, flinging mud and snow, snapping branches as he plowed through the bushes frantically waving his flashlight and yelling incoherently like a mad-man. He felt a hand on his shoulder. It was Boylan.

"Gus," he said softly. "We've looked all around there. He's not here. Come on, let's go inside and tell the police we found the bike and get you a change of clothes." Gus looked at him and at all the men standing with their heads down, their eyes not wanting to meet his.

Gus wheeled the bike into the garage. He gazed upon it as if it was a holy relic; the last thing Jack touched. He caressed the handle bars and his bottom lip began quivering.

What was going on? He knew it wasn't good…knew something awful had happened. Again he thought of Victoria. His only hope now was that she, in a fit of anger about having to stay at the hotel – or about something else – got somebody to take Jack while she distracted Gus with her phone call. He needed to find her – or the people she spoke with at the Holiday Inn.

He ran into the house to call her again. The house was a hive of activity; dozens of people were coming in and out of the front door…a lot of faces he didn't know. Who were they and who was letting them in?

Then a rush of panic swept over him and made him nearly lose his breath. Lilly! He hadn't seen Lilly in more than an hour. His entire focus devoted to finding Jack, he had forgotten about her. All these strange people in the house!

He ran to her bedroom door, which was closed. He swung it open and exhaled deeply when he saw her sitting on the bed, Vera and Lauren and her cousins sitting with her. She was crying and they were consoling her.

"Hi," Gus said. "Hi honey." He rushed over and took Lilly in his arms, hugged her and kissed her wet cheeks. "We're looking for Jack. There's a lot of people helping – the police, all the neighbors. They're walking though the swamp and woods now in case Jack got lost or hurt."

He wiped the tears from her face. "We're going to find him. Don't be sad, okay?" Lilly buried her face in his shoulder and bawled. Her body shook.

"I know. I know. I promise you Lilly, I will find Jack. I won't stop looking even if it takes me the rest of my life. But we'll find him." He rocked her in his arms for a few minutes and then placed her back on the bed. "Now you stay with your aunt and grandmother, okay? Don't leave them." He lifted her chin so she was looking at him and he smiled a loving smile. "Don't let her out of your sight," he said to Vera and Lauren. "There are a lot of people here who I don't know, so watch her."

Gus paused at the doorway. "Mom, you told me God would never give me more than I could handle. You were wrong." Then he walked out to call Victoria.

The doorbell rang and Gus answered it. A short, wiry man, wearing a long black overcoat, stood at the door. "Good evening. My name is Detective Boyd and I'm looking for Gus Delaney," he said. Gus had called him and left a message on a voice service. He was surprised to see him so soon, and he was surprised that though he was completely bald, he looked young, at least younger than a guy with twenty years experience.

Boyd asked immediately if Gus had heard from Victoria. "No," Gus said. "But that's what I called you about. I phoned the Holiday Inn and they said Victoria spoke with a couple in the hotel bar for a few hours last night. I asked the clerk for their phone number or address, but he said they didn't leave any information."

"Hold on a second," Boyd said. He began writing the information down. "Okay. Did the hotel have their names at least?"

"Yeah. They said they signed the register Mr. and Mrs. John Smith."

"Hmm. That's interesting."

"Oh, I almost forgot," Gus said. "I think I saw these people. My dad and I drove Victoria to the hotel and we helped a couple jump their car. I'm certain it's the same couple."

"What kind of car did they drive?" Boyd asked.

"It was a brown Pinto."

"Did you get the license plate number by chance?"

"No, I didn't. But the guy did say they lived in Cape Cod." Gus described the man and woman to Boyd and Boyd said he'd go down to the hotel and try to get more information. Gus told him he wanted to go too, but Boyd said he wanted to go alone and would call him if he found out any more information. "Can you ask them for her phone records so we can see who she called and what she said? Is it possible to get the tapes of people's conversations?"

"Don't you worry Mr. Delaney," Boyd said. "I'll check everything out and let you know. Is there somewhere quiet we can go to talk," he said, looking around at the chaos.

"Yes, let's go to my bedroom." Once in Gus's bedroom, Boyd spoke briefly about his experience and the approach he would take. He asked Gus many of the questions the others had all asked, but he did it in a way that made it sound like he would put a specific use to the answers he received; that he had a plan that would lead to finding Jack. Boyd told him his fees, Gus agreed, and Boyd said he would start by going to the Holiday Inn. "I'll let you know if I find anything; otherwise I'll be back first thing in the morning."

That night was the longest of Gus's life. He spent it trying to reach Victoria, running through all the possibilities of what could have happened to Jack, consoling Lilly, talking to the police, and planning for the next day's search.

CHAPTER 15

Abraham

The man had black, wet, slicked-back hair that came together in a ponytail. He was built like a panther; long and lean and muscular and dark. His nose was a crooked beak, but his eyes were not bird-like at all. They were deep pools of incandescent blue, radiating and compassionate, and they dominated his face. A gangling, wispy, black beard hung loosely from a pointed chin to complete that face.

"This is Abraham," the woman said.

"Thank you Elizabeth. You may leave us now," Abraham said. She bowed and left the room. Abraham smiled. He had straight, white, perfect teeth. He gestured for Jack to sit on the bed. Jack didn't move.

"Don't be afraid, come," he said as he sat on the bed and patted the space next to him. Jack did as he was told and sat on the bed. Abraham put his arm around him. "Do you know why you are here, Augustine?" he said.

"My name is Jack," Jack said. Abraham smiled and then spoke.

"You go to church, Catholic Church, I believe, right?" Jack nodded.

"You probably attend Sunday school?" Jack nodded again. "Good. Then surely you've learned about the sacraments – baptism, communion, confirmation, et cetera. Well think of this experience here like a new church experience…a new faith experience in which you are going to be re-baptized, re-confirmed – *reborn*." Abraham's eyes widened and he said this last word.

"Just as you are confirmed historically in the Church at the age of seven – the age of reason – and given a new name, casting off the old, so you will adopt this name, Augustine, which we have chosen specifically for you. You are seven years old, aren't you?" He moved his hand to Jack's knee.

He didn't wait for Jack to answer. "Have you heard of Saint Augustine?" Jack shook his head no. "He is a very special saint and there is a reason you have been given his name. You will learn about him in time."

"But I don't want his name," Jack pleaded. "I like Jack." He looked down at Abraham's long, manicured fingers on his knee and began to squirm away from him. Abraham squeezed his knee hard.

"Don't do that," Abraham said.

Jack shuddered and began to sob. He was shaking. "I want my mommy!" he cried.

"Your mother is dead," Abraham said. "You will not see her again and you must accept that. You will meet your new family tomorrow and they will love you and care for you and save you and, in time, you will love them too."

Jack's body shook. "What did you do to her!" he yelled. "Where's my daddy?"

"We are watching your daddy, and your sister too. If you don't do everything I say, we will kill them. They are sinful and impure, and will inhabit the fiery pits of Hell for eternity for their sins. Augustine, this will not be your fate. You can still be saved from that destiny. We are here to save you, to sanctify you with the grace and happiness you would never have found with those sinners that were your mother and father."

"Augustine, you have no other family except this one now. We will be your protector and guide." He raised his hand in the air and looked toward the ceiling. "Rejoice, and be glad. You are saved."

He lowered his hand and continued. "Saint Augustine lived by the exhortation of the Epistle to the Romans in 13:13: 'Let us walk honestly, as in the day, not in rioting and drunkenness, not in chambering and wantonness, not in strife and envying.' He confessed his sins and devoted his life to God. He had been a wicked and wanton man, but he found God, and he found salvation. Now you must do the same."

Abraham's hand patted Jack's thigh. "As the New Year dawns, you will be cleansed with the saving waters of baptism; you will receive the spiritual seal, the spirit of wisdom and understanding, the spirit of right judgment and courage, the spirit of knowledge and reverence, the spirit of holy fear in God's presence. Guard what you receive. You will be marked with the sign – Sacramentum!"

Jack didn't understand any of what Abraham was saying. The words didn't make sense to him. He thought of his mother and wished more than anything she would come and wrap him in her arms and tell him it was just a bad dream. He prayed silently that he would wake up and smell her perfume and she would kiss him on the cheek and brush his hair out of his eyes and tell him everything was ok. Dead? He didn't understand what that meant. He didn't understand anything. He didn't know if this was real or if he was having a nightmare.

Abraham got off the bed and walked to the bathroom from which he had first come. "Take off your clothes," he said and then he closed the door behind him.

Jack heard water running and Abraham chanting. His heart raced. He jumped off the bed and ran to the door. It was locked. He ran to the window and looked out. He saw the Pinto sitting in the driveway.

"I said, take off your clothes!" Abraham roared so loudly that Jack jumped. He hadn't noticed he had returned to the room. He held a crystal bottle containing red liquid. Jack trembled and tears rolled down his face and dripped from his chin.

Abraham smiled a kind smile. "Augustine…be not afraid. Everything we do, everything I ask you to do is to help you…to save you." He paused to wait for Jack's response. Jack didn't say anything.

"And remember what I said. Everything you do will determine whether your father and sister – Lilly, right? – will be saved too. If you don't do what I ask of you, they will be killed immediately. They are sinners and deserve to die, but I will let them live if you do exactly as you're told. You decide if you want them to live or die."

"Leave them alone!" Jack wailed.

"Then take off your clothes right now."

Jack undressed at the window where he stood. "Underwear too," Abraham said as he took something out of a canvas bag. Jack shivered and covered his private parts with his hands.

"Come here."

CHAPTER 16

The Basement Prison

A man pushed Jack into the basement bedroom. "Go to bed," he said. "I'll be back for you soon." The man closed the door. Jack tried to see in the dark bedroom, but everything was fuzzy. He was dizzy. He could hear snoring coming from one of the beds and thought he saw a small bubble underneath the covers – another child, he thought, or a small woman. He climbed underneath the covers of the other bed and cried. He didn't remember falling asleep.

The ringing of an alarm jarred him awake. Pale sunlight filtered in through the window. Jack sat up and, for a moment, he didn't remember where he was. He felt like when he had had the flu and missed a week of school in November. He vomited on the bed and on himself. "Daddy!" he yelled and he started crying. He looked across to the other bed and saw another boy, a little older than he, blinking and rubbing his eyes and staring at him.

Each boy looked at the other for a few minutes, neither one speaking. The boy in the other bed crinkled his mouth and put his hand over it. "What did you do?" he asked. "That's disgusting!"

The boy got out of bed and walked over to the dresser. He was wearing the same white shiny and smooth undergarments that Jack noticed he himself had on. Jack's had a vomit stain on them and they were wet and sticky and clung to his cold legs. He knew he had peed the bed too because he could smell it and he could see a yellow stain mixed above the reddish color of the vomit.

He remembered Abraham had put the underwear on him the night before, telling him he must always wear them. He had dunked him in the bathtub and Jack thought he was drowning him. Then Abraham spoke words Jack didn't understand and told him to put on the – he called them sacred…Jack couldn't remember the name because he had been woozy from being dunked in the bath water and from the red stuff in the bottle that Abraham made him drink.

"Moses is not going to be pleased when he sees what you did in here," the boy said. Then he pulled a white robe from a hook on the wall. Jack's eyes followed his movements. When the boy finished putting on the robe, he stood at the foot of Jack's bed. "What's your name," he asked.

"Jack."

"Really? Jack? That's a funny name," the boy said.

"Why is it funny? That's my name."

"I dunno, I haven't heard a name like that before."

"What's your name?" Jack asked.

"Emmanuel."

"Well I don't know anybody with that name," Jack said. He didn't like this boy who thought his name was funny.

"You better wipe your tears and get ready. He'll be here soon and he doesn't like it when you aren't ready," Emmanuel said.

" Who is coming to get us? How do I get ready?"

"You put on this robe they gave you." He picked up a robe folded at the foot of Jack's bed. It was white and shiny like Emmanuel's. "But you'll have to clean up first."

"Why do we have to wear it? Why do I have to wear these?" he asked, gesturing to his underwear.

"Those are the sacred garments. They are our spiritual shield and protect us against the powers of evil. You wear the robe during morning prayers, which is where we're going."

"Prayers?"

"You ask too many questions," Emmanuel said. "You must pray this morning for God's forgiveness and grace. Abraham teaches that we shall choose the right path if we ask God to show us the way each day. He will show us the truth and the light. Everything will be revealed."

Jack glanced out the window at the early sunlight. Emmanuel spoke like Abraham. Jack didn't understand what his words meant either. He began to cry again. He was ashamed to cry in front of a strange boy he had just met, but he couldn't help it. "I want to go home. I don't want to go to prayers…I just want to go home."

Emmanuel looked confused. "Why would you want to go back?" he asked. "This is your home. You should never want to leave because then you'll go to hell and the demons will tear your flesh forever."

"I don't care," Jack said, crying harder now. "I want to see my mother and father." Emmanuel's eyebrows furrowed. "What do you mean, your mother and father?" he asked.

"My mother and father," Jack said. "Don't you have a mother and father?"

"Yes, Abraham is my father. He is father to us all. And Sarah is my mother."

"Abraham is NOT my father," Jack said.

"You better never let anyone hear you say that," Emmanuel said.

"Why? He's not! I already have a father and a mother and I wish they would come and get me."

"Nobody is going to come for you. You are here and you better do what everyone says. You will learn that Abraham is your father and guide," Emmanuel said.

"Don't you have a real mother and father?" Jack asked.

"Abraham and Sarah!" Emmanuel yelled angrily. "They are my real and only mother and father. If you ask any more questions I'll tell Abraham. He will not be happy."

There was the sound of a key turning in the door. A man burst into the room. It was the man from the night before. He wore the same white robe that Emmanuel wore, the same robe Jack held crumpled in his hands.

"Come on boys," the man said. "Let's not be late for prayers." He sniffed the air. "What's that smell?" he asked.

"Jack got sick," Emmanuel said.

The man stepped toward Jack and with his heavy, meaty hand slapped him hard across the mouth, sending him sprawling to the ground. "That's not for getting sick," he said. "That's for forgetting your name." He stood over Jack with his hands on his hips. "Now what's your name?"

Jack looked up at him. "Augustine," he whimpered.

"What?" the man barked. "I can't hear you."

"Au-Augustine."

"That's better. Don't you forget again and I won't have to remind you." He inspected Jack. You haven't even had your sacred garments for one night and you've gotten sick all ove

Jack got up and took the clothes off. "Now put them in the sink and put your robe on. r them. And is that...did you pee on them too?" Jack looked at the yellow stain on the white underpants and the vomit stain on the undershirt and pants. "Take them off!" the man roared. You will wash them later."

"Come with me, Emmanuel. Augustine, you wait here. I'll come back for you." The man, called Moses, led Emmanuel out the door. Jack heard the key turn in the lock. He put the robe on and tied the belt tight. He was sticky and cold and uncomfortable.

Looking out the window, he saw a barn at the edge of the woods to the left. A barren garden enclosed by a chicken wire fence was between the barn and the house, not ten feet away from the window. At the end of a long sloping snow and ice-covered lawn, perhaps fifty yards away, the ocean, gray and cold chop, crashed against the shore wall.

He grasped the window frame and tried to open the window, but it was sealed shut. He thought that if he could get outside, he could escape through the woods. None of the kids at home could catch him when they were chasing each other in the woods, not even Bobby – not even the older kids. Unlike on the bike, he could dart through the trees and bushes like a rabbit when the others plodded more like Clyde, the Boylan's old bulldog. If he were to try to escape though, he would have to find his clothes – his jacket, pants, and sneakers at least – so he wouldn't freeze in the winter frost.

He noticed the barn door spring open. A woman walked out carrying a basket. It looked like it was heavy because she struggled. She wore strange clothes – a bonnet and a long dress with an apron. She looked like the pictures of the Pilgrims in the book about the Mayflower that Jack's dad had. He watched her until she staggered around the corner of the house out of sight. Then he sat on the bed and shivered…and waited.

After some time, Jack heard the lock turn in the door. Moses was back. He led Jack through the basement and up the stairs. Jack yawned a few times and Moses squeezed his hand hard. "You better pay attention at prayers and stop yawning. You're not starting off well."

The house looked different bathed in the pink light of morning. Less like a haunted house, more like a museum. The light showed the faint covering of dust on the furniture and the wood floors. Jack was led into a large room with wrought iron bars on the windows, through which he could see the tea-colored ocean.

Thirty-two people sat in a circle on the floor. Half of them were kids. Jack seemed the youngest, except for a little girl with blond hair and light freckles. She looked about his age or younger. Everyone sat with their legs crossed Indian-style and rested their hands on their thighs, palms facing up. He saw the woman from the night before, sitting across from him, legs crossed like everyone else.

Abraham sat on the floor in the same manner, surveying the group. Candles were lit on a table underneath the windows. The same spice smell as the night before in Abraham's room. Moses dragged Jack over to Abraham. He leaned in and whispered something in Abraham's ear. Abraham frowned and then nodded.

"Welcome Augustine," Abraham then said in a friendly voice. "Come sit." He gestured to a space beside him. "Today you will continue your journey to salvation." Then he closed his eyes and chanted some words in a language Jack recognized from church. He didn't know what it meant, but he knew the sound of it.

"Amen," everyone in the room said after Abraham finished. Then Abraham continued chanting and every few minutes the group said amen. They all closed their eyes the whole time. Jack watched them. They all wore the same white robes.

Jack looked at the girl. She sat directly across the room from him. Her eyes were scrunched tight in concentration.

She glanced up suddenly and caught Jack looking at her and immediately bowed her head and scrunched her eyes tighter and mouthed her prayers more fervently. Jack quickly shut his eyes and pulled his robe as far down toward his ankles as it would go so no one would see that he had no underwear.

After about 20 minutes of the chants led by Abraham in the church language, it became quiet for a few minutes. Then everyone in the room clasped each other's hands to form a circle around the room. Abraham broke the silence.

"Brothers and Sisters," he began. "I want to introduce the newest member of our family...Augustine. Let us give him a warm welcome." Everyone in the room clapped. They all smiled and yelled, "Welcome Augustine!" Abraham smiled during the applause and then a serious look spread across his face.

"Augustine was baptized last night into God's divine love," he said as he scanned the others in the room. He put his hand on Jack's shoulder. "Augustine, like the saint for whom he has been named, was wicked. He was lost. He lived a life of sin and was destined for the fiery pits of hell. But we plucked him from the flames and now he will be saved and God will welcome him at the gates of Heaven."

Jack heard a few of the group shout, "Amen!"

"Augustine, look around you," Abraham continued. "This is your new family. They will help you stay on the right path – the path of righteousness. Listen to them and they will teach you how to live to deserve God's blessing and find salvation. You cannot trust anyone – anyone – except them. Do not fall into the trap of believing the lies that people outside of your family here will tell you, for they know not the path to Heaven."

"In the coming months you will prepare for your confirmation – the most important day in your spiritual journey. Seek the counsel of your new spiritual family and you will gain the kingdom of heaven."

Abraham stood. Each person continued to hold hands in a circle around the room. Then they began to sing. The words were the same strange church words Jack knew but didn't understand.

His head swam in a whirlwind of hunger, exhaustion, the scent of pee he could smell from his sticky legs, and the strange singing in the queer words. Suddenly, the voices all dissolved and were taken over by one voice. It was a nice voice. It was the blond girl's voice. Jack was surprised at how such a small girl had such a strong, clear singing voice.

He watched her, so still. So unafraid – not shy – but not forward or showy. Fervent, just like she was during the prayers, her bright almond eyes and long lashes scanning the room as she sang. They fell on his briefly then looked away as she sang the hymn.

Jack looked around and noticed again that he was the only one with his eyes open – except Abraham. Abraham was watching him. Jack closed his eyes quickly and listened to the girl's crystalline voice. It was the first time he wasn't scared.

When she finished, Abraham said some words about following the path to enlightenment and then asked everyone to proceed to the dining room. He spoke some words to a woman sitting next to him and she took Jack's hand and led him down the long hallway to the dining room.

She brought him to a large wooden table in the center of the room, big enough to hold everyone. She pulled out a seat. "This is your seat," she said to Jack. "You will sit in this seat for all meals." A teenager that Jack had noticed at prayers sat in the seat to his right. Jack scanned the room to see where the little girl was. He didn't see her. He twisted and turned in his seat looking for her.

Moses sat to Jack's left. "Hello Augustine," he said. "You better pay closer attention during evening vespers than you did to the morning prayers. If you don't, bad things will happen. You understand?" Jack nodded his head. His cold thighs chafed and irritated him.

The woman – Jack learned her name was Sarah – came over and whispered something in Moses's ear. He frowned. She whispered again, more insistent. Moses jerked out of his chair and mumbled something that Jack didn't hear. Then Sarah gestured with her hand to someone behind Jack. The girl.

CHAPTER 17

One Found

"Gus, you should try to take a nap," Vera said as the sun came up the morning after Jack's disappearance. "You haven't slept a minute."

"I can't sleep. I can't do anything. I don't know why I'm even standing here, doing nothing. Jack's out there somewhere, waiting for his dad to find him and bring him home and I'm just standing around!" He was shouting at this point.

"Honey, calm down," his mother said. "You're too hard on yourself." Gus resumed pacing back and forth, quickly like a tiger paces in a cage in a zoo, constrained within the steel bars but ready to spring and devour anything thrown within its vicinity.

"You won't do Jack any good if you put yourself in the hospital with exhaustion.

The phone rang again. Gus ran to it and picked it up. "Hello?" he said.

"Hi Gus, I want to talk to the kids." His heart began beating fast. It was Victoria.

"Victoria! Do you have Jack?" he yelled.

"What are you talking about? You have Jack."

"Victoria, please tell me, did you have someone pick up Jack yesterday afternoon? Do you have him somewhere?"

"Gus, what the hell are you talking about?" she said. "What's going on? WHERE'S JACK?"

Gus's stomach turned queasy. His heartbeat throbbed irregularly; Gus could feel it in his chest. She didn't have him.

"Jack's missing," he said. "I've been trying to call you but nobody could find you."

"What do you mean he's missing?" Her voice rose to almost a shriek.

"Since yesterday about four. It happened when I was on the phone with you and Jack was riding his bike out front and I yelled for him to come in and he was gone."

She was crying now, her voice pregnant with panic. "My baby! How could you Gus? How could you?"

Gus had no stomach for a fight. "I'm sorry. We're doing everything to find him. We've been looking all night. The police are looking—"

"Why didn't you tell me he was missing yesterday when I called?" she wailed. "You hung up on me!"

"I'm sorry. I should have, but at that point I thought he was at a neighbor's house or had ridden his bike somewhere. I didn't want to worry you unnecessarily."

"You should have told me!" she yelled. "I'm his mother!"

"I tried to reach you all night. I must have called thirty times. I called Donna. I called your parents. Where have you been?"

"It's none of your goddamn business!" Gus didn't immediately know how to answer this. Why did she not want to tell him?

"Victoria, I'm not accusing you of anything and I don't really care where you were, but I'm just telling you that I tried to reach you. The police were trying to locate you too."

"Why do you think I had Jack? Why'd you ask me if I had someone pick him up?" she asked.

"Because I didn't want to think about what it meant if you didn't!" Gus yelled, his voice hoarse with emotion. "I actually prayed that you had taken him because then at least I'd know he was safe." He thought of the couple at the hotel.

"Victoria, who was the couple at the Holiday Inn that you spoke with? We called the hotel looking for you and they told us that you spoke with a couple in the lounge for a couple of hours."

"They were just having dinner at the restaurant. I went down there to get something to eat and we were the only ones there so we started talking. Why?"

"Did you know them?"

"No I didn't know them." Gus could sense anger building in her voice. "We just talked in the lounge – the only people staying at a hotel on Christmas Eve. Why are you asking about them?"

"I don't know. They were the same couple I gave a jump to in the parking lot. Big guy with a long beard, wispy woman, dressed in black, right?"

"Yes, that's them."

"What did you talk about?" Gus asked.

"Oh just where they were from, what they were doing for Christmas, what I was doing there."

"And what did you tell them?"

"Nothing. We just talked. Small talk." She changed the subject. "What are the police saying?" she asked. "He's not with Bobby or any of his friends? He was just out front riding his bike and he disappeared, just like that? Nobody saw anything?"

"Yes, believe me, I've checked with everyone. We've had hundreds of people scouring the swamp and woods looking for him, all the neighbors know and are helping look for him, my parents and sisters are here—"

"Where's Lilly?" she said suddenly, frantically.

"She's here, she's in her room. My mother and Lauren have been with her. She's having a real tough time with all of this."

"I want to talk to her. Please get her."

"Yes, she'll be glad to hear from you. Hold on one minute." Gus got Lilly and handed her the phone. All the upheaval and fear within the child came pouring out to her mother. She could hardly get the words out, but the words were clear: she wanted her mother. After a few moments of anguished pleas, Lilly handed the phone back to her father.

"I'm catching the next flight up there," she said. "I'll be there as soon as I can." Victoria was crying too, her voice halting. She was sniffling. "You had him one day, Gus. Only one day and you couldn't keep him safe! I'm on my way." She hung up.

Gus hung up too and then picked up the phone again and dialed another number. "Hi, may I speak to Detective Boyd please?"

CHAPTER 18

Frances

"Augustine, I want you to meet Frances." Frances sat in the chair next to Jack. "Pleased to meet you Augustine," she said. She smelled faintly of flowers.

"Hi," Jack said. "You sing nice."

"Thank you."

A woman placed a plate containing an egg and a slice of buttered sourdough bread, a bowl of oatmeal, a glass of orange juice, and a cup of tea in front of Jack. She placed the same in front of Frances. Everyone at the table received the same meal. Jack waited for the others to begin eating but no one did. Each just looked expectantly at Abraham.

A minute or two after all the food and drink were set on the table, Abraham cleared his throat. "Frances, will you lead us in prayer this morning."

"Yes prophet Abraham," she said. Then she grasped Jack's hand. The boy next to him reached over and clasped Jack's other hand. Everyone bowed their heads.

Frances closed her eyes and began. "Here this morning we most humbly offer our prayers and supplications to the great Lord and Ruler of Nations and beseech Him to pardon our transgressions."

"Dear God, perfect what is lacking in my faith and in the faith of my brethren at this table. We thank you for bringing Augustine to us. Please convert and recover him and make him a man after thine own heart. Save us from all enemies and false brethren. Save our heathen neighbors – the unbelievers – from themselves and protect us from their wicked ways. Reform all sinners, and where sin hath abounded, may your grace superabound. Reform thy world O Lord."

"Dear God, we here repent our sins and past transgressions and seek your redemption. We surrender ourselves to you. Finally, God, we thank you for the blessings of this bounty before us. May you guide us and protect us today. Amen."

"Amen," everyone said in unison.

"Thank you Frances," Abraham said. Then everyone began to eat.

Jack wolfed down his breakfast. "What are you doing?" Frances asked. Jack's plate was clean and the bowl empty. He noticed that Frances had hardly touched hers. "Slow down," she said. "Temperance is one of the virtues in which we abide."

"Why does everyone talk funny?" Jack asked.

"What do you mean?"

"You use funny words, like church words."

"We use the words God spoke to us. We use the words in the Bible. The word of God."

Jack wanted to ask her if Abraham was her father or if she had other parents before coming here. Instead, he asked her if she had always lived at this house, if she grew up there.

"Yes, I grew up here."

"You weren't brought here from somewhere else?"

"No," she said. She frowned. "This has been my only home. This is my family, and now you are part of my family. This is your family now too. We must care for each other and protect each other and love each other always."

Jack leaned in close to Frances. She smelled nice, like the lilacs in the backyard by his father's garden. "But I *have* a family already," he whispered. "I don't want another family."

"You mustn't say that Augustine. You must forget all about them. God demanded that his disciples bid farewell to their old lives and actually hate their life in the abnormal society from which they came, to take up their cross and follow Him. For just as He gave up His life for our sake, so we must give up our sinful lives for His sake." She paused and read his face to see if he understood. He didn't. He had never heard any kid – or any adult for that matter – talk like that.

"Augustine," she continued, "I heard that your family was wicked and had brought God's wrath upon them. God told Abraham to rescue you from their wickedness and take you up as his own and teach you God's way so that you could be saved. You have been given a great gift."

"My family is not wicked," Jack said. "I love them. They are my family."

Frances smiled and lightly touched her hand on his forearm. "I know it's hard," she said. "But you will soon be glad you've been brought here and taken from the evil path you were on." She paused and looked toward Abraham. She saw he was not looking and continued.

"I heard your parents are divorced and they fight over you and your sister. I heard that they say the most horrible things to each other and that they live in drunkenness and that your dad has many girlfriends who share his bed." Jack listened to Frances more closely. How did she know about his parents?

Jack's parents were the only parents he knew who were divorced except for Billy McCabe's, and Billy was a mean bully. Were you bad if you were divorced? Did God not love you if you were divorced? Were his parents really doomed to hell because they didn't love each other?

He had prayed to God every single night as he lay in bed for his parents to get back together. He prayed when he used to go to Saint Andrew's on Sundays that his parents would love each other again and not scream at each other all the time and that they would all be a family again.

Grandma told him that she didn't pray for his parents to get back together; she said she prayed only that they would all be happy. This made Jack mad. She said sometimes mommies and daddies don't love each other anymore and fight too much and it is better if they get a divorce. But she said they didn't do anything wrong, that's just the way it is sometimes.

Then Jack wondered if God was mad at him and his parents because they didn't go to church anymore. He thought about how God must feel about them not going to church when the priest always said that it was one of the most important things a person can do for God.

Jack knew that missing church was considered a mortal sin – the worst sin you could commit. Maybe God was punishing him for missing church. Maybe he was teaching him and his mom and dad a lesson.

"But even if you get divorced, can't you go to confession and God will forgive you?" he asked Frances.

"God will forgive you if you are truly sorry," Frances said. "But you can't just say you're sorry; you must show God you are sorry by repenting your sins, by changing your ways and devoting your life to Him. Your parents continue to lead a sinful life, and you were leading a sinful life, a life not devoted to glorifying God."

"We glorify God every day here – every hour, every minute. Our whole reason for being is because Jesus died and suffered horribly so that we could have this life. You must embrace that and accept it and then God will welcome you into His kingdom. Living here is your purification from the evil that is all around in the outside world." She patted his wrist while she said all this. She smiled at Jack, a full smile that showed all her tiny white teeth. Her eyes shone – beautiful, big, clear eyes.

"But I am not evil!" Jack protested.

"You cannot see it now, but you will soon, and you'll be glad and rejoice that you are here."

Jack decided to change the subject. "Did you have Christmas here? What did Santa bring you?"

Frances looked at him and blushed. "You still believe in Santa? Don't you know?" she asked.

Jack squirmed in his seat and scraped his fork across his plate as if trying to scoop any lingering crumbs. "Know what?" he asked.

"Santa's not real. Christmas is not supposed to be a time when you get a bunch of presents and everyone shops and spends a lot of money on stuff that nobody really needs and stuffs their faces with turkey and roast beef and cakes and cookies and sweets until their stomachs explode and they feel sick. There is so much greed and waste when so many of our brothers and sisters are in need and have nothing – no home, no food. Christmas today is so sinful and not in the spirit in which Jesus taught us to live."

Frances took a small bite of her bread and continued. "Christmas is a time when we reflect on the great gift God gave us – his only son. We celebrate the birth of Christ. We fast and pray and sing hymns of praise. We are humble. We bring food and clothes that we grow and make ourselves to those who need them. There are no presents, no feast, no wrapping paper and no prideful displays."

"You will see how we live humbly, as God asked us to. You will see why it is the right way, and you will be thankful that you have been chosen." She spooned some of her uneaten eggs and oatmeal onto his plate. "Eat these. Soon you must fast. You need your strength."

Jack didn't know why he had been chosen. He wished he hadn't been. He liked presents and cookies and Santa Claus. He liked Christmas lights and Christmas decorations.

A boy came and took all the plates. The children and adults scattered. Some went outside to the barn. Some went down the stairs leading to the basement. Others went upstairs. Frances wished him luck. He didn't get a chance to ask her for what. He watched her petite figure as she walked out quickly with all the others.

Sarah took Jack's hand and walked him along a corridor. They walked past the entranceway and the large front room with the fireplace that Jack had seen the night before and ended up in a windowless library with leather couches and a desk pushed against the wall.

CHAPTER 19

Lessons

"Sit here," Sarah said, pointing at the desk. She placed two books before him. The first one was a Bible. The second was the *Catechism of the Catholic Church*. "For the rest of winter you will study the Bible and pray and meditate to prepare for your confirmation, when your life will change forever. This catechism will help you. You must focus every waking moment on God and ask His guidance and forgiveness."

"What happens at my confirmation? What is confirmation?" Jack asked.

"That I cannot tell you. You must wait until it happens. But mark me well, Augustine, it is a day in which you will move closer to God. It is a most special day." She paused. "But you have much work to do before that day. You will be tested. We must focus now on being worthy of God's grace."

"To become worthy, first you will enter a period of fasting – three full days of nothing but water. After that, for 40 days, you will eat only breakfast and a collation at night. You must cleanse your body as well as your mind."

"Each day we will take an account of your moral assets and liabilities. Self improvement is our daily goal and each morning you will make a vow to God to improve that day."

She told Jack that he would join the group for morning and evening vespers each day, but would not eat with them or attend school with them or participate in any recreational activities until he was deemed worthy through confirmation, which would occur sometime in the early spring.

"I'm going to read a few passages from the Bible and the catechism and then we'll discuss them, okay?" Jack nodded his head. Sarah sat down next to him and began to read, in a low rhythmical chant, alternately, passages from the Bible and the book of catechism.

"I am the light of the world; he that follows me shall not walk in darkness, but shall have the light of life— John 8:12," she said and looked at him to gage his reaction.

"And all the people who give up mothers and fathers, sisters and brothers, relatives and friends to be disciples will, in turn, live in our house and receive an abundant social life with those hundreds of new brothers and sisters, mothers and fathers and children." She paused and searched his eyes to determine what thoughts might be behind them. She continued.

"The first thing He commanded His original twelve disciples to do was to leave everything behind — homes, farms, parents, relatives, friends, children, brothers, sisters, jobs, and ambitions — and set out with Him on His mission. He demanded that they, His followers, should uproot themselves, that they should abandon the safety of the status quo and the security of their own domains."

She placed the book on the desk and put her hands on Jack's shoulders and moved her face about ten inches from his. She spoke in a softer, but more urgent voice. "Augustine, these words of God were the most direct and powerful words He spoke concerning a person's salvation. These very precious words were the unmistakable good news of how to escape death. God demanded loyalty and devotion to Him and to His commands. Be mindful of this."

She ran her hand through his hair lovingly. "Augustine, do you know what this all means?" Jack looked at the floor and shook his head no.

"You have been given a great gift. You can't see it now, but you will soon. You're thinking of your old life, your old family. You must forget them, as God has told us to do. You must devote yourself to Him alone."

Jack listened and hoped that his mother or father would knock on the door and rescue him from these people. Sarah interrupted his thoughts.

"Augustine, do you know what it means to be chosen? You have been chosen as one of God's disciples. There is no greater glory in all the world. But now you have to prove yourself worthy of being one of the chosen. That is what we will teach you."

"You must become who you were created to be. There is nothing better. You were not going to do this with your old family, full of sin. Rejoice and be glad, for now you will become who you were truly created to be in God's eyes."

Nearly two hours had passed, and Jack was having a hard time listening to Sarah anymore. He was tired and hungry and still didn't understand what she was telling him in that strange way she spoke. "I'm hungry," he said. "Can we eat lunch?"

"No, Augustine. I told you – you will not eat again for three days. Your period of fasting has begun." Jack thought for a moment about not eating for three days and tears streaked his cheeks.

"You mustn't cry Augustine. Fasting will cleanse your body. You can do it. Meditation will help you. Listen to me now. We're going to meditate and you will forget about hunger and sleep and your family. Focus. God will come to you…you will find God when you master meditation."

Sarah made Jack sit on the floor. "Cross your legs, bow your head, and close your eyes," she said. She told him he would meditate many times every day to quiet his mind and focus on what he needed to do to live a worthy life and please God. She also asked him to concentrate on a mantra. Jack didn't know what that meant.

She told him to think of it as a personal code word or group of words or sound. This code word would be a secret that Jack could not share with anyone else. Jack decided on "Da Doo Ron Ron" his favorite song by Shaun Cassidy. He began to repeat it to himself.

After a few minutes, he began to fidget. Sarah scolded him and told him to focus on his breathing and repeat his mantra to himself over and over. "Focus on the sound, the vibrations of your mantra, and each breath," she said.

Jack tried to stay still and focus on his breath and mantra, but he couldn't concentrate. His stomach began making funny noises and he worried that Sarah would hear them. Jack closed his eyes and listened to his breathing and repeated his mantra in his head. It was no use. He kept thinking about not eating. He looked up at Sarah. "I can't," he said.

"Okay then," she said. "Let's continue our Bible study." She read the Bible and catechism to him for many hours until a woman named Teresa came and told them that it was time for vespers. Sarah closed the Bible, took Jack's hand in hers, and led him to the same room where the morning prayers had been held. He was surprised when he looked out the window to see it was dark outside. They sat next to Abraham.

"Before we begin, I'd like to welcome Brother Augustine to his first evening vespers," he said. He smiled at Jack. "I've heard that you had a productive afternoon of Bible study, meditation, and prayer with Sister Sarah."

"We have evening vespers every night, and you will find that we use vespers to share our experiences from the day, to praise God for a day well lived, and to thank Him for the gifts He hath brought to us."

"We also use the time to be mindful of God's will before we return to bed for the evening. Vespers is our last opportunity as a community to make sure we have focused properly on the Lord and lived for Him entirely during the day…to think about how we will live tomorrow to deserve His glory. Let us begin."

Vespers began with singing. Abraham sang a line and then everyone would repeat. "Deus, in adiutorium meum intende. Domine, ad adiuvandum me festina.

Gloria Patri, et Filio, et Spiritui Sancto. Sicut erat in principio, et nunc et semper, et in saecula saeculorum. Amen," he, and then they, said. "Alleluia."

Sarah, who stood next to Jack, whispered to him. "That means O God, come to my assistance. O Lord, make haste to help me. Glory be to the Father, and to the Son, and to the Holy Spirit. As it was in the beginning is now and ever shall be world without end. Amen. Alleluia."

A boy then sang a hymn. He had a nice voice too, but not as good as Frances's.

Bible passages were read by various members of the community. Sarah leaned in and whispered to Jack. "These are the psalms, do you remember them?"

Abraham sang a sentence, and everyone sang after him. "Whom should we pray for?" Abraham asked. Three people offered prayers for names Jack didn't know.

Vespers was different from morning prayers. There was more singing, which Jack liked except that Frances did not sing. Abraham said a few prayers then everyone said the Our Father. Jack knew the Our Father and recited it along with them. Then Abraham made the sign of the cross and vespers was over.

CHAPTER 20

The Arrival

G us was speaking to a reporter from the Lowell Sun about his latest efforts to find Jack. There was a buzz of conversation – white noise – among the dozen or so people in the living room. Then came a tornado. Victoria burst through the door, shrieking and crying. Her eyes glanced, darted across the room until they found Gus.

She bolted over to him. Then she hit him as hard as she could with her purse, causing a gash at the top of his eye out of which blood began flowing. "How could you?" she wailed, and she hit him again and again, screaming. "What have you done to Jack?"

Gus put his arms over his face. She continued wailing away, flailing, hysterical, hitting his arms and screaming and crying. "How could you! How could you lose him?" Sean Boylan and Bill O'Connor came to pry her away, and it took all their strength to pull her off Gus.

Gus knew then, without a doubt, that she was not involved, at least knowingly, in Jack's disappearance.

"Where's Lilly?" she asked through sobs as the men held her.

"She's in her bedroom," Gus said.

"Let go of me!" she said to Boylan and O'Connor and she ripped her arms free and rushed to Lilly's bedroom. "Lilly!" she called. "Lilly!"

Gus followed behind her. She threw the door open, saw Lilly and her tear-stained face sitting on the bed with Vera, Lauren and her cousin Tricia, and stumbled to her and hugged her and kissed her cheeks. Gus stood at the door, holding a cloth to his forehead to stop the bleeding. He had never in his life seen her like this. She pulled Lilly to her breast and mother and daughter sobbed.

Vera and Lauren left the room, but Gus remained in the doorway. After fifteen minutes, Victoria spoke. "What happened darling? Do you know?"

Lilly shook her head. "I'm scared."

Victoria rocked her. "Don't be scared honey. Mommy's here. It's going to be okay." She looked at Gus as she said this; a look full of hate. "Now tell me what you remember."

Lilly wiped her eyes. "Me and daddy were on the phone with you and Jack was riding his bike. Daddy called him to come in but he was gone. We thought he went to Bobby's but he wasn't there. Mommy, where is he? He's all alone and he must be scared." She buried her head against her mother's shoulder and cried.

"I know honey. We're looking for him now and we'll find him."

"I don't want you to go away again," Lilly said.

"I won't honey. I'm not going anywhere. I want to talk to Daddy for a minute though, okay? Will you go find Grandma and I'll be right out?" Lilly nodded yes. Gus called to Vera and asked her to watch Lilly.

"Close the door please," Victoria said. Gus wondered, after her earlier outburst, if she was going to attack him again, but she seemed to have calmed somewhat. She wasn't hysterical.

She wiped her eyes. "Gus, where's Jack?" Her tone had changed. She had said the same thing a few minutes earlier, but earlier it had been a desperate cry; now the tone had an accusatory vibration.

"What are you talking about? You can't think I have something to do with this."

"I don't know what to think," she said. "I just know you had him and now he's gone. I don't know how he could have disappeared if he was biking in front of the house."

She was not going to put more guilt on him than he already had. "Victoria," Gus said, his voice rising in volume, "I was on the phone with you. As soon as I realized he hadn't just wandered off and wasn't at a friend's house, I called the police and they came down and asked me a bunch of questions and searched Jack's room. They even called your mother."

"They called my mother? Why did they call my mother?"

"We were trying to find you!"

"Where are they now?" she asked. "I want to talk to them."

"I think they're questioning neighbors," he said. "Honestly, I don't have a lot of confidence in them. I hired a private investigator. He's from Lowell. Supposed to be an expert on child abductions, got like twenty years as a detective. He was here last night."

"You hired a private investigator without consulting me? I'm his mother for Christ's sake! You can't just go hiring people and doing things without asking me first!"

Gus steeled his voice. He spoke clearly and forcibly and punctuated his words with his finger pointing at her face. "Listen. I don't have to clear anything I do with you when it comes to finding Jack. I'm going to do whatever I think will get Jack back, and you will not question me. All I want is to find him. We want the same thing. If this guy helps us get Jack back, then that's all that matters."

Just then Boyd knocked at the door. He had gone to the Holiday Inn and taken fingerprint and hair samples from the room the couple had stayed in and had gone to the FBI field office earlier in the morning to see if he found a match in the FBI database. He didn't. He began to tell Gus that the Holiday Inn did not have any more information than they gave Gus the night before but he stopped abruptly when he noticed Lilly clinging to Victoria.

"Mrs. Delaney?" he asked.

"Yes."

"Hi, I'm Detective Will Boyd and I've been asked to assist with the investigation into your son. Do you mind if I ask you a few questions?"

"I've already been interviewed by the police," she said.

"No you haven't!" Gus said. "You were just asking—"

"Well I will be interviewed by them as soon as I find them," she interrupted. "I don't know who you are. My husband hired you, right? I'm not comfortable answering questions from you."

"Oh come on Victoria," Gus said. "He's just trying to help us get Jack back."

"That's okay Mr. Delaney," Boyd said. Then he turned to Victoria. "Mrs. Delaney, I understand this is a difficult time for you, and I'm sorry about your son. There's nothing I'd like better than to help you get him back. If you don't want to talk with me right now that's okay. But after you speak with the police, if you have any questions or if you think of anything that might help me find Jack, just call me. Here's my card."

Victoria nodded and took his card but didn't say anything. Just then the man who offered to print posters walked in carrying a box. He placed it on the floor and pulled out a poster for Gus to look at.

"These are great, thanks," Gus said. "There are a bunch of people in the kitchen asking what they can do. Lots of people have been coming by asking to help. Can you organize them and start putting these up on store windows, handing them out to people at the grocery store, stuffing them in mailboxes?"

"Yes, I'll get a group together and do that," the man said. Boyd examined the posters but offered no comment on them.

CHAPTER 21

The Sin

Moses led Jack and Emmanuel down to their room in the basement. Jack wondered where everyone else slept. He wondered what their rooms looked like. Where did Frances sleep?

"You come here," Moses said to Jack. He grabbed his arm and pulled him over to the sink where his spiritual underpants or whatever they were called lay soaking. "You need to scrub these and then hang them on the rack over there. Use that bar of soap and face cloth and scrub the garments under the hot water on that washboard." He pointed to a rectangular wooden frame with corrugated metal in the middle of it hanging on the wall next to the sink. "I'll be back in 15 minutes to check on you."

Jack scrubbed the undergarments and hung them on the rack. The kitchen was cold and he had splashed water on himself, which made him shiver. He walked into the bedroom and found Emmanuel kneeling at the side of his bed praying. Jack walked over to his own bed and knelt down and pretended to pray too. He had prayed all day and didn't feel like praying anymore.

He was thinking of his bedroom at home and all his toys that he got for Christmas and never got to use when Moses returned. "Okay, time for bed," he said. "You better get some rest; you have a busy day tomorrow." He closed the door and Jack heard the key turn the lock.

Jack hopped into bed and pulled the covers up. "How did your first day go?" Emmanuel asked.

Jack yawned. "Okay, but I'm really hungry and I don't feel good. Why can't I eat?"

"You are being cleansed – your soul of course, but also your body. The food we eat we grow and harvest ourselves. There are no chemicals in them – just wholesome and pure food from our gardens and animals. So you've got to flush all the bad chemicals out of your body."

"I don't eat chemicals."

"Yes you do. The food out there is loaded with chemicals and preservatives and the way it is produced is unclean. Abraham taught us that our bodies are our temples, and just as we nourish our souls with God's grace and don't expose our minds to anything sinful and impure, so we must do the same with our bodies."

Emmanuel sat up as he said all this. Satisfied that he had provided a good lesson to Jack, he lay down in the bed.

"But when will I eat again?" Jack asked.

"You shouldn't question Abraham. You must endure quietly and humbly, as God wills it and not complain in such a selfish manner," Emmanuel said. "Those who are concerned with earthly pleasures are wicked and not welcome in the kingdom of Heaven."

"I don't care if I'm welcome in the kingdom of Heaven," Jack said.

"What? What did you say?" Emmanuel sprang upright in his bed.

"Nothing, I didn't say anything," Jack said.

"I heard you Augustine. Your words might jeopardize your confirmation. You must ask God to forgive you for uttering such a blasphemous statement. I will say a prayer for you. The Bible, in Psalms, says 'I had rather be a doorkeeper in the house of my God, than to dwell in the tents of wickedness.' Remember this and repent."

Emmanuel told Jack that if he were to die in his sleep, he would go straight to hell for what he said. Jack was sick of the Bible and never wanted to read it again. He pushed that thought out of his head and prayed to God to forgive him for thinking it and for what he said and to help him be better.

He hoped he wouldn't die that night in his sleep. Sarah had told him all day how bad Hell was. He was scared of Hell. He didn't feel good, but he didn't think he was sick enough to die. He turned over, pulled the covers tightly to his chin, and fell into a troubled sleep.

The buzzing alarm jarred him awake in the early morning. He glanced out the window and watched the sun creep above the horizon and turn the sea pale pink. Emmanuel turned off the alarm and got out of bed. Jack pulled the covers over his head to try to go back to sleep.

"What are you doing?" Emmanuel asked as he pulled the covers off Jack. "We have to get ready for morning prayers."

"I don't feel good."

"You have to go to morning prayers. Abraham will not abide you sleeping through prayers.

Suddenly a key rattled in the lock and the door opened. Moses came in and, seeing that Jack was not ready, roared at him and began to move toward him. "Why don't you have your robe on! We're late for morning prayers!" Jack felt the warm trickle of pee down his leg and a dark stain began to creep across the front of his underpants. Then he felt the hard slap of Moses's hand across his face. Then everything went dark.

A cold splash of water on his face revived him. "Wake up, Augustine." It was Moses. "You have disgraced yourself and God again by soiling your spiritual garments and for not being ready for morning prayers. And Emmanuel told me that you blasphemed our lord and savior last night. Your sins must be brought before the community and you must show repentance."

Moses told him to put his robe on and brought him and Emmanuel to the meeting room. Everyone was there waiting for them. Abraham frowned as Moses whispered in his ear.

"Brother Augustine, please step forward," he said when Moses finished. Jack froze. "Brother Augustine, step forward!" he yelled. Jack took a step.

"You have sinned and must confess your sins to the group and to God and ask his forgiveness. Please confess your sins." Jack thought for some seconds. He didn't know what to say.

"What did you say to Emmanuel last night?"

"I asked him when I would be able to eat," Jack said.

"And what did you say when he told you that to get to the kingdom of Heaven you must fast?" Jack looked at Emmanuel and then at Moses.

"I don't know," Jack stammered.

"Don't lie to us!" Abraham bellowed. "What did you say to Emmanuel?"

Jack's voice cracked. "I'm sorry. I…I didn't mean what I said—

"WHAT DID YOU SAY TO EMMANUEL!!!"

Jack began to cry. "I said I didn't care if I went to the Kingdom of Heaven," he whimpered.

"Thank you," Abraham said calmly. "Augustine, one thing you will do here is always tell the truth. If you lie you make your sin far worse. There now, don't cry. We are here to help you. What you said last night angered God and brought disfavor to our community. But I believe you are sorry and ready to repent your sin and again be looked upon favorably by your family here, are you not?"

"Yes, I am sorry for making God angry and I won't do it again. I do want to go to Heaven with God."

"Thank you Augustine. And is there anything else you did for which we should pray?" Jack looked at him and then glanced around the room. No eyes gave him any answer what to say. "I don't know," he said.

"Please open your robe," Abraham said. Then Jack remembered. He had a big yellow pee stain on his spiritual garment. He turned bright red.

"Please Abraham…I am sorry for all my sins and I will pray really hard today to ask God to forgive me for them."

"Go ahead – open your robe so everyone can see." Jack slowly opened his robe, just a little bit.

"Open your robe!" Abraham yelled. Jack opened it all the way. He felt a chill. His eyes never left the floor.

"Now turn around so everyone can see." Jack turned around and kept his head down. He didn't want to see anyone, especially Frances.

"Augustine has soiled his spiritual undergarments both nights he's had them. Thank you Augustine; you may go back and sit now." Jack walked back without looking at anyone, sat down, and gazed blankly at the ground, tears dripping off his chin.

"Let us pray for him to abandon this disgusting habit," Abraham began. "And let us pray to God to forgive him for his mortal sin last night. Let us also ask for God's wisdom to teach Augustine how to live to bring glory to God's name." Everyone bowed his head and said silent prayers for Jack.

Jack did not go to breakfast with the others. Sarah brought him straight to the library for his studies. If he weren't so hungry, he would have been glad not to have to endure sitting next to Frances, with everyone looking at him, knowing that they had seen that he peed his pants.

"Let us begin," Sarah said.

Sarah read some of the same passages she had read the day before. Strange Biblical chants – whispersongs from her lips – blurred together and made his head hurt: "I am the light of the world…shall not walk in darkness…and all the people who give up mothers and fathers…to be disciples…He demanded that they…uproot themselves…loyalty to Him…to cling to anything…forfeit eternal life."

After reciting passages from the Bible and catechism for hours – the 'word of God' as she called it – Sarah told Jack that they would practice meditating again. She told him to sit and cross his legs, his arms extended, resting on his lap, palms facing up. Then she told him to bow his head and chant his mantra. He closed his eyes and concentrated.

She smiled. "It's not easy, but you'll get it. Focus." Jack closed his eyes. His mind kept filling with thoughts. Thoughts about his family. Thoughts about his friends. Thoughts about his school and his bike and his father's banana pancakes and the swamp in summer. He tried to move them from his head and make them disappear. He tried to use the lessons he learned in karate classes about discipline and breathing and repetition. Nothing worked.

Hours went by and he felt weak and dizzy. "Okay," she said finally. "Come with me." She grabbed his hand and led him out of the library.

The house was quiet. "Here, put these on," she said, and she handed him his pants, which lay folded on a table. His sneakers also sat on the table. He put them on. Then she took from a hook by the front door an old olive jacket with a big fur-laced hood, like ones the Eskimos wore in pictures Jack had seen, handed it to him, and led him outside.

The sky was shadowy gray. Snow fell softly. He didn't know what time it was. Sarah led him to the side of the house and down a dusky path through the woods. The air smelled crisp in Jack's nostrils and snapped him out of his lethargy. He looked to the left and right of the path and saw only woods on either side. The thick trees hid the weakening sun's light so that night prematurely invaded the woods.

He had an impulse to break free from Sarah's grip and run.

CHAPTER 22

Escape

He didn't know if the fence he saw at the entrance to the driveway where Moses opened the gate extended around the entire yard, but he was certain that even if it did he could climb it.

He would find the first house he came to and knock on the door and ask them to call his father. He knew the number. Suddenly the silence of snowfall was broken by shouting and laughter somewhere ahead of them down the path. Jack decided to wait to see where she was taking him.

They came to a clearing and a frozen pond. Everyone from morning prayers was ice skating. Some of the boys raced around the edge of the pond on the dull ice. Jack saw some of the girls skating in an inlet on the far side. Frances was skating with them.

She glided smoothly, in and out, around and around, carving figure-eights in the ice. Jack watched her. He had skated since he was four years old at Billerica Memorial High School's rink and played on a pee-wee hockey team before he moved away with his mom.

He wished he could play hockey on the pond with the other kids. He wished he had his Bobby Orr jersey. He would show Frances what a good skater he was. Sarah watched Jack watching the other children. "Do you know how to skate?" she asked.

"Yes, I can skate good. I used to play hockey," Jack answered.

"Well, you will not play hockey again. It is immoral and we do not allow it. But you'll be able to skate with the other children if you study your Bible well and pray faithfully every day and are worthy of confirmation. However, you cannot skate, or participate in any of the approved recreational activities for that matter, until you are confirmed and are in good standing with the community."

"Do everything you are asked," she continued, "and you can play with the other boys and with Frances too." She smiled. Jack thought if he was home and wanted to skate, all he had to do was ask his dad and he would take him to the ice rink, or they would skate on the frozen swamp.

Why was hockey immoral? His dad had taught Jack to skate and stick handle the puck on a pond at the town park. He liked hockey. Everyone loved Bobby Orr – they said he was the best.

Sarah and Jack stood on the path at the edge of the pond and watched the skaters for a little while longer and then she took his hand and led him up the path back toward the house. It had gotten noticeably darker.

Now was the time to run. He played out in his mind his escape. He didn't like the woods in the dark, so he thought maybe he should try to escape during the day. But he didn't know if he'd be outside again anytime soon, and maybe escaping in the dark would be better because he could hide easier. If he didn't escape, Moses would beat him. He worried that he would pee his pants in the morning again. So he made up his mind that he had to go now. He waited for a good place to run and got ready to break her grip and dart into the darkness of the woods.

Then he thought about what Abraham said. He would kill his dad and Lilly if Jack didn't do what he said. Jack could call and warn them, but what if he didn't find a house in time? Maybe, he thought, he should wait until he could escape without anyone knowing and give himself a head start.

He thought about what Bobby would do. Bobby would try to escape. He wouldn't be scared of the woods. He shivered. This might be his best chance. Caught in his indecisiveness and fear, he saw the chance was passing – the house came into view 50 yards ahead through the trees. Soon it would be too late. *Be brave…be brave*, he repeated to himself.

They reached the edge of the yard. It was too late. Soon they'd be back inside the house. He would wait. They came within the shadow of the house, menacing and cold. Without being fully conscious of what he was doing, Jack ripped his hand free and bolted back down the path and cut into the woods. "Augustine!" Sarah shrieked. "Come back!" Jack didn't look back but he knew she was running after him.

He raced through the trees like a hare chased by a fox, ducking under branches, jumping over logs, and snapping through bushes. His only thought was to run as fast as he could until he found someone who could help him. He heard Sarah's voice grow fainter. Either she stopped chasing or he was as fast as he thought he was and she couldn't keep up.

He burst upon a clearing and saw some houses ahead through the trees. *Thank you God*, he prayed. He rushed to the first house at the edge of the woods. It was a small wooden cottage. It was dark, but Jack knocked at the door frantically. There was no answer.

He raced to the next house. It was the same style. He saw a dim light flickering in the window. He banged on the door. This time a woman answered. She saw his face, ashen with terror, and started. "Oh my goodness!"

"Please help me!" Jack blurted. "There are people who took me from my parents and they locked me in a big house near here. I just escaped through the woods. They're coming after me. Please help me," he begged.

"Who's coming after you?" she asked, looking out behind Jack.

"Please...please let me in before they get me," Jack wailed.

"But who's trying to get you?" the woman asked again.

"Some people who kidnapped me from my daddy's house and took me to another house – a really big house. They said they killed my mother and if I don't do what I'm told they will kill my daddy and sister too. I need to call my family and warn them and tell them to come get me."

"Come in," the woman said. She directed him to a living room. It had plain wood floors, an old couch and chair, and a wooden coffee table. There was a rocking chair in the corner. An oil lamp burned on the table next to it. "I don't have a phone," the woman said. "But sit down for a moment and tell me how you escaped."

The woman pointed to the couch. She sat in the rocking chair. A shawl was wrapped around her head and Jack couldn't see her face because it was hidden in shadow.

"Now you say you were kidnapped?" the woman began. Jack noticed a Bible resting on the coffee table. He sat on the edge of the couch and tried to see the woman's face. He noticed that she was dressed like the woman he had seen come out of the barn and his stomach dropped like it did the time he had gone on the roller coaster at Canobie Lake Park.

The woman saw the terror in his eyes. "You poor thing!" She smiled. "Would you like a cup of tea...I'm sorry, what is your name?" She got up to go to the kitchen.

"No I don't want any tea, I have to go," Jack said. He stood.

"Go? Why do you have to go? Sit down. I'll help you," she said. "But first let me fix something for you to eat. You must be terribly hungry." Jack looked nervously out the window. He saw the *Catechism of the Catholic Church* lying on the table by the rocker. He sat on the edge of the couch and his hands clung to the coffee table.

"I'm sorry, I really have to go," he said. He stood and raced to the door. The woman swooped over and grabbed his arm. "I'm sorry Augustine. What you did is very bad and you will be punished severely. I cannot let you go or I will have sinned in the eyes of the community, and worse, in the eyes of God."

Jack jerked his arm from her grip and bolted out the front door. "He's here, he's here!" the woman yelled. She began to ring a bell. It sounded like the bell his father used to call him and Lilly in for supper.

"Augustine, you can't escape!" she yelled. "Give up now or it is going to be much worse for you." Jack kept running. He thought of home and his family and those thoughts pushed him forward. Suddenly he heard dogs barking ferociously in the distance. Did they have dogs chasing him? His face paled and his heart raced.

He knew if he didn't find a fence to climb over soon, or a house to help him, the dogs would catch him. No matter how fast you are, dogs always catch you. He knew that. He ran straight ahead.

Jack looked wildly around him. The barks became louder. He fled across the clearing of cottages toward the other side of the woods from which he came. He heard the dogs so loudly now that he turned around, expecting to see them right behind him. He did see them. Two Doberman pinschers burst from the woods and raced across the clearing after him.

CHAPTER 23

Fire

"Help me!" he cried. "Somebody please help me!" He reached the woods on the other side. He raced up a tree just as the Dobermans caught up to him. The two dogs stood at the bottom of the tree barking ferociously, jumping up on the tree trunk – up and down, frenzied – trying to reach him. Jack edged higher up the tree. His heart beat like mad.

Soon he heard a man's voice yell to the dogs. "Max! Rebel! Good boys!" He appeared and held out something in his hands. "Good boys! Come here!" The dogs left the tree and took whatever was in the man's hand. The man looked up at Jack shivering in the tree.

"Augustine, I'm afraid your actions today will not please Abraham." Jack recognized him from morning prayers and breakfast. His name was Timothy and he was about eighteen years old.

"Please Timothy, please don't take me back to that house! I'm begging you, please let me go back home to my family," Jack shrieked.

"Augustine, you have to come down from that tree now. I have to take you back," Timothy said. His eyes were kind as he said this, and he smiled, flashing a mouthful of crooked teeth. "It's hard for you now, I know, but you will eventually love it here and never want to leave. I promise you."

"What's going to happen to me?" Jack said. He hadn't budged from the tree branch to which he clung.

"I cannot tell you that, Augustine. Only Abraham knows. You will be punished, of that I am certain, but I do not know what form it will take." Tears trickled off Jack's cheeks onto the ground, like drops of water dripping off leaves after a rainstorm.

The dogs, finished with the snack he had given them, looked up at Jack and growled. "Max! Rebel! Stop that!" he commanded. They stopped growling.

He noticed that Jack was watching the dogs. "They won't hurt you with me here." He moved toward the tree and extended his hand. Jack moved to a higher branch and shook his head no.

"Augustine, I will leave the dogs here and you can stay up in the tree all night. If you try to get down they'll rip your flesh from your bones. Do you want me to do that?"

"No!" Jack screamed. "I want you to let me go to my parents where I belong!"

Timothy shook his head. "Augustine—

"And stop calling me Augustine! My name is Jack!"

"Augustine," Timothy repeated. "If I have to leave and bring back Moses or Noah to get you, it will be much worse. Then you will be punished twice – first by them and then by Abraham. Each punishment will be harsh. If you let me take you to Abraham now, you will only be punished once and I will pray that his punishment is lenient."

Jack searched the landscape around him. He saw only woods – just trees and darkness. No fence to sprint to, no safe house nearby, though now he didn't know if there were any houses safe for him. He clung so tightly to the tree limbs that his arms became sore. He glanced at the dogs, menacing, circling the tree. He saw no other alternative than to go with Timothy.

He climbed down the tree and Timothy grabbed him by his shirt collar and yanked him forward. Sarah met them at the edge of the path by the big house. She grimaced. She said nothing but Jack could tell she was hurt. Timothy brought Jack into the house and Sarah told them to wait in the same bleak entry hall he waited in the night he arrived. This time, however, a fire blazed in the fireplace in the room with the books and paintings.

Sarah returned after a few minutes. "Come with me," she said. She took him up the winding stairs. Jack knew where he was going. His lip quivered, and he shivered off a chill. His legs wobbled, his strength sapped from the chase through the woods, the lack of food and drink, and his nerves.

Sarah knocked on Abraham's closed door. "Please enter," Abraham said. Jack remained still. Cement shoes. Sarah pulled him in. Jack saw Abraham and froze. His body stiffened, paralyzed. "Augustine. I cannot tell you how disappointed in you I am," Abraham said. He held a sledgehammer.

"We've given you a great opportunity for eternal life – the greatest gift you can be given, in fact." His hand caressed the handle of the hammer. Jack shrunk into Sarah's bosom. She stood beside him and held him so tightly by his shoulders he winced. "And how do you repay us?"

Jack couldn't speak. Abraham paced the room and looked from the floor to Jack and back to the floor again. "Do you think God is happy that you tried to run away from a community – a family – that is trying to bring you closer to Him…trying to help you understand Him and what He wishes for you?" Jack looked up at Sarah.

"Look at *me*!" Abraham yelled. Then he walked over to the dresser and took a small metal figurine. He placed it on the floor. He heaved the sledgehammer in the air over his head and slammed it on the object. He picked it up and waved the mangled mass in front of Jack's face.

"I think the proper punishment for running away should be to make it impossible for you to run again," he said. "What do you think Sarah?"

Sarah hesitated. Then with a catch in her voice she said, "Whatever you decree is the correct course Abraham."

"Your sin is great, Augustine, so should your punishment be. I shall smash your toes so they are more twisted than this little figurine." Jack turned to Sarah. He clutched her leg and his eyes pleaded with her eyes to intervene. Abraham pulled a chair from against the wall and placed it in the middle of the room. "Sit here," he said.

"Please!" Jack cried. "I'm sorry. Please! I won't run away again, I promise!" Abraham watched him. He didn't answer for a few moments. Jack's body shook with fear and he clung to Sarah's leg. Tears flooded his eyes.

"Augustine," Abraham said. "Your tears are a sign of weakness, of selfishness, of lack of faith in God's will. You must learn to face your punishments with courage and resignation. 'Though he was harshly treated, he submitted and opened not his mouth; like a lamb led to the slaughter, he was silent and uttered no cry.' Now sit down." Sarah pushed Jack toward the chair. He began screaming and wriggling to break free. Sarah could not contain him.

"Timothy, Moses, please come here!" Abraham shouted. They appeared instantly. "Help me place Augustine in that chair." Jack flailed and scratched at Sarah and screamed to let him go. She struggled to hold on to him.

Timothy ran over and grabbed Jack's neck with one hand and his arm with the other. He twisted Jack's arm up behind his back. Pain shot through his elbow and he yelped. Timothy pushed him roughly down on the chair.

"Good," Abraham said. "Now put out your foot." Jack squirmed, trying to wriggle free, but every time he moved Timothy pulled his arm so that it felt like it would snap at the elbow. Moses seized his leg and pulled it out so his foot was exposed. Abraham hoisted the hammer in the air and brought it crashing down. Jack closed his eyes and screamed.

"You have no need to scream Augustine," Abraham said a second later. "I did not hit you." Jack opened his eyes. Abraham stood, stroking his wispy chin-beard. "I have a better idea." He put the sledgehammer on the bed. "Bring him to the fireplace in the front room."

Timothy and Moses pulled Jack off the chair and pushed him down the stairs to the fireplace. Abraham followed. Jack looked for Sarah, but she had disappeared. "Take off his shoes," Abraham commanded. Timothy and Moses did as they were told.

"Now, Augustine. I think this will be a more effective punishment. When you sin against God your soul is banished forever to the fiery pits of hell. Flames a thousand times hotter than the flames of that fire." He indicated to the fireplace. "And the inferno of Perdition will blister your feet forever. Do you understand what awaits you when you sin – what surely awaited you until we plucked you from that certain fate and gave you a chance to redeem your soul and find God's love?" Jack did not respond. He was numb.

"We will show you an example of hell's flame and you can decide if hell is where you want to spend eternity," Abraham continued. He looked at Timothy and Moses. "Put his feet in the fire and don't pull them out until I tell you." Timothy and Moses looked at each other. "Now!" Abraham said.

Jack kicked and screamed and writhed. He tried to break free, but they were far stronger than he and, though they struggled, they held firm his ankles and pulled his feet close to the flames. Jack felt the heatsting. He listened for Abraham to tell them to stop.

Timothy and Moses must have thought he'd tell them to stop too, because when they got close enough so their hands felt the sting of the fire, they stopped and pulled back a little. "All the way!" Abraham roared. "His feet must be engulfed by flame for him to know truly the horror of hell!" The two men carrying out the punishment looked at each other again.

"I command you: put his feet in the fire! St. Madeline said 'As iron is fashioned by fire and on the anvil, so in the fire of suffering and under the weight of trials our souls receive that form which our Lord desires them to have.' This is a trial young Augustine must face to become what God wills him to be."

Timothy and Moses looked at each other, an unspoken conversation occurring between their faces. Then they quickly put his feet in the flames until they were fully engulfed. Jack shrieked. Timothy and Moses recoiled as the heat burned their own hands, and they pulled his feet out a second later. Jack continued screaming, agonizing wails of pain, until he blacked out.

CHAPTER 24

The Holy Light

Jack awoke in a strange room in a small bed, his feet wrapped in linens. Woozy, he cringed and grated his teeth as the pain in his feet shot through him. "You've been asleep almost 15 hours," he heard a voice say. Then a woman walked into the room. It was Sarah. She placed her hand on his forehead and rubbed his hair gently. Jack said nothing.

"You're going to be fine," Sarah said. She continued to rub his forehead. "You have second degree burns on your feet. They will heal in two weeks." Jack shivered in the bed and Sarah pulled another quilt from a chest and placed it on top of the other blankets covering him.

"Do you understand why Abraham did what he did?" she asked. Jack shook his head no. She smiled a kind smile. "Everything he does is to teach you lessons so you will learn to accept God. Augustine, you did not seek God, but God sought you. And he found you through us. He called you here to us." She looked toward the ceiling. "Thy will be done."

"Why does everyone do what Abraham says?" Jack asked.

Sarah looked at the door. "Have you heard the term *ex cathedra?*"

Jack shook his head no.

"Ex cathedra avows the authority imbued in certain individuals by the Divine Redeemer. For example, the Catholic Church – a flawed church, but one in which you are familiar – teaches that when the Pope speaks ex cathedra, he utters the infallible expression of doctrine, faith and morals revealed to him from God…that he speaks with the authority of God."

"Abraham speaks with the authority of God. God speaks through Abraham. God reveals His purposes to us when we listen to Him. Abraham's teachings will manifest themselves to you when you reflect upon them and listen to God."

"Lux in Tenebris. Light in darkness. Augustine, you run to the night, when you should cry out for the day. Let God reveal his purpose to you through Abraham. Let His light envelop you. Abraham's lesson last night: find the Lux in Tenebris." Jack winced in pain.

Sarah unwrapped the bandages and examined his feet. She stood up and walked into another room and returned with a bowl and a cloth. She sat down on the bed, dipped the cloth into the bowl and cleaned his feet with cool water.

It hurt and Jack moaned. She then wrapped his feet in new bandages. "It is going to be painful for awhile, but I'll be able to put something on them tonight that will help. In the meantime, just try to get some rest."

Then she kissed his cheek. "Your feet will heal," she said. "It is your soul I worry about. Did you hear what Abraham said about the anvil?" Jack indicated no. Sarah repeated what Abraham had said before he put Jack's feet in the flames.

"You must experience Christ's suffering through sacrifice. This is why you must fast, for example. Your suffering last night was to fashion the iron of your soul so it is in the form that the Lord desires. Only in the fire of true suffering can your soul be saved. Only when you are punished properly will you recognize your sins and repent."

"How come God talks to Abraham and not everyone else?" Jack asked after a moment.

"I will tell you Abraham's story and how it came to be that God talks to him some other time," she said. She stood from the bed on which she had been sitting at Jack's side and gazed upon him.

"For now you must rest, little one, and remember these words from St. Teresa of Avila: 'They deceive themselves who believe that union with God consists in ecstasies or raptures, and in the enjoyment of Him. For it consists in nothing except the surrender and subjection of our will – with our thoughts, words and actions – to the will of God.'"

"You will resume your lessons tonight." She left and closed the door behind her. Jack looked around him. The room was strange. It was not his room in the basement. He looked out the window to the right and saw a clearing and woods. He was not in the large house. He must be in one of the cottages he had seen earlier.

The room was sparse. One bureau, a bookcase full of books, a quilt hanging on the wall, a small writing desk. Groggy, he laid his head back on the pillow and stared at the beams on the ceiling. He listened. The house was silent. Outside was silent. He wondered if he was alone.

He wanted to get up and look around, but he knew he couldn't walk on his feet, and he was afraid that if he got caught out of bed, he'd be punished again. So he just lay there and looked at the ceiling for awhile and tried to block out the pain in his feet. He closed his eyes and dreamed about what his dad and Stacy and Lilly were doing. He pictured them at the dining room table eating spaghetti and meatballs. He could smell the dinner. Then they would watch *The Muppet Show*, or *Little House on the Prairie*, or *The Incredible Hulk*.

He drifted off to sleep. Someone unwrapping the bandages from his feet woke him. The room was dark, lit faintly by a small candle on the dresser. He could only see the figure in shadow. A girl. The girl dipped a brush into a jar and brushed something gooey on his feet. The substance tingled: icecool goop, good goo.

When she had covered his feet with the goop, in silence she rewrapped his feet in new bandages and pulled the quilt over him. Then she whispered: "Don't worry. I'll help you."

Jack tried to see who it was. Small. "Frances?" The moment he said the name, she slipped from the room. "Frances, is that you? Come back! Please!" Jack yelled.

Jack watched the candle flicker. He breathed in the slight scent of lavender and stared at the ceiling. The balm didn't last long. After about a half hour the skin on his feet screamed again. He saw a light coming toward the doorway of the room and he raised himself up on his elbows. Sarah walked through the doorway holding a kerosene lamp. She placed it on the bed table and walked out the door. She returned a minute later carrying a Bible, the catechism, and another book.

"How are you Augustine? Ready to resume your studies?" she asked. She dragged the chair from the desk to Jack's bedside. Jack said nothing. "You have an important day coming and you must prepare yourself."

Sarah read some of the passages she had read in the library the day before— was it the day before? Jack didn't know. "Light of the world…walk in darkness…give up mothers and fathers…forfeit eternal life."

After reciting passages from the Bible and Catechism for some time – more 'word of God' – it was time to try meditating again. "Sit up in the bed," she said, "and lay your hands, palms facing up, on your lap. Now bow your head and chant your mantra." He closed his eyes and concentrated.

"Listen to your breath," she said. "Breathe. Quiet your mind. Feel the vibrations of your mantra." Jack breathed, slowly, deeply. He repeated his mantra to himself – da doo ron ron, da doo ron ron. It didn't work.

Sarah sensed his fidgeting. "You need to trust your instincts and let go of your thoughts," she said again and again. This reminded Jack of something, but he couldn't remember what. He tried to think where he had heard that saying before. He closed his eyes tightly and breathed. *Star Wars*! He remembered!

In the movie *Star Wars* when Luke was flying his X-Wing fighter to destroy the Death Star, Obi Wan told him "Let go, Luke. Trust your feelings. Use the

Force." He imagined that meditating was like the Force, a great mysterious power that he might be able to harness if he quieted his mind just like Obi Wan told Luke to do.

He changed his mantra to the buzzing sound that the lightsabers in *Star Wars* made, like an electronic bee, and focused on that sound. He emptied his head of all thoughts – just the buzz, buzz, buzz until he didn't recall the physical act of thinking about the buzz and it just happened automatically and he was no longer aware of place or time or himself.

At some point he became aware of a voice, soft and soothing, rhythmic and rhyming, repeating words; words he had heard before, he thought. He felt warm. He opened his eyes and saw Sarah seated across from him, light emanating from her. She glowed like an angel from a movie.

The light was intense – intense yet comforting. Jack couldn't keep his eyes off of her. He felt as if he was in the presence of some spirit or energy form – the Force, he thought – and he wanted the light to move within – and emanate from – him as well.

She continued to glow, a bright halo around her head, holy and good, like the paintings of the saints on the church windows when the sun shined through. She repeated the words from the Bible she had said before: "I am the light of the world; he that follows me shall not walk in darkness, but shall have the light of life…I am the light of the world; he that follows me shall not walk in darkness, but shall have the light of life…"

Suddenly, Jack became aware of Sarah grasping his hand. He forgot where he was. She noticed the startled, frightened look on his face. "Good," she said. She still glowed as she walked out of the room. Strange tears rolled down Jack's eyes. He didn't know why he was crying. His head felt woozy and he didn't feel his feet.

Sarah returned and lit twelve candles that made the room smell like spice. She continued to read passages to him and instruct him in meditation. "Breathe, clear your mind," she said. "Send your thoughts to the sky like balloons that disappear in the clouds." She reminded him to repeat his mantra and to feel the vibration of it deep inside his brain. Buzz….buzz…buzz.

"Augustine," she whispered, breaking the trance he was in. Jack saw the light around her again. "I want to pray with you now to ask God's forgiveness for your sins. You must thank Him for bringing you here." Jack closed his eyes and asked God to forgive his sins. Then he asked God to forgive his mommy and daddy for their sins.

"Please, God, help them to be good and forgive them for their wickedness," he prayed silently. "Teach me what I need to know so I can go back to them and help them to be better."

After awhile, there was a knock at the door. Sarah stood. "Must be time for evening vespers," she said. She left the room. The incandescent glow followed her. She returned with Timothy. Jack gazed placidly at him, still intoxicated in spice-scented luminous fervor.

"Timothy will carry you to vespers," Sarah said.

Timothy swaddled Jack in the bed's blankets and gently picked him up. He felt safe and warm in Timothy's strong arms, different – so different – from when he cowered in horror as Timothy was about to place his feet in the fireplace. That seemed so far away, an act done by strange hands – not the hands that cradled him now – and an uncaring face, not the benevolent face that now looked upon his face.

The brisk wind slapped Jack's cheeks when Sarah opened the door and Timothy carried him outside. He shuddered in the cold. They walked across the clearing, the glow from the swollen moon bathing them in pale light. Then they slipped down a path into the darkness as the woods swallowed them. Thick woods. Dark woods. The previous night Jack had run through these woods, scared of Timothy and not the woods, and squirmed to break free of his harsh grasp. Now he clung to him, rested his head in his warm chest. Safe.

They came to the gabled main house and Timothy carried Jack to the large room where prayers were held. Everyone was there, exactly as they had been before – all seated in a circle, all wearing white robes. Jack was glad to see them. The only people he had seen the whole day were Sarah and Timothy, and whoever had placed balm and wrapped new bandages on his feet.

Timothy placed Jack next to Abraham. Sarah sat on his other side. Abraham smiled at Jack and Jack flinched and burrowed into Sarah's breast. He clung to her robe. His eyes wandered across the room until they landed on Frances. Her eyes were looking intently at Abraham. Jack realized everyone was looking at him. After a silence of about five minutes, Abraham began. He never mentioned that Jack had run away. He didn't say why Timothy had carried him into vespers, or why Jack was wrapped in blankets. He didn't make him stand in the middle like the other morning.

Jack could hardly keep his eyes open for most of it. The fear of making a mistake and being punished helped him fight his exhaustion, but it was a struggle he barely won. His feet hurt. Finally vespers ended and Jack was carried back to the cottage. Timothy placed him on the bed. Sarah said prayers with him and kissed his forehead. Then she dressed his feet with clean gauze and goop. "Goodnight Augustine. I'll see you in the morning." She blew out the candle and closed his bedroom door.

All alone, Jack gazed out the window from which a faint light lit the room. He thought about Sarah and the light and how safe he felt in Timothy's arms. He wished she would stay with him through the night. He looked forward to seeing her in the morning. He wondered if he would get to eat breakfast. He had had nothing but water for the past two days.

The next day was the same as the day before. Timothy carried Jack to morning prayers, then he had lessons with Sarah in the cottage all day, then Timothy carried him to vespers and back to the cottage for bed. He saw the light again around Sarah during meditation. She told him that his feet were healing and that he would be able to walk soon.

The following morning Timothy came as usual. "Let's try out those feet and see if you can walk."

"He's not ready, Timothy," Sarah said. "His feet are still raw and swollen. It will be another week at least." Timothy examined Jack's feet. He gingerly tried to put a shoe on Jack's foot, but it wouldn't fit and Jack recoiled in pain when he tried to force it.

"Okay Augustine. I'll carry you to prayers for another week." He laughed. "But don't get used to it!" So he carried him again through the woods to the gabled house for morning prayers. After prayers, instead of carrying him back to the cottage, Timothy brought him to the breakfast room. Jack's face lit up. He was going to eat! He hoped Frances would be sitting next to him again at the breakfast table.

He hadn't been able to talk to anyone the last two days except Sarah and Timothy, and sometimes Moses. Breakfast was the same meal as the first day – an egg, oatmeal, bread, and tea. Frances sat next to him. "Good morning Augustine," she said after the blessing. "How are your studies? Sarah is a wonderful teacher and I'm sure you are learning the great blessings of the Lord."

Jack told her that he had learned to meditate and that he had seen a beautiful light surrounding Sarah and that he didn't know what it meant but it made him feel happy. "Oh good!" Frances said. "You've seen the divine light, a preview of the beatific vision. I'm so happy for you!" She touched his arm and smiled as she said this.

Her joy at him having seen the light surprised him and encouraged him to share more of his experiences with her. He told her what he had learned and the Bible passages he had memorized and she squeezed his hand and told him how proud she was of him.

After awhile, she leaned in and whispered, "How are your feet? I heard that you tried to run away. Oh, Augustine, please tell me you won't do that again. I don't want to see you punished any more. I know that Abraham knows what's best and that the Lord works in mysterious ways, but…oh, still I can't bear to see punishments carried out. So please don't try to run away again."

Jack promised her he wouldn't and that since he had seen the divine light he hadn't wanted to leave. He wanted to learn all about the community and how he could live a life worthy of being accepted by everyone in it. He asked her to tell him all about the community and about her. She did.

First he learned that all of the others except Abraham, Sarah, Moses, and Emmanuel slept in seven cottages on the compound, just like the one he was sleeping in now and the one with the old woman. He had only seen the two. He was curious what the other cottages looked like on the inside.

The children, Frances said, had specific chores assigned to them each day according to their talents, likes, and the needs of the community. Frances liked animals so she worked in the barn a lot. She milked the cows and goats each morning and collected eggs from the hens. She brushed the horses. She fed all the animals. She said she did all this before morning prayers.

"What time do you get up?" Jack asked. She told him she got up at five a.m. and finished a little before seven and then washed and came to morning prayers.

After breakfast, she said, the children had school, which focused on Bible study and reading, writing, arithmetic, and practical skills, such as woodworking and sewing. Everyone ate lunch together in the dining room, and then they all either studied or worked until recreation time. After recreation, they performed afternoon chores and then cleaned up and helped prepare dinner. Dinner was followed by vespers, which was followed by bedtime.

In the winter, the women made quilts, knitted blankets, and wove baskets. The men built furniture – chairs, desks, bureaus, tables – and crafted fishing lures from lead they collected at the Bourne Dump and then melted into molds.

In the summer and fall, the women gardened, collected antique furniture at flea markets and auctions, made butter and cheese, and picked apples. The men fished, pulled lobster traps, dug clams and quahogs, chopped firewood, and also attended auctions to buy furniture that the men and women both refinished and sold.

They sold their wares, in winter and summer, at a market in the village of Van Winkle. The market was an eclectic general store, located next to the post office and underneath the shade of a towering oak tree in front of its porch. They called it The Mayflower. The community sold vegetables and flowers from their gardens, milk and cheese from their cows and goats, furniture, quilts, blankets, fishing lures that they made, and the seafood they caught.

She told him the community did not sell other items that other general stores sold. They didn't sell newspapers or magazines. They didn't sell candy or lottery tickets or cigarettes. They didn't sell beer, wine, or liquor. But she said it was a popular store. The craftsmanship on the furniture they made and refinished was intricate, unique, and highly valued.

He learned all these details, but she wouldn't tell him about the thing he wondered about most. "Frances," he said, "what happens to me at confirmation?"

"You must wait. It is our special and secret ceremony, and you can only learn its secrets if you are deemed worthy by Abraham." Jack was disappointed that she wouldn't tell him. If she wouldn't tell him, he knew nobody would.

CHAPTER 25

The Beating

Jack studied his catechism every day. For two weeks, his days didn't vary much. Timothy came for him in the early morning and gave him a piggyback ride to the main house for morning prayers. This was followed by breakfast and then lessons with Sarah: Bible study, catechism, St. Augustine's *Confessions* and other religious texts sprinkled in. He meditated and took comfort in the tranquility, clarity, and happiness he gained through it. He consistently saw the holy light around Sarah – pure joy.

Sarah changed his bandages three times a day. Two weeks after he was burned, she told him his feet had healed well enough for him to walk. He stood up tentatively, expecting a jolt of pain when his feet hit the floor. He didn't feel any discomfort at all.

He walked over to Sarah and hugged her. She knelt down and he buried his head in her bosom. Happy. She rubbed his hair. "See," she said. "I told you your feet would get better." She caressed him for about ten minutes. He held her tightly.

"Trust in me, Augustine, for I will not let harm come to you if you do as I tell you. I will always care for you, because I love you very much."

"I love you too," Jack said. She smiled and raised her eyes heavenward in gratitude.

That night after prayers, Jack was not brought back to the cottage in the woods. He was led to the basement room in which he had slept the first night. As he walked through the door to the bedroom and saw his old bed, a disturbing thought came to his head. He had forgotten to worry about peeing his bed while in the cottage. He had not, in fact, committed that great sin since the night he tried to run away.

Now in this room he worried about peeing his pants again and being punished. He knelt at his bedside and asked God to help him not to pee the bed. As he was praying, Emmanuel came into the room. Moses poked his head through the doorway after him. He smiled.

"Welcome back Master Augustine. Good to see you healed quickly under Sarah's care. I'll see you in the morning. Lights out now boys."

Emmanuel joined Jack and knelt down beside his bed to pray in the dim light of the lantern flame on the bedside table. After several minutes of silence, both boys fervent in their prayers, Emmanuel spoke. "Augustine, I've prayed for you. I want you to be happy here. I want you to know you are surrounded by people who love you."

"Abraham's ways may seem cruel, but he acts as he does to open the gates of heaven to you. Everything he does readies your soul for heaven." He gestured toward the window. "The world's an evil place, Augustine. Fortune smiled upon you when Abraham chose you to join our community."

"Thank you, Emmanuel." Jack turned out the lamp and slipped into bed. He breathed deeply the musty covers. The blankets and sheets on the bed smelled like they had not been used in awhile, like they had just been pulled from a storage dresser, and Jack liked the smell. He shivered to warm up his bed.

Jack knew it was a really big deal in the community to be confirmed. Everyone talked about how it would be the best thing to ever happen to him – how it would change his life and how then he would be a full-fledged member of the community and be able to join all the others in activities.

He vowed that the next day he would commit even more ardently to learning and understanding God's purpose for him. He would study extra hard. He would read the Bible at night before bed and first thing upon waking. He would learn all the prayers and psalms.

He thought that once he was confirmed and proved that he had committed his life to God, Abraham would let him go back to his family to save them and show them how to serve God. He didn't want to abandon them.

Abraham and everyone else said he had to leave them forever and forget them, but Jack thought maybe Abraham would change his mind if he showed him that he was devoted to God as much or more than anyone else in the community. He drifted off to sleep excited about the next day.

The following weeks Jack threw his heart into his lessons with Sarah and a woman named Esther who also began to tutor him. They worked him hard in preparation for confirmation, but Jack pushed himself even harder. He began to understand what had been so strange to him during the first few days with the community.

He now understood the language – the strange words they spoke and the peculiar manner in which they spoke it, and he began to assimilate their way of speaking into his own speech. Each day was the same – morning prayers, breakfast, studies in the library with Sarah and Esther, an afternoon walk with

Timothy through the woods to the lake, a collation in the evening, vespers and, finally, bed in the musty basement room.

Breakfast was by far Jack's favorite part of the day. He looked forward to sitting next to Frances to learn more about the community and what she and the other children did each day. She was always nice and never said anything about him peeing his pants.

He became used to the schedule and comfortable knowing what each day would bring. He began to enjoy it and he thought back to how scared he was when he first arrived. It seemed so long ago.

Then one afternoon while he was studying the catechism with Sarah, Moses burst into the room and announced that Abraham wanted the community to meet in the barn immediately. There was a great rush of excitement; unlike the many vespers and morning prayers held in the meeting room, gatherings in the barn were rare and meant a significant announcement was going to be made.

When Jack entered the barn, he saw everyone standing in a circle. In the middle of the circle stood a teenaged-boy. It was Timothy! He was naked and shivering. He held his hands over his private parts.

Abraham stepped forward. "Brethren," he said. "We are gathered here because Timothy has brought shame upon himself and us. He was caught fornicating right here in the barn with a girl from town. He has brought the sin of the outside world into our community. I fear we will face God's wrath for this egregious act, so we therefore must act swiftly and surely to gain again God's grace."

Timothy stood and looked at the ground while Abraham spoke. Jack couldn't see his face. He did see more than a few members of the community bless themselves and heard a few of them gasp. He felt bad for Timothy because it was cold in the barn and he was shaking violently in front of everybody.

He remembered when Timothy didn't let him go and threatened him with the dogs and then burned his feet. He had wished bad things to happen to him. He had hoped Timothy would suffer some day for not helping him. But he had since grown to love Timothy and now felt pity for him. He did not want to see him suffer.

Abraham's voice was filled with both anger and disappointment. Jack wondered what Timothy had done. He didn't know what the word Abraham had used meant.

"Timothy has broken two of our community's most important rules. First, he brought someone from the outside world into our community without my permission. And then he curried God's great displeasure and stained our home by the grievous sin of fornication. He must be punished and he must repent. What have you to say brother Timothy?"

Timothy fell to the floor prostrate and groveled. "Forgive me Lord, for I hath brought shame upon myself and the stain of my sin upon our community. I am weak and succumbed to the devil's temptation. Please teach me, Prophet Abraham, the folly of my ways and forgive me. I accept any punishment that you have planned for me to wash away the stain and return God's favor to us. Bless me and protect me from evil, O Lord."

Suddenly, with a swift and violent lunge, Abraham raised a horse switch high in the air and brought it down on Timothy's back. The sound of the switch snapping against Timothy's skin followed by his screams scared Jack. Then Abraham whipped him again.

Abraham had a wild, excited look in his eyes. Jack had seen a similar look when he put his feet in the fire. He had also seen that terrible look once before on his father's face when he and Lilly were fighting over a record and his father, after asking them three or four times to get along and share the record, had had enough and ripped the record from the player and smashed it on the floor. Then he threw the record player itself against the wall.

"There," he said. "Now you don't have a record player so you won't fight over it anymore." Afterwards, he had hugged them and told them how sorry he was that he lost his temper. But he hadn't hit them, only scared them.

Now Jack saw that same angry look in Abraham's eyes as he whipped and whipped Timothy. Timothy pleaded with him to stop, but this only seemed to make Abraham whip him harder and he continued until Timothy moaned and then made no sound at all.

Abraham gestured to Moses and another man named Peter. "Take him to the shed." They each ducked their heads under Timothy's shoulders and carried him outside into the frigid air. His eyes wobbled, half open, and his lifeless legs dragged across the wooden floor of the barn.

"Sarah," Abraham said calmly. "Please get some clothing and blankets and bring them to the shed." Then he spoke to the group. "Brother Timothy's sin is great. His punishment must also be great if he is going to see how wicked his acts were. Without appropriate punishment, Timothy would not truly repent and then he'd spend eternity in the hot flames of hell."

"Timothy will be shunned for two full weeks. He will be banished to the shed and I forbid anyone from visiting him except Sarah to bring him sustenance. Only by doing this can Timothy be saved."

"God will look with favor upon us now for addressing this sin and teaching Timothy repentance. It must be. The Bible teaches us that 'He who spares the rod hates his son, but he who loves him is careful to discipline him,' and 'The rod of correction imparts wisdom, but a child left to himself disgraces his mother.' These are from Proverbs and I ask you to study Proverbs tonight when you pray."

"Let us all learn what is in store for any of us if we sin thus. Now let us pray for Timothy that he will see his evil ways and repent. Let us pray that Timothy will seek God's redeeming grace and guidance and be welcomed into His kingdom again."

He reached out and everyone clasped hands and bowed their heads. They were all silent, except Frances weeping softly. Jack whispered a prayer for Timothy. His eyes filled with tears and he asked God to forgive him for wishing that Timothy would suffer.

CHAPTER 26

Suspicion

For a few weeks Gus's home was like a train station. People filtered in and out constantly, asking to help, bringing food, offering support. Gus didn't know many of them, but they were either connected through his family – his parents' or Lauren's or Ellen's friends; the schools – former teachers, coaches; the town – the town selectman, the school board, the churches. Even Senator Ted Kennedy called and offered his campaign volunteers.

Gus's colleagues at Fidelity also helped. His co-workers all took days off to join the search and help Gus coordinate efforts. Gus hardly cared about work or the stock market. He told his boss he was going to take a month of unpaid absence. His boss told him somewhat coldly to do what he needed to do. Ned Johnson, the founder of Fidelity Investments, called him personally and told him to take as much time as he needed and offered any help he could give.

Others had seen the story on the news or read about it in the newspaper and didn't know Jack or anyone in the family but wanted to help. So many people called his home that Gus installed an additional phone line for people to call with information. He put the new number on all the posters and pamphlets.

The Billerica police told him it was unnecessary because they already had a dedicated phone number at the station for people to call. But Gus wanted to have a direct line to his home so he'd have more control and be sure to get all the information first-hand. He had been frustrated with the police because he thought they were stingy with what information they shared with him regarding the calls that came in and leads they were getting.

This way, Gus had volunteers man the phones in shifts all day and late into the night, and he could relay the call information to Boyd and have him analyze the credibility of the tips and follow up on any leads.

Gus was surprised at the outpouring of initial support after Jack disappeared. Hundreds of people had come from all over. They gave up their days and nights for weeks, spending hours doing whatever they could to help. They told him that they prayed for him. They asked him if he was getting enough sleep and eating right. They worried about his health.

Jack's old class at Hajjar Elementary – Miss Monaco's class – led a letter-writing campaign and each child wrote about their memories of Jack and how they missed him and hoped they would find him soon. The letters were sweet; perhaps the nicest gesture in a hundred nice gestures from people after Jack disappeared.

Despite all this support and the work of both the Billerica Police and Detective Boyd, weeks passed and they were no closer to finding Jack than they had been the night he disappeared. Plenty of people called claiming they knew where Jack was or saying they had seen him at the mall or walking along the side of Route 3A or at the movie theatre, especially when Gus increased the reward money to $15,000 – a reward, incidentally, that he didn't yet know how he would pay.

Most people had good intentions, but there was a small percentage who tried to cash in on Gus's misfortune. It was amazing how many psychics were in the area who had visions of where Jack was and demanded the reward money up front before they would share these visions.

One of the reasons why they were no closer to finding Jack, Gus thought, was because the cops continued to suspect Gus in Jack's disappearance. They certainly treated him more like a suspect than a victim. They continually sent in different people to ask him the same questions about that night – why he had waited so long to report Jack missing, where he was and to whom he had spoken the hours immediately after Jack disappeared. They asked him further questions about his marriage and divorce and dug out the details of the previous custody hearing. They were trying to catch him in a lie; he wasn't dumb.

Boyd – as well has Gus's family – suspected Victoria of somehow orchestrating Jack's disappearance. But Gus knew in his heart that she had as little to do with it as he did.

He could see in her eyes every day when she came to the house that she suffered as much as he did, and that she was as scared as he was. He never thought she cared deeply about the kids, but her reaction to the news that Jack was missing, her utter devastation, showed him something in her he had never seen.

Victoria took Lilly to Donna's where they stayed for a month before going back to New Jersey. It was the only time Gus was glad that Lilly was with her mother. He couldn't devote enough attention to her and he knew it. His focus every minute of the day was on the investigation, on looking for Jack.

It was hard for Gus to admit, but Lilly needed her mother right now. She cried all the time, blaming herself for Jack's disappearance. "If only I had watched for him and made sure he came in too," she said. Gus told her over and over that it was not her fault and to stop blaming herself, but she couldn't get rid of her guilt or grief.

One other thing that Gus knew was that Jack did not run away. The police and psychologists could say all they wanted until they ran out of breath about unhappy children of divorced parents and kids running away from a bad situation. As bad as it ever got, Jack was loved, and he knew he was loved.

Gus thought about this often. He regretted every time he had lost his temper. He regretted every time he had been too busy, or tired, or hung over to play with Jack. He thought about Christmas Day and tears filled his eyes. Oh, if he could have that morning back – every morning back that he took for granted!

Despite all his regrets and these moments that passed in a continuous loop through his head each day, he believed in his gut that Jack had been a happy boy. He would not have run away. The other thought that Gus believed in his gut was that Jack was alive.

Three months passed, however, with no breaks in the case. The news stations and newspapers began to lose interest in the story and move on to other things. Gus, at Boyd's suggestion, increased the reward money every couple of weeks until by mid-March it was up to $50,000, or more than the value of his house. Doing so, Boyd said, would give the reporters something to write about. It would keep the story in the news. Gus wanted it in the news. He wanted people seeing Jack's face all the time. He wanted people to be reminded constantly that his little boy had still not been found.

But Gus also hadn't returned to work and he was running out of money. The church had set up a fund for him, so people were donating to help with his piling expenses. But far more money was going out than coming in and Gus's savings were going to run out sooner rather than later.

And despite spending a small fortune on Boyd and devoting every minute of every day to finding Jack, nothing was happening in the case – no new information had come out in weeks, no credible leads, no ransom notes, no arrests, no remains or clothes found. The Pinto and the couple from the Holiday Inn had not been found. The story was fading. Then something happened that all the news organizations – local and national – covered that brought the story back and changed everything, much to Gus's regret.

CHAPTER 27

The Day After a Funeral

The custody trial that had been scheduled for early February was postponed until March. Victoria had initiated the hearing the previous year to request full-time custody of Lilly and Jack, including summers and school vacations. Her rationale had been that, based on information she was receiving from the kids, she was concerned that Gus had an alcohol problem and that the increased demands of his job kept him at the office late at night, leaving the children with his parents and babysitters most of the time.

Jack's disappearance strengthened her case, according to her lawyer, who wrote as much in a letter to the judge. Gus received a copy of it. The letter said Gus had the children less than 24 hours and in his care one of them had disappeared. It made Gus so angry when he read it that he tore it up like confetti and threw it so it scattered across the kitchen.

Gus was glad when Victoria took Lilly while he focused on finding Jack. But he soon realized how much he missed his little girl.

He spent a week preparing a binder full of information about the benefits of Lilly living with him. He was confident that their existing agreement – him having Lilly for the summers and school vacations and alternating holidays – would remain intact, but he hoped he could make a successful argument to reverse the current arrangement so he would have Lilly during the school year.

His main argument was that he was going to cut back his hours when he returned to work and would be able to spend more time with Lilly. He would also try to convince the judge that he did not have an alcohol problem and that Jack's disappearance was beyond his control and not a case of negligence. And finally, he would argue that when he was not with Lilly she would still be with family – his parents and her aunt and uncle and cousins lived less than 10 miles away.

At this time, after such a traumatic experience, it was important for Lilly to have a good support network of family around, he'd argue. Victoria worked full-time, even though he sent her money every month, and paid one of her girlfriends to babysit Lilly for a couple hours each day after school until she got home. She had no family in the area to help her out, and having friends and acquaintances was not the same as cousins and grandparents and an aunt, who was also her godmother, living right down the street. Gus believed Lilly would be better off being near all of them. He – and they – could better help her through this than Victoria alone.

Gus researched the schools and their reputations and offerings. He outlined a series of activities and self-enrichment programs that he would sign Lilly up for, such as dance class, softball, piano lessons. Victoria's lawyer was a man with a great reputation who had won many cases in his distinguished career.

Despite this, a few days before Gus was to leave for New Jersey for the trial, he was confident. He woke early, put on the coffee, and walked to the end of the driveway to get the paper. When he opened it and read the headline he stopped dead. On the front page, top of the fold, the boldest, biggest headline in the *Lowell Sun* screamed: "New Suspicions About Father of Missing Boy."

Gus seethed as he read an account from an unnamed source in the Billerica Police that said they were now looking at Gus as a 'possible suspect.' "That fucking coward," he said. He knew it was Goddard. His eyes scrolled down the text. Victoria was quoted in the story as saying the police had spoken to her about new allegations against Gus and that she was hopeful the truth would come to light soon.

"New allegations?" he spat. "What new allegations? How convenient this came out now three fucking days before the trial." He stormed back into the house, picked up the phone, and dialed. "I'd like to speak to Lieutenant Goddard." After a few seconds Goddard came to the line. "What the hell is this bullshit in the Lowell Sun?" he yelled.

"Mr. Delaney," Goddard said. "I'm sorry about that. I don't know how that got out. We are doing an internal investigation to determine—"

"Bullshit!" Gus yelled. "You know damn well how that got out. You're a coward; hiding behind the unnamed source banner!"

"That's not true," Goddard said.

"What new allegations are there against me? What is the paper talking about?"

"We're doing our due diligence, investigating every angle…"

"Am I a suspect?"

"Everyone is suspect, Mr. Delaney. You are naturally under suspicion simply because you are the father in the middle of a custody battle for his kids whose son went missing. Your wife is in the same category. We cannot rule anything out. We are still investigating all information that comes in and that is as much as I will say about it."

"What information has come in that you are investigating?"

"That is all as I'm going to say about it."

"You're a useless coward!" Gus yelled. "And when am I going to get Jack's blanket back? I've been asking you for two months now. I want it back."

"I'm sorry Mr. Delaney, it is part of our case file. I can't give it back to you until the case is closed."

"That's bullshit! You told me I'd get it back when you were done with it."

"Well we're not done with it yet."

"You can't keep it! I want it back!"

"When the case is closed."

"You're a fucking lying coward!" Gus yelled and he hung up. He grabbed the edge of the kitchen table and flipped it over. Then he picked up a pot lying in the sink and threw it as hard as he could against the wall, putting a hole through it. He ripped his shirt off, popping the buttons, and ran to his bedroom, where he punched the mattress over and over. It took him an hour to calm down.

Three days later Gus sat in a courtroom in New Jersey. Charlie, Vera, and Stacy had driven down with him. He sat and watched and noticed the back of the courtroom was filled with print and television reporters. There were seven cameras. He had welcomed news before. Not anymore.

His stomach churned when Victoria's lawyer greeted the judge warmly and chatted for some five minutes before the hearing began. As the hearing unfolded however, and her lawyer inexplicably stumbled a few times and Gus's lawyer hammered Victoria on her prescription for a bi-polar disorder, Gus grew more confident that he could win his case to get custody of Lilly for the school year.

At the very least, Victoria wouldn't get Lilly during the summers and vacations in addition to the school year.

After Gus's lawyer made his closing argument and Victoria's meandered through his, Gus sat back in his chair and almost dared to sigh in relief. Then the judge returned from his chamber.

"This is a difficult case," he began. "It is even more tragic because of the disappearance of your son. Mr. and Mrs. Delaney, you have both been through a lot in the last couple of months and it saddens me that you could not work out some arrangement on your own." Gus leaned forward now in his chair. The judge continued.

"At the end of the day, however, we must do what is in the best interest of the child. Based on what I've heard, I think the best thing for Lilly is to remain with her mother, so I am granting full custody of Lilly to Victoria Delaney."

"No!" Gus gasped. He slumped in his chair and looked over at his lawyer as if to tell him to do something. The lawyer just sat there scribbling in his notepad.

"Mr. Delaney," the judge said. "There are a few reasons why I made this decision. One is the fact that Jack disappeared on your watch, which leads me to fear that you may not be the most careful or attentive minder of a child." Gus felt the muscles across his shoulders and neck tighten.

"More importantly though," the judge continued, "is my fear of your mental state right now and whether it is wise for Lilly to be exposed to you. Your drinking has increased according to our witnesses, you've had violent outbursts toward the police on the case of your missing son, you haven't worked in three months. You are unstable at the moment."

He glanced up from his notes. "And your commitment to finding your son, your obsession really, while understandable and in many ways commendable..." he took off his glasses. "I don't think you're capable of focusing enough attention on anything or anyone else at this time and I think Lilly would suffer for that."

Gus gripped the rail in front of him and squeezed hard. The tightness in his neck moved across his upper back. This could not be happening. The verdict left him stunned. How could the judge punish him because he thought he was trying too hard to find his son?

He looked over at Victoria, her lawyer hugging her and tears of happiness, of victory, streaming down her cheeks. "This is horseshit," he muttered.

Gus spent the few days after the trial sifting through leads that came in daily. When leads first began coming in Gus followed up on every one of them. Boyd told him this was a waste of his time, but he insisted on calling back every person who left a message on the hotline saying they knew where Jack was or that they had seen him.

Most of them were crackpots. Sometimes it was a well-intentioned person who thought he saw Jack but it always turned out to be someone else. The worst, though, were the scam artists who were making up stories trying to get their hands on the reward money. Gus was disgusted by how many of these people there were.

Then on Wednesday morning the week after the trial, Boyd called him to say police had found the remains of a child in Merrimack, New Hampshire, about thirty miles north of Billerica, in a creek in the woods.

The cops brought the skeleton back to the coroner's office to check the dental records. Gus sat at the kitchen table and drank a six-pack of Old Milwaukee while he waited for the result from Boyd. It had to be Jack, he thought. What were the chances that remains of a child thirty miles north of where Jack disappeared would not be him?

Tears rolled down his cheeks. He paced the living room. A skeleton. The thought nearly made him go mad it was so incomprehensible. That beautiful, vibrant boy, adorable and happy, was now just a pile of bones found in a creek. His boy. Gus's jaw quaked uncontrollably and he could hardly see out of his eyes he was crying so hard. He punched a hole in the living room wall.

His boy was dead. He had prayed every day that Jack was still alive and that he would find him soon. Now he had a sinking feeling in his stomach. The skeleton found lying in the creek was his little boy. It was more than he could bear. He sobbed, guzzled three more cans of beer, and collapsed on the bed, nearly convulsing, loud sobs pouring out of him.

The phone ringing jarred him awake. He had fallen asleep on the bed, emotionally exhausted. It was Boyd. "Gus, it's not Jack. It's a boy that disappeared from Camden, Maine two years ago."

Gus noticed that he was alone in the house. The house had been filled with people every day for the first month and a half. The numbers diminished somewhat after that, but there were always at least a few people, neighbors or friends, who stayed to answer the phone or bring food…until the Lowell Sun article and the trial.

Gus's messy personal life had been displayed in all the papers. The details of his temper, his drinking, and suspicions about whether he was involved in Jack's disappearance all helped to sell papers, boost ratings, and drive people away from Gus.

Even Gus's parents and sisters and Stacy didn't come every day. They all had exhausted themselves, physically and emotionally, and couldn't take the upheaval anymore. Gus had exhausted himself more than anyone.

He was smoking two packs a day – more than he ever had – and drinking more as well. He hardly ate anything anymore. His face took on a yellowed pallor, sickly, and he had lost twenty-two pounds. His clothes hung off him in a baggy mess. His hair looked lifeless and unwashed and had been falling out. He'd wake up and the pillow would be covered in hair, as if a shedding dog had slept on it. "You need to take better care of yourself," Stacy told him again and again.

Gus looked around the empty, quiet house on that day in early April. It reminded him of when someone dies and there is a funeral and then a party at the house with loads of relatives and friends around so that you are not alone with your thoughts and your sorrow. But then after the party everyone goes home to leave the mourner alone to walk zombie-like in the home where the living once trod. Gus, the yellow-faced, choleric corpse, went to Jack's room and cried unheard tears.

CHAPTER 28

Back to Work

Gus decided to go back to work. He had no choice. After more than three months' unpaid leave, the money he invested in the search, the cost of hiring Boyd, lawyer fees, and the increased child payments – an additional insult to the determination to give Lilly to Victoria full time – had cut into his savings and he needed to make money.

He called the office and arranged to begin the next day. He hadn't so much as looked at a financial paper in the past three months. He spent the day sitting at his desk reading piles of documents – company reports, industry trends, market movements.

On his second day he attended a three-hour meeting with the equities analyst team and didn't recall a single word said during it. He spent the three hours thinking about the leads Boyd had told him about the day before. Each day they received dozens of tips and none of them ever led to them finding Jack.

At the end of his third week back at work, Mr. McKenna called Gus into his office. He was a bald man with a mustache and a dour look etched permanently on his face. He sat behind his big mahogany desk. "Gus, sit down," he said. He folded his hands on the desk. "Talk to me. What's going on?"

"What do you mean?"

"You really need me to answer that?" he asked.

Gus thought for a minute. "Well, yes. Please elaborate."

"Well, frankly I was a little aggravated that you took three months off after you said you'd only take one. And now, the Gus Delaney who came back here is not the Gus Delaney who left."

Gus shifted in his chair and leaned forward, his lips crinkling into a scowl. McKenna noticed it.

"Gus, I understand your situation, but—"

"Do you? Do you?" Gus shouted, nearly jumping out of his chair. "Do you understand what it's like to lose a child and not know where he is? Not know if he's alive or dead, if he's in pain or being tortured or raped? Do you know what they say happens to the majority of kids who are abducted in this country?"

Gus's emotions were right at the surface, about to breach and send waves crashing onto whatever object was agitating them. "Do you know what that's like Bob?"

McKenna unclasped his hands and leaned back in his chair. "No I do not Gus, and we all feel for you. We've all tried to help you…joined the search, bent over backwards to accommodate you…" Gus's grimace began to turn into almost a growl now. "But we have a business that we need to run," McKenna continued.

" The Elysium Fund has had a horrible first quarter and we need our top analysts fully engaged. I'm not sure you're passionate about doing this anymore. Do you agree?" he asked and he leaned forward again.

Gus sneered. "The fund isn't doing well because no funds are doing well. The economy is in the crapper because that moron Jimmy Carter has his head stuck up his ass." Gus pounded the desk, the emotion creeping ever closer to bursting from its fragile confines.

Gus said this and believed it was mostly true, but he also couldn't deny what McKenna said. He didn't care anymore. His job used to be his passion, but now he didn't care. He couldn't focus. His eyes glazed over financial reports and he often put them aside and called the police station and Boyd to see if any new information came in, see if they were able to track down the couple from the Holiday Inn.

He couldn't do it; didn't want to anymore. He needed to spend every waking hour figuring out what happened to Jack. Whatever had happened, even if he was dead, he needed to know.

But when everything was telling him that Jack must be dead, when the precedent of thousands of cases before and the percentages should have led him to conclude that Jack was most certainly dead, his instinct, something deep inside – a sixth sense – told him that Jack was alive. He knew. He just did, and unless he saw evidence that he wasn't, he was going to keep looking, full-time.

Jack was out there somewhere, relying on his dad to find him and bring him home. So the police could give up. Stacy could give up. Victoria could give up. His parents, sisters, neighbors and friends could give up. And they could say he should give up too; that he should resume his life, move on; there was nothing more he could do. But he would never, ever give up.

"Bob, you're right." Gus stood. "I'm sorry but I just have no interest in this job anymore. And you can tell everyone who is so concerned about the Elysium Fund earning a 70 percent return again that they can shove it up their asses. I'm going to find my boy."

He walked out of McKenna's office, past the trading desk, and out of the building without speaking to anyone. He wouldn't worry about going back to work now. He'd focus on the only thing he could: finding Jack.

It was a beautiful day at the beginning of May as Gus pulled up to his house. He decided to take a walk in the woods. He could smell spring. The creek was swollen. The sun was shining. The woods were alive with chirping and rustling. Yet, this only made Gus more melancholy.

His soul was stuck in the gray, barren ice of winter, stuck in the cold afternoon five months ago when Jack was taken from him.

He walked back to his empty house. He was sitting on Jack's bed when Stacy arrived home. "Gus," she called when she walked into the house. "What are you doing home so early?"

"I quit," Gus said, gazing blankly in front of him. "I just couldn't do it. I couldn't focus. I thought about Jack constantly, and spent more time on the phone with the Billerica police and Detective Boyd than I did studying companies."

Stacy sat on the bed next to him. She didn't say anything for a few minutes. Then she spoke softly. "Gus, what are you going to do for money? I mean Detective Boyd is expensive and all the flyers and advertising, and the mortgage and child support…you sure it's a good idea? Can we manage it financially? I mean I can help a little, but I don't make that much."

Gus put his hand on her knee. "I just have to tighten the belt a little," he said. "Well, a lot. I'm going to let Detective Boyd go. I've been studying for three months what he does and there's no reason I can't do it myself. That will save money. I still have some in savings and I can take from my retirement if I have to. But right now I just need to keep looking for Jack." He put his arm around her.

"But Gus, how long do you plan to keep it up? How long can you keep going without an income? I mean, what if it takes a while to find Jack? What if it takes a year…or longer? Sometimes it takes years and sometimes…" She stopped.

"What?" Gus asked.

"Sometimes they never find out what happened."

"As long as it takes," Gus said. "I'm going to look for him until I find out what happened. I'm going to find him."

"Gus, if it takes years, I don't know how you could not work."

"I'll cross that bridge when I come to it," Gus said. Then he softened. "I'm sure you never envisioned all this when you first went out with me. I mean you knew about Victoria and the kids and all, but instead of an ambitious, young analyst in the financial world, you've ended up with a poor, unemployed basket case."

Stacy brushed his hair with her hand. "I didn't date you because of your job, and I certainly didn't date you because I enjoyed being your ex-wife's punching bag. I dated you because I loved your intellect, I loved your confidence and how you attacked life. I loved your humor and generosity. I loved the way you loved your kids. I want to see that Gus again. I want to help you find Jack and find peace in your heart...find that part of you again, hidden somewhere deep. I'll help you."

Gus hugged her as if he never wanted to let her go. He thought about the engagement ring sitting in a box hidden in his sock drawer. He never told her that he had planned to ask her to marry him that week that Jack disappeared, and he didn't know when the time might come for him to ask her in the future. A wedding, just as work, was the furthest thing from his thoughts. "Let's go to Papa Ginos for pizza and see a movie tonight. Does that sound good?"

"Yes, yes it does. I'd like that very much."

CHAPTER 29

The Voices

"Wake up," a voice said. Someone shook his shoulder. Jack bolted up in his bed, sitting in darkness. It was cold. He didn't know where he was for a few seconds.

"Who's there?" he asked.

"Come on," the voice said. "You're coming with us." It was a man's voice. Jack didn't recognize it and this frightened him.

"What time is it?" he asked.

"Don't worry about the time," the voice said.

"But it's the middle of the night," Jack said. He looked across the room to Emmanuel's bed to see if he was there, but he couldn't see anything. The shade was drawn over the window and his eyes hadn't yet adjusted to the dark.

"Put this on," the man said.

"Who are you?"

"The voice of truth," the voice said. "You must do everything I say." Jack felt a cloth being placed over his eyes – a blindfold. Then the man pulled it tight and tied it at the back of his head.

"Ow!" Jack said. Jack pulled at it to try to loosen it, but the man grabbed his hand and told him not to touch it. "Why do I have to wear a blindfold?" he asked.

"All will be revealed in time," the voice said. "Now here is your robe; put it on." The man helped Jack put on his robe and then grabbed his arm and pulled him forward.

"Where are you taking me?" Jack said, his voice shaking.

"All will be revealed." The man placed his hand on Jack's shoulder and pushed him forward. He guided him to the kitchen. Jack then heard a door open and felt a blast of wet, cold air rush across his face and up his thin robe. It was the door that opened to the back yard. It was raining and he shivered.

"It's freezing!" he cried. "Can I have a coat?"

"No," the voice said. "Your sacred garments will be sufficient." Jack's feet felt the wet grass when he stepped outside, and the chill made them tingle as if pricked by needles. He began shaking violently.

"Augustine, everything will be okay," another voice said over the blowing wind and rushing rain. It was a woman's voice. "Just do everything we say."

"Who are you?" he stuttered. "What are you doing?"

"I'm the voice of trust," she said. "Open your mouth."

"I want to go back inside."

"Open your mouth. This will help." Jack opened his mouth and she poured a warm, spicy liquid into it. He gagged and spit it up. The liquid dribbled down his chin and neck and chest. He shivered.

"Open your mouth again and drink it this time," the woman said. "It will warm you." She poured more of the liquid into his mouth. It tasted like spicy black licorice and Jack nearly gagged again. "Swallow it!" she said.

Jack swallowed. The liquid felt warm going down his throat and he could feel it warm in his chest. The man gripped Jack's shoulders and continued to push him along. He felt strange – dizzy and dazed like he was in some sort of trance.

"Open your mouth," the woman said, and she poured more of the liquid licorice into his mouth. They pushed him along the grass of the back lawn.

"Augustine, you must go out into the darkness and put your hand into the hand of God. Though you tread now into the unknown, you must have faith that this road is the right way," the woman said.

"Recall the words of St. Madeline," she continued: "'As iron is fashioned by fire and on the anvil, so in the fire of suffering and under the weight of trials, our souls receive that form which our Lord desires them to have.'" Jack remembered Abraham saying the same thing right before he burned his feet in the fire. He shuddered.

Jack stood on the grass, blind, shivering. "You must walk into the unknown to truly know," the voice of truth said. "Let nothing disturb you. Let nothing frighten you. Everything passes away except God. God alone is sufficient." But Jack *was* frightened. Were they going to kill him? Sacrifice him to God?

"Repeat after me," the voice of trust said. "I am in God's hands. The kingdom of God is within me." Jack repeated the words. "Here, drink again," she said. Then Jack's whole body felt warm and tingly. Then he fell.

CHAPTER 30

The Island

Jack woke and he couldn't see anything. He panicked until he realized the blindfold was still tied over his eyes. He was soaking wet, lying in a pool of water, his robe drenched. He shivered as he pulled the blindfold from his eyes to discover that he was floating in a boat. It was still dark – still night – and a light rain pecked his face.

The boat bobbed, a big buoy in the sea. He was not in the pond, of that he was certain. On one side of the boat he saw only the sea and the black night, but on the other, about fifty feet away, he saw the silhouette of shoreline and trees.

He sat shaking in the boat, still groggy from the licorice potion the voice of trust had poured down his throat. He didn't see the outline of any homes on the shore – only woods. He also didn't recognize it as the shore of the compound, though he had never seen it from the bay and wasn't sure what it looked like from that view.

Jack looked for oars, but there were none in the boat. There was a rope tied to the bow, though. It plunged straight down into the black water. Jack pulled at it to see if it was tied to something, but he couldn't move it. He rested for a minute and then yanked again. It didn't budge. He examined the knot and tried to untie it, but this too proved impossible. The knot was wet and tight and he couldn't loosen it. He looked for something in the boat to cut it, but the boat was empty.

Jack was not a good swimmer. He had not been able to swim the length of the pool a year ago during his swimming test at the Lowell YMCA. Instead he doggy-paddled to the side of the pool about halfway down. He remembered Bobby made the whole length of the pool on his first try. It took Jack three tries. He was a better swimmer now, but it was a much further swim to the shore than the length of the pool at the Lowell Y, and it was in the ocean, in the rain and at night. The waves crashed against each other in little whitecaps.

He worried about a current or undertow or what might be below the inky surface. He knew about a movie with a shark that had come out a year or two ago. He was too young to see it, but Seth Boylan's sister saw it and told him it was about a shark in Cape Cod that lurked in the water at beaches and pulled people underwater and ate them. Jack shuddered thinking about what creatures might be in these black waters ready to bite his kicking, splashing legs.

But he had to find somewhere to get dry and warm and find something to eat. His ears were numb and his toes and fingers ached. His thin robe offered no protection from the wind and cold, and anyway it was wet. "Hello!" he yelled. "Is anybody here?" He waited a moment and strained to hear for an answer, but all he heard was the wind, rain, and water lapping against the boat.

"Help me! Please, somebody help me!" he yelled. He waited. Fifteen minutes passed. He yelled again, and again nobody answered. He tried to undo the knot again, but he couldn't loosen it a speck. He began to feel weak and dizzy from hunger. He could sit in the boat and wait and freeze or he could jump into the ocean and try to swim to shore. He thought he could make it, but he dreaded the water. It would be freezing and a shark or man o' war stinging jellyfish might attack him. He waited.

An hour went by. Jack sat on the plank of wood resting across the boat that served as its seat and shivered, and every few minutes he shouted into the rain for someone to help him. He waited until he knew nobody was coming and the only thing he could do was swim to shore.

He looked to the sky and said a prayer while rain pelted his cheeks and chin. "Please God, guide me. Show me what I must do." Then he said the Lord's Prayer. He repeated the last line: "Thy kingdom come, Thy will be done…Please God, help me through this and I will praise thy name and offer my every breath to you for the rest of my life on Earth."

As scared as he was of what might be below the black water, he had to swim for shore and find someone to help him and to figure out where he was and why he had been taken from his bed in the middle of the night. Who were those people, the voices of trust and truth, and what had they done to him?

He stripped off the robe because it was wet and heavy and he worried that his feet would get tangled if he tried to swim in it. All that he wore now were his sacred underpants. He crossed himself and in one quick burst, before he could change his mind, he jumped into the black, churning sea. He felt the salt water surround him and rush up his nose and into his mouth. Cold. Then he popped up like a buoy. He coughed and spit up a mouthful of water.

He treaded water in the chilly ocean and thought that at any time a shark might come and pull him under. Then something touched his foot and he screamed and swam as fast as he could toward shore. It was hard because the waves were high and splashed his face. He paddled his hands and kicked his feet and wished he was in the pool and could grab the side.

He kept paddling and realized the shore had looked much closer when he was sitting in the boat. His arms were dead and heavy and he said a prayer to ask God to forgive his sins in case he drowned. Suddenly, his toe scraped against a rock. It hurt. Then his knees scraped the sand under the water. He was on shore. He made it. He stood up and looked ahead and saw ten-foot high cliffs with woods lining the top of them. He turned around to look out at the water. He couldn't see the boat anymore.

He stepped gingerly up the rocky beach. He said a prayer to thank God for helping him reach the shore safely. He thought he heard a voice call to him: "Thou art in God's hands! Ye must walk in the darkness and you will find the light." Jack strained to hear where the voice was coming from, but it swirled in the air above the sea until it was swept away to silence.

Again: "We must all walk in the darkness of faith and trust that God will bring us to the light of His love. Walk in the wilderness. You must endure every trial with humility. Pray. Meditate."

Jack looked up and down the beach and then towards the dark woods at the top of the cliffs. Was he imagining the voice? Was it the voice of trust or truth? Where was he? Was this an island? He reflected on the lessons he had been taught in the last months. Was he being tested in some way? Was this all to see if he was worthy of entering into the fellowship of the community and into God's grace?

He had worked so hard and endured so much. He couldn't fail now. He said a silent prayer again and hoped God would hear him. "Please God, show me the way. Make me see. I submit myself to your will: 'Thy kingdom come, Thy will be done.'" He then said the full Lord's Prayer and blessed himself.

"I endure this joyfully, knowing that your will guides all things, and I shall greet the unseen with a cheer," he said, quoting a poem Frances had read him. He thought of some of the hymns they sang at the morning mass and he thought of Frances. She believed in him. She had faith in him to make his confirmation and become a great leader in the community some day, she had told him.

Jack wanted to see the joy on her face when he passed confirmation. He also wanted to make Sarah, who had spent so many hours teaching him each day, proud. If this was somehow part of his preparation, he would do his best to listen for God's guidance. He would try to apply the lessons he had learned.

He stumbled past the trees and shrubs and rocks. The thorns from prickly vines throughout his path snared his legs and tore his flesh raw. His nose was running, dripping off his upper lip. His ears, despite the cover of the bandana, ached with cold. He staggered through the dripping, prickly woods; he had to find a place soon and get help. The muscles in his legs were cramping. He had a headache. He began to get frustrated with God. Why isn't God listening, he thought. Why won't he help me?

"Please God, please help me!" he cried. He kept thinking that he would come to a road or house eventually, but the woods went on, it seemed, forever. There was no end. But there had to be an end.

He plopped down on the ground and sat in the lotus position that Sarah had taught him for meditation. He rested his hands on his lap and closed his eyes and hummed his mantra. He breathed and tried to relax his cramped, paralyzed body. Eventually, he got his muscles to stop shaking and he forgot about the cold. His body was overcome with lightness.

He opened his eyes. Looking around he saw a bed of moss underneath a beech tree about fifty feet away. He walked to it and lay down for ten minutes to try to sleep, but, even though he had become adept at clearing his mind of all external forces, he could not clear it of the cold his body felt.

He got up and continued trudging through the woods – underneath the barren branches of elm trees and between holly bushes and naked saplings, across dead meadows and listless beds of fern, the smell of dead leaves and rotting wood filling his nostrils. At least it had stopped raining.

He came to a creek, about a foot deep and three feet wide, and followed it until he emerged from the woods. The salt water creek expanded and carved shallow rivulets through a gray-gold marsh. Jack saw his reflection in the still, clear water and he realized for the first time that the sky had turned from black to gray. It was morning.

He cut through the long, squishy grass of the marsh and followed the main stream until he came to a sandy beach on the edge of a bay. He could see land about a quarter mile across the water. Is that where he had come from? Was the compound somewhere over there? He looked, but he didn't see it. He wondered whether he was on an island and had reached the other side or if he had somehow walked in a circle.

The gray light of the sky was brightening as he walked along the beach looking for a house or shelter – anywhere that would offer warmth and something to eat. "Please God," he said, "help me find a house and people who will help me."

He promised that he would offer himself up to God and spread His good news to anyone he met.

He saw a rickety boathouse along the shore in the distance. He ran toward it. It was set on a hill and was falling apart – the dock pilings stood crooked in the sea and the dock that they had once held up hung off the beams like a roller coaster track careening straight into the beach, broken pieces of wood half buried in the sand. The windows of the boathouse were boarded up with plywood.

Jack climbed underneath the boathouse, over slimy rocks covered with seaweed, and looked up through the rotted floor. He started to climb up to see if he could get into the house, but he slipped on a rock and decided not to. He walked back out and climbed up the hill. Once he got halfway up the hill he saw a roof in the distance. Climbing further, a whole house came into view.

It was an old house with a few boarded-up windows and no shutters, sitting on the edge of the woods. Jack trudged through the wet grass of the lawn toward it. At the edge of the house he stepped on a piece of broken glass and cut his foot. He lifted his leg to see how deep the cut was and blood dripped out of the gash.

He limped toward a large window and saw a group of people inside. He said a prayer asking God to protect him and then he knocked on the door.

CHAPTER 31

House of Heathens

"Who the fuck are you?" a young man with ripped jeans and long, greasy blonde hair said when he opened the door. Jack looked up at him. He was shaking again. "I…I'm Augustine. I'm lost."

"Who is it?" Jack heard a woman's voice from inside the house call out.

"Some kid," the greasy-haired guy said. He turned back to Jack. "So how did you get here and what the hell are you wearing?" he asked. A pretty girl with glasses and black, curly hair appeared next to him.

"Dillon, look at him! He's shivering. Where are his clothes? Oh poor thing. What happened to you?"

"I…I don't know." Jack stammered. "Someone…someone took…me." He looked at their faces. The curly-haired girl's face showed concern. The greasy-haired guy's mouth crinkled in a frown.

"What's your name?" the woman asked.

"His name's Augustine," the greasy-haired guy, Dillon, said. "Hey, what the hell is that that you are wearing?" he asked again. Jack didn't answer. He tried to see beyond them into the house, but they were blocking the doorway. He looked to the right, down the side of the house, and then to the left, not sure what he was looking for, but he now regretted knocking on the door.

"Here, come in and let's get you warmed up, and get you some clothes," the girl said.

"What are you doing?" Dillon asked. "You can't just let in some stranger who shows up out of nowhere in his underwear and knocks at our door. We don't know who he is or who he's with!"

"Oh Dillon, look at him! He's just a baby, and he's cold and wet and scared. You can't be serious."

"Maybe he's a plant or something. Who's he with? I mean, don't you find it a little strange that this kid wearing some weird shiny white underwear shows up at our door all the way out here at 9 o'clock in the morning?" he asked.

"Dillon, stop! You're paranoid! Look at him!" The girl then turned to Jack. She smiled. "Don't listen to him. He's an idiot. Come in." Jack stood on the doorstep. "What's the matter?" she asked.

"I cut my foot. It's bleeding."

"Let me see." She kneeled down and lifted his leg and examined his foot, which was dripping blood. "Oh yeah. You have quite a gash there. Hold on and I'll get a rag and wipe it. I doubt we have any bandages here."

Jack waited at the door while his foot bled. Dillon waited with him. "You still haven't answered any of my questions," he said. "When we get inside I want you to tell me where you're from and how you got here, okay?" Jack nodded his head.

The woman returned with a wet face cloth and a tee shirt. She wiped the cut with the cloth and then took him inside. The living room carpet was mildewed and gold-colored with holes in it. They walked down a hallway and turned into a kitchen. Jack let out a startled gasp when he saw the room. There were five people sitting in a haze of cigarette smoke drinking Schlitz beer at a big table in the middle and two more on chairs against the wall underneath the window.

Four men and three women, all young looking – older than high school kids, but not much older. They passed around a cigarette and a bottle labeled Johnny Walker. It was morning!

"Dexter, give him your seat for a minute," the girl said to a guy wearing a Boston Bruins baseball cap. "He cut his foot and I want him to hold this shirt to it to stop the bleeding."

"Why do I have to give up my seat," the guy named Dexter said. "Who is this?"

"Just get up," the girl said. "This is Augustine and he got lost and is cold and wet and he cut his foot."

"Lost! No shit, really?" Dexter with the Bruins hat said, and he laughed. "Look at him! I guess so!" He got out of his seat. "What the hell is he wearing?" He faced Jack. "What are you wearing?" he asked Jack. "It's not Halloween yet. Or did you just get back from playing cupid in the school play or something?" Jack didn't answer. He just stood there looking at the room.

Dirty dishes were piled high in the sink. The counters were covered with crumbs and dirt. There was a trash bag in the corner overflowing with garbage – mostly beer cans. Spider webs hung from the corners of the ceiling and across the large picture window.

The people sitting in the chairs looked dirty too, like Dillon. The guys had stubble on their chins and necks, which looked more like dirt than the beginnings of beards and indicated less that they were trying to grow beards and more that they were just too lazy to shave. They wore dungaree jackets – dirty, ripped, and stained – and dungaree pants and boots – the kind construction workers wore.

The girls also wore dungarees, and three of them wore dungaree jackets. One, the girl with the glasses and curly black hair, wore a black sweater. None of them had washed their hair in awhile. It was greasy and clung to their heads.

"Sit here Augustine," the curly-haired girl said, motioning to the now empty chair. "Hold this tight against the cut. Can you do that? Good."

"Wait, you're not with that bunch of Quaker freaks over in Van Winkle, are you?" a large guy with red hair and pimples all along his stubbly chin asked. Jack looked down at the floor.

"You are, aren't you?" pimple guy said.

"Who are you talking about?" Dexter asked.

"The bunch of Quakers or Puritans or whatever the hell they are over in Van Winkle. Haven't you seen them? They have that shop that sells the furniture and herbs and stuff. Pretty famous. People come from all over Massachusetts to go to the shop. They're some sort of cult."

"Oh, yeah," Dexter said as he took his cap off his head, ran his fingers through his unwashed hair and put the cap back on. "I know that store. They dress like they just walked off the Mayflower, with those fuckin' crazy beards and bonnets."

"Nobody ever sees them outside of that place," pimple guy said. "I heard all they do is pray all day. Is that right?" he asked Jack.

Jack just sat there and looked at the floor.

"Well, are you with that cult?" pimple guy pressed. Jack remained quiet, looking at the floor.

"What's the matter?" he asked. "Cat got your tongue?"

"No," Jack said. He looked at each of them. They puffed on cigarettes and drank from their beer cans.

"Look, he's shaking, poor thing," a girl with long blond hair in a pony-tail said.

"Oh my God, I forgot," the curly-haired girl said. "Come with me and we'll put you in some warm clothes." She stood and took Jack's hand.

The guys whistled and cheered. "Wow, you usually have to get her stoned before she takes you to her room," a guy with hair past his shoulders said.

"Be gentle. Remember he's only seven," pimple-face guy said.

"Don't you think that's moving a bit quick for a first date, even for you?" Dexter said. The girl turned around and stuck her middle finger in the air.

"Fuck you, you losers," she said. Jack heard them all laughing as she pulled him up the dirty carpeted stairs, stained with spilled drinks, into a bedroom with soiled laundry scattered around the floor. There was a big mattress in the middle of the room and empty Ruffles potato chip bags lying next to it, as well as two plates with hard spaghetti and congealed sauce still on them, half-eaten.

"I'm Ciara," she said as she opened a dresser drawer and pulled out sweat pants, a sweatshirt, a tee-shirt, and socks. She also handed him a pair of girl's underwear. They were white with rainbow-colored dots on them. "God, you're soaked. Here, put these on. Don't worry, I won't look. I'll turn around."

"I don't need the underwear, I have mine on," Jack said.

"They're wet!" she said. "You've got to change them." Jack insisted that they weren't wet.

"Let me see," she said, and she felt them on the side of his leg. "You've got some weird underwear," she said. "But they're drenched. Put these on and you'll feel much better."

"I can't," Jack said.

"Why not?"

"Because I'm never supposed to take these off."

"Well, what do you do when they're dirty?" Ciara asked.

"I have another pair."

"Well it's silly to wear wet underpants. Won't you feel better with some nice dry ones?" Jack shook his head no. He was not going to take them off. It was forbidden to wear anything but the sacred garments. "All right," Ciara said. "Wear the wet ones then." Jack put the sweatpants, tee-shirt, and sweatshirt on. They were all too big and the sleeves of the sweatshirt hung over his hands, but he didn't mind because they were warm. He was relieved that she let him keep his sacred garments on, even though they were cold and wet. Abraham would approve.

"Do you feel better?" she asked. Jack nodded yes. "Good," she said. "Now tell me, how the heck did you end up here, soaking wet, wearing only your underpants?"

"I don't know," Jack said. "I don't even know where I am."

"You're on Bassett's Island, off Cataumet in Red Brook Harbor. How long have you been here?"

"Since last night."

"When last night?"

"I don't know, the middle of the night sometime."

"The middle of the night? How did you get here?" Jack hesitated. He wasn't sure what he should tell her. If he told her the truth, would he get in trouble? Though he didn't recognize the voices of truth or trust, he thought they must be associated with the community in some way – a son or daughter of Abraham. They had quoted scripture and told him to pray and meditate.

If he told her that some people took him in the middle of the night and made him drink some potion and left him floating on a boat on the ocean, she might call the police or something. Then Abraham would punish him and beat him, probably worse than Timothy.

"I was trying to find my puppy and I got lost," he said.

Ciara arched her eyebrow. "Wait a minute. You went…to look for a puppy…in the middle of the night? You do know you're on an island? Why would you think the puppy would be on this island? And how would it have gotten here? It's half a mile to shore." She knelt down. "Tell me the truth."

"I…I ran away, and then I got lost," he said.

"How'd you get here?"

"What do you mean?"

"Did you take a boat?"

"Yes, I had a boat."

"And where'd you run away from? Are you really from that cult that Dexter was talking about?"

"Cult?" Jack asked.

"That group – like he said, the ones who run that store, who live on some farm somewhere in Van Winkle and dress and talk funny and quote the Bible all the time. They're weird. They act and dress like they're the Pilgrims or something. Everyone thinks they are a cult. And you are wearing some sort of special underwear that you refuse to take off."

"Why don't you like them?" Jack said.

"So you *are* with that group," Ciara said. "Why did you run away?"

Jack shrugged his shoulders. "I don't know."

She examined his eyes and after a few seconds said, "We can talk about that later. For now let's go downstairs and get breakfast. Are you hungry?" Jack nodded. "I thought you might be," she said. She smiled at him.

He was glad it was breakfast time – the one meal he was allowed to eat while he was in his period of fasting. She held his hand and walked him back to the kitchen.

"The lovers return," pimple face guy said.

"Fuck you," Ciara said. She opened a cabinet door and pulled out a box. "Do you like Cap'n Crunch?" Jack nodded. He had eaten the same meal every morning at the compound – an egg, oatmeal, a slice of toast, and tea. He couldn't believe he was going to get to eat Cap'n Crunch – and it was the Crunch Berries kind, his favorite. He sat and leaned over the bowl, bowed his head and made the sign of the cross quickly and said a prayer thanking God for the food before him.

"Look at this – he's praying before eating his cereal," Dexter said.

"So, I guess that confirms where this kid comes from," said a fat guy with large glasses that made his eyes look like fish eyes against the glass of a tank.

"Yes." Ciara paused, considered. "He is from Van Winkle and he ran away from home."

"Then he *is* one of the freaks!" fat fish-eyed guy said.

"Look who's talking!" Dillon, leaning against the counter, said. They all laughed.

"They are not freaks," Ciara said. Jack devoured the cereal as they talked about him.

"They're a bunch of crazy moonbats," a skinny girl with a big nose said.

"I agree," Dexter said. "Who the heck would isolate themselves from the world like that? I heard they don't believe in going to the doctor, even if they are really sick."

"Yeah, yeah," pimple-face guy said. "They were on the news years ago because one of the children got pneumonia and had a fever of 105 degrees and they wouldn't take him to the hospital because they don't believe in that and the kid died." He took a draught of his beer and looked at the others. "Do you remember that? It was all over the news."

"Yes, I remember," a girl with red hair and freckles said. "People thought the parents should go to jail for child neglect but they got off, right?"

"Yes," ponytail girl said. "They did. They should have been thrown in prison. Who would stand by and let their child die and say it's God's will when they could have saved him easily if they just went to the hospital?"

Jack had never heard about this. He wondered if it was true. He didn't think Sarah would let a child die if she could help it. But Timothy almost died. Jack thought at the time he should definitely have gone to a hospital. Especially when the sores on Timothy's back became infected with streaks of yellow puss where the wounds were, when he smelled like rancid meat. Sarah said she trusted God to give her the wisdom to save Timothy. She nursed him and he was lately recovering. At least he wasn't going to die.

"Hey kid, what's your name again?" Dillon asked. "Augustine? Oh yeah, Augustine. Augustine," he continued, "did you see any of that shit going on over there with those Jesus freaks?" Jack shook his head no.

"No? You sure? Have you lived there all your life?" Jack didn't answer.

"Did you grow up there, or did your parents join the group as converts and drag you in too?"

Jack hesitated. He watched the fat guy with the glasses take a long puff on his cigarette, which Jack noticed wasn't shaped like a normal cigarette. "My parents brought me there," he said finally. They were not smoking just cigarettes, he knew. They were smoking joints too. The smoke smelled different than the cigarette smoke. He knew how cigarettes smelled from his father. He had always hated the smell. The smoke hovering in the kitchen stung his eyes and made them water.

He also noticed they weren't using tweezers. He thought when you smoked joints you used tweezers. He didn't know why, but he remembered that Seth Boylan told him that once. He noticed freckle-face girl looking at him.

"Hey, you people don't smoke over there, do you?" she asked.

"No, I was taught that God said that harming your body is immoral," Jack said. "The Bible says that our body is the temple of the Holy Ghost and that we must glorify God in our body, so we're not supposed to smoke." He looked down at his empty cereal bowl. "Or eat certain things," he said softly. Freckle-face girl burst out laughing and Jack felt his cheeks turn warm.

"Did you hear that?" she asked, looking at the others sitting around the table. They were all laughing too. "My body is a temple!" She took a cigarette from a pack – it looked like a normal cigarette and not a joint – and offered it to Jack. "Here, try one," she said. She giggled.

"Christ, he's only seven," pimple guy said. "What the hell are you doing?"

"I don't know," she said, still smiling. "I think he should break out and have a cigarette. They smoke when they're seven over in England. My cousins used to smoke when they were his age."

"Yeah, but aren't they dwarves now?" fat fish-eye guy said.

"Ha, very funny." She turned again to Jack. "Here, take it. Give it a try. It won't kill you." Jack shook his head no while his eyes faced the floor.

"Oh come on! Give it a try. Just do it once! Go crazy!" she said, giggling. "You can say a prayer before you smoke if that makes you feel better."

"No, I don't want to," Jack said. He didn't want to do anything to jeopardize gaining God's grace and getting into heaven. Already he had heard them swear, take God's name in vain, drink, smoke, and do drugs. He had to get away from them or God would not look with favor upon him and he would bring shame back to the community…or worse: be banished to hell.

"I really should get home now," Jack said. "How do I get off the island and get to Van Winkle? Which way do I go?" He heard a few of them snicker.

"Swim, kid. Or maybe you can walk on water," big-nose girl said.

"You can go after you smoke a cigarette," freckle-face girl said.

"Stop it!" Ciara yelled. "Leave him alone."

Ciara looked over into Jack's empty cereal bowl. "Wow, you are pretty hungry, aren't you," she said. "Do you want some more?" Jack thought for a moment and nodded yes.

"Whoa, whoa, whoa," fat fish-eye guy said. "Are we running a soup kitchen here? That's the last box."

Ciara filled Jack's bowl again. "Calm down. I'll buy another box tomorrow. Besides, you could stand to miss a few breakfasts anyway, you fat fuck."

"Why don't you suck my fat dick, you slut," he answered.

Ciara glared at him. "I don't know if I could find it under your belly."

Fat fish-eye guy undid his belt and unzipped his pants. "Here, I'll show you where you can find it," he said, and he moved to pull down his pants.

"For god's sake, stop!" ponytail girl and freckle-face girl both shouted at once. "There's a kid here, and besides, I don't want to throw up," freckle-face girl said. Fat fish-eye guy stopped and zipped up his pants.

"Fine," he said. "That cereal better be replaced tomorrow."

Jack listened to them yell at each other as he ate the second bowl of cereal. He couldn't believe the mean things they said to each other and how often they swore. He had never heard language like that…except a few times when his parents fought and screamed mean things to each other.

"I'm going to bed," pimple-face guy said. "I'm exhausted."

"Me too," Dexter, said. He motioned to freckle face-girl. "You coming?" She nodded and stood up and he took her hand.

"Wait," Ciara said. "Can anyone take him to the mainland right now?"

"Are you serious?" fat fish-eye guy said. "I'm so fucked up right now I'd drown trying to cross a kiddie pool. No way." Ciara looked to each of them with pleading eyes, but nobody offered to take Jack.

"I'm too tired," the guy with the shoulder-length hair said. "I'm going to bed. Maybe later." Jack couldn't figure out why they were all going to bed when it was morning.

"Why don't you take him yourself," the girl with the big nose said. "You can row the boat, can't you?"

"No, I can't row all the way by myself," she said.

"Let me get some sleep and I'll bring him over later," Dillon said. Then he also left the kitchen and disappeared up the stairs, leaving Ciara and Jack alone.

"Why is everyone going to sleep and it's the morning?" Jack asked.

Ciara flopped onto the chair beside Jack. "Because we were partying all night. We didn't go to bed, just drank straight through." Her eyes were red and Jack could tell that she was tired.

"But how am I going to get home?" he asked.

She leaned over and patted his head. "I'll get you home...after I get 40 winks. Just a little nap." She slurred her words. Jack hadn't noticed it before, but now she swayed back and forth on the chair and Jack thought she might fall into him.

"But they'll be worried at home."

"I know. I know." She had trouble focusing on him. "But I'm in no condition to take you right now. I need to sleep...and you need to sleep. Why don't we take a nap and then go? Is that all right?"

Jack watched her teetering. The longer he stayed there, the more disappointed God would be. And Abraham. He felt he was tainting his soul staying with these unrepentant sinners. He didn't want to jeopardize his confirmation, which Sarah kept hinting was going to happen soon. But he hadn't slept either and he was exhausted. Maybe it would be okay if he took a nap, and then, refreshed, he would be on his way in a couple of hours.

"Okay," he said. "I'll take a nap. Can we go right after that?"

"Yes. That's what we'll do."

She took him back to the bedroom where he had changed. Dillon was splayed out on the mattress, snoring. Ciara quietly pulled a pillow and blanket from it and laid them on the floor. "I'm sorry, we don't have a spare bed so the floor's gonna hafta do. Is that all right?" Jack nodded and lay down on the floor and pulled the cover up. The dirty gold carpet smelled like mildew and beer.

Ciara tripped over something on the floor and fell into the mattress. "What the fuck?" Dillon said. Ciara whispered sorry and got under the covers with him. In a few minutes she began snoring too. Jack listened to them for a while. He said a silent prayer to God to forgive him for being in this house but thanked Him for giving him shelter. Ten minutes into his prayer, he too fell fast asleep.

CHAPTER 32

Confession

He woke up drenched with sweat. He bolted upright and realized it was dark outside. How long had he slept? He looked over at the mattress and saw it was empty. He ran downstairs to find Ciara. When he reached the kitchen he was out of breath. Pimple-face guy was the only one there. He sat slouched on a chair, his feet up on the kitchen table, a cigarette in one hand and a can of Schlitz in the other. A glass ashtray rested on his round belly.

"Sleeping beauty woke up," he said. "I thought you were going to sleep right through the night."

"Where's Ciara?" Jack asked.

"Whoa. I guess you don't want to talk to me? She's out back at the bonfire, I think." Jack ran out the front door. It was a cold, clear night. He ran around the house and saw a large fire in the middle of the yard. Seven lawn chairs surrounded it. Ciara was sitting in one, smoking a joint. Jack ran up to her.

"Well, you finally got up," she said. "You must have been pretty tired."

Jack stood at the side of her chair. "Can you take me home now?" he asked.

"Oh Augustine, I think you're going to have to wait until morning," she said. His eyes asked why. "It wouldn't be safe to go over in the dark."

Jack looked over at Dillon. Dillon held over the fire a stick with hot dogs stuck to the end of it. A few empty cans of beer were at his feet. "Can you take me?" Jack asked him.

"I could have five hours ago," he said. "I'm not going over there now. I'll take you in the morning." He turned the hot dogs over. "Have a hot dog. Do you want one?" Jack was starving. He wasn't supposed to eat any meal except breakfast and a small piece of bread at night until after he was confirmed. He thought of St. Madeline and the anvil. He must be strong. He was too close to confirmation. Even if Sarah or Abraham would never know he ate a hot dog, God would know, and he'd be compelled to confess.

"No thank you," he said.

"No? You don't want one?" Dillon said. He pulled one off the stick and put it on a bun that he had ready on a plate. He poured ketchup and mustard on it and took a huge bite. "They're good. You sure?"

Ciara sucked a deep suck of the joint. "Have one. Aren't you hungry?" she asked.

"No," Jack lied.

"You haven't eaten a thing since breakfast," she said. "Don't be shy," she said. "Have one if you want one."

Jack thought for a second. "I'm not supposed to."

"Not supposed to what?" Dillon said.

"I'm fasting. I'm only allowed breakfast until I'm confirmed."

"Wait a minute," Dillon said. "You're telling me you only eat at breakfast – nothing else for the entire day?" Jack nodded yes.

"How long have you been doing that?" Ciara asked.

"Since January."

"What?" Dillon said. "You're not serious, are you? For four months you've been fasting, only breakfast?" Jack nodded again. "They really are moonbats over there," Dillon said to Ciara.

Jack looked into the fire. He could feel its warmth at his feet and he winced.

"Where is everybody else?" Jack asked. "Can anybody take me?"

"Drunk, and probably not," Dillon said.

"Do you all live here?"

"No. We just come on weekends, mostly, though it might look like we live here. Sometimes some of the others stay here longer, but most of us work during the week. It's nice out here because nobody bothers us. We can do what we want," Ciara said. "It's our little hang-out."

"Like a secret fort or something?"

"Yes, kind of like that. Did you ever have a secret fort?" She took a deep suck from her joint and sighed. Her glazed eyes peered into the fire.

"Yes, I used to have a fort in the woods with my friends. We had carpet and our toys and we'd have club meetings there. We covered it with pine branches so it blended with the woods and was hard to see."

He remembered the time in the fort last summer when Bobby dared him to kiss Sally Boylan. A bunch of the neighborhood kids were in the fort eating Twinkies and playing truth or dare, and Bobby dared Jack to kiss Sally on the lips. Sally had made a face and said *no way*, but Jack had to do it and he kissed her and she said *ew* and *gross* and wiped her mouth. Jack wiped his mouth and said gross too, but he didn't mind it. Sally was pretty. But that was a long time ago.

"That's cool," Ciara said, and she took another puff from her joint. Jack watched her. He was sad that she sinned so much because he would like her to go to heaven.

"Aren't you afraid of going to hell?" he blurted.

Ciara turned and looked at him quizzically. "Where the hell did that come from?" she asked. "Why do you think I'm going to hell?"

Jack glanced at the marijuana joint in her hand and then at her face. "I don't know," he said. Then he looked around at the empty beer cans strewn on the ground in front of the fire. "Well, you drink and smoke and do drugs. And you swear and call people mean things. And you—"

"Okay, enough already. Who died and made you Mother Teresa?" she said. She had an aggravated expression on her face. "You're acting a little holier than thou, aren't you? I mean, if you are a good person, and you help people and – like me helping you for example." She took another deliberate drag from the joint.

"I didn't have to help you when you showed up at our door this morning. But I did. I gave you warm clothes. I fed you. I let you sleep in my room and offered to let you stay at our place out of the rain and cold until you could get back home. And I even offered to take you back tomorrow."

She continued. "Wouldn't God say, 'Wow, Ciara has a kind heart and did a good deed and I want her to be in heaven. I mean, I do all that and you tell me I'm going to hell because I smoke or get high or have a beer? Why does God care if I smoke? It doesn't hurt anybody, does it?"

Jack looked at her stringy, greasy hair and reddened eyes as she took a great puff from the joint. Her clothes were dirty and smelled like musty sneakers that had gotten wet in the rain. Her life was not lived to glorify God; it was lived for decadent pleasure. Pleasure was the goal, not self-improvement or reflection, or humble service to neighbors or God.

Jack stared into the fire and thought about what she said. She wasn't hurting anyone, except when she called the fat guy cruel names. He recalled the exhortation that Saint Augustine lived by: *Let us walk honestly, as in the day, not in rioting and drunkenness, not in chambering and wantonness, not in strife and envying.*

Ciara and the others lived in drunkenness. They lived in wantonness. They lived in envying and strife – everything that Saint Augustine rejected when he discovered God's calling. And the worst part was Ciara knew she was sinning and still she sinned and dared God to strike her down.

Yet she had been nice to Jack, and if he were deciding, he wouldn't want her to suffer in hell, so he'd probably let her into heaven. But he didn't decide. God was the judge. He wondered if he was sympathetic to Ciara's sin, if he was friendly to her and let her sin stand without saying anything, then was he guilty too? Yes, he must be guilty – just as guilty as a boy who watches another boy beat up a wimp and steal his lunch and stands by and lets it happen.

Sarah had drilled him on questions just like these, over and over again. She would have taught Ciara why what she was doing offended God. She would have told her she'd been tempted by the devil and had succumbed, and for her earthly fleeting moment of pleasure, she could look forward to an eternity in the fires of hell.

Jack continued to gaze at the fire. He thought of Frances. Frances would have also answered Ciara, telling her that smoking and drinking, just like indecent relations, all are pleasures of the flesh. They are all sins because they hurt the body and the body is not your own. It is a gift from God. Anything that you do that destroys that gift is sinful. Anything impure you put into it is an affront to God.

"My teacher taught me that you cannot sin against your own body because the body is the temple of the Holy Spirit, who lives in you and who was given to you by God," Jack said meekly.

"Listen kid," she said. "My body is my body. I can do with it whatever I want as long as I don't hurt anyone. And who the hell says my body is God's body anyway? Tell me where you heard that."

Jack's mouth hung open a little as she was saying these words. Abraham would whip anybody in the community if they ever said anything blasphemous like this. "The Holy Spirit is God's breath in us, and God's breath gives our bodies a divine life and energy," he said. "We do not belong to ourselves but we belong to God and when we put impure things into our body, we offend God."

Dillon started laughing, shaking his head from side to side. Ciara smirked and then laughed a little too. "I have never heard a seven-year-old talk like that," she said. "You people are…interesting. But we're all just food for worms. Live for today, I say. If I'm a good person, then I'll go to heaven. And if I don't, I don't care." She shook her head and took the second hot dog from the stick. "You won't mind if I eat this?" she asked. "I know it's impure, but I'm hungry."

She took a few bites from her hot dog while she gazed alternately from Jack to the fire. About halfway through her hot dog she spoke. "How do you know what happens after you die?" she asked. "How do you know there even is a heaven or hell?"

Jack knew the answer, so he answered her as he'd answer Sarah if she asked him in class. "Because the word of God, which has been handed down to us, says so," he said.

"Where the hell did you learn all this?" Ciara asked.

"I've been studying it with my teacher to prepare for my confirmation."

"When's your confirmation?" she asked.

"I don't know. Soon I think, but they won't tell me."

"Who's they?"

Jack thought for a second. He'd never had to describe the community to anyone else before. "My teachers," he said finally. "They are preparing me."

"Well I don't really believe in all that," she said. "I used to go to church with my family, but I stopped going when I was in high school. I think it's all a waste of time, if you ask me…and sooo boring," she said, and she rolled her eyes.

Jack's eyes grew big and he blurted, "I used to go to church too with my family and I thought the same thing and then we stopped—" He caught himself. Ciara stared at him. He remembered sitting in church with a coloring book, not paying any attention to the priest. He remembered fighting with Lilly and his mother and father scolding him and telling him to pay attention. When they stopped going to church, he didn't think much about it.

"What?" she said. "Go on."

"Nothing. Just that I used to think the same as you – that church was really boring and I didn't want to go. But I didn't *understand*. Once I understood I realized that life is meaningless if not lived in the service of God. I was doomed. I was unclean and impure but God has washed away my sins."

"Saint Augustine, for whom I've been named, said: 'I *believe* in order to understand; and I understand, the better to believe,'" Jack continued. "I didn't understand before. Now I do. You can too." Ciara held the joint to her lips for a few moments then pulled it away.

"God will clothe you in grace, if you only let Him, if you only listen for His voice," Jack added.

Ciara stared at him, mouth open slightly. She rolled her eyes. "You can recite all those lofty words and platitudes, but at the end of the day, how do you know any of it is really true?" she said. "How do you really know what happens to us after we die?"

"I told you," Jack said in an urgent voice, "the Bible—"

"It's a crock of shit," Ciara said. "You actually believe that God spoke directly to these people and they wrote down what he said and that's that?" Just then they heard leaves rustle. Jack looked behind them and saw the fish-eye guy appear out of the darkness. He sat down beside them.

"What's going on?" he asked. He sipped from the can of Schlitz.

"Augustine is trying to bring me religion," Ciara said.

"Religion! Who said that famous statement about religion? Was it Hegel? No, no, not Hegel." He snapped his finger and thumb together repeatedly in quick bursts. "It was…it was…do you know what I'm talking about?"

Ciara shook her head. "I don't have a clue."

"Goddammit, it's on the tip of my tongue," he said. Jack shifted his weight from his left to right side and looked away.

"'Religion is the opium of the people', he said – Marx, it was Marx. Religion is the opium of the people." Fish-eye guy looked into the fire, a satisfied frown on his face.

"I've never heard that," Ciara said. She was lying back, gazing at the night clouds. Purple clouds. She leaned up on her arms to face him. "What did he mean?" she asked.

"He meant – give me a hit of that," fish-eye guy said, and he reached for the joint. He took a deep drag. "He meant that religion is like a drug for people to escape the reality of life. It is an illusion and people get addicted to this illusion far more strongly than to pot or heroin or any traditional drug."

He took another long puff from the joint and handed it back. "It has the same effect – to take them away from the struggles of life." He looked at Jack and then back to Ciara. "I mean look at some of these people who go to mass three times a day and cling to the fantasy that they will be rewarded after they die and sent to some paradise where angels will be playing fucking harps all day or something. All because they went to mass and didn't eat meat on Fridays. It's a bunch of bullshit."

He turned to Jack and saw his sullen face and added quickly. "No offense, but you gotta admit it's some racket, at least organized religion is. Why don't people just shoot up some heroin instead? That way they don't have to wait until they die for paradise; they can get it right away." He reached for the joint again and Ciara passed it to him.

"That's how I feel," he said. "Live for today. No one knows what comes next, so enjoy life in the here and now and stop worrying about pleasing some all-knowing, all-powerful *being* you think is out in the clouds but may not be." He held the joint out in front of his face. "This is my God," he said, and Jack gasped.

This was certainly the devil trying to tempt him, he thought. This was a test of his faith and if he didn't pass, if he denied God in front of them, or didn't speak up, God would be angry at him and bad things would happen. He was about to speak when Ciara spoke.

"I do think there is something out there," she said. "I don't think we'll know until we die, but I think a person can be spiritual and pray to God. But what I don't like, or don't understand, is the idea that if you don't pray a certain prayer, or like you said, follow rules like not eating meat on Fridays, you're a bad person. So if I eat a cheeseburger on Friday I'm a worse person than someone who doesn't eat meat but is a dick to people, or a hypocrite?" She started speaking in a more animated manner, her hands conducting in front of her and her voice rising to a louder pitch.

"Why do I have to go to a priest for confession? Why can't I just confess to God directly?" she said and she looked at Jack. "Tell me that." Jack gathered his thoughts. Before he could answer, she began again.

"Why is it a sin to have sex outside of marriage? What difference does a ceremony and a piece of paper make? Tell me," she yelled.

"Or why can't you marry again in the church if you get divorced? It's ridiculous," interjected Dillon, who had been focused on cooking and eating two more hot dogs for the past few minutes. "If people don't love each other anymore and want to marry someone else who will make them happy, I think it's bullshit that the church says they can't do that."

Jack listened to Ciara, Dillon and fish-eye guy's back-and-forth silently. He thought of his parents and how they didn't love each other so they did what Dillon said and got a divorce. But then they stopped loving him too, and divorced him too. They didn't even try to find him. It made him sad to think about it.

He wished Sarah or Rachel were there. They would be able to tell them why they were wrong – much better than he thought he could. They always made everything so clear. Frances too. It all made sense when Frances explained why every detail of their commitment to God was important.

Just then he thought of his vow to God when he was in the boat and prayed to God that if he helped him swim safely to shore and find someone to help him, he would proclaim God's word to all those he met. He worried that if he didn't defend God as best he could, he would be banished from heaven and sent to the hot fires of hell forever.

He wanted to tell them that God desired all his children to be saved and to come to the knowledge of the truth. He searched his memory for teachings or passages that would show them that they were wrong; that God was real and that the lives they were living – lives lacking faith and humility and service to God – would lead to eternal suffering. He wanted them to see that the body is not to be used for sexual immorality, but to serve the Lord.

Perhaps he could reach them and save them. As Jack had learned, God can cause good to emerge from evil itself; God gives life even to the dead. "I have been taught," he began, "That those who are dominated by the sinful nature think about sinful things, but those who are controlled by the Holy Spirit think about things that please the Holy Spirit. A sinful nature is always hostile to God. It never did obey God's laws and it never will."

"I've learned that if our life is upright, our heart will be open to welcome the light shed by the dogmas of faith, and that God's word is a lamp to your feet and a light to your path."

"And we know that God exists because God's only son came down and died on the cross and rose from the dead. We know God through Jesus, who walked among us." He stopped to look at them and see if they were interested in what he was telling them.

Dillon shook his head. "Kid, what the hell are you talking about? You're seven and you sound like the priest at St. Margaret's. Where did you learn to talk like that?" The question surprised Jack. Did he really talk differently? He didn't think so. The words simply flowed out as naturally as if he had been speaking them his entire life.

"I speak only the word of God, as it has been taught to me," he said. "God wants more than anything to give eternal life to all those who seek salvation by patience and well-doing." Jack continued to tell them how God desired all men to be saved and to come to the knowledge of the truth. They listened for awhile as they passed the joint back and forth, giggling and rolling their eyes at each other after most of Jack's statements.

Jack wanted them to learn what he had learned. He wanted them to be as happy as he was that he had discovered God's great love…that his heart had been moved by the Holy Spirit. He tried hard to convince them that they too could discover the grace achieved through faith. He spoke with such earnestness that, though he did not persuade them to change, he won their affection.

"You know what kid? You're all right," Dillon said. "I like you."

Ciara laughed. "I'm going to call you the midget monk," she said. "I don't think you can convert us, but your heart is in the right place."

Jack stopped talking, turned away and stared into the fire. He was sad that they were not interested in learning about God. His cheeks flushed. He was a little embarrassed about the zeal with which he had spoken about his beliefs to these adults like a teacher to students.

"I'm sorry," he said. He looked down at the ground. "I just promised God when I landed on this island that if He helped me find some shelter and food I'd praise His name. And He helped me find you." Jack looked at Ciara. "Thank you for helping me today," he said quietly.

"You're welcome," Ciara said. She leaned over low to the ground to see his face. "Aw, you look so sad. Don't be sad." Jack's chin quivered and his eyes welled up.

"Oh don't cry," she said. "What's wrong? Are you sad that we don't believe in what you are telling us, or are you homesick?" Jack nodded his head yes and the dam of his eyes burst and tears poured down his face. His small body shook.

"Oh my, what happened?" fish-eye guy said.

"Come here," Ciara said. She pulled Jack to her chest and hugged him. She rubbed the back of his head and held him against her. "It's going to be all right. I'm going to bring you home first thing in the morning and you'll be okay." She took his face in her hands and looked into his eyes. "I'll say a little prayer for you." She wiped the tears from his cheeks. Jack nodded. He didn't know why he was crying; only that he couldn't stop.

CHAPTER 33

Escape Again

After sitting around the fire for an hour or so more and then walking to the beach on the other side of the boathouse to see if the rowboat was ready, Ciara brought him to the bedroom where his makeshift bed was still set up and the plates of half-eaten spaghetti were still sitting on the floor, untouched.

Ciara put him to bed and pulled the blanket up to his chin. She kissed him on the forehead. "Good night Augustine. Try to get some sleep." Jack tried to sleep, but this time the floor felt hard and uncomfortable and his nose was stuffed up. The room was cold. He shifted from side to side for an hour, miserable because he couldn't breathe, when Ciara and Dillon stumbled into the room and crashed onto the big mattress. Jack pulled the covers over his head and pretended he was sleeping.

They giggled and talked to each other in loud whispers. "Shhh!" she said. "Don't wake up Augustine."

Jack heard them kissing. He peaked over the covers to look at them. There were no shades on the windows, so he could see them in the faint blue light of the moonlit room. They were kneeling on the bed, facing each other, kissing, lips to lips, and then Dillon kissed her neck and she let out a soft mmm sound.

Suddenly, Dillon took off her shirt. She had no bra and Dillon kissed her breasts. Then Ciara started undoing Dillon's belt and Jack pulled the covers quickly back over his head. He could hear them breathing heavily and then they both began moaning and panting. Jack crossed himself and asked God to forgive him for watching Ciara with her top off.

He should try to leave, he thought. They began to get louder and louder and the mattress shook. Jack remained hidden under the covers, horrified. He peeked to see if he might be able to crawl out without them noticing. Ciara was on top of Dillon and she was rocking furiously back and forth. Her behind, bare, bouncing in a sort of circular motion now, was facing Jack.

He crawled along the floor, dragging the top blanket with him. Shimmying past the bed, he saw them grinding against each other, Ciara's mop of hair flying around. Dillon's low grunts and Ciara's heavy breathing and moans, their movements, arms flailing, heads bobbing, torsos going back and forth made them sound and look like wild animals to Jack. This must have been what Timothy had done. Surely this was fornicating.

Jack turned the knob and began to open the door – slowly, ever so slowly. It creaked. "Oh my God, Augustine!" Ciara yelled. Jack pushed the door open and ran out without looking back. "Augustine, wait!" he heard her yell. He didn't wait.

He ran down the stairs and out the front door, into the cold April night. He wrapped the blanket around himself and then realized it wasn't his to take. Nor were the clothes he wore – the sweat pants, socks, and sweatshirt. The only thing that belonged to him was his sacred garment. He had sinned enough. He could not compound his trespass by stealing their clothes. They had, despite their rejection of God, been kind to him.

His soul was dirty, filthy, and God would be disappointed and angry with him. Abraham would surely make him confess his poor judgment in staying with heathens for a whole afternoon and evening. He may even be shunned. By staying with them and witnessing their sloth, drug and alcohol-fest, profanity, contempt for God, and finally their animal sex outside of the marriage bond, Jack had abandoned God's way and fallen from His grace.

He couldn't remember what type of sin his was – a sin of commission or omission, or something else – but he knew, though he had not done the acts himself, it was sinful just to willingly witness them. He would bring an unclean soul and, with it, God's disfavor to the community. The only way to fix it, he thought, was to repent his sin and beg God to forgive him…to cleanse his soul.

To do that, he must suffer. Redeem himself, purge his soul, and commit himself to do better. He shed the sweatpants, sweat shirt, tee-shirt, socks, and blanket, and left them on the front step. As when he arrived at the house, he wore only his sacred garment. *As it was in the beginning, is now and ever shall be.* Dust to dust, naked to naked. It was cold outside, but at least it wasn't raining.

Jack ran around to the back of the house where a shed stood fifty yards from where the bonfire had warmed him a few hours ago. The fire still smoldered. Something had caught his eye when Dillon had emptied a trash bag into a large bin next to the shed. Leaning against the wooden structure, amidst a pile of lumber, an old, rusted lawnmower, and a ripped lawn chair…were two oars. He grabbed them and began to pull them down the steep slope of the lawn.

About halfway down he heard the front door open. Ciara stood on the steps and called his name. She had gotten dressed in the jeans and black sweater she had worn that day. She saw him in the grass. "Augustine, wait!"

She jumped off the steps and ran across the meadow-lawn. "Where are you going? Why did you take off your clothes? Aren't you cold?" Jack didn't answer and resumed pulling the oars. "What are you doing?" she asked. She stepped on them. "Answer me!"

"I have to go," Jack said. "I'm sorry."

"Where?"

"Home."

"Right now? It's 11 o'clock at night. Why don't you wait until the morning when I will take you over?"

"You keep telling me you'll take me. All day you've said, 'I'll take you after dinner...I'll take you after I take a nap,' and then you don't. I can't wait anymore!" he said, bursting into tears. "Please let me go!" Jack tried to pull the oars, but her foot remained on them. "I have to go," Jack repeated.

"You're not seriously going to try to get to the mainland by yourself, are you?" Jack nodded yes. "You're crazy," she said. "Listen, I'm sorry you saw that in the bedroom. I thought you were sleeping and—" She broke off and looked up to the house. Jack had a scared and confused look on his tear-streaked face. "It doesn't matter. I'm sorry. I shouldn't have done that with you in the room. You're just a little kid." She noticed Jack shivering.

"Listen, come back and put on the clothes I gave you so you don't freeze to death. I'll take you back now if you really can't wait until morning. There's no way I'm letting you go out in the ocean by yourself because I'm afraid you wouldn't make it across and I don't want you to drown."

She walked over and kneeled down in front of him and put her hand on his shoulder. "I'm really sorry," she said again. "You're a good kid and your parents must miss you terribly. I should have taken you back immediately. Come on and put the clothes on. You can keep them. I'll take you to the mainland in the boat now, okay?"

Her lips curled up into an uncertain half-smile, but her eyes were big and kind. "Okay," Jack said.

CHAPTER 34

A Choice

Ciara led Jack to a small rowboat not unlike the boat he had found himself in the night before. It had a small engine on the back of it. Jack looked out across the black water. Both remained silent for some ten minutes. Ciara spoke first. "Augustine, I don't know you or understand how you live or how your family lives, or what it's like growing up in a group like your people, so religious, but I hope you won't need to run away again." Her face, pale to begin with, shone paler still in the moonlight.

She spoke softly, the soothing effect of her voice enhanced by the lapping water against the hull and the gurgle-buzz of the motor. "I hope you won't think less of us because we do certain things that you've been taught are bad. We have good hearts. I suppose we, in turn, shouldn't criticize the way you live. I'm sorry for that." Jack sat perched on the bow, twisting his body every few seconds to see how close they were to the land ahead.

He watched her face as she steered. She smiled – not the pursed, nervous smiles of earlier, but a big smile that showed her slightly crooked teeth. He had condemned her not a half hour earlier, in his mind calling her wicked and begging God's forgiveness for even talking to her. She was everything, did everything, that God abhors – everything that Abraham and Sarah and Frances called wicked, evil.

But when she smiled at him then, Jack couldn't call her evil. Sinful? Yes, she was sinful. But she was kind. Jack didn't want to like her. He told himself over and over during the boat ride that the community would banish him if they knew he allowed his eyes to see the wickedness of this heathen. Should he pray for her? Yes, he would.

The small boat slipped through the water and the shore came fast, until the hull scratched and scraped against the sandy bottom and came to a grinding stop. Ciara pointed ahead toward a sloped lawn and Jack saw the looming steep roof of the place he now recognized as home.

"Here you are," she said. "I think that's your place right there." Jack wanted to run up the hill, but she was not done. "Augustine, one more thing." He paused, one leg hanging over the side of the boat. "Keep me in your prayers!"

Jack raced up the lawn and around to the front door of the big house. It was late, well past midnight, and he worried that the door would be locked and that nobody would hear his knock. He turned the knob. He pushed the heavy door open and froze.

On a leather-bound chair in the foyer sat Abraham, arms folded, an intense, stern gaze on his face, upon which shadows from the light of a candle on the table beside him danced. Jack's knees buckled a little. "Where have you been?" Abraham asked in a cold, even voice.

"I…I tried to get back, but I couldn't," Jack stammered. "Somebody took me in the middle of the night…the voice of trust. I was on an island and I couldn't get back, though I begged them to take me back."

"Who did you beg? Who was on the island with you?" he asked, his eyes widening and penetrating through Jack.

"Forgive me, Master Abraham, but I stumbled upon a group of sinners, and though I did not participate in their trespasses, I did witness much wickedness." Though Jack had stood by while the boy beat up and stole the lunch of the wimp, at least now he could tell the principal and in this telling might be forgiven and commended for doing *something*.

"And what did you think of these people and their activities?"

"I prayed to God often and asked Him to forgive me for witnessing this evil and asked Him to cleanse my soul of these iniquities which I did witness."

"And what sin did you see?"

"The worst sins I ever witnessed. Please forgive me, I did not seek to witness them, and when I discovered the sinfulness I tried to flee from it. When I could not flee, I tried to spread the Word of God. I tried to tell them how important it was to commit their lives to God."

Abraham remained silent for some seconds, folding and unfolding his fingers slowly. Jack felt beads of sweat form on his forehead. "What wicked acts did you witness," Abraham asked finally.

"Oh, I witnessed the most horrible acts," Jack said. "I witnessed unspeakable vile sins not fit for an animal."

"What acts did you witness?" Abraham pressed, leaning forward now in his chair.

Jack was certain that when he told Abraham the sins he had seen he would be beaten. He braced himself for a blow across the face and slowly recited what he had seen. "I saw…I saw drunkenness, drugs, profanity, idleness…gluttony. And I saw improper relations between a man and a woman outside of marriage."

Abraham leaned forward so much he looked ready to spring out of the chair. Jack flinched. Abraham did not strike him. He stroked his beard. "They live in filth," Jack continued. "They are unclean in body and spirit."

"And how did these sins make you feel?" Abraham asked.

"It made me sad. But mostly it disturbed me. It made me wish to flee and get as far away as I could to cleanse my soul of what I'd seen, and I finally did."

"Sad?"

"Sad that they choose to reject God…sad that they do not care at all about living to serve God. They said many horrible, blasphemous things about Him and I tried to tell them how to seek God's grace, but I failed to convince them. Please forgive me. I tried to teach them what Sarah has taught me. I tried. But they choose to live sinful lives."

"Tell me again how you came upon this group," Abraham said. "Where did you get these clothes?"

"Please forgive me," Jack repeated, bowing low, "but I was stuck on a little boat and I had to swim to shore and I could not swim with my sacred robe. I had to leave it on the boat," Jack said. He stared at the ground. "Forgive me, but I was cold and they – a girl – gave me these clothes and said I could keep them. But I didn't take off my sacred garment, Father Abraham. I still have that on and never took it off."

"That is well. You will discard those clothes immediately, yes?" Jack nodded yes. "And Moses will get you a new robe." Abraham leaned back in the chair and stroked his beard. Then he gestured with his hand. "Please continue."

Jack told him how he was taken in the middle of the night and given something to drink and woke up on a boat and how he couldn't untie the boat. He told him again how he had to swim to shore in the rain. He told him how he had been cold and wet and sought shelter and found a house and didn't know it was a den of sin and how they told him he was on an island and that they promised to take him home but kept delaying him even though he begged them to bring him home.

"And where did you ask them to take you?"

Jack looked at him for a moment. "Here."

"You believe this to be your home?" Abraham asked.

"Yes. Yes. I begged them to bring me here and they promised over and over but didn't." Jack paused, trying to read Abraham's face.

"Continue," he said.

Jack told him that he prayed for them, prayed for God's forgiveness and guidance, and prayed to return as soon as possible to the community. He told him fervently and sincerely. Abraham listened silently, but retained a stern look on his face. Jack fell on his knees. "Oh father Abraham," he pleaded. "Please forgive me and help me purge this sin from my soul and make me clean again."

"Augustine, I'm glad you witnessed this evil. What those people do on that island is the foulest weed, the blackest serpent of sin there is. That is what I saved you from – a life of waste and filth and pain and eternal black death. That is the road the outside world has chosen, and it is a road that heads straight to eternal damnation."

Abraham stood and put both hands on Jack's shoulders. "Tell me child. You have a choice. Is that the world you want to go back to – a world of drugs and cruelty? A world of sex and disease? Do you want to go back to hate and anger, hedonism and permissiveness, war and chaos?" He gripped Jack's shoulders tighter as he spoke. Jack looked up at him, eyes searching.

"Do you want to live like your friends on the island, whose reward for their affront to God will be a thousand years in a charred wasteland, with searing heat but no light? They will be cast into the abyss of darkness and never know the ultimate joy beyond all joy, to bask in the reflected glory of God's visage."

Abraham let go of Jack's shoulders and sat back down in the chair, reclined, hands joined together as if formed for a prayer. "Now tell me what you would like to do. Tell me your choice."

Jack stared into Abraham's intense blue eyes. What choice was Abraham now giving him? Was he saying that he was free to leave, to just walk away? He thought about when he tried to run away before, about being up in the tree while those Dobermans growled below, snapping their sharp teeth at his feet.

He thought about Abraham burning his feet in the fire so he wouldn't be able to run away again. If he walked away now, would Abraham really let him leave? Or would dogs chase him again, or a car pull to the side of the road some day when he was riding his bike and Moses snatch him up and bring him back. He must have misunderstood. "I...I don't understand," he said.

Abraham smiled and the candlelight flickering on his face gave him a ghoulish appearance, like a body-less spirit. "It's very simple Augustine. You have a choice. You can stay with us and continue your spiritual journey, the journey to live in God's grace, to devote your life to Him and Him only; to live humbly and piously in the service of the Lord."

Abraham leaned forward and spoke now in almost a whisper. "Or you can choose the easy path where the demon lurks at every turn, where your soul will become so polluted it will fester like a never-healing sore, where temptations follow you and lure you to live in the cold dark night that shall never see morning and never see God, and where pain and suffering will be yours forever."

He leaned ever further forward as he spoke and Jack recoiled. "This is the path of the seven deadly sins and eternal death," he continued. "You can leave here now and walk back into that world from which you came. But be mindful, Augustine. Be mindful that if you choose the road of sin now, you can never come back and your soul will be black as coal and you will go to hell where the devil's foulest fiends will rip out your intestines and gouge your eyes."

Jack shuddered. He thought of his mother and father and Lilly and the thought of them in such an awful place frightened him. He had asked Sarah about saving them too by bringing them to live on the compound. She told him it was impossible. They could not be saved.

Jack had persisted one day after class, telling her that when he learned more and was confirmed, he wanted to find them and save them. He asked her if she'd go with him. If they didn't want to be saved, he said, he would return with Sarah to the compound and never leave again. But he thought they would want to be saved and that if he found them they'd come back to the compound with him.

"Is my mother really dead," he had asked. Sarah took his hand and crouched down next to him.

"Her soul is dead," she said. "Augustine, I did not wish to tell you this, but you must know." She looked him in the eye. "Yes, your mother is dead. And your father no longer hopes to find you. He has gone back to work and back to his life. He stopped looking for you. He has Lilly now and doesn't need you."

She stood and faced the wall and pulled out a book. "And he has fallen deeper into the blackness of sin," she said, her back facing him. "He is always drunk and often violent. His house is a den of iniquity – prostitution, drugs, violence. He has cursed God – denounced Him –and has rejected a life of faith."

"How do you know this? Have you seen?" Jack asked quickly. Sarah turned around.

"No, I have not seen him. I have heard this from friends who have seen him and say he is the town embarrassment, walking always in drunkenness, screaming obscenities at women, and cursing God. He can't be saved Augustine, and I think you should focus on your life here and not trouble your thoughts with such wickedness."

Sarah had told Jack all this in the middle of March, nearly a month ago. Now he stood before Abraham, who was seemingly giving him a chance to walk away from the compound and go back to his family. His eyes welled and a single tear rolled down his cheek.

"What troubles you?" Abraham asked, still sitting, but now reclined. Jack looked at the wooden floor.

"I just…I just…"

"Speak freely," Abraham said and leaned forward again. "You are free to accept or reject God. What do you choose?"

CHAPTER 35

Confirmation

"Augustine," Abraham said, candlelight reflecting in the pupils of his eyes. "Do you choose this life with us, devoted to serving God? Do you reject the evil of the outside world, reject living among them and their barren, faithless wasteland? Do you commit yourself to prayer and reflection, to measure your soul each day and strive to make it a vessel of God's faith and love?"

"Yes Father Abraham, I do." Jack searched his face, his eyes. Should he say more? Should he promise more? He waited for Abraham to lead.

"You will have to give up things that you want, that you think God wants, but He doesn't. Just as you water a flower for it to bloom, gaining no benefit from the water yourself except the sweet scent of the flower, so you must love, loving for others so that they may blossom, and not for your own benefit. Mark my words well, Augustine. This is not a decision to take lightly." He shook Jack gently by his shoulders.

"Once you commit to serve Him, you must seek His truth and live a life that is upright. You must each day take the measure of your moral assets and liabilities and seek to tip the balance evermore toward perfect harmony with God's will."

"God has called you to serve Him in spirit and in truth. Are you prepared to answer that call now? Are you ready to walk in faith, and by faith submit completely your intellect and your will to God here with us?"

Jack bowed low before him. "Yes Master Abraham. I am."

"Good," Abraham said. "Very good. Now get ye to bed and rest. You were born anew by baptism; in the morning your faith will be strengthened by the sacrament of confirmation."

Jack skipped down the stairs to the basement room. He could hardly believe his ears. He had passed the test. He was going to be confirmed! He looked up the stairs behind him and realized that this was the first time he had gone to the room on his own, without Moses escorting him.

He opened the bedroom door. Emmanuel was in bed, asleep. Jack closed the door behind him. There was nobody on the other side locking it this time. He smiled and skipped to his bed. He had worked so hard to reach this day when he would be brought into the community. After tomorrow, once he was confirmed, he'd be among the elect, among the chosen few who had been deemed worthy to have the chance to see God's face.

He slipped underneath the covers and his mind pictured the next day. He didn't know what happened during confirmation – nobody had ever told him, but he stayed awake for almost forty-five minutes envisioning the ceremony, imagining what it would be like to attend class with the other kids, to do chores with them…to be one of them!

He couldn't wait to see Frances. How proud of him she would be! He drifted to sleep where these happy thoughts formed blissful dreams.

A knock at the door in the early morning woke him. It was Moses. "Augustine, today is your big day," he said. "Wash up and put on this robe and meet me in the front hall in fifteen minutes." He handed him a blood-red robe. "This is your confirmation robe." Jack noticed that Emmanuel was not in bed.

He met Moses in the front hall. "Where is everybody?" he asked.

"They are waiting for you."

Moses led him inside the barn. Everyone from the community stood in two lines opposite each other at each side. They wore their white robes, but with a red – it looked like a scarf – cloth draped over their shoulders.

Straight ahead, elevated on an altar made of wood built for the occasion, wearing a magnificent red robe with a red scarf with purple embroidery and an ornate hat that must have been two feet high, stood Abraham, his hands extended upward and outward.

Sarah stepped forward from the side and took Jack's arm and walked him toward the altar. When they reached it she let go of his arm and stepped aside. A beam of morning sunlight streamed though a crack in the roof and fell upon Abraham's face, making him look like God Himself. This reminded Jack of what he thought the beatific vision must look like.

In a booming voice, with his eyes raised to heaven, Abraham prayed. "Bring us, O Lord God, at our last awakening, into the house and gate of heaven, to enter into that gate and dwell in that house, where there shall be no darkness nor dazzling, but one equal light; no noise nor silence, but one equal music; no fears nor hopes, but one equal possession; no ends nor beginnings, but one equal eternity; in the habitations of thy majesty and thy glory, world without end."

"Augustine," Abraham said fixing his gaze on Jack. Then he paused and looked out over his people standing, mesmerized by his magnificence. "Since God could create everything out of nothing, he can also, through the Holy Spirit, give spiritual life to sinners by creating a pure heart in them."

"You have reached a crossroads in your spiritual journey toward an ultimate perfection yet to be obtained. Today you will choose the destiny God wills for you – you will receive the sacrament of confirmation to complete your baptismal grace."

"With his sacrament," he continued, "comes the special strength of the Holy Spirit as witness of Christ and the duty to spread and defend the faith by word and deed. Do you come here freely to accept this duty?"

Jack looked over at Sarah, who mouthed "I do." "I do," Jack said. Once Jack said this, Abraham raised his hands higher, closed his eyes, and recited a long prayer in Latin. Jack watched him, enchanted by the cadence of the words and the glow of Abraham's face.

Abraham touched Jack's cheek. "Pax tecum." All the members of the community, in unison, said, "and also with you."

Abraham put his hands on Jack's forehead and said: "All powerful God, Father of our Lord Jesus Christ, by water and the Holy Spirit you freed your sons and daughters from sin and gave them new life. Send your Holy Spirit upon them to be their helper and guide. Give them the spirit of wisdom and understanding; the spirit of right judgment and courage; the spirit of knowledge and reverence. Fill them with the spirit of wonder and awe in your presence."

Abraham then dipped his fingers in a chalice on a small table next to him and made the sign of the cross on Jack's forehead and said: "Accipe signaculum doni Spirtus Sancti. I sign thee with the sign of the cross and confirm thee with the chrism of salvation, in the name of the Father, and of the Son, and of the Holy Ghost."

"You are now a soldier of Christ. Recall each day that you have received the spiritual seal, the spirit of wisdom and understanding, the spirit of right judgment and courage, the spirit of knowledge and reverence, the spirit of holy fear in God's presence. Guard what you have received. God the Father has marked you with his sign; Christ the Lord has confirmed you and has placed his pledge, the Spirit, in your heart."

"God's word will be a lamp to your feet and a light to your path." Abraham then led Augustine past the community members lined on each side of him along the length of the barn. When they passed Frances, Jack glanced over and saw she was beaming. He noticed they all were. He couldn't remember ever being happier. He was now one of them.

CHAPTER 36

Missing Lilly

"I want to see Lilly," Gus said.

"No. I don't think that's a good idea."

"It's been eight months since I saw her. Why are you doing this to me? I'm her father!" Silence on the other end of the phone. Gus waited. He hadn't seen Lilly since Victoria took her to New Jersey at the beginning of February. He had asked many times to see her in the spring and summer and Victoria refused every time. She had only let him speak to her a half dozen times over the phone. How could the law dictate that a father never see and hardly talk to his daughter? Wasn't it enough that he had lost his son? To also lose his daughter was too cruel.

"I can't trust you," Victoria said at last. "I don't have to let you see her."

"Please," Gus pleaded. "Give me one weekend. That's all I ask."

A few seconds passed. Then: "I'm visiting Donna next month for Columbus Day weekend. I'm taking Lilly. It's a long weekend. Let me talk to her and maybe she can stay with you for one night." She called him back an hour later and told him Lilly could stay with him Saturday – sleep over Saturday night – and she would pick her up Sunday morning. Gus was shocked. He ordered an ice cream cake from Carvel – Lilly's favorite – and began thinking about things to do.

Victoria dropped Lilly off on a cool Saturday morning the following month, as promised, and without incident. "How have you been holding up?" was all she said. Gus told her he'd been okay. "I'll pick her up at nine tomorrow morning, okay?"

Lilly had changed physically. First, she was a few inches taller than when he had seen her in February. Her hair was cut short in a bob. She was ten now; still a little girl, but seemingly closer to a fourteen year old than a nine year old. This was revealed more in her attitude toward him than her appearance.

Once they entered the house, where Lilly hadn't been since the chaos after Jack's disappearance, Gus hugged her. She pulled away. "What's the matter?" he asked. "Is it too much to ask for a hug from my little girl?"

"Come on dad, stop," was all she said as she pulled away from him.

"How's school?"

"Fine."

"What's your favorite class?"

"I don't know." She walked into the living room and turned on the television. Gus followed her.

"What do you mean you don't know? Don't you have a favorite class?"

"Recess," she said, flipping through the channels.

"What about boyfriends? Any boy you have your eye on?" he teased. She shot him an annoyed look.

"Please forgive me if I just thought I'd try to find out what's new in my daughter's life. I haven't seen you in nearly a year, and you hardly ever talk to me on the phone." Lilly stared at the television. Gus tried again.

"What do you want to do today?" Lilly shrugged her shoulders. "Do you want to go for ice cream?"

"No."

"Do you play any sports?"

"I play soccer."

"Do you want to kick a ball around?"

"Do you have a soccer ball here?"

"No, but we can buy one."

Lilly shook her head. "It's too cold to play soccer."

"Well, what do you want to do? I'm not a mind-reader you know."

"I don't know," Lilly snapped.

Gus sighed. "How about going to Boston? We can get lunch at Quincy Market and go to the Museum of Science."

"Dad, I'm not five."

"You used to love the Museum of Science."

"That's when I was little."

"Oh, okay. We don't need to go to the Museum of Science. We can look at the shops, go to Downtown Crossing, look at clothes at Filene's Basement. I don't know. Maybe there's a Red Sox game."

"How far a drive is Boston?"

"Well, I thought we could take the train. It's about a forty-five minute train ride."

"Okay. Maybe Quincy Market and the shops," she said, turning her gaze to him momentarily before turning back to a *Brady Bunch* rerun.

"Good," Gus said. "Let's get ready then. Turn off the TV and put on your shoes and we'll catch the next train." They rode without speaking for the entire train ride. Gus tried to engage her at the beginning but gave up when it became clear to him she wasn't interested in opening up about her life in New Jersey. So he read the Boston Herald and she stared out the window.

The awkward silence continued while they walked from North Station to Faneuil Hall. "Hey, I want to show you something," Gus said. "Do you know any of the history of this country or Boston?"

She shrugged her shoulders. "I don't know."

He pointed at a red line painted on the sidewalk. "Do you know what this red line is?" She shook her head no. "It's the Freedom Trail. It marks how America gained its independence from Britain. I used to work down the street and sometimes I'd walk along it during lunch. It reminds me how lucky we are to be free." Lilly didn't say anything. She just stared, bored.

"Come on, it will be interesting. I'm sure you must have learned about the American Revolution in school." She shrugged her shoulders. They walked away from the steel structures piercing the Boston sky. Gus had looked down from the top of one of them every day not too long ago.

They walked away from the cluster of financial district office buildings to the North End, where worn-out red brick three-story apartment buildings were tucked amid Italian pastry shops, restaurants, and shoe stores. They walked up bustling Hanover Street, smells of baking bread and warm sewers hanging in the humid air, and then turned left into a red brick courtyard.

"Look," Gus said.

At the other end of the courtyard a white, wooden spire jutted out over the red brick buildings and leafy branches of the trees. "Do you know what that is?" Gus asked.

"What what is?" Lilly asked.

"That big white steeple."

"I don't know, some famous church I guess," she said.

"Yes, Old North Church. And that's Paul Revere," he said, pointing to a statue of a man on a horse. "That's the church where Paul Revere hung his signal lanterns in the steeple to warn America that the British were attacking."

"Oh," Lilly said. They followed the Freedom Trail to Quincy Market and Faneuil Hall.

"Faneuil Hall used to be the major trading post where boats delivered coffee, tea, fish and other supplies." Gus looked at her. She seemed interested in what he was saying so he continued. "The second floor served as a meeting hall where talk about King George's tyrannical treatment toward the colonies sparked the revolution for independence."

"Here, look at this," he said. He pointed to a copper plaque on the side of the building. *"This is Faneuil Hall, the cradle of liberty built and given to the town of Boston. Still used by free people, 1930."*

They continued on the red brick path until they came to Tremont Street and the Granary Burying Ground. "Look Lilly – this graveyard contains the last remains of three signers of the Declaration of Independence, Ben Franklin's parents, Paul Revere, and Samuel Adams. What do you think of that?"

"It's boring," she said. "Who cares about a graveyard and a bunch of dead people."

Gus told her how lucky she was to live in a country where she was free to do and dream so many things that little girls in other countries would never do. But Lilly wasn't listening and the only time she showed interest in anything else for the rest of the day was when he bought her new Adidas sneakers.

On the ride back, hypnotized by the clacking of the train on the tracks, she fell asleep. Her head bobbed and it fell onto his shoulder. She slept resting against him for the rest of the ride. And that moment erased the rest of the uncomfortable, dispiriting day and Gus smiled and his eyes welled a little.

When they got home he ordered pizza for dinner and they watched Barbara Mandrell and the Mandrell Sisters. In the morning Victoria came and took her away again after another strained goodbye hug.

Part III

CHAPTER 37

A Sighting

G us drove to the Billerica Mall to pick up some grass seed and fertilizer at Kmart. He found himself gravitating to the toy section. *Star Wars, Return of the Jedi* action figures filled the shelves. Luke Skywalker in his black Jedi uniform. Han Solo. The Ewoks. He pulled all the figures off the shelf and put them in his cart.

He had saved all of Jack's *Star Wars* figures and space ships and stored them in boxes in the attic. He would buy the new ones too, just in case. He pushed the cart down the aisle toward the lawn and garden section. Then he stopped. A few aisles down, a teenage boy held a pump squirt gun. Gus studied him. "Could it be?" he stammered to himself.

He looked around. He didn't see any parent. The boy walked around to the next aisle and looked at puzzles. Gus followed him. He looked again for adults with him. There were none. He walked closer. He stood five feet from the boy. He picked up an electronic game called Merlin and pretended to examine it while studying the boy.

The boy was taller, of course. His hair was longer. Gus tried to get a good look at his face. Then the boy turned and looked at him. "Jack?" Gus asked. The boy had a blank, uncertain look on his face and then he turned awkwardly to look at the puzzles again.

"Jack! It's me!" Gus said. "Don't you remember me?" he stood in front of the boy and held his face in his hands. "Look at me!" The boy jerked away. "I'm not Jack!" he yelled. "Get away from me!" Gus saw fear in his face.

"Jack! It's me! It's me! Daddy!" He pulled him close and enveloped him in a hug. "Oh Jack! I knew you were alive. I just knew it."

"Get off of me!" the boy cried. "I don't know what you're talking about."

"Listen," he said. "I know who you are. It's me, daddy. You don't have to be afraid anymore. Whoever took you, and whatever they did to you, it's over now. I'll protect you."

"I don't need you to protect me. I don't know what you're talking about," the boy said. "I'm not Jack and you're not my father. Please leave me alone!" He thrashed to break free of Gus's grip.

Gus was certain that this boy was Jack and that he was afraid to reveal himself because whoever had taken him had instilled some sort of terror in him.

They probably had brainwashed him too. Gus had read all about Stockholm Syndrome and how kids didn't want to leave their captors. He had to rescue Jack from them and make him remember.

"Get away from me," the boy yelled. "I'm not Jack! You've got the wrong person!"

"Jack, I don't know what you've been through but—"

"I'm not Jack!" the boy yelled. A woman pushing her cart past the aisle stopped and looked at them before moving slowly past.

"Where are they?" Gus asked. "Are they here?"

"Where are who?"

"The people who took you."

"Nobody took me. I told you, you've got the wrong person. I'm here with my mother."

"Where is she?" Gus grabbed the boy by the arm and pulled him down the aisle. The boy struggled to break free. "Where is she?" Gus yelled as he dragged the boy along with him looking down each aisle. The boy couldn't break his grip. He began thrashing and yelling.

"Jack, I know this is hard. They've really done a number on you. But don't you remember me? Don't you remember Lilly and Stacy and your mom?" Tears rolled down Gus's cheeks. Patrons of Kmart watched him drag the boy toward the registers. Nobody interfered until the manager of the store rushed up to them.

"What is going on here?" he demanded.

"This is my son Jack. He was kidnapped seven years ago. You might remember. I've finally found him and I'm looking for the son of a bitch who took him from me and wrecked my life." The boy pulled free and began to run.

"This man is crazy!" he yelled. "He is not my father and I am not Jack." Gus ran after him and caught him by the arm. He stumbled and fell onto the boy. They crashed into a display of soccer balls and knocked them over. The store manager yelled to a cashier to call the police, and a security guard yanked Gus off the ground and away from the boy.

A crowd gathered and a woman burst through the onlookers. "Andrew!" she yelled. She ran over to the boy. "What happened?" Andrew was shaking violently.

"This man tried to take me," he said. "He thinks I'm his son. He keeps calling me Jack."

"Which man?"

"Him!" The boy pointed at Gus, who was being held by the security guard. The woman, with all the fury of a tornado, marched up to Gus.

"What the hell are you trying to pull?" she said. "Who are you and why are you harassing my son?" Gus dug in. This boy was Jack and he had been brainwashed. He kept thinking about what he had read about Stockholm Syndrome. Jack's memories of him were suppressed. They had been blocked from his mind.

"That's my boy – Jack Delaney. He went missing seven years ago, and that's him!" He gestured at the boy, who continued shaking.

"No he is not!" the woman roared. "This is my son – Andrew Gray – and you better stay the hell away from him!" Gus looked from her face to the boy's. Then he glanced at the faces in the crowd. Angry faces, anger directed at him. Why were they mad at him? He was the one whose little boy was taken from him. He's the one who lost everything that Christmas afternoon – both his kids; his boy and then his little girl.

Now he had found his son and wanted him back and these people were looking at him like he was a criminal. "Don't you think I know my own son?" he yelled to the crowd. "That is my son!" he pointed to the boy, whose mother pulled him closer to her.

"The police will be here in a minute, Sir, and we'll sort this out," the store manager said.

Gus scrutinized the boy. A crack of doubt filtered to his conscious. Had he lost the ability to identify his son? Did he really know what his son looked like seven years later? Jack would be 14 now. He would have changed a lot, but he would still be Jack. Gus would still be able to see in his eyes the flash of familiarity, wouldn't he?

He remembered suddenly that Jack had a birthmark on the left side of his stomach. "Wait, lift up your shirt," he said.

"Why? Are you some kind of pervert?" the woman said.

"No, Jack has a birthmark on the left side of his stomach. Just lift up the shirt and I'll know." She lifted up the shirt. There was no birthmark. Gus became quiet. The crowd jeered at him. He looked at the woman – the boy's mother. He sighed, a deep, heavy exhale of air. The woman shook her head and yelled something at him, but he didn't hear what she said. He looked at the boy. He looked so much like Jack. He knew he screwed up. He began to walk over to the woman but the security guard restrained him.

"Please," Gus said. "I want to tell her I'm sorry. I had the wrong kid." He wanted to apologize and leave Kmart as fast as he could. The guard nodded okay and Gus walked up to the boy and his mother, who held him to her.

"I'm so sorry. I thought this was my boy who was taken from me seven years ago."

"You should be ashamed of yourself," she said. The boy didn't say anything. He clung to his mother. Gus began to speak and then stopped. He couldn't think of anything to say. Two police officers arrived. The Kmart manager scurried to them.

Gus watched the manager point at him and point at the boy and his mother as he explained what had happened. Then the cops walked to the boy and his mom and questioned them. After a few minutes one of them walked over to Gus. His badge said 'Batchelder.'

"How are we today, Mr. Delaney," he said in a condescending cop voice.

"Pretty crappy, actually."

"Do you want to tell me what happened?"

"I thought that boy was my son – my boy Jack. He disappeared seven years ago and we've never found him."

"I know," Batchelder said. "I'm familiar with the case. So what happened?"

"I was sure it was him. He looks just like him. I wanted to take him to the registers to call you —"

"Call me?"

"The police – and ask them to help me identify him."

"But the boy says he told you repeatedly that he was not your boy, that he was not Jack."

"I thought he was afraid. I thought he might have been brainwashed – Stockholm Syndrome or something."

"What syndrome?" Batchelder asked.

"Stockholm. It is when the captive becomes emotionally attached to the captor. Like with Patty Hearst."

"Yes, yes. Stockholm," Batchelder said. "But you've determined that the boy is not your son?"

"Yes," Gus muttered. "Jack has a birthmark on the left side of his stomach. I forgot about it at first. This boy doesn't have the birthmark." He looked over at the boy and his mom. She was still talking to the other cop. "I told them I'm sorry."

"She's pretty upset you know," Batchelder said. "She can press charges if she wants to."

"Press charges?"

"Yes – assault, kidnapping…yeah, she could press charges."

"Are you serious? I didn't assault the kid or kidnap him. What are you talking about?"

"According to the kid you grabbed his arm and forcibly dragged him against his will. I've got a dozen witnesses who saw the whole thing. The boy's got a gash on his arm he says he got from you knocking him into the display."

"But I wasn't kidnapping him! I asked him to take me to his mother. Ask him! I was trying to find the people I thought kidnapped my son and I really thought this boy was Jack and that he was too scared or mentally tortured during the past seven years to tell me."

"Mr. Delaney, that's quite an imagination you have. You can't just take the law into your own hands. Next time you think you've found Jack, call the police and let us handle it. It's our job, not yours."

Gus felt the blood rushing to his cheeks. "If you guys had done your job my son wouldn't still be missing!" Gus was tired of talking. He wanted to go home. Charge him with assault and kidnapping! Did this guy give a shit about what he'd gone through the past seven years?

Everybody had moved on and thought he should too. Time heals all wounds, they said. The passage of time had done little to heal his heart. The only change time brought was that the pain now was a dull ache, a chronic debilitating illness that he had learned to live with – not the searing agony that felt like a knife stabbing through his neck, a bone snapping, flesh tearing – that he had felt for the first six months of Jack's disappearance.

"You'd better watch your step now, Sir," Batchelder answered. "You're treading on thin ice here and it is not in your best interest to start bashing cops."

Gus looked him in the eye as he spoke. He clenched his fists at his sides. "Look," he said. "When my son disappeared, you treated me like a criminal. You accused me of kidnapping my own son. It was all over the newspapers. My life was hell when I lost my boy, and you made it worse. Then my ex-wife got full custody of my daughter because you cast a taint of suspicion in the judge's eyes about me regarding how Jack disappeared."

Gus continued, his voice rising. "All in all it's been a pretty crappy seven years. If you're going to arrest me because I thought I had finally found the one thing I've been looking for all this time, the only thing I have left, then go ahead and arrest me. Do your worst, and it couldn't begin to approach what I've been through already." Gus stood, his fists still clenched, the vein in his neck throbbing.

Batchelder thought for a moment. "Wait here," he said. He walked over to the woman. He said something to her and her mouth opened and her arms flailed as if she was conducting an orchestra. Her face was animated, angry. Batchelder spoke again and the woman answered again with active arms. Then she nodded and looked over at Gus – an unkind, unsympathetic look. Her mouth trembled and twitched.

Batchelder came over to Gus. "Look, the woman's pretty angry. She wants to press charges. I'm trying to talk her out of it, but she's not there yet. She agreed to let me bring you over to apologize and tell your side of the story. Think you can do that?" Gus looked at him sheepishly. He was sorry he had made the crack about the cops not doing their jobs.

"Yes," he said. Then, as Batchelder led him over to the woman: "Thank you."

"Just remember this next time you think that we're the bad guys, always out to get you." Gus nodded. The woman, squeezing her child's hand, waited for him to speak. Gus didn't say anything. He just stared at her and the boy. The resemblance to Jack was uncanny, but how could it have come to this, where he didn't recognize his son anymore?

He had thought this boy – this stranger – was Jack. He had been certain. Had he forgotten what Jack looked like? His mannerisms?

The thought scared him. What if Jack had come into his presence and Gus hadn't recognized him? How would he ever find him if he was out there and looked so different as to be unrecognizable? Batchelder nudged Gus and cleared his throat. "Mrs. Gray, Mr. Delaney wanted to apologize to you again," he said.

Gus woke from his thoughts. "Mrs. Gray," he began. "I cannot begin to tell you how sorry I am. It's just that…" He struggled with his words. "It's just that if you ever lost a child, you'd know why I did what I did." He looked at the boy, Andrew. Andrew stuck close to his mom and listened.

"I thought for sure that your boy was my Jack. He disappeared seven years ago and we've never found him. I know he's out there somewhere. I've lost everything since that day. My boy, my daughter, my career – everything I love. But I won't stop looking until I find him."

"I meant your boy no harm. I wasn't trying to kidnap him. I just wanted to know – to find the truth, that's all. Please understand. I meant no harm." His voice trailed.

"You really scared Andrew," she said.

"I know. I'm really sorry." The woman's facial expression softened.

"I'm sorry about your boy. His name was Jack?"

"Yes, Jack. He'd be 14 – he is 14. He's out there somewhere, I just know it."

"Well I hope you find him," she said. She turned to Andrew. She put her arm around his shoulder and pulled him close to her. "You've had quite an ordeal," she said to him. "You ready to go home now or do you want to stop first at Baskin Robbins?"

Andrew's face lit up. "Baskin Robbins!"

"Okay, okay," his mom said. She smiled. "Officer, can we go now? Are you through with us?"

"Yes ma'am, if you don't need us any further, you can go." She walked away and Gus issued another awkward apology and thanked her as she left. He looked at Batchelder.

"Okay, Mr. Delaney. Looks like you're free to go."

"Thank you."

"Just a word of advice. You're lucky that she changed her mind. You could have been in some trouble here and we don't want to see that. Next time promise me you'll contact us and not try to take matters into your own hands."

"Yes sir," Gus said. "I will." He left Kmart and his cart full of Star Wars figures in aisle five and slinked home, chastened, embarrassed…humiliated.

CHAPTER 38

Stacy Leaves

"Did you get the fertilizer?" Stacy asked when he walked through the door.

"No," Gus said and he went into the kitchen and opened a can of beer.

"I thought you were going to get seed and fertilizer and work on the lawn," she said.

Gus guzzled the beer. "What are you doing?" she asked.

"I had a little problem at Kmart."

"What do you mean?" she asked. Gus took another can of Old Milwaukee from the refrigerator and cracked it open. "Gus, why are you drinking like that? What happened at Kmart?"

"I don't want to talk about it," he said between gulps of beer.

"You never want to talk about anything," she said. "Why won't you tell me what happened at Kmart? Are you in trouble?"

"No, I'm not in trouble. I've just had a bad day and I don't want to talk about it, okay?" He walked out the front door and sat on the steps. He ran his hands over his face and through his hair. He was neither sad nor moved. Just numb. The breeze blew the sweet air of late spring and scattered pollen from the trees around the lawn in swirls. He thought about what might have been. What should have been.

Stacy came out fifteen minutes later. He was still sitting on the steps. "I can't do this anymore," she said. "It's been seven years since Jack disappeared. I know it's impossible to ask you...life goes on Gus. Look at me!"

Gus moved his hands from his face. Things had not been going well with Stacy for years, but for some reason she hung on. They had gotten married two years ago, but something was missing. Not something: Gus was missing. Stacy gave everything she had to the relationship, but Gus couldn't give back. They had tried to have children, hoping the gurgling and giggling of babies would fill the hole in their lives, but Stacy couldn't.

"What do you want from me?" Gus said.

"I want you to live. I want you to understand that there are other people in this world who love you, but you've pushed them all away. You're stuck trying to relive a life that doesn't exist anymore. Look around you. There are other things to live for besides Jack—"

"You cannot possibly understand what I've been through and you never will," he said. He got up to go back into the house. Stacy ran up and grabbed his arm.

"Oh no you don't," she said. He tried to pull away. "You run away every time someone tells you something you don't want to hear. Not this time. Sit down! You're going to listen to me. I do understand what you've gone through, because I've been at your side through all of it, every minute." Gus stood at the doorway.

"I was there when he disappeared; I was there for all the sleepless nights for months and years; I was there searching the swamp and the woods for him; for the court hearings; each time you buried your head in my chest and my blouse grew drenched with your tears. *So don't tell me I don't understand!*"

Gus didn't say anything. He walked into the house. She stormed in after him. "Gus, I don't love you anymore, not like before," she said. "I'm leaving." Gus kept walking to the kitchen.

"Please leave me alone," he said. "I just want to be left alone right now."

"Don't worry about that, you'll have plenty of time to be alone the way you're going. Gus, it's too late for me. I've tried and tried, but you've kept me at a distance for too long. This has been building in me for a long time now. Just listen to me – get help. Don't ruin the rest of your life because you can't get past the past."

And with that she turned around, walked out the door, and drove away. Gus walked out after her and watched the car drive down Kingsbury Lane, slow at the corner, and turn right on Carriage Road until it was out of sight.

He stumbled into his shed and pulled out his father's old weed-wacker, which looked like a golf club with a jagged blade at the end in the shape of a crocodile's snout. Gus took the blade and thrashed the long grass and weeds around the garden. He hacked and hacked until he dripped sweat and his arms hung heavy, exhausted.

He sat on the rusted swing set in the backyard for a few minutes in a daze. Then he walked toward the swamp. He entered the green woods, the oak and maple trees bursting with fresh leaves, birds chirping, a warm breeze blowing like sweet breath on his neck.

He walked along the path between the cattails. The same path on which Jack and Lilly had run so many hot summer days with the other kids – the same path that Bobby and Betsy, Seth and Greg, and Michael and Elizabeth continued to chase each other on, giggling, laughing, enjoying everything a child is entitled to enjoy.

Gus was denied the right of every parent to witness the exuberance and innocence – the happiness – of youth in his own children. Stacy was right; he *had* pushed people away. He knew the day she'd leave was coming. He was surprised only that she had stayed for as long as she did. He had taken her for granted. But he couldn't have acted any other way. Because she was wrong about one thing: she could never fully understand.

Every day – every minute of every hour of every day – for the past seven years he thought about Jack, how his whole life, his whole reason for living had been taken from him. But that wasn't the worst part. The most difficult part was not knowing what happened to him. Where was he? Was he running around in woods similar to this somewhere? Why didn't he know anything more seven years after he disappeared than he did seven days after? Not knowing gnawed at him.

He returned to the house and called his mother. "Yes, I know," Vera said. "She called me and told me."

"She did?"

"Yes. I'm sorry Gus. She's a nice girl. I love her like a daughter. You know that, don't you?"

"Yeah," he said. "I guess it just wasn't meant to be." He paced impatiently back and forth across the dining room, stretching the phone cord.

"I don't know about that, Gus. She talked to me all the time about you…trying to figure out how to make you happy, how to get you to enjoy life. She really loved you Gus. It was just too hard when you never responded to her. I know you're not over Jack, but you can't forget about all of us who are here and love you. Don't forget about what you do have."

Gus paced and fidgeted with the cord. "I know," he said. "I can't help it. Listen, I gotta go. I'll call you back later."

Gus still believed with his entire being and soul that Jack was alive. He didn't know why he was certain of this. Odds said that he was dead within the first two days of when he disappeared. But something deep inside Gus told him that his boy was alive and wondering why his father had never come to get him.

He would keep looking, no matter what anyone thought or said. He would keep looking until he found Jack – dead or alive. Only then could he rest; only then, perhaps, could he sleep through the night without medication. If this pushed people away, so be it.

Gus decided to walk around the neighborhood. He walked up Carriage Road and came to the path that led to Whale Rock. He walked down it. The path was overgrown with long grass and weeds. Gus hadn't been there in nearly five years. It looked different – smaller. Whale Rock looked smaller, and the ditch looked smaller – everything smaller and overrun with weeds and bushes.

He walked back and went to the swamp. He stumbled upon the old fort, which the kids no longer used as a clubhouse. Some of the boards were rotting and the roof was falling in. There was no lock on the door. He walked in. Some strips of the golden shag carpet, excess from Gus's living room, still lined the floor, along with a few blankets and pillows.

Gus thought of Jack's old blanket. He had never gotten it back from the police. He had begged and pleaded and hired a lawyer to try to get it back, but he was unsuccessful. Gus looked around the fort. There was also an old telephone, a *Star Wars* coloring book, and a weathered Winnie the Pooh bear sitting on a shelf, both eyes plucked out. Jack had had a Winnie the Pooh bear just like it. Gus took the bear and continued walking aimlessly in the woods.

CHAPTER 39

Lilly's Last Visit

G us sat in the kitchen, shirt soaked, drops of sweat dripping on the floor, and drank a tall glass of Country Time lemonade. It had been a month since Stacy left. He had called her a dozen times asking her to come back, asking for another chance. "I gave you seven years' worth of chances," she had said. "I can't give you any more."

During their last phone call she said simply, "I have to move on with my life." Since then, she stopped returning the messages he left on her answering machine.

Gus realized how much she had meant to him, how patient and understanding she had been long after he deserved it. *Love knows not its own depth until the hour of separation*, he had seen written on a tea bag or something. How true. He was alone now. His father had died of prostate cancer two years ago. His mother visited every couple of weeks, but most of the time he was a solitary figure sitting on his couch, drinking a beer, or calling the missing children's center and FBI offices to ask about new leads. Sweating in the kitchen, his thoughts turned to Lilly.

He last saw her at his father's funeral. The school photographs of her that Victoria sent each spring were of a girl in the early stages of becoming a woman, a girl he didn't know anymore. He walked into her bedroom. He had kept it just as it was when she was there the Christmas Jack disappeared. Time stood still, not only in Jack's room, but Lilly's as well.

Her childhood effects lay displayed as if her room was a time capsule from 1977, an abandoned museum with Gus as the curator. Raggedy Ann, Winnie the Pooh, Strawberry Shortcake and Blueberry Muffin sat on the dresser, along with a black jewelry box with pink roses painted on the side. The same flower quilt covered the bed and the same white wallpaper with pink and blue daisies covered the walls.

Gus returned to the kitchen and dialed Victoria's number.

"Hello?"

"Victoria, it's Gus. I want to see if Lilly can come to visit this summer."

"What? For the rest of the summer? What are you talking about? I don't think so Gus."

"No, not the whole summer. A couple weeks." He paused. "A weekend." He winced as soon as he said this – he wanted a week, at least, preferably two, but he hadn't spent more than two weeks with her total in the last seven years, so he didn't know why he'd expect something to change now.

"I don't know. Lilly's pretty booked this summer. She has riding camp and we're going to France for two weeks in August and—"

"Riding camp? What do you mean? Horses?"

"Yes horses. She's been going to this camp for years."

"I had no idea."

"Haven't you ever asked her what she does?"

"Don't start. I hardly ever talk to her and you've conditioned her to despise me so that the couple of times a year I do talk to her, she clams up and doesn't want to tell me anything," he yelled. "And it's nice that I pay for riding lessons and trips to France but I can't be involved in my daughter's life."

"Listen Gus, I just don't think it would be the best thing for Lilly."

"What are you talking about? Lilly needs a father and I want to be involved."

"She has Roger. He's—"

"Roger is not her father!" Gus screamed. "I'm her father! Don't you ever say that again!"

"I know you are her father, you idiot. But you haven't been in her life for years because you haven't been…stable enough. And Lilly doesn't want to visit you."

"Give me a fuckin' break. I haven't been in her life for years because you took me out of it. Listen, I just want a weekend. I'll pay for her flight. Please. Let me talk to her. I'm her father for Christ's sake. It's not right to keep her away from me."

"Listen to yourself. Why should I let her go to you when you talk to me like that? I don't have to. You know what the judge said."

Gus began chewing the phone cord. He wanted to reach through the phone and rip her head off. She held all the power. Getting angry was fruitless. He had to kiss her ring if he had any chance.

But he couldn't. "Yeah, you remind me all the time what the judge said. You can't keep her away from me! I don't give a fuck what the judge says – she's my daughter!"

"Are you through, because I've had enough of this conversation," Victoria said.

"Please…" Gus's voice cracked. "I miss my little girl. I've got nothing. Please let me see her, just for a weekend." He paused for a few seconds. "Stacy left me."

"Oh," she said. "I'm not surprised." Gus immediately regretted telling her. "Let me talk to Lilly about it and let me see if there is a weekend that works and I'll call you back, okay?" she said.

"Okay…thanks," he sputtered.

"You're welcome," she said in a condescending tone. "I'll call you in a couple of days." Then she hung up.

"God I hate her!" Gus yelled. He slammed the phone into the receiver.

Victoria called a week later and agreed to let Lilly stay over the third weekend in August. Gus had given up hope that it was going to happen at all. She said she planned to come up to visit Donna and would allow Lilly to stay a night. She repeated that Lilly didn't want to stay with him but she told her to. She must have initially thought Gus wouldn't be able to accommodate her largesse on such short notice. But the short notice didn't bother Gus; he had no plans.

The day arrived and Gus waited on the front step. They were driving up and due to arrive at lunch time. It was 12:05 p.m. He saw Betsy O'Connor riding her bike toward him on the street.

"Hey Betsy," he yelled. "Can you come here for a second?" Betsy wobbled up to his mailbox and stopped at the end of the driveway. Gus walked down to her.

"Hi Betsy. Lilly is coming this weekend and I want to do some stuff with her but I don't know what sixteen year-old girls like to do. Do you have any ideas? What *do* sixteen year-old girls like to do?"

"I don't know," Betsy said. "I like to go to the Burlington Mall with my friends and see movies. We talk about boys we like or music."

Great, Gus thought. I don't think she's going to want to hang out with me. "Anything else?" Gus asked.

Betsy thought for a moment. "Nope, that's about it."

"Okay. Thanks. Tell your mom and dad hello." Betsy said she would and continued biking along Kingsbury Lane. Then she disappeared down Carriage Road. Gus thought. He wouldn't take her to Boston again. Maybe the beach. Or Canobie Lake Park. That was close, only a half-hour away. They'd go there.

Sweat dripped from his chin while he sat, smoking. His shirt clung to his chest. He hadn't seen Lilly in two years. What did she look like? Sixteen years old. God. Not a little girl anymore. He had missed her growing up. He hoped this visit wouldn't be awkward like it was last time. Would she hug him? Shake his hand? Just say hello?

He watched a car drive down Carriage Road and slow and turn onto Kingsbury. He leaned forward. It passed. He wiped his brow and looked next door where Eleanor Schroot pulled weeds from the flower bed along the front of her house. She had stopped coming by to chat and bring over baked banana bread and lasagna five years ago. She had stopped inviting him over for dinner about the same time.

None of the neighbors bothered with him anymore. Oh they'd say hello when they saw him in the yard, which was not often, but they continued jogging or walking the dog or biking and didn't stop to say anything more or ask how he was doing, like they used to. They now took the Beatles song as their mantra with him: Hello, Goodbye.

Gus stood to walk back into the house when another car rambled down Carriage Road and turned onto Kingsbury Lane. It slowed in front of his driveway and pulled in. Gus smoothed his shirt, patted it down over his slight paunch and ran his hand through his hair. He began to walk down the steps and then stopped.

The car idled in the driveway. The doors remained closed. He saw Victoria and Lilly behind the glass of the windshield arguing. Lilly kept shaking her head from side to side. Gus stood on the step and slowly moved to the next one. Then he stopped again. And watched. Why didn't she turn off the engine? He walked to the passenger side and waved to Lilly. She scowled and waved back. Gus opened the door. "Hey, aren't you coming out?"

Lilly turned to Victoria. "Mom," she whined.

"Go on," Victoria said. "I'll be back to pick you up tomorrow afternoon."

"Fine," Lilly said and she got out of the car. Gus moved to hug her. He leaned in and put his arms around her and she stood like a lump and didn't make any effort to hug him back.

"What's wrong?" Gus asked.

"Nothing."

"I can't believe I haven't seen you in two years," he said.

"Yeah," she mumbled. She glanced over at Mrs. Schroot, who was watching them as she weeded.

"Let me look at you." He held her by the shoulders and turned her chin from Mrs. Schroot to him. "Wow, you've gotten tall," he said.

"You've got a beer belly," she said.

"What are you talking about?" Gus looked down at his stomach. "You haven't seen me in two years and that's the first thing you do – insult me?"

"No," she said. "But you have a beer belly because you drink too much."

"I see you take after your mother. This isn't from beer, it's from eating too much ice cream."

"Yeah right."

"Any other comments you have?"

She examined his face. "You smell like cigarettes. You're losing your hair. That's from smoking too much. Why don't you take care of yourself?"

"Great, nice to see you too." He felt the crown of his head and peered into the passenger window to see Victoria's expression. He turned back to Lilly. "Well, you're right. I should take better care of myself, but I didn't want to see you just so you could tell me I have a beer gut, I'm going bald, and I smell bad. How would you like it if the first thing I said to you was that you must be hitting your gawky years or that you look goofy with braces?"

Lilly turned and went back into the car and slammed the door shut. "Shit," Gus muttered. "Why the hell did I say that?"

"Mom!" Lilly said from inside the car. "Why do I have to stay with him?"

"Lilly, I didn't mean you were gawky, I meant *if* you were gawky and I said that, you wouldn't think it was very nice. Well, that's how I feel when you say those things about me. I was just trying to make a point. You're beautiful, you really are."

"All you said when you saw me was, 'Wow, you're so tall'"

"Geez, I wasn't saying it as a bad thing. Do you think you're too tall? I was just saying you've grown in the past two years. Why are you acting like this? What did I do?"

"Nothing," she said.

"Go on," Victoria urged. Lilly reached over the back seat and grabbed a pink backpack and then opened the door and trudged toward the house, not saying a word. Victoria remained seated in the driver's side. The car continued to idle. Gus walked over to her window.

"What's wrong with her?" he asked.

"She doesn't want to stay with you. I told you over the phone."

"Why not?"

"She doesn't know you. She just feels funny. You know how kids can be around strangers."

"I'm not a goddamned stranger! I'm her father!" he yelled. "Of course she doesn't know me!" he continued, leaning across her window. "You've kept her away from me for seven years." He noticed Mrs. Schroot still kneeling in the dirt but not weeding as vigorously as she was listening. He didn't care. Maybe she'd see what he'd been dealing with all this time.

He tried to collect himself. He couldn't blow it now. He knew Victoria could change her mind at any moment and take Lilly back with her.

"You wonder why I keep her from you?" she shouted. "Because you're filled with rage. I mean, look at you. You can't control your temper. You steam like a tea kettle every five minutes, and that's why you can't keep a job or a relationship."

Gus clenched his fists. He was tired of her making him out to be a no-good drunk to his daughter. "The reason I don't have a job is because I've chosen to spend my time trying to find Jack."

Victoria looked toward the house. "And what's your excuse with Stacy?" she asked.

"None of your business."

"It's my business if you want my daughter to stay here."

"I told you, Stacy and I broke up and that's all I have to say about it. You happy?"

"She finally saw the light and left you, you mean."

"Fuck you."

"That's nice. It's no wonder she left you. I know you probably drove her away with your temper."

"No, the only time I have a temper seems to be when you're involved. You say I'm full of rage?" he said, stepping closer to her, hovering over the door. "I wouldn't be so full of rage if my only son hadn't been taken from me and if I hadn't then been accused of harming him in all the newspapers. I wouldn't be so full of rage if you hadn't taken my only daughter away to New Jersey and now she hates me because all she knows about me is whatever you've told her in the past seven years."

"So am I full of rage? Yeah, because of you and what you've done to me." He pointed his finger in her face.

"Get your hand out of my face!" Victoria yelled, and she swatted his hand away. "Forget it! I can't leave Lilly here with you like this," she said. "Lilly, get in the car!"

"What do you mean?" he said. "We had a deal. You promised Lilly could stay with me this weekend. I have a bunch of things planned. Come on Victoria! You can't do this to me again! Please," Gus pleaded. "I haven't seen her in two years."

"She doesn't want to stay. Get in the car," she said again to Lilly, who had been standing next to the passenger door holding her backpack. Lilly opened the door and got in. Gus stuck his head in Victoria's window and spoke across Victoria to Lilly.

"Please Lilly," he said. "Don't you want to stay with me? I was going to take you to Canobie Lake Park. We can go on the rides and play games in the arcade, win a stuffed bear, get a nice lunch. Please, just stay. We'll have fun." Lilly just looked at him and looked at her mom and didn't say anything.

Victoria put the car in reverse and began to back down the driveway. "Stop! Wait!" Gus yelled. He reached for the door handle but she locked it just as he pulled and the door didn't open. He reached inside the car to unlock the door from the inside and Victoria began to roll up the window.

"Get away!" she yelled. "She doesn't want to see you! You're never going to see her again."

"What have you told her?" Gus yelled. As he pulled up the lock and swung the door open, she dug her sharp nails into his arm and gouged his flesh, then pulled, tearing his skin. Gus screamed and grabbed a handful of her hair at the back of her head and slammed her face into the steering wheel to get her to stop.

Lilly screamed and cried. "Stop!" she yelled. The car, still in reverse, continued rolling backward. Blood gushed from Victoria's nose and lips. Woozy, she was no longer steering. Gus saw a car coming down Kingsbury Lane as Victoria's car rolled down the driveway toward the road.

"Hit the brake!" he yelled. He tried to climb in. Victoria, like an angry drunk, swatted him in the head and fought him off. She swore at him. Blood continued pouring from her nose. Lilly screamed and cried.

"Hit the brake!" Gus yelled again. He reached his leg in to try to press the brake but Victoria's attempts to gouge his arm again kept him from reaching it. Then she suddenly slammed her foot on the brake and the car jolted to a stop. She sprawled forward against the wheel and Gus crashed into the dash. Blood from her nose sprayed everywhere. Then, just as abruptly, she took her foot off the brake and slammed on the gas.

The car lurched down the driveway, swerved to the left, crashed into the mailbox, and careened into the street. Gus heard brakes screech and then felt the smash and skid at impact and heard glass breaking and the crunch of metal. Then everything was still.

CHAPTER 40

The Accident

Gus lay face down on the pavement next to the curb where the impact of the crash had thrown him out of the car and onto the ground ten feet away. He had banged his head. He was dizzy. Victoria's car rested diagonally, off-kilter, on Kingsbury Lane. He couldn't see the other car, but in a few seconds he saw sneakers walking from the back of Victoria's car toward the driver's side.

The sneakers stopped at the door. "Oh God…call 911!" a man's voice said. Gus pulled his face from the pavement and spat out the sand and gravel from his lips. He looked up. The man was not facing him, not talking to him. Gus rested his cheek back on the road.

"What have I done," he murmured. He watched the sneakers walk towards him.

"Hey buddy, are you okay?" the voice said to him.

"Yes. I think so," Gus said. "I banged my head…I think on the road." He started to push himself up. The man grasped his arm to help him. Gus got to his feet and he felt so lightheaded that he fell to his knee.

"Whoa, why don't you stay down here and don't move. We've called an ambulance," the man said.

"What about Lilly?" Gus asked.

"Which one is Lilly?"

"The girl. She's my daughter. She was in the passenger seat."

"She seems fine," the man said. "She's standing over there." He gestured to the Schroot's yard. "But the woman – is she your wife? She looks like she's in rough shape. There's a lot of blood and she's not too with it."

"She's not my wife," Gus interjected.

"Oh," the man said. "Well, anyway, we called an ambulance." He started to walk back to the car to check on Victoria and then stopped and turned to Gus. "What happened anyway? Did she have a seizure or something? An epileptic fit?"

"No, she didn't have a seizure." Gus stood, wobbled, and walked over to the car. "Victoria, I'm so sorry," he said. He held her hand. "Are you okay?"

"Get the hell away from me!" she screamed. Her face was covered in blood.

What did I do? he thought. He looked over the roof of the car to find Lilly. He saw her standing on the Schroot's lawn, crying. Eleanor Schroot consoled her. Bud Schroot had also come out. Eleanor seemed to be explaining to him what had happened. She pointed to the car and then to Gus, and then pointed down the street where the other car had come from.

Gus looked at Lilly's shoulders heaving as she cried and he buried his head in his arms on the roof of the car. *I've just broken the nose of the mother of my daughter,* he thought. He had slammed her head into the steering wheel as hard as he could. It was a spontaneous reaction to the immense pain. He didn't think of consequences – he didn't think at all, he just reacted blindly.

He had never laid a hand on a woman like that before. Even when he felt such hatred toward her, he had never hit her. Her face was a bloody mess and his daughter was scared to death of him. He could see it in her eyes. *She was afraid of him.*

He lifted his head off the car roof and saw that the people who lived across the street had come out of their house and walked over to the Schroot's. The Mahoney's were walking over too; they must have heard the loud crash. Then sirens blared in the distance.

Gus hobbled over to Lilly. She shrank in Eleanor Schroot's arms when Gus approached. He fell to his knees and held out his arms. "Lilly, I'm so sorry. I didn't mean it." She clung to the old woman and sobbed. "Please Lilly. Please know I wouldn't do anything to intentionally hurt your monther. It was—"

"Yes you would," Lilly blurted. "You hate her."

"I don't hate her, Lilly. I really don't," he lied. It was no use lying though. He did hate her, and Lilly knew it. But he wouldn't ever hurt a woman. He thought of his mother. She would be disappointed in him. She didn't raise him that way. She didn't raise a son who would smash a woman's face so hard that it would be covered with blood, no matter what the circumstances were. Mrs. Schroot had a sad, dismayed look on her face. She frowned and her eyes looked alternately from the ground to him; heavy eyelids, sad eyes.

The sound of the sirens grew louder and within a minute an ambulance, followed by two police cars and a fire truck, barreled down Carriage Road and screeched onto Kingsbury Lane.

It was quite a scene now in front of Gus's house – two cars crumpled in the middle of the street, a woman with blood covering her face sitting groggy in one of them, a little girl standing, hysterical, on the neighbor's lawn twenty feet away, and enough flashing lights to light up a disco.

Two paramedics rushed to Victoria's side and began tending to her. Gus stood on the sidewalk. A fat cop labored to climb out of the closest cop car and surveyed the scene. Gus recognized him immediately. It was that goddamn Goddard.

He sauntered up to Gus. "Well Mr. Delaney, what happened here?" Gus thought he detected a faint smile creep into Goddard's face as he said this, as if he enjoyed Gus's misfortunes.

"We had an accident," Gus said.

"An accident, huh? Is it an accident like the one you had at Kmart a couple of months ago?" he sneered. "Oh yeah, I know all about that. You seem to have quite a few more accidents in your life than the average guy. I'm surprised she didn't press charges, dragging her son away like that, scaring him to death." Gus didn't answer.

Goddard leaned in close and spoke in almost a whisper. "You're lucky it was Batchelder there and not me. I'd have told her to press charges." He pulled back, a smirk smeared on his face. "Well," he continued, "tell me how this one happened? Is that Mrs. Delaney in the car?" The other cop walked over and now stood beside Goddard. Gus didn't recognize him.

"Hello, Mr. Delaney," he said. *Jesus*, Gus thought, *all the cops know me.* He scratched his head.

"Yes, that's Victoria. She's not Mrs. Delaney. She re-married five years ago. She was backing out of the driveway and –" The man from the other car – Sneakers – came over. He had been talking to the paramedics but now stood next to Gus and listened. Gus continued. "She was backing out of the driveway and she hit the gas instead of the brake and swerved into the mailbox and out into the street and hit this man's car."

"What caused her to hit the gas instead of the brake?"

"I don't know," Gus said.

"Can you tell us what happened?" Goddard said to Sneakers.

"Yes, I was driving down Kingsbury Lane here and this car flew out of the driveway and slammed into me. I tried to swerve out of the way but it came at me so fast."

Goddard turned to the other cop. "Can you ask this man some questions, get all the information?" Then he turned back to Gus. "You just wait here Mr. Delaney while I talk to your ex-wife, your daughter, and your neighbor to see what happened."

"I told you what happened," Gus said.

"I want to hear it from them," he said, and he turned to walk away.

"Asshole," Gus said under his breath. Goddard stopped abruptly and turned around.

"What did you say?"

"Nothing. I was talking to myself," Gus said.

"You better watch your step Mr. Delaney." Then he turned again and walked to Victoria, who was sitting on the Schroot's lawn being tended by paramedics. Lilly and Eleanor Schroot stood next to her.

Gus watched Goddard interrogate them all. He saw Mrs. Schroot point over to him with an angry look in her eyes when answering a particular question. The other cop remained with Gus and Sneakers. "So tell me again what happened," he said. Gus explained that Victoria was supposed to leave Lilly for the night but she got angry and changed her mind.

Gus had pleaded with her to let Lilly stay and she began backing out while his head was in the window talking to Lilly. She hit the gas hard and the car lurched back and smashed into the other car.

"It looks like she broke her nose," the cop said. "How'd that happen?"

"Well after she hit the gas she slammed on the brake and her head flew forward and her face hit the steering wheel. Then she hit the gas again and smashed into the other car."

Goddard came back after about fifteen minutes. "It seems like you weren't telling me the whole truth Mr. Delaney. Both your wife—"

"She's not my wife."

"I don't give a fuck who she is," Goddard said. "Both she and your daughter say you caused the accident by trying to take over the car. They say you slammed her head into the steering wheel. Your neighbor says she saw the whole thing. Now we have three people telling me one thing and you telling me something different."

"Do you want to tell me what really happened, because now we're talking assault and battery and that's pretty serious."

This was a repeat of seven years ago, Gus thought, and he didn't like it. He began speaking quickly, his heart beating like a hammer against his chest. "Listen, I told you the truth. I told you we got in an argument because she was supposed to leave Lilly and she started backing up while I was still – I was leaning in the window talking to Lilly. She drove off and I yelled at her to stop so we could talk."

"Talk?" Goddard said. "And what about you slamming her head into the steering wheel? Is that part of the talk?"

"I didn't mean to. She dug her nails into my arm and—look!" he said, showing Goddard the gouges in his bleeding arm. "She tore the flesh off and I just reacted to get her to stop."

"So you broke her nose because she scratched you because you were trying to take over the car."

"You haven't changed at all," Gus said. "You're still the condescending asshole you always were."

"Mr. Delaney, you better watch it now, if you know what's good for you." Goddard snapped.

"Fuck you."

Goddard stepped forward and got right in his face. "I don't like guys who get their kicks from beating up women." His breath stunk. "And I don't like guys who kill their kids and get away with it."

No sooner had these words left his lips than Gus punched him as hard as he could in the nose. He snapped. A blind madman. His punch knocked Goddard to the ground and before he even landed Gus jumped on top of him and began wailing away at his head, screaming profanities much like Victoria during her fit in the car.

Suddenly from somewhere someone sprayed something in his eyes. It burned like acid and blinded him. He shouted in pain. Then someone was on top of him and something hard, like a baseball bat, hit him in the head. He felt his arms pulled behind his back and cuffed.

Then he was yanked off the ground and dragged over to the police car. He looked over at the Schroot's lawn and saw Lilly looking at him. Hatred was in her eyes. Hatred and disgust. A hand pressed down on his head and pushed him into the back seat of the police cruiser.

At the jail a young cop processed him. Took his fingerprints and then had him sit in a chair for his mug shot. A sign on the wall behind the camera said, *Smile.* Gus scowled.

He was thrown into a cell about the size of a walk-in closet. It had a metal bench attached to the wall. The only items in the white, antiseptic cell were an aluminum sink and toilet. He wondered if the bench was supposed to serve as a bed or if it was a holding cell and he'd be moved to a cell with a bunk bed like he saw in movies. He discovered later that the metal bench was his bed.

One of the cops came in and told him he was allowed to make one phone call. He called his mother. When he told her what had happened, he could hear the disappointment in her voice – not worry or concern. Disappointment was what he heard.

"I'm going to need a lawyer," Gus said to her. He looked over at the young cop, a kid who looked like he was barely out of high school, sitting at a desk watching him. Gus turned away and spoke quietly. "A good one."

Vera Delaney bailed him out. The prosecutor recommended withholding bail, reasoning that Gus, having no family, was a flight risk. The judge didn't impose that on him, however, and allowed him to stay at home if he didn't leave the state.

At the trial, Gus's lawyer argued that Gus, under great duress at that moment, was provoked by Captain Goddard. He argued that Gus was not in command of his ability to reason and was not fully responsible for his actions, much like an insane person. His actions were not premeditated.

The trial lasted three days. "I have come to a decision," the judge said. "It was a fairly easy decision, a straightforward case in my opinion. I find the defendant—" Gus closed his eyes and inhaled "—guilty on the count of assaulting Lieutenant Richard Goddard and guilty on the count of assault and battery of Victoria Bozzolo on August 20, 1984." He heard his mother behind him let out a small cry.

Gus blew his breath out in a huge exhale and opened his eyes. "I sentence Mr. Gus Delaney to 36 months in the Billerica House of Correction." His mother was crying now. He did not turn around to try to comfort her. He couldn't bear to see the sadness he knew was etched on her face.

Her only son had become an alcoholic, unemployed, flabby, pasty, balding, single and alone middle-aged man, a man who couldn't move beyond December 25, 1977. Now, to add to that list and finally reach the Death Valley of his descent, he would add the title convicted felon.

His life had reached the deepest, darkest caves of suffering and humiliation in the span of seven years. If Jack's disappearance was the greatest suffering he had ever endured, going to jail for assaulting a woman and a cop was the greatest humiliation.

The bailiffs led him out in handcuffs. He glanced at his mother, who clung to his sister and wept. She had aged. His sister stood expressionless, gazing into the ether in a trance. He saw Victoria and Lilly standing toward the back of the courtroom. The sight of Lilly caused his legs to nearly give way.

His sadness and disappointment in himself turned first to embarrassment and then to anger and hatred toward Victoria and life in general. She had brought Lilly in to witness her father's final humiliation, escorted in handcuffs on his way to jail for three years. Victoria wore the same condescending sneer on her face he had seen a hundred times before. He couldn't believe she would kick him so hard when he was down in the mud already. She would have this final triumph and she would revel in the completeness of her victory.

Gus knew he would never see his daughter again. He would never be granted access to her by Victoria, and she would never let her visit him in jail. Even though she'd be eighteen years old by the time he got out and able to make her own decisions, the look on her face conveyed all the contempt toward him that he had ever seen from another human being. She would not want to see him.

He had harbored hopes that once Lilly reached eighteen and had the ability to act on her own she'd slowly make time in her life for her father and want to see him. He knew at this moment that he had lost both of his children forever.

CHAPTER 41

A New Sensation

Jack rested his foot on the pitchfork. He smiled and his eyes followed Frances as she walked past the garden carrying the scib of eggs to the house. She was smiling too, he saw. He watched the curl of her blond hair peeking out of her bonnet, the sun gleaming on her face. A face full of joy. He found himself looking at her breasts and tiny waist then caught himself, ashamed that he was looking at her this way.

He glanced around quickly to see if anyone had seen him. Moses was watching him from the hammock on the other side of the lawn. He returned to the barn and pitched the hay with renewed vigor. He noticed that a rush of excitement flowed through his body – that he became hard – whenever he saw Frances lately. It made him uncomfortable. He had to stop this lust in his heart.

Suddenly a loud voice behind him interrupted his thoughts. "Hey Brother Augustine!" Moses said. He had snuck up behind Jack and startled him. "I would like a word with you." He had his hands in his pockets and he rocked back and forth from the heels to the balls of his feet.

He remained silent for a while as he worked a blade of grass in his mouth and rubbed his bearded jaw. "I've been watching you. I see the way you look at Frances," he began. "Your sin may be hidden from others, but it is not hidden from God, and it is not hidden from me."

"What do you mean, Brother Moses?" Jack asked, returning to his fork to pitch the hay. Moses walked over and grabbed the pitchfork.

"I want to warn you that you better not get too close to her. Surely you must know that she has been chosen for Emmanuel for many years? Abraham himself decreed the match. So she is betrothed to him." His eyes narrowed. "Do you understand this, Augustine?"

Augustine had never heard that Frances was promised in marriage to Emmanuel. She had never spoken of it. In fact she had never spoken of marriage at all when referring to her own life. Nor had Emmanuel. Jack was angry at himself for his indiscretion. He knew the devil was tempting him and his will had to be stronger to fight the temptation.

"I am sorry if you have misconstrued my looks of only the purist form of love for Frances, the same heavenly love with which I look upon all our brothers and sisters here," Jack said. He smiled a full, warm smile. "I did not know that Frances was betrothed to Brother Emmanuel, but you needn't worry Moses. I couldn't be more pleased for her or for Emmanuel and wish for a most blessed union between the two."

Moses cocked his head and his eyes narrowed as he examined Augustine's facial expression. "Well then. Tis good. But I warn you; you should not be so intimate with the members of the fairer sex, particularly one who is to be another man's wife. You should practice some distance in your relations with Frances."

Jack continued to smile. "Indeed I will," he said. "Thank you so kindly for your good words. I shall pray to thank God for granting Frances such an auspicious gift. I shall also pray for God's guidance in my endeavors with her so they may be deemed appropriate and worthy in the eyes of the community and the Lord."

"Well spoken Augustine. With much reflection you may live up to your austere namesake yet." With that, he turned and walked back to the hammock to read the catechism. Jack's smile disappeared. He laid down the pitchfork and walked to the beach, along the sand to the jetty.

He hopped from rock to rock until he got to the end, and then he sat and stared at the sea. He looked across the horizon and up at the endless sky, bright blue. The news of Frances's betrothal troubled him. He wondered if she knew and didn't tell him. She always confided her deepest thoughts to him.

Perhaps this promise of her nuptial life to another had been withheld from her. He didn't recall any particular closeness or affection between her and Emmanuel that might have hinted that they were bonded together for the remainder of their time on Earth. She was always kind to him, but she was kind to everyone, and didn't seem excessively so toward him. For his part, Emmanuel didn't speak of her much.

Jack searched his soul for the source of the tormented thoughts now swimming in his head. Did Abraham have someone picked out for him? There was nobody else in the community whom Jack could view as his future wife; but he had never really thought about having a wife. He was young, just 16, and marriage, if that was God's will, was far in the future.

What he pondered now was that he must distance himself from Frances. He knew he had become far too intimate with her – and she with him. Their smiles to each other had taken on a new character lately – he knew not what, but he *felt* it was different than before, and that it was immoral.

He thought back to when he first arrived; how he had been so scared. If not for her, he would never have gotten confirmed. He had wanted to be confirmed for many reasons – to be accepted into the community, to be closer to God…but when he was honest with himself, he knew he wanted to be confirmed most of all to please Frances and win her affection. In her he confided his fears and she in turn guided him and comforted him. He became gloomy if she didn't respond to him with her usual cheer, or if for some reason he didn't see her after class during chores.

He was supposed to give himself entirely to God, but she had some grasp on him. He needed to break free of it, and he decided on the rocks that he would do just that. He prayed to God to give him the strength to let go of Frances.

He recalled the lesson he had been taught by Sarah on his first day of class and in every subsequent class: that he must be prepared to abandon all earthly pleasures and relationships; leave everything behind — homes, farms, parents, relatives, friends, children, brothers, sisters, jobs, and ambitions — and set out with God on His mission.

He had left childish things behind – his childhood home and childhood father and mother. It had been hard at the time, he missed them terribly for many months; but he didn't think of them much or miss them anymore. No, he was thankful that he had left his childhood sins behind.

Looking out at the sea, he committed himself now to do the same with Frances. "God will tell you what to do; you need only listen humbly and His purpose will be revealed to you," he said out loud to himself.

Yes, he must be prepared to leave Frances behind if he was going to truly devote himself to God. He thought about his parents and Lilly, a fleeting thought, as he followed the flight of a seagull. He sometimes didn't remember if they had been real or just a recurring dream. It was hard to tell the difference. They were just fuzzy pictures in his mind.

He remembered that he had left something – whether real or in a dream. And that he had cried every night for a long time – the tears were real. But he knew it was God's will that he had left them and joined Abraham to learn to live a holy life. He knew his old life, the one he could barely remember anymore, had been sinful and selfish and would have led him to unhappiness and ultimately pushed him far away from God's grace.

He didn't think about his old life much anymore. Through the years he thought mostly about the joy he felt when he was with Frances, and how much he cherished the afternoon walks to the pond with her. He thought about improving each day, his woodworking, and living a life devoted to God. And he thought about the beauty of the ocean and the woods surrounding the compound.

He watched the seagull hovering in the wind, then swooping and dipping, then flapping and gliding, until it disappeared in the horizon. He tried to form a more concrete image of the people that had haunted his dreams. A pretty woman in furs. A tall, strong man who built forts for him once upon a time. A little girl with black hair.

He stood and breathed deeply the warm salt air, stretched his arms to the sky, and walked back to the barn to finish cleaning the stalls and pitching fresh hay to the horses – resolved to push Frances from his mind just as he had his parents and sister when that seemed the most impossible thing in the world to do.

CHAPTER 42

Pushing Away

D uring the following months, Jack avoided Frances. When he did come in contact with her he'd walk by without making eye contact or saying hello. When her birthday came in May and the community threw a birthday party for her with a funnel cake and pear juice from the tree in the garden, Jack didn't go. He told Emmanuel that he wasn't feeling well and he remained in the room, gazing out the window at the ocean.

She seemed to adopt his lead and stopped speaking with him. But Jack couldn't avoid seeing her each day – at morning prayers, breakfast, vespers, classes, or during chores. He wanted to run away so he wouldn't experience the pain of seeing her. If he could just leave and go somewhere far away, maybe he would forget about her. But every mass, every encounter, became torture. When she sang about love for God, Jack imagined that she was singing those words of devotion for him.

One day she confronted him. "Why do you not talk to me anymore? What's wrong?" she asked when she caught up to him on the path leading to the pond. Jack walked briskly.

"What do you mean? Nothing's wrong," he said.

"Yes there is. You've been distant for months now. You never stop by the barn to help with the animals, you never walk with me to the pond, you ignore me at breakfast and you avoid me whenever you see me. Something is wrong."

"I'm just trying to focus on God's will. As the Lord taught us, 'Thy kingdom come, Thy will be done, on Earth as it is in heaven.'" The part of her face between her eyebrows crinkled. Her eyes searched his eyes. He stared ahead down the path and tried not to meet her gaze. He felt her hand press lightly on his arm.

"Augustine, I don't understand what you mean. What is God's will for you that you cannot talk to me?" Jack broke from her grip and walked faster. This was the first time Frances questioned him on a point of faith. She had always taught him what God's will meant. Now she was asking him.

Didn't she realize he couldn't confide in her as he did when they were children? Didn't she understand what unfamiliar feelings were fluttering through his body every time he looked at her? Perhaps she didn't feel at all like he did and couldn't possibly recognize why he was avoiding her. Was he perceiving affections that were not there? He struggled every day to drive lustful thoughts of her from his heart, and she, like a puppy who keeps coming back and licking your face no matter how far you throw the stick and tell it to stay, continued to seek that same intimacy which he could no longer give.

Jack stopped walking. He looked into her eyes, eyes reflecting so much love. "Read St. Teresa of Avila," he said: "'*They deceive themselves who believe that union with God consists in ecstasies or raptures, and in the enjoyment of Him. For it consists in nothing except the surrender and subjection of our will – with our thoughts, words and actions – to the will of God.*' Heed her words. I must follow my namesake. It is God's will." Then he abruptly turned and continued walking down the path.

She did not continue walking with him. Jack didn't look back. He struggled to keep walking and keep his tormented thoughts to himself. Then he ran, slowly at first, then as fast as he could. He ran along the wooded path that circled Heath's Pond until he reached the high point. The pond was forty feet below him.

There was a large rock that jutted over the ledge out past the trees and gave a clear view of the water below. Jack climbed onto it and buried his head in his hands. He cried out the words of Saint Augustine:

"O rottenness, O monstrousness of life and abyss of death! Could you find pleasure only in what was forbidden, and only because it was forbidden?"

"Saint Augustine, help me! God please drive this lust from my heart!" he yelled to the pond below and sky above and all the trees around. "I am wicked. Help me!"

He sat on the rock for many hours thinking about what God's purpose was for him. Was it incompatible for him to live obediently and humbly, devoted to God, and devoted at the same time to Frances? To love her? God commanded his children to love thy neighbor as you love Him. Did he not command that?

Was not loving others the same in God's eyes as loving God Himself? Jack knew his love for Frances was wicked because she was willed to love somebody else. But who willed it? Did God will her to be promised in marriage to Emmanuel? Or did Abraham will it, and did he will it because God told him it must be?

Or did Abraham arbitrarily choose Emmanuel? Was there another reason Emmanuel was chosen? Maybe Jack could ask Abraham. No he could not. Perhaps Sarah. Yes, he would ask Sarah what the arrangement was and why it was thus.

Why was his soul tortured over this? He did not want to get married. Only adults got married, and he was still a child. But he wondered; everyone else in the community had someone chosen for them to marry eventually. And the one girl from the community whom he ever thought he could marry, from the day he first saw and heard her singing, the only girl he wanted to marry to this day, was picked to marry somebody else.

Gabriel had married Rachel three years ago when he was eighteen and she was only fifteen. And a couple years before that, Pius, twenty at the time, married Teresa, who was seventeen. Jack would be eighteen in just over a year. Would Abraham pick someone for him? Who was left? There was Bernadette, but she was only a child – seven years old. He couldn't marry her.

But was she promised to him? Nobody had told him that. According to Moses, Frances had been promised to Emmanuel since she was a young child. If she knew this, she never revealed it to Jack.

Did all-knowing God have another plan, unknown to Jack, for his life? Was it God's will for him to remain chaste until the end of his days and never marry, like St. Augustine after his conversion? If so, then it must be and Jack must trust in God that this was his fate and accept it.

As Sarah had taught him many times, faith is often lived in darkness, and his faith would often be tested. Was this such a test? He thought of Job and Job's steadfast trust and faith in God despite the evil, suffering, injustice and death dealt to him by Satan.

Jack continued to churn the possibilities around and around in his mind as he sat on the rock and watched the sun dip below the tree line. Was there someone else God had chosen for him to marry? Someone he had not met yet? But how could that be; in nine years he had never met anyone outside of the community. He was banned from working at the store. He didn't understand why.

He was the only one – besides Timothy – who was not allowed to work at the store. And he knew that Timothy was forbidden because he had fornicated with that girl whom he had met while working at the store those many years ago.

Even if he did meet someone, they were forbidden to marry outside of the community. Those people were morally corrupt and damned. But couldn't Abraham find someone for him and bring her in and save her, the same way he saved Jack?

Jack listened to the chickadees chirping and the wind rustling the leaves on the maple trees. He looked out at the pewter water, dappled silver from the sun's glare shining a rippled swath across it. He thought about his recurring dream…another life in another place long ago. Blurry images like the water.

He remembered certain things at certain times; nothing all together at all times. But the things he remembered, like a fort in the woods, he remembered vividly. He thanked God for calling Abraham to bring him here to this beautiful place where he could live a humble and obedient life devoted to the Lord; where he could find purification from all infidelities of his past life. When he thought of how depraved he must have been before he was saved, it made him sick.

He was also happy God had called him here because he had met Frances. Though he was tormented by having met her, at the same time he was happy she had been a part of his life. Now he had to seek God's help to accept that she was going to occupy a different place in that life, and not the intimate role of life's companion. He had to cut her out. That was the only way. Satan was leading him into temptation through her. Just like he did with Job. He had to push the sinful thoughts of her – lustful thoughts – from his mind.

God had asked him to abandon all earthly pleasures and in return would give him the one true good, the greatest happiness of all, the beatific vision – the eternal and direct vision of God – enjoyed only by those who attain heaven. He had committed to this life long ago at his confirmation – to live, grow, and persevere in the faith until the end – until he saw God face to face.

His soul had been dead. The light of salvation had woken it. God had given the light of faith to him, through Abraham. He had shaken his dark, dormant soul from its slumber. Now he was in danger of blackening it forever through the lust now in his heart. Frances was not his. It was not God's will.

He breathed the warm summer air into his lungs and looked to the sky to again ask for God's help. He resolved to accept his fate and submit completely his life to God's will. God would reveal to him His divine plan for his life at a time and a place of His choosing. Jack had simply to listen. He would walk into the night of faith, and he would walk it alone if he was so called.

CHAPTER 43

Love

Jack began to walk back to his basement bedroom. The afternoon sun had slid behind the trees and its light had weakened. He turned and ran to the barn instead. He had neglected his afternoon chores and would face a reprimand from Moses. He slipped into the barn unnoticed. It was quiet and empty. He stocked the hay and filled the troughs with chicken feed and slop. He finished and walked back to his room to clean up for dinner and vespers.

He sat in his appointed seat at dinner. Frances was already there. She looked at him with her big eyes and smiled and began to say something to him. Jack ignored her and turned rudely to Gabriel seated in the chair to his right. He asked him how the fishing had gone that morning.

He never heard Gabriel's answer. Though he outwardly ignored Frances, inwardly his whole being was riveted to her presence. As hard as he tried to appear interested in Gabriel's story about fishing, he didn't hear a word. Prudence interrupted them to ask Gabriel a question and he began an animated conversation with her.

Jack turned to his meal, which had been placed in front of him on the table, and cut his beef into small pieces. He snuck a glance at Frances. She was talking to Jacob, seated on the other side of her, who was focusing intensely on her as she spoke. He burst out laughing at the end of her story. She laughed too.

Jack stared across the table and silently watched the others eat. He picked at his food. He tried to catch Gabriel's attention to resume their conversation, but Gabriel was enraptured by whatever Prudence was telling him. How stupid he was for not having anyone to talk to! Frances would have been talking and laughing with him instead of Jacob if he hadn't shunned her. "It must be," he muttered. "God has willed it. Abraham has decided it. I must abide by it."

Frances did not try to speak to him again during dinner. She didn't even smile at him. When dinner was finished, she left her seat before Jack. Jacob walked with her. Jack's eyes followed her as she walked out the door, still joking and laughing with Jacob. Jack banged the table with his hand. He looked for Moses. He didn't see him. Good. Finally not watching. He didn't want another lecture about his fondness for Frances.

Jack pulled Sarah aside. "Sarah, can I talk to you about something?"

"What do you want to talk about?" she asked. Jack paused. He waited for the others to clear the room. She noticed the torment on his face. "Shall we walk?" she asked. "I sense that something troubles you. It is a beautiful evening. We can walk around the pond and you can tell me what's bothering you." Jack nodded in agreement.

They wandered in silence down the wooded path. After a few minutes Jack spoke. "Sarah, my soul is troubled. I cannot sleep at night. I have so many questions that I have not been able to answer." He paused. She said nothing, just listened.

"What is God's will for me?" he asked. "What is it I'm supposed to do?"

"What do you mean?" she asked. Jack walked a few steps, gathering his thoughts.

"Am I to marry? Has Abraham picked somebody for me, and if he has, who is it? How does it work?" Sarah puckered her mouth, as if she had just sucked a lemon.

"Augustine, I'm disappointed in you. You mustn't worry about such things. If you've prayed and meditated about it with the devotion and focus required, God will reveal the answer."

"Forgive me Sarah, but that is all I have done. I've prayed about it every minute of every hour of every day. I've meditated about it. I still don't know the answer."

"Then you haven't prayed or meditated enough," she said with her lemon-crinkled mouth. "And in your prayers you must listen for God, for He will answer you if you listen with an open heart. He may not tell you the answer you want to hear, but you must be open to his desires. Trust in God to show you the correct path."

"Augustine, you have to see the difference between what you want to do and what God wants you to do. You must discern what comes from your will and what comes from God's will." Jack listened. They came to one of the cottages in the clearing and paused. The woods rustled with the calm warmth of a summer's afternoon.

"But what if I know what I want and I think it would also please God for this to happen, but circumstances I don't understand prevent me from pursuing this course?" Jack said. Sarah looked at the sky.

"We have some time before vespers. Let us continue walking," she said. They turned left along the edge of the woods until they came to the path that led to the pond. She began talking once they reached the path. "Augustine, you learned that by faith – by your covenant to God when you were confirmed – you submitted your life and your will to God. You swore obedience to Him alone."

She walked in silence for about twenty yards before speaking again. "Tell me, Augustine, what do you believe God's will is for you?" Jack's cheeks flushed. He wasn't sure he should reveal his thoughts to her.

"Augustine," she said. She placed a hand on his forearm and turned to face him. "I want you to know that you can share anything that is in your heart. I will guide your prayers to help you discover God's will for you. You must trust in me, as you trust in Him. What is it that has been troubling you, keeping you from restful sleep, tormenting your soul?"

"Well," Jack began. He looked at her face. It was open and loving. "Can you tell me if I am to marry and have a family, or am I to live a chaste life with no companion to share my happiness with? What does God will?" Sarah's expression changed. A cloud passed over her eyes and her brow furrowed.

"What hast brought these thoughts to you, Augustine? You are still a boy, only sixteen, and marriage should be far from your mind."

"But Jacob was married last year and he was only eighteen. And…and…" He swallowed. "Emmanuel already knows that he will marry Frances. He is seventeen and she is sixteen." His voice cracked.

"Who told you that?" Sarah asked, her voice edgy. Now he was in trouble. He knew if he told her that Moses told him she would talk to Moses. Moses would whip Jack for telling Sarah and he would tell Sarah about Jack looking at Frances in an impure manner. And Sarah would then tell Abraham and Abraham would whip him and make him confess his lustful thoughts publicly to the community and Frances would shun him for looking at her with sin in his heart. She would never talk to him then. He regretted ever beginning this conversation with Sarah. What could he do now?

Jack decided he could not tell Sarah. He thought of someone else. Timothy! Why didn't he think of Timothy? He remembered when Timothy had been whipped and shunned many years ago – only a few weeks after Jack had arrived. He had been in love with a girl too – someone outside of the community, and had in a weak moment succumbed to the same carnal passion, the impulse for intimacy, that Jack felt for Frances.

Ever since his shunning and repentance, though, Timothy had been a model of virtue and an example Abraham held up for the younger folks in the community. Even after his grievous sin, he was able to marry Rachel and they had had a child together. He seemed happy. How did he do it?

"Augustine, tell me what you believe your destiny in God's eyes is," Sarah said, interrupting his thoughts. He would not confide in her now. He would talk to Timothy first and see what he said.

"Mother Sarah, I will pray and meditate about it some more before I trouble you with my burdens. You are right. I haven't listened closely enough to hear God's answer."

She stopped walking and smiled. "Augustine, you must bear your sorrows with the deep reserves of strength God has given you. He will never give you more than you can bear. Have faith that he will guide you and be mindful that faith is often lived in darkness. We will be tested, just as Job was tested. But, like Job, we must remain steadfast in our profession of faith."

"Walk into the night of faith," she continued. "Te Deum Laudamus – we praise thee, O God. You must pray to God to take from you everything that distances you from Him, and give you everything that brings you closer to Him." They came back to the clearing and cottages. "Go now and get ready for vespers. I will see you there and I will pray for you."

Jack entered the house and went straight to his bedroom. He fell to his knees at the foot of his bed and prayed. "Oh heavenly Father, bring me light to end this darkness. Light my path. Show me the way." He asked God, as Sarah had suggested, to bring him the things that would draw him closer to Him. He pledged to serve God first: "Oh God, you are the first and the last, the beginning and the end. Please let me see to see." He blessed himself, put on his robe, and resolved to seek Timothy's counsel that evening after vespers.

Jack sat in his appointed position at vespers. He ignored Frances and refused to look at her. Looking at her was too painful. Then her voice – that voice! – hovered in the air, clear and strong, as she sang Simple Gifts. Then he couldn't keep his eyes off this beautiful creature any longer as she sang with a mix of fervor and purity available to her voice alone.

Her eyes remained looking at the ground before her. Jack watched her and his chest swelled. His heart nearly burst from its casing, thumping—an ardent drum. Love, lust, which was it that he was feeling? Weren't they kindred flames fueled by the same spark, fed by the subsequent consuming fire? No. Jack loved her. Love, not lust. Not sinful. She made him want to be a better person. She in fact did make him a better person. How could his devotion to her be sin?

He studied her. She was the most beautiful human being he had ever seen. He scanned the others standing in the circle listening to her. They looked dull and ugly in comparison. Her eyes were more luminous, her porcelain skin more pristine, her lips more tender. Beautiful – inside and out. Her small breasts poked against her robe. Lust.

She lifted her gaze from the floor and her eyes fell on Jack's. There was a dispassion in them that she expressed to his eyes. He blushed and turned away, glancing across the group. They were all looking at Frances...except Moses. Moses was looking at him, watching him with bitter eyes. Jack looked at the floor and shook his head slightly side to side, angry that he had been caught again. He looked again at Frances. Love. Love with every fiber of his body and soul. He wanted his soul intertwined with hers for the rest of his life on this Earth, and beyond and evermore.

Jack sought out Timothy after vespers. "Timothy, can I talk to you?"

"Sure, what's on your mind?" Timothy asked. They sat on the windowsill in the room, bright moonlight filtering through the glass pane of the windows.

"I'm struggling with God's will for me. I have strong feelings for someone and I cannot push them from my thoughts. I don't know what to do and Moses has warned me about being too affectionate with this person."

"Hmm. I think I can guess who this person is."

"You can? How?"

"Augustine, it is clear. I see the way you look at Frances. You light up whenever she walks in the room. You're attentive to her – you finish your chores early so you can help her with hers. You hide behind the haystacks to listen to her singing when she works. You pick her flowers. Oh, it's obvious what your feelings are for her."

"Oh no," Jack said. "Has everyone noticed? I have tried to hide my feelings but I fear I haven't concealed them too well. Moses caught me watching her and he told me to distance myself from her."

Timothy's eyes widened. "He did?" He looked out the window. The darkness concealing anything there was to see, he turned back to face Jack. "Well yes, I understand. And yes, I think your feelings for her are written all over your face whenever you are around her." He turned his glance from Jack back to the window. "And I'm afraid she feels the same way about you." Jack's sadness vanished from his face, replaced by a radiant glow that rose to his cheeks.

"She does? You really think so?"

"Augustine, it doesn't matter how she feels about you or you about her. Abraham decreed long ago that it is God's will for Frances to marry Emmanuel."

"Do you really think she feels the same way about me?" Jack asked, hope expressing itself in his bright eyes.

"I do not know her mind or heart, I only know what I see written on her face when she's with you. And frankly, I didn't really know how strongly you felt about her until now, but I'm beginning to get a fuller picture and it troubles me."

Jack didn't care that it troubled Timothy. He didn't care about anything else. Any thoughts about abiding by a destiny that did not include her faded. All he thought about was that he loved Frances and that she might actually love him the same way back. God surely must will it that they be together. Why plant the seed of desire and not allow it to blossom. If it was pure and good, as Jack believed it was, God – and Abraham – should bless the match.

"Augustine, there is another reason why you cannot marry Frances. Abraham has expressed it many times, though not in your presence." Timothy looked out the window. He had a troubled expression on his face. "I will not – I cannot – tell you the reason, but you must trust that it is so and not pursue it any further. Abraham has made up his mind and you tempt his wrath if you pursue it further." He looked back to Jack. His eyes were sad.

"But I don't understand, brother Timothy? Please tell me, and perhaps it will become clear to me and this torture in my heart will end. What is the reason?"

Timothy looked at him for a long time. Then he shook his head. "I'm sorry brother Jack. My love for you is great; you know that. But I cannot tell you the reason right now. Please drop this matter. Please accept that Frances is betrothed to another and be content with the gifts God has bestowed upon you."

Jack just looked at him, pleading with his eyes to help him. Timothy began to speak and stopped. Then he began again. "Augustine, I am certain that Sarah taught you something when you first arrived, and no doubt you have heard this many times since: loyalty to the Lord must come before all things, including all of your own possessions. Possessions are not only the material things that you own – things that you control – but also the things that control you. This includes relationships, loyalties, passions, opinions, and ideas. To cling to anything, no matter how well accepted by society or the religious establishment, is to forfeit eternal life."

Jack shook his head. Yes, he had heard this many times, and had prayed about it. He knew that to cling to anything on this earth was to abandon God. It had been seared into his soul. God came before all, and to become enveloped in the flame of passion toward possessions, ideas, or loved ones was a certain path toward not witnessing the pure joy of seeing God's face in eternity.

But as he shook his head, he decided he could not devote himself entirely to God at the exclusion of all other things beautiful in his life. He was not Saint

Augustine. He was simply Augustine, and he was not going to live the life of a monk. He could love Frances and devote himself to God too – it should not be an either/or proposition.

He would confront Abraham and ask him to revise his decree. He would find out the reason that Timothy would not tell; he would ask to know the truth about why, when everything demonstrated a future blessed union between them, Abraham had decreed otherwise. Surely Abraham would see that Augustine's love was pure and good and that God would approve the match.

CHAPTER 44

Deceit

The next day after they were walking back from a hike through the woods, Jack pulled Sarah aside. "I have one further question if I may ask you."

"Yes, anything," Sarah said.

"Why did Abraham choose me?" Jack asked her.

"What do you mean?"

"Why did he decide to bring me here and save me from the world of sin?" Sarah quickened her pace. She didn't answer immediately. Jack kept up with her. "Why did he bring me here?"

"You mustn't ask these things," she said.

"I asked you once why everyone listens to Abraham; how it came to be that he was chosen to be God's one, perfect and unsurpassable Word. You said you would tell me Abraham's story one day, but in all these years I've never learned these truths."

Sarah looked behind them. Then she glanced around. She took Jack's arm and led him forward. "Come with me and I will tell you."

They climbed the path along the pond until they were at the edge of a cliff high above the water – the place where Jack often went to contemplate alone. "Sit here," she said, pointing to a rock. She sat on another one facing him.

"Abraham chose you because you reminded him of someone – someone he loved dearly and lost."

"I don't understand," Jack said. "How could I have reminded him of somebody when he had never met me?"

"Let me correct myself. Your situation reminded him of something he experienced many years ago that changed his life forever and led to God revealing Himself to Abraham."

"You see," she continued, "Abraham's parents divorced when he was a boy. He was fourteen or fifteen years old. He had a younger brother and sister. His brother Jeremy was about your age, seven or eight, and his sister was ten when it happened."

"The divorce was hard on the children, and the brother and sister didn't handle it well, though they had witnessed years of fighting. Their father had beaten their mother whenever he was drunk, which was most nights."

"Even so, they witnessed even worse after the divorce. Their parents were so caught up in their own problems they didn't pay attention to their kids. Their dad moved a couple towns away. Abraham lived with him, and his brother and sister lived with their mother. Abraham learned from them that his mother brought home different boyfriends every night and smoked marijuana all day."

"Abraham's brother started to spend time with a bad crowd and dropped out of school not long after he reached his teens. He started hanging out on street corners and doing drugs. He began stealing to pay for the drugs." Jack noticed Sarah's eyes had grown moist.

"Why are you sad, Sarah?" he asked.

She wiped her eyes. "Forgive me. It's nothing."

"One day the police came to the house and told them that Jeremy was dead. He had overdosed on heroin. When Abraham heard the news he was devastated. And he was furious that his brother's so-called friends had allowed him to overdose and then just left him, dead, lying in an alley."

"He blamed himself for not being around and for not being strict enough when he heard what was going on. He said over and over that he should have physically pulled him by the collar and thrown him in jail or a detox center where he couldn't get out until he cleaned up and changed his ways. He said that he should have kept him away from those bad influences at any cost. He felt tremendous guilt." Sarah's eyes filled with tears again.

"It was about all he could handle, and Abraham had hardly recovered from the reality that his brother was dead when his sister then also succumbed to the evil influences in the world."

"She started doing drugs and then started sleeping with men to pay for the drugs. She lived on the street in filth and it looked like, despite Abraham's efforts to not make the same mistakes he had made with Jeremy, she would come to the same horrible end." Sarah stopped speaking and wiped her eyes. She gazed out over the pond.

"What happened to her?" Jack asked.

"She was saved. She turned her life around, all because of Abraham. After Jeremy died, Abraham devoted himself fully to God. He studied the Bible and meditated and prayed. He was raised Catholic, but he studied other religions and the works of enlightened gurus," she said.

"Then one day God spoke to Abraham. He told him that he was the chosen one and that he must build a society apart from the one that killed Jeremy and was claiming his sister." She took Jacks hands in hers.

"God told Abraham that he must lead this group and that they would become the chosen ones, the elect, who would enter the kingdom of heaven. Abraham's father owned a large company that Abraham inherited. Abraham sold it to buy this compound."

"He brought his sister here and introduced her to God and saved her. He brought other seekers whom he had met at prayer groups. In all, twenty-two people came and formed this community. Some married here and had children here and as you can see we've grown since then."

"Abraham is father to us all. He is our leader and guide. God speaks to him directly as He did in the beginning. Yes, you asked me many years ago why everyone listens to Abraham and does what he tells them. This is why: because God spoke to him in a revelation and God continues to speak to him and tell him what we all must do to enter His kingdom."

"How do you know all this?" Jack asked.

Sarah took a deep breath and let out a long, slow sigh. "Because that girl – Abraham's sister – that girl was me."

"What?" Jack gasped. "You are brother and sister? You...you were a prostitute?"

"Augustine! Please do not speak so loudly," she said as she stood and moved to him and pulled him close to her. "Yes, I was," she whispered. "And I have carried that shame and stain with me all these years."

"Does anyone else know?" Jack asked.

"No, I have never revealed my past life to anyone. Only Abraham knows. You mustn't share what I've told you with anyone. I told you only because I think it will help you finally understand why Abraham brought you here."

Jack couldn't believe Sarah had been a drug addict and prostitute. He thought of Ciara on the island. He walked to the edge of the ledge that overlooked the pond and began to throw rocks far into the water. He watched the point of the splash and the ripples that rolled outward.

"Augustine, what is it?" Sarah asked.

"It's just that I would have tried to save that girl Ciara but you told me she could not be saved; yet now you've told me that you were saved and you did far worse in the eyes of God than I ever saw Ciara do."

Sarah stepped back, a look of surprise on her face. "That's not true," she said. She paused. "She indeed could not be saved. You have to want to be saved. You have to choose God and decide to give up your sinful life."

"From what you told me, she and the others with her did not want to repent their wicked ways; they thought the way they were living was fine and they wanted to continue on their black paths. I wanted to be saved. You have to choose to devote your life to God and I was ready to do that."

"I did not choose to be saved," Jack said. He looked at her coldly. He noticed that her look turned from surprise to concern.

"Augustine, where is this coming from? Why do you say that with such anger? Why do you look upon me with hatred in your eyes? You were a child. A child cannot understand what is best for him. You were the perfect age – seven, the age of reason. You would never have had an opportunity to learn about God and how to live a life in service of Him if we hadn't—"

Jack's face was hot. "You must remember that you did have a choice," she said. "Abraham gave you a choice before and during your confirmation and you chose this life. So you did, in fact, have a clear choice – to accept God or reject God and I'm happy for your eternal soul that you accepted God and saved yourself from eternal damnation."

"Yes," Jack remembered. "Yes I did." He threw a rock as far as he could and watched it plop in the pond. "I must go now," he said.

"Where are you going?"

"I'm going to pray on this." Jack ran straight to the main house. He saw Moses in the reading room. "Where is Abraham?" he asked.

Moses looked at him with a curious look. "Abraham is in his chamber and is not to be disturbed," he said. Jack turned around and bounded straight toward the stairs leading to Abraham's room. "Augustine, I told you he is not to be disturbed!" Moses yelled. He chased Jack up the stairs. Jack reached the top and pounded on the door while Moses yelled after him to come away from there.

Abraham opened the door. "What is the meaning of this?" he asked. By this time Moses had caught up.

"Forgive me Master Abraham. I told Augustine you were not to be disturbed."

"Augustine, why have you disobeyed Moses' orders and disturbed me during my meditation?"

"Forgive me Master Abraham. I want to talk to you about an important matter." Abraham paused and looked from Jack to Moses. Abraham told him to come back to the house after chores and before dinner and he would sit with him.

Jack attended class and studied the Odyssey in the Greek text. After class they were sent to do their chores before lunch. Jack saw Frances walk into the barn to clean the stalls and fill the feed troughs, so he went to the garden to pull weeds. He would continue to avoid contact with her until Abraham gave his blessing to their union. He ran though his head what he wanted to tell him. He tried to think of Bible passages that supported his plea.

In the end, he believed that his love for Frances strengthened his love for God. She made him a better person – more in tune with what God wanted. She had always guided him and he felt he had, overall, lived a good, pure, faithful life, in no small part thanks to her support. As his partner on his earthly life's journey, he would continue to draw from her example. And if God blessed them with children, the children would be reared in a way pleasing to God.

Jack thought his argument was strong. It was Abraham who had seated Jack next to her that first breakfast morning. Abraham had told Jack many times to seek out Frances for guidance. If Timothy had noticed their affection for each other, surely Abraham had seen it too, and had done nothing to discourage it. How could he refuse a match that seemed as though God had willed it?

The warm spring sun beat down on his face as he pulled weeds from the dirt and put them in a basket. He smiled. It was the first time he had smiled in a long time.

After chores Jack ran to his basement room and washed up. Then he ran upstairs where everyone would soon gather for dinner. He found Abraham in the prayer meeting room gazing at a passage in the Bible. When he saw Jack he smiled. "Augustine, God's greeting to you this afternoon. Now what is it that you would like to talk to me about?"

Jack felt his cheeks go warm and a trickle of sweat roll down his temple. He wiped it with his sleeve. His neck was wet. "Master Abraham. I seek your blessing on something that has been on my mind and in my heart for many years." He stood and waited for Abraham's acknowledgment to continue. Abraham turned and placed the Bible on a chair, then turned back with a serious expression on his face.

"Is this regarding your affection for Frances?" he asked. Jack felt the sweat now dripping down his neck. *Timothy!* he thought. How else could Abraham know? Timothy must have told him. Jack had confided in Timothy and he had betrayed his trust and told Abraham.

"Yes," Jack began. "I wanted to ask your permission to—" Abraham held his hand up, indicating for Jack to stop.

"Augustine, I'm disappointed in you. One of the first things you learned nearly ten years ago when you arrived was that you must give up all earthly pleasures and devote yourself – sacrifice yourself – fully to God. Nothing matters except your relationship to our Savior, and each day lived must be lived for Him."

He placed his hand on Jack's shoulder. "You rely too much on your love for Frances. Your affection for her has diverted and diluted your love for God. I see it Augustine. You are more focused on her than on what you need to do to improve and be worthy of gaining entrance to heaven."

"Augustine, do you not remember Proverbs? *Many are the plans in the mind of man, but it is the purpose of the Lord that will be established.* You must refocus on living a life for God, as your namesake did, and reject the earthly pleasures you seek from a union with Frances. You must drive lustful thoughts from your heart. These thoughts can only lead down the dark road to hell."

Jack's wet shirt stuck to his back. "But Father Abraham I have not abandoned or lessened in any way my devotion to God. My life here I have dedicated to God alone, but the Bible also says when we love our neighbor, we love God." He wiped his forehead.

"I do love Frances," he continued. "But I love her within the grace of God's love. My love for her enhances my love for God. Our love here, love for all God's creatures, can only strengthen our love and appreciation for God."

"No, you are wrong Augustine. Search your heart, search your mind, think upon everything you have learned. Your love for her is a physical love. It is a sexual, lustful, impure love. Search your heart. You are seventeen years old – an age when the pull of the opposite sex is strongest. It is springtime. Flowers bloom, birds sing, and young boys' blood boils with romance and passion."

"You are caught up in the moment Augustine, and cannot see clearly. You must pray to God to forgive you for this weakness."

Jack thought about what Abraham was telling him. Yes, it was true that he did have impure thoughts about Frances. But he had tried to push these thoughts out of his mind and the result was too many sleepless nights. If only he could make his love for her – his physical and emotional love – sanctified through marriage, then it would not be a sinful or impure impulse, it would be blessed – the foundation of the marriage vow.

"Forgive me Abraham," he said, "But this is not a passing fancy or a springtime blooming. I have felt this connection with Frances for many years. I have loved her from the day I met her, ten years ago." Jack forgot about the sweat on his neck and he spoke with an urgency and intensity that poured out unfettered.

"I was scared. I had just arrived and didn't know anyone or understand why I was brought here," he said. "Then Frances sang at the first mass you took me to, and then – only then – did I feel comfort. I had felt only misery and fear after being taken from my parents—" Abraham stepped toward him and in a quick, fluid motion, slapped Augustine so hard across the face that the blow knocked him down.

"How dare you," he said as he shook his hand out. "After all I've done for you." The unexpectedness of the slap shook Jack more than the actual physical impact of the blow. He remained on the ground as Abraham loomed over him.

"You were doomed to a certain fate that you cannot fathom; a fate I rescued you from," he said, wagging his finger to punctuate his point. "You cannot imagine the horrors of hell, and now you're willing to throw away eternal life, the chance to touch the face of God, for the pleasures of the flesh!" These last words he spat out in a spray of bile. "Don't ever say that you were taken from your family as if you regret it – as if you regret that we – that I – rescued you from untold pain."

"Have you not had a good life here? Have you not learned how to live in God's grace – the greatest gift you could ever be given?"

Jack withered on the floor underneath Abraham's pointing finger.

CHAPTER 45

Jail

Gus was given a number – 866 – and an orange jumpsuit – like Elvis's but without the rhinestones and eagles. More like an airplane mechanic's. He was asked to empty his pockets, take off his clothes and put the jumpsuit on. "This is what you'll be wearing every day for the next three years," the smug guard said. "Sorry it's not as nice as those fancy suits you used to wear at Fidelity. But look on the bright side: you'll save a fortune on dry cleaning." He smirked.

They are all assholes, Gus thought. He continued looking straight ahead and didn't let his expression betray the anger creeping up his tensed back. He was escorted to his cell. His new home. He looked around. There was a bunk bed, one toilet with no seat, one sink, a 40-watt light, one outlet. There was also an 18-inch black and white television. The beds had two sheets, a blanket, and a pillow – a relief after the cold metal bench-bed at the police station.

He flopped on the bottom bed and stared at the underside of the top bunk. So it had come to this. He recalled the words his mother had told him so often: God will never give you more than you can handle. "Yeah right," he muttered. You make plans and God laughs – that had a more appropriate application to his life. He turned on the television but all he got was snow. He jiggled the antenna and flicked the channels, but no matter what he did he still couldn't get a picture. So he stared at the bare walls of his new jail cell for an hour instead.

"Can I have a book or something?" he shouted finally to the guard.

"What do you want a book for?" the guard yelled.

"Well I'd like to read one!" Gus shouted. "Dickhead."

"What kind of book?"

"I don't know. Anything to pass the time. Maybe something off the best seller lists? You got any recommendations?"

"Hold on, let me see what I can do," the guard yelled. He appeared a few minutes later and threw a book through the bars. "Try this," he said.

Gus picked the book off the ground. "The Bible? I don't want this! What the fuck am I going to do with the fucking Bible!" He threw the book against the bars.

"I don't care what you do with it. You can read it or wipe your ass with it for all I care."

"I don't want the fucking Bible!" Gus shouted again. "Just get me something else!"

"That's all we got," the guard said. "Why don't you read it – maybe you'll learn something."

"Fuck you." He lay on the bed, closed his eyes, and thought about summer afternoons splashing in the cool pool with Jack and Lilly and the neighborhood kids.

He wondered if he had the cell to himself or if he had a roommate. He didn't have to wonder long when the door buzzed and clanked and a Puerto Rican guy with his shiny black hair tied in a pony tail walked in.

"Get out of my bed," he said. "You're in the top bunk."

"Sorry," Gus said. He got up and walked to the back wall and leaned against it. He stood while a few minutes of awkward silence passed. "I'm Gus." He walked over to shake the man's hand. The guy, now sitting on the bed, looked up at him for a second and then looked toward the television, which was off. Gus walked back to the wall. More awkward silence.

"So what are you in for," Gus asked finally.

"None of your fucking business."

"Well fuck you too," Gus muttered.

"What? What did you say?" the guy said. He stood. He was a skinny, wiry guy. Probably weighed about a hundred and forty pounds, couldn't have been more than five foot seven – half Gus's size. He only had about half his teeth.

"I said go fuck yourself if you're gonna be that way. I'm just trying to make conversation. You don't have to be an asshole."

The guy sprang on him in a flash. Gus felt the guy's fists crash against his face and ribs. They came so fast he couldn't react. Soon Gus was gasping for breath. Punch after punch pounded his head. Gus flailed and tried to grab him but the guy was too quick. Then he grabbed a hunk of Gus's hair and smashed his head against the bed rail.

By this time Gus was screaming for help. "Where the fuck are you people?" he wailed. He dropped to the cement floor and felt the warm blood pouring down his forehead, into his eyes. He couldn't see. He heard the buzzclank of the door opening.

"Get some towels!" a man said. Gus tasted blood and spit it, blood-drool dripping off his chin. He heard another man's voice and felt someone pressing a towel hard against his forehead. He held it there.

"Oh shit – he's getting blood everywhere," the guy said.

"Can you sit up?" the other guy asked him. At this point Gus realized they were two of the guards. "Here sit up," one guard said. Gus wobbled.

"Think you can get to your feet?" the guard asked. Gus nodded yes. They pulled him up and searing pain shot to his head. He had trouble breathing.

"Let's get you down to the infirmary and have Nurse Brown take a look at you. Looks like you're going to need a few stitches. You've got quite a gash there. Can you hold this to your head? Press it hard." The guard guided Gus's hand to the spot and Gus held the towel – wet and warm with blood – against his forehead.

"Okay, here we go Mr. Delaney," the other guard said. "Walk with me."

"Not a good first day, I'm afraid," the other one said. Gus nodded and staggered out of the cell, down a long corridor and down some stairs. They brought him into a room and a woman in a nurse's uniform told him to sit in a chair. She lifted the towel from Gus's head.

"We're going to need to bring in the doctor," she said. "He's going to need some stitches." She replaced the sopped towel with a dry one. She was cold toward him; all-business, no small talk. She left him sitting there for the doctor. Ten minutes passed and an older man entered the room. Not the doctor – this man was dressed in a police uniform.

"Well what happened here, Mr. Delaney?" the man asked.

"My cellmate attacked me." Gus began to feel dizzy.

"That's unfortunate. At least now you know what it's like to be attacked. Maybe in the future you'll think twice before attacking and beating an officer." Gus studied the man, whose bearing, facial expression, and voice were that of an arrogant father giving a stern lecture to a good-for-nothing son. Gus didn't want any lectures right now.

He looked at the man's cranky, condescending face. "Fuck you," he said.

"Exactly the response I'd expect from a dirt-bag like you. Maybe you can sit here awhile and think about adopting a better attitude."

"I don't need a lecture from you. Just get me a fucking doctor before I bleed all over your jail."

"He's on his way, so just sit there and keep your mouth shut," the man said. Then he left.

After the doctor came and stitched him up – eight stitches – and checked his ribs and ability to breathe, Gus was taken to a cell. It was a different cell, though it had the same spartan features. There was no roommate at the moment. Gus lay down on the bed. His head throbbed and his chest hurt every time he inhaled. Did those fuckers purposely put him in a cell with a violent lunatic to get back at him for lashing out at Goddard?

He tried to sleep, but sleep didn't come. He stared at the bottom of the mattress above him. Same view as in his old cell. The buzzclank of the door opening roused him from his aimless thoughts. Another inmate walked in, also a Hispanic guy. "Get out of my bed," he said. Great, Gus thought. Another asshole.

Gus sat up and became so lightheaded he thought he was going to vomit. "Sorry boss, I didn't know," he said.

"Oh shit," the guy yelled. "Did you get blood all over my pillow? Fuck!" Gus looked at the pillow.

"Yeah, looks like I did." A hint of a smile crept into the curl of his lip. The Hispanic inmate was waving his arms up and down, swearing and telling Gus to look what he did to his pillow. Good, Gus thought. Too fucking bad. But when the guy wouldn't shut up and kept going on about his stupid pillow, Gus told him he could have his.

"Just take this and give me the one with blood on it, all right?" The guy snatched the pillow from him and turned on the television. This one worked. Gus looked for a clock. There was none. No windows either, so he couldn't tell what time of day it was. He was starving. It had to be close to dinner time. He had missed lunch, he assumed, while he was waiting for the doctor. He didn't bother asking his cellmate for the time. He was engrossed in Star Trek, his 300 pound carcass splayed on the bottom bunk like a hairy jelly fish.

Gus fell asleep on his bunk. He was awakened by the buzzclank of the cell door. "Chow," a guard announced. All the inmates lined up outside their cells and walked single file to a large dining facility, where an elderly female cafeteria worker slopped runny mashed potatoes and something that looked like leather that had been left out in the sun.

Gus sat at a long table and looked around. The prisoners segregated themselves into like groups – the Asians with the Asians, blacks with blacks, Hispanics with Hispanics, and whites with whites. He noticed only then that he had sat down at a table with young Asians. They spoke to each other in their native language – whatever it was he couldn't tell; Chinese, Vietnamese – and gave dirty looks to Gus. He focused on his leather beef and ate silently.

After dinner came two hours of recreation time. During this time prisoners could go to the library, gym, outside yard, ball field, a day room with couches and a 36" color television, or the weight room. Gus walked to the gym, which had a basketball court. A group of guys – all black – played a pick-up basketball game. They trashed talked to each other – called each other bitch and nigger and challenged the guy guarding them to just *try* to stop them from scoring at will. You risked losing an eye or at least getting smacked hard in the head if you tried to drive the lane for a lay-up.

Gus watched for awhile, wanting to play but knowing it would be weeks before he could do anything physical. He went to the library and scanned the bookshelves. It was mostly crap. Then he saw a book by Peter Lynch, the investment legend from Gus's old firm. The book, *Beating the Street*, was a best seller. Lynch had gone on to manage the most successful mutual fund in history, the Magellan Fund. Gus had gone on to read Peter's book from the Billerica House of Correction.

He put Lynch's book back, depressed, and pulled out the Count of Monte Cristo by Alexander Dumas. Every day during his first week in jail was the same. He was told when to get up and when to eat. He was told when to recreate and when to stand in line for the 12 daily inmate counts. He was told when to shit.

Each meal he sat at the table with what he found out was a group of Vietnamese gang members. He didn't talk to them and they didn't talk to him. He didn't want to talk to anybody. He ate his meals and listened to the rhythms of the cafeteria and then went to the library to read Monte Cristo.

CHAPTER 46

Father Driscoll

One morning, about a week and a half after Gus arrived, a priest appeared at his cell. "Do you want to receive Holy Communion son?" He was an older man, perhaps in his 60s, slight and bald with warm eyes. He spoke in a lilting Irish accent.

"Do I know you?" Gus said.

"I'm sorry, no we haven't met. I'm Father Driscoll. I'm the chaplain here. Pardon my interruption."

"Is it Sunday?" Gus asked.

"Tis. I'm sorry I missed you last week. You hadn't shown up on my list yet."

"What list?"

"I have a list of all the Catholics here at the House of Correction. You filled out your religious affiliation when you were booked in. You're Gus Delaney, right?"

"Oh. Yes." He didn't remember filling out his religious affiliation.

"You can receive communion if you want to," Father Driscoll said.

Gus didn't care if he received communion or not, but he realized he had rudely greeted this man who seemed to be kind and earnest and he didn't want to compound his rudeness. "Sure, thank you Father." Father Driscoll said a small prayer, Gus said amen, and the priest slipped a thin wafer onto his tongue.

"I hear confessions before mass on Sundays." He paused. "Do you mind if I have a seat for a minute?" he said, gesturing to the bed.

"Sure," Gus said. Great, here comes the lecture.

"How are you doing?"

"Besides the fact that I'm in jail with 12 stitches in my head, I'm doing just great Father."

Father Driscoll looked at the floor and shook his head slightly. "Yes, I understand. Listen Gus, I've just got to ask you…what the fuck were you thinking?" This jolted Gus. He had never heard a priest swear before.

"What do you mean?"

"Well, breaking your ex-wife's nose on the steering wheel and then attacking Lieutenant Goddard. I mean, *what were you thinking?*"

"I wasn't thinking. It just happened."

Father Driscoll slapped his hands on his thighs and sighed. "Ah yes. That's the problem. You've got to think, Gus." He shook his head and looked at the floor as he said this.

"So they told you why I'm here? You know all about me?"

Father Driscoll nodded. "I saw it in the papers first," he said. "You were on the front page of every newspaper. You were the lead story on every local news station. How could I not know about it?"

"I guess so." Gus shrugged.

"But what I want to know is how a talented guy like you is in here. A guy who should be doing great things with his life is instead going to spend the next three years locked up."

"That's a good question," Gus said. "I wonder that myself."

"I'm sorry about your son," Father Driscoll said. "You have a tough time with this still, don't you?"

How did he know all this? Gus wondered. "Yes," he said, looking at the ground. "Yes I do."

"I want you to know that I am available to you for any of your spiritual needs. I will pray that God will give you strength to get through this difficult time and that your son is safe somewhere and that you will be reunited with him in the future."

"Thank you Father. I appreciate that."

Just then Gus's fat-ass cellmate arrived. He gave a dirty look toward Father Driscoll for sitting on his bed. Father Driscoll stood and shook hands with Gus. "I'll be back to check on you again soon. Keep faith that God is with you always, even – especially – when you're in your darkest hour. There is mass every Sunday you know; we have a chapel right here at the jail. I hope I'll see you there." He shook Gus's hand again, made the sign of the cross, and left.

Gus kept to himself the following week. He didn't bother speaking to his cellmate any more. He ate his food with the Vietnamese gang members and neither spoke with them nor looked at them. Father Driscoll approached him again one afternoon while he read in the library.

"Why don't you get a job?" the priest blurted as a greeting. "Maybe it would be good for you."

"A job?"

"I think it might be helpful for you to get a job, become part of the community."

"What do you mean get a job? Here at prison? And you think I want to become a part of this… *community*?"

"Yes, right here. They have lots of jobs," Father Driscoll said. "It would make the time pass quicker."

"Jobs like what?"

"You could get a job mopping floors, dishwashing in the kitchen, folding laundry, or working in the canteen." Father Driscoll must have noticed the frown on Gus's face. "They're not so bad," he said. "Don't be too quick to disparage honest labor –"

Gus cut him off. "No thanks Father. I'll pass."

"You get paid you know," Father Driscoll said.

"Yeah, how much?"

"A dollar thirty an hour."

It took all of Gus's power to keep from bursting out laughing at this priest who so earnestly thought Gus would want to mop floors and do dishes for a dollar thirty an hour.

"I'm sorry, but what the hell am I going to do with a dollar thirty an hour? I could buy a car after thirty years maybe."

"You'd be surprised. It adds up and there are lots of things guys use the money for – cigarettes or gum at the canteen, they send it home – you can find a lot of uses for it. Besides, are you doing anything better?"

"Yeah, I'm reading the Count of Monte Cristo here and I'm enjoying it a lot more than cleaning toilets or whatever it is you think I should be doing."

"Very well then. I hope you'll at least think about coming to mass on Sunday. I didn't see you last week."

"I'm sorry Father. I'll come this week."

"Good man. I think you'll be glad you did. I'll look for you on Sunday then."

Gus turned back to Monte Cristo. He finished before the end of recreation and repeated the last sentence a few times in his head: *All human wisdom can be summed up in two words: 'wait' and 'hope.'* "Ha," he said. "No shit."

Gus continued his routine for the next two months. He didn't talk to anybody. He watched the brothers play basketball, not joining even though his body had healed. He read in the library. Despite his promise, he didn't attend mass. One day one of the young guards named Daly approached him in the library as he read V.C. Andrews' *Flowers in the Attic*. "Mr. Delaney," he said. "I was wondering if I could ask you a question."

"Sure," Gus said. Daly had never spoken to him before except to give commands like telling him to line up for count. "I just opened an account at Fidelity and I was wondering if I could talk to you about what kind of investments I should look at."

"Why do you want to talk to me about it?" Gus asked.

Daly looked confused. "Because you're…good with finances."

"How do you know who I am?"

Daly smiled sheepishly. "You're kind of our celebrity inmate. Everyone knows who you are."

Gus continued the game. He wasn't inclined to help any of the guards who not only kept him imprisoned here but also chastised him for his former success – even if they seemed like decent guys like Daly. "Who does everybody say I am?"

"You're the financial guru – number one in your class at Wharton, manager of the Elysium Fund, the best fund in the country when you were running it. I've read all about you."

"Yeah, and did you read that that was seven years ago and that for the past seven years I've been an unemployed alcoholic, a washed-up woman beater?"

Daly looked at the ground. "Yes, I've read about all that. I'm sorry about your son. I remember when it happened. I don't know how anyone who went through what you've gone through could survive. I think I might have killed myself."

"Don't think I didn't contemplate it," Gus interjected. "Thank you though. As far as the investing, I've been away from it so long I don't think I could help you." Gus knew he could help him but he didn't want to get involved. He just wanted to read and not be bothered.

"Okay, Sir. Sorry to interrupt your reading." Gus watched him as he walked out of the library. Did he just call me sir? He was the first polite, respectful guard he had seen in the House of Correction since he'd been there. The others treated the inmates like animals. Granted, most of them were animals, but the guards could have tried a little harder not to strip all traces of dignity from them.

The day after Daly's request Father Driscoll appeared at Gus's cell. "Do you mind if I sit down and talk with you for a little while?"

"I don't know; I'm booked solid with meetings and events today," Gus said. He couldn't help but smirk at his own joke. "No, not at all Father. I'm sorry I haven't been to mass." Father Driscoll pulled in a chair from the hallway.

"Gus, what's been troubling you? I've been watching you – you haven't noticed, but I have. I know a little bit about you and I think you have great gifts to give the world. You were once an up-and-coming star in the financial world and now look at you. It makes no sense to me and I want to help." Gus groaned.

"I know you don't want help from me," Father Driscoll continued. "But I spoke to your mother when she came to visit you last month. I didn't want to tell you. She made me promise to talk to you, to try to help you. She loves you very much you know, and she worries about you as much too."

"She is a lady of great faith," he continued. "I gave her my word that I'd talk to you and do everything in my power to help you. Since then I've watched you from afar. I've noticed you make no effort to make friends with anyone. You don't speak to anybody. You don't get involved in anything." Gus fidgeted on his bed, alternating from staring at the ceiling to looking at Father Driscoll.

Father Driscoll continued speaking. Gus was his prisoner – a captive audience. "Officer Daly asked you for your advice in a field in which you know more than everyone in this prison combined and you refused him. You must realize that the guards are not bad guys. They're just doing a tough job."

"I beg to differ," Gus said.

"Of course there are some bad eggs – that's true everywhere. But most of them are decent, dedicated men and you'd like them if you got to know them. Most of the guys they're dealing with are gang members – dangerous guys. None of the other inmates have your intellect, your education, your talent, or your potential – and yes, you still have potential to do great things in this world if you just open your heart to it."

Gus sighed, an audible sigh like a child makes when a parent is scolding him for something and he doesn't want to hear it. "You have so much anger in you," Father Driscoll said, leaning forward in his chair. "I know where it is coming from; you've gone through something that no human should ever have to go through. I want to give you a little prayer to think about." He pulled out of his pocket a folded sheet of paper and handed it to Gus, who unfolded it. It had a hand-written prayer on it. Father Driscoll stood and walked toward the cell door.

"Winston Churchill once said, 'If you're going through hell, keep going.' Keep going Gus," he said. Then he waited at the door while Gus looked at the piece of paper. Gus sat up in the bed and read the prayer.

I asked God for strength, that I might achieve...
I was made weak, that I might learn humbly to obey.
I asked for health, that I might do greater things...
I was given infirmity, that I might do better things.
I asked for riches, that I might be happy...
I was given poverty, that I might be wise.
I asked for power, that I might have the praise of men...
I was given weakness, that I might feel the need of God.
I asked for all things, that I might enjoy life...
I was given life, that I might enjoy all things.
I got nothing that I asked for, but everything I had hoped for.
Almost despite myself, my unspoken prayers were answered.
I am among all men, most richly blessed.

"I sure don't feel blessed," Gus said. He put the paper on the bed. "You spoke with my mother?" Father Driscoll nodded. "She once told me God would never give me more than I could handle. I want to tell you Father that God, time after time, has given me more – much more – than I could handle."

"Gus, you are not aware of the reserves of strength you have within you. God—"

"God! Please don't talk to me about God. God did shit for me! He abandoned me a long time ago!"

"No Gus. You abandoned Him. Only with God at your side, in your thoughts, do you have the strength to conquer the hardships of your life."

"Father, forgive me, but I went to Sunday school and church and all that and learned all about God and how He would care for His children. I've heard it all and it's a bunch of crap."

"Gus, there is a big difference between knowing *about* God and *knowing* God. If you *knew* God, as opposed to simply knowing about Him, you would find comfort."

Gus lay back down on the bed and stared at the ceiling. "I don't know Father. God wasn't there for me when I needed Him; the Catholic Church was never there for me – through my divorce, when Jack disappeared. Everyone else from the town came out and offered their help – people from school, people from Jack's little league, even the town selectmen. But not Father Dwyer. Not Father Gugino."

"I never saw them." Gus's eyes followed a crack in the ceiling. "I never heard of any prayers or collections taken up at St. Andrews, or any attempt to round up volunteers. Oh, people from church joined the search and prayed, but they did it of their own volition with no prompting or support from the church."

Gus turned his head and glanced at Father Driscoll. The frail priest was looking at him with such a pained expression on his face that it startled him.

"What's wrong Father?" He sat up in the bed again.

Father Driscoll remained silent for a second. Then he said, almost in a whisper, "I'm here for you now Gus. I can't account for what happened in the past, but I want you to know that if you'll let me, I'm here for you in whatever way you want to use me. And whatever you might think, God is here for you too. If you seek Him humbly and sincerely, He is here for you."

"You have never properly grieved," Father Driscoll said, changing the subject. He walked back to the chair but didn't sit. He stood next to it, resting his hand on its back. "Those who experience trauma and deep grief feel shock, emotional numbness, emptiness, anger, depression – a jumble of complex emotions." Gus leaned forward on the bed. This man, who hardly knew him, looked like he might break down and cry at any moment.

"You need to free yourself from what was and adjust to what is. You need to build new, positive, constructive experiences."

"Father, I'm fine as I am, honestly. I'd rather just be left alone with my books, jog on the treadmill, and eat my meals in peace. I don't need to make any friends here in prison, or build positive experiences." The cell door clanked and fat-ass walked in and scowled at Gus and Father Driscoll.

"You're in my prayers, Gus," Father Driscoll said. He made the sign of the cross and left.

CHAPTER 47

The Kiss

Jack went to the jutting rock overlooking the pond to think about what Abraham had said. He took a Bible with him and he read passages from it. A rustling in the woods nearby startled him from his intense reading of Psalms. It was Frances.

"Augustine," she said. "I thought you'd be here."

Jack ignored her and continued reading. "Why must you do this to me?" she asked. "We used to be dear friends and now you never talk to me. You used to confide your deepest thoughts and ask me mine and now you ignore me."

"Why do I do this to you? Why do you do this to me!" he said. "You follow me around like one of the puppies wherever I go and no matter how hard I try to avoid you, you always find me and want to talk." A hurt look entered her eyes; she looked like she might begin to cry. Then her eyes did fill and with a blink one, then another teardrop overtopped the bottom lids of her eyes and rolled down her cheeks.

"I'm sorry," she said. "I thought you were fond of me. I thought you enjoyed my company." She began to run away, slowly at first, then quickly. "I shall never bother you again," she called over her shoulder, and though Jack could no longer see her face, he could tell by the tempest in her voice that she was weeping. "You didn't have to be so cruel!"

He stood up and ran toward her. "Wait!" he yelled, but she kept running. He stopped for a moment and then sprinted after her.

"Wait! Please!" he said. He grabbed her by the arm and spun her around. He stood facing her, holding her shoulders.

"You don't understand at all," he said. "It is torture for me to see you each day or confide in you not because I am not fond of you but because I am *too* fond of you." He looked into her almond eyes, the same eyes – the only eyes – that had given him comfort on the first day he spent with the community. When everything was turmoil, she was the one lullaby that calmed him.

Her eyes didn't understand and they told him to explain.

"Frances," he said. "I'm more than fond of you. You must know this by now. I love you more than I've ever loved anyone in my life." She opened her mouth to speak but he cut her off.

"You have an inner, joyful music about you that makes my heart dance. I can't breathe in the morning before I think of you, and at night you are the last vision in my head before I drift to sleep. I don't know if you've ever felt this way about me, but I've felt this way for about you for a long time."

He shouldn't have been telling her all of this, he knew, but he had nothing to lose. He had to tell her. He let go of her arms. "None of that matters because you've been chosen for someone else; you've been promised to Emmanuel and I can never marry you. That is why I've avoided you and ignored you and treated you poorly."

"Forgive me," he said. "I speak too boldly, but I need to tell you my heart. I didn't mean to hurt you; it was self-preservation. I had to accept fate. I had to accept that I could never be joined with you in the way I have dreamed about almost since the day I met you."

Tears rolled down Frances's face, though the look on it had turned from sadness to joy, as if a cloud had passed to reveal the sun. She looked at the ground and then into his eyes. She spoke softly, barely above a whisper.

"I have loved you too. It became clear ever since that day nearly two years ago when we hiked along this same rocky path around the pond and you took my hand in yours to help me climb the boulders. I had been fond of you before then, but something changed that day and I could not stop my feelings, no matter how hard I prayed." She looked at the ground. "I love you still."

A surge, like an electrical current, went through Jack's body. Each limb had grown excited by the jolt. Frances looked into his eyes again.

"But I realized the same thing you did," she said. "It cannot be. I am betrothed to Emmanuel and I have known it for some five years now. Just this afternoon Abraham told me we are to marry in four months, in September. This is God's will and we must abide—"

Jack stepped forward, took her face in his hands, and kissed her, all the energy flowing though his body and rushing to his lips as they met her soft, moist lips. He trembled. It was his first real kiss.

The kiss lasted but a few seconds before she pulled away. She trembled as if she might faint, then regained her strength. "Augustine, it cannot be! You mustn't tempt God's displeasure."

"How could God ever be displeased that we love each other?" Jack asked.

"I am not yours," she said. "Do not covet thy neighbor's wife."

"You are not his wife!" Jack said. "How do we know God's will truly? How do we know that God's will is not for us – you and I – to join in the bond of marriage?"

"Because Abraham has said thus," she said. "God speaks to Abraham. He is the prophet and knows God's plan for us. In four months I *will* be Emmanuel's wife."

"Does he Frances? Does Abraham really know God's will for us? Why would he pick Emmanuel for your husband? Do you love him?"

"It is not for me to decide," she said. "Emmanuel is a fine boy and will make a fine husband."

"Yes, but do you love him? Prudence is a fine woman and will make a fine wife, but I don't count the stars dull next to her smile. I don't hear the songbird's voice as a shriek next to her voice. To me, there's only one smile and one voice that compares to the stars and the lark."

"Augustine, you are treading towards blasphemous thoughts right now. You know it can't be." She was still crying. "You must see me differently...and I, you."

"I will never see you differently than I do now," Jack said.

"You must, and I—" Jack kissed her again; mouth to mouth, their bodies pressed against each other. She tried to pull away.

"Don't," Jack said. He looked into her eyes. "There must be a way."

"I'm sorry," she said, tears dripping off her chin. "There is no way." She pulled away and ran. Jack took a few steps to follow her, then stopped and watched her dart through the woods until she was out of sight.

He stood at the edge of the jutting rock. He couldn't stay in the community then. Not if they couldn't be together. He had prayed for years asking God to give him strength. But his prayers had gone unanswered and he no longer had the ability to endure the suffering that each day spent near Frances – but not with her – brought. He was not Job.

He decided where he would go – at least for a little while – to clear his head. He went to his room and packed a few toiletries, two blankets, a pillow, and extra clothes. Then he snuck into the kitchen and took enough food to last for a couple weeks, some matches, cider, and candles. He put them all in the sack with his clothes and hid it underneath the basement stairs. He would leave that night after everyone had gone to bed.

That evening, Jack spent all of vespers studying Frances's face. He knew every aspect of it by heart – the tiny mark above her left eye from when she cut it on a tree branch as a child; the pock mark on her forehead that served as a reminder of the time she had chicken pox; the curl of her mouth...and those full lips, lips he had kissed only twice but whose sticky softness he would never forget.

That night he snuck out of bed, dressed in the basement bathroom, and took the full sack. He tip-toed out the front door and scurried around to the back yard, down to the ocean. The air was warm against his face. He walked along the beach wall toward the wooded area where a small, unused rowboat rested in the tall grass.

Jack struggled to pull it over the wall onto the beach. Then he threw his sack in the boat and dragged it to the water. He hopped in and rowed toward the dark mass a half mile in front of him. The salt-sea air smelled good as the boat cut silently through the waves to his metronomical beat.

After forty-five minutes, the bottom of the boat scratched against the sand. Bassett's Island. He pulled the boat up the beach and hid it within the shadows of the rickety boathouse that he had not seen in ten years.

The dock had collapsed and lay half-buried in the sand, and the roof of the boathouse had fallen in. Jack rushed up the hill through the long grass toward the house. It loomed in the moonlight. It too had deteriorated since he last saw it – the windows were all boarded up.

He knocked on the front door. Nothing. He knocked again. It didn't seem like anyone was there. He turned the knob. Locked. He ran to the side door by the kitchen and tried that door, but it was also locked.

There was one window that was not boarded up, a narrow one by the side porch. Jack pulled a two by four from in front of the shed and slammed it through the window. He wiped the glass away and shimmied through.

The house smelled musty and stale. The kitchen table was in the same location as ten years ago, and the two chairs remained underneath the window. He opened the cabinets and was surprised to find a few cans of Campbell's soup, a box of Cocoa Puffs, and a box of elbow macaroni. He wondered if someone had been there recently.

He opened the refrigerator and the rancid smell from it nearly made him vomit. He ran upstairs to the bedroom. The mattress was still there, and the bureau, but nothing else. The window was boarded up. He pried the board from the window so it wouldn't be so dark and gloomy. He wanted to see the light of the moon and the sun when it shined in the morning.

He remembered how nervous he had been the last time he was here; how much he had disliked all of them and how anxious he was to leave. Now he wished they were all here. The house was lonesome without them. Unlike before, he was glad to be able to stay for as long as he wanted.

The mattress was covered with mold on one side, so Jack spread one of the blankets from the sack over it. He put the pillow and other blanket on top of it.

Then he took out the Bible and placed it on the dresser, and kneeled beside the window and prayed.

"Please God, guide me, for I walk in darkness and have walked thus for so long. Please show me what I must do and forgive me for my sins. If this goes against thy will for me, forgive me, for I know not what else I can do right now."

"I've tried for many years to accept that Frances is betrothed to Emmanuel; that it is Your will that has been sent to Abraham to pass to me. But I cannot bear the torture of seeing it executed, seeing her smile with him knowing that her heart beats for me."

"I cannot bear that he will share her nuptial bed in four months and she will bear his children and they will praise Your name together while I praise it alone the remainder of my days. And if not alone, I will praise it falsely wed to someone I could not possibly love as I love her."

Jack spoke his words aloud – to the walls and the window and the world. "Forgive me that I do not endure selflessly! Forgive my wickedness! Give me the wisdom to see the right and the strength to abide by it." He bowed his head. "But now let me stay here and try to find concord from this discord. Amen." Then he crept under the covers and slept.

The sun shining through the window woke him and he went outside and built a fire where Ciara and – he forgot the boy's name – once sat next to a bonfire and talked about God and sin and life. Jack thought about these same things now as he ate oatmeal and drank tea.

He remained on the island for a week. He prayed and meditated every day. He walked along the beach and through the woods, contemplating what to do. He decided that he must go back to the community and live the life God had called him to live. He must endure whatever test of faith life brought him.

The last day on the island he begged forgiveness for his sinfulness and selfishness and promised God he would rededicate himself to serving Him. He knew he would be punished and possibly flogged by Abraham, but he knew he must go back and regain God's grace.

As he shoved off from the shore in the tiny, wobbling rowboat, he shouted the prayer written by John Donne that he had read often in one of the community's prayer books. "Oh my God, I commend my spirit! Declare thou thy will upon me, O Lord, for life or death in thy time; receive my surrender of myself now; into thy hands, O Lord, I commend my spirit."

CHAPTER 48

Rock Bottom

Gus had watched the basketball games nearly every day for three months. He looked at his paunch. He was certain he'd gained more weight in prison. Though the jail had a training room with weights and treadmills, he hadn't used them. He smoked two packs of cigarettes a day. He might either have a heart attack trying to run up and down the court or he would embarrass himself out there – or both.

He decided finally to shoot a few baskets before they started the afternoon recreation game. He stood two feet from the hoop and shot one-handed shots over and over again – all from two to four feet. Slowly he moved back to six feet, then eight and then ten. All one-handed. This is how he had been taught by John Havlichek at a Red Auerbach summer basketball camp he attended every year as a child.

"Look at Larry Bird shooting from two feet out," one of the black guys said.

"Someone better tell Whitey that they stopped using the one-handed set shot in the 40s," another one said. They all laughed.

"That shit ain't gonna do you no good when I send it back into the stands," the first guy added. Gus glared at the guys. He had watched them every day and they were athletic, but not skilled. He knew back in his college days he would have run these guys off the court. They were young and thin and muscular, not an ounce of body fat. He looked down at his own bulging belly. He was a doughy, middle-aged, balding, cigarette-smoking, slow man. Yet he couldn't resist the competitive fire that burned inside of him.

"Yeah? You wanna see what I got?" he said. "See if you can stop me?"

They all looked at each other with incredulous smiles on their faces. "Did Whitey just challenge us?" one of them asked.

"I think so," another one said.

"Oh it's on! Let's see what Larry Fucking Bird's got." They picked teams and began. The guy Gus guarded called for the ball. They gave it to him and he backed into Gus hard, banging against him. Gus banged back. The guy shot a turnaround jumper and missed. Gus's team got the rebound.

"Give the ball to Larry Bird. I want to see what he's got." The point guard threw Gus the ball. *Let's have some fun,* Gus thought. He jab-stepped to the right. Then he brought the ball up high and faked as if he was passing the ball over his opponent's head, toward the basket. He held the ball over the guy's head for a split second and then pulled it back. The guy whirled around looking for the ball. He turned back around, confused.

Gus stood smiling, the ball firmly in his grasp. Then he faked a jump shot and the guy jumped as high as he could to try to block it. While the guy was in the air, Gus dribbled past him, faked left with a crossover dribble when a second guy came to guard him, and flipped the ball in the hoop, an easy lay-up.

"Looks like Whitey can play some ball," Gus said. "Next time do you want me to tell you how I'm going to beat you before I do it?" He laughed and jogged back to play defense. Gus's man called for the ball again, and again he missed his shot. He gestured for the point guard to give Gus the ball. Gus took it at the three point line and got into triple threat position – a stance in which he was ready to pass, dribble, or shoot.

"Come on Whitey," the guy said. "Try that shit again." Gus faked a pass. The guy lunged and then recovered. Gus jab-stepped to the right again and the guy jumped back, knocked on his heels, and then tried to regain balance. That split second when the guy was off balance was all Gus needed. He crossed the ball to his left side and blew past the younger, quicker man.

As he drove toward the basket, another guy moved toward him to block his path, leaving the man he had been covering open under the hoop. *Too easy*, Gus thought. He looked toward the basket as if he was going to shoot and then began to pass the ball to the open man. Suddenly from behind, an arm came across Gus's head, smacked him hard across the face, and then pulled him down. Gus fell backwards to the ground, clothes-lined.

Gus sprang up and turned around. It was the guy who had tried to guard him. Gus ran up to him and punched him in the face. The force of his punch knocked the guy to the ground. Immediately, five guys came after him. They knocked him to the ground. A kick in his ribs stole his breath. They kicked him over and over in his back and ribs. Then one kicked him in his head. That was the last thing he remembered.

Gus, woozy, woke in a strange bed. He didn't know where he was or remember what had happened. There was an ice pack on his nose, a sling on his arm, and a wrap around his torso. He turned gingerly to his side. Father Driscoll was sitting in a chair with his eyes closed, rosary beads clutched in his hands, mouthing prayers.

"Father Driscoll!" Gus said. It hurt to talk. "Where am I?"

"You are at Lowell General Hospital. They beat you up pretty badly."

"What are you doing here?"

"I was praying for you," he said. "I was asking God to give you strength and peace."

Gus turned his head gingerly toward him and stared at him for a few moments. The priest's face was gentle and earnest.

"Thank you Father," he said. "I need it."

"We all do Gus." Father Driscoll smiled and Gus was sorry that he had never gone to his mass.

"How are you feeling?"

"I've been better. How long was I out?"

"You've been sleeping for about four hours."

"Four hours?" Gus pushed himself up into a sitting position. "You've been here the whole time?" Father Driscoll nodded.

"Why?"

"Because I was worried about you. You had a collapsed lung and you have a few broken ribs."

"But I don't understand—" Gus saw that Father Driscoll had something else in his hands. It was old and tattered. A blanket. "What is that you have?"

"Do you recognize it?"

"Is that Jack's blanket?" Gus strained forward to see it better. "Do you have Jack's blanket?" He braced himself for disappointment. Father Driscoll nodded.

"But how—how did you get it? I tried for years to get that and they told me they lost it in some warehouse."

"They had it Gus, along with these items they took as evidence that day." He leaned over and picked up a small box and brought it and the blanket to Gus. "They should have never kept these from you. I'm so sorry." Gus smelled the blanket. He could not smell Jack in it anymore. Inside the box were Jack's coloring books and drawings that Goddard had taken the night Jack disappeared. Tears rolled down Gus's face.

"Thank you Father." Gus held the blanket against his wet cheek. "You can never know how much this means to me."

"I promised your mother I would look after you. And I believe in you Gus. I also believe in God's power to help you. But you must listen, *really listen*, before you will hear Him and find the answers you seek. The kingdom of God is within you." Gus nodded.

"But how did you—"

"I haven't been chaplain here for fifteen years without making a few friends among the police officers along the way," he said. "Now get some rest, and promise me you'll do three things once you are better: go to mass on Sundays; teach Officer Daly finance and ask him to teach you self-defense in return; and, finally, pray – talk to God each day. 'Faith, mighty faith the promise sees and looks to God alone; laughs at impossibilities and cries: it shall be done.'"

CHAPTER 49

Cracks

Jack stumbled up the lawn during afternoon chores. Gabriel and Isaac stopped hoeing the garden when they saw him. Prudence and Teresa stopped picking flowers and stared at him. Moses dropped his tiller. "Abraham!" he bellowed.

Just then Jack saw Frances run out of the barn. She froze just outside the doorway and watched Moses hobble over to Jack and grab his arm. Jack saw her take a few steps toward him and then stop when Moses glared in her direction.

"Come with me, Brother Augustine. I hope you have a good excuse for your absence or it's a whipping you're going to have."

Jack explained where he went and why he went. He told Abraham how he had struggled and needed to get away to share his thoughts alone with God – to meditate and pray without the distractions that plagued him daily in the community. He told Abraham that after much contemplation, God had shown him the right path and that he had come back to rededicate himself to God, to make a new covenant of his faith.

Abraham told him that he would be punished and would have to confess his sins before its members in a public meeting. He would accept his punishment, which Abraham must administer to regain God's grace.

"Take off your clothes!" Abraham said. Then he asked Moses and Jacob to bring him to the barn and he asked Sarah and Elizabeth to gather the community there for a public confession. Jack did not fight or struggle. He walked to the barn unclothed with his head bowed. He stood before them, his hands folded in front of his nakedness.

Abraham stood among them and began to read from a book: "The Lord hath given us leave to draw our own articles. We have professed to enterprise these and those accounts, upon these and those ends. We have hereupon besought Him of favor and blessing."

"Now if the Lord shall please to hear us, and bring us in peace to the place we desire, then hath He ratified this covenant and sealed our commission, and will expect a strict performance of the articles contained in it; but if we shall neglect the observation of these articles which are the ends we have propounded, and, dissembling with our God, shall fall to embrace this present world and prosecute our carnal intentions, seeking great things for ourselves and our posterity, the Lord will surely break out in wrath against us, and be revenged of such a people, and make us know the price of the breach of such a covenant."

"Brother Augustine hath brought shame upon himself and this community," he continued. He held a switch in his hand. "He hath breached his covenant with God by committing grievous sins this week. He broke two of God's commandments: he stole food from the community and he has coveted his neighbor's future wife."

"He has confessed these sins to me. In addition, he left the community under the dark of night without permission, when he has been forbidden to do so, and he went to a place known to be inhabited by heathens, drug users, fornicators, and derelicts. Surely with his actions he has brought the Lord's wrath to this community. What have you to say, Augustine?"

"I confess these sins to you and to Almighty—"

"Get on your knees!" Abraham roared and he lunged forward and brought the whip down so hard across Jack's back that it knocked him to the ground. "Now tell us your sins and repent!"

"I confess to stealing food so that I would not grow hungry while I spent the week in seclusion and reflection," Jack said. "I will earn it by working extra hours in the gardens." He looked over at Frances. She was not looking at him but was staring toward the ground, hiding her face. Jack could hear that she was weeping.

"I also confess that I have coveted someone who does not belong to me. It is the reason I left – to reconcile my earthly desires with God's will. Please forgive me and guide me. I am weak. I have walked in darkness in search of God's divine light to guide my path. Forgive me. I understand now what I must do."

Jack felt the blow of the whip again against his bare back. He winced.

"Please forgive me Father Abraham. I did not intend to bring shame upon the community. I only intended to strengthen God's grace in my life." The whip cracked against his back and he fell prostrate on the dirt.

"You must be punished to purify your soul, and to bring the community back into God's favor," Abraham said. "Your sin is great; therefore your punishment must be commensurate." The whip cracked against his back again. The pain shot across his torso and drool dribbled down his chin.

Abraham continued speaking – for how long Jack couldn't tell. He couldn't hear all of the words but he heard "Let this be a lesson…" and "Let us pray that Augustine will repent…"

Then he felt two arms pull him off the ground and carry him outside. They dropped him on a bed in the shed – the same shed where Timothy had spent three weeks during his shunning after he was beaten. The door closed and Jack howled in pain.

About fifteen minutes passed. Jack writhed and wailed on the bed, the searing pain like someone was running a hot iron across his back, branding him with the seal of shame. His brow dripped with cold sweat.

Then the door opened. It was Sarah. She carried a basket of cloths and balms. "Here, let me look," she said and she bent over to inspect his back. Jack saw her wince.

"Augustine, you shouldn't have done that," she said. "Especially after I told you how guilty Abraham felt for not being stricter with Jeremy when he strayed down the dark path. You must have known punishment would be severe."

"This is going to sting but it will help it heal," she said. She applied a balm to his back with some sort of brush. Jack clenched his teeth then yelled in pain. "There, I know it hurts, but you'll get better soon." She sat on a chair beside the bed.

"Augustine, Abraham punishes you to help you improve. Proper love means proper discipline. Parents who love their children discipline their children, and Abraham loves you very much. Do you understand that?"

Jack didn't answer. "He does," she said. "He loves you as a father loves a child, with all his heart, and only wants the best for you."

"Why doesn't he want me to marry Frances then?"

"You cannot understand all of the reasons; we cannot question God's motives," she said. "We simply must abide. As you well know, God reveals Himself to Abraham, and He revealed to him that Frances and Emmanuel are to marry, and you must struggle with the corruptions in your heart and abide."

"Abraham is trying to protect you from God's wrath and help you lead a godly life, but you keep thwarting him, and for that you were justly punished."

"But I left the community to see rightly, to reflect and know more clearly how to move beyond my selfish love for Frances and live a humble and obedient life dedicated wholly to God."

"You know you are forbidden to leave the community," she said. "You told nobody your intentions. You stole from us. And then to go to a place that had once been a den of sin…I don't know what you expected or hoped to find there. And, worst of all, you have confessed both to me and Abraham that you covet someone whom you know is marked to be someone else's wife."

"When you were absent from morning prayers and breakfast, and you were not found in your bed, Abraham became gravely worried," she continued. "He cried out, 'My child! My child! What have you done?'"

"He searched all the grounds for you the entire day, and he commanded everyone to forgo chores and studies to look for you. He dispatched Moses and Timothy to Van Winkle to search for you in the town. You shouldn't have made him worry so, Augustine."

"It is true; I do not understand Abraham's ways, or God's," Jack said. "I did not tell anyone of my plans because I was uncertain myself what I would do. I didn't know if I was coming back, and I wanted time alone to meditate and determine my course. I did not hope or expect to find anyone on the island," he lied.

"I'm glad you decided to come back," she said. "You must remember that the community strengthens each other. Our aim is to be a pure community of Christians and we are here to guide you, to help you fight against indwelling sin and do what is right before God. You must seek spiritual guidance from us always if you have moral failings that need to be addressed."

Jack thanked her for her love and said he would seek spiritual help from community members in the future. But he thought about how he had sought counsel from many members of the community, including Sarah and Abraham on this matter, and none of them ever brought him to a better understanding.

Their guidance only frustrated him more and led to his desire to seclude himself apart from the community for a week to search within himself and with God and to unlock any secrets hidden in the sea or the trees or the marsh of the island.

In fact, the week spent on the island did more for his spiritual well-being than any recent conversation with anyone in the community. His faith in God had changed in ways he was just beginning to realize. In some ways, it grew stronger.

He knew he would still struggle with his conflicting feelings for Frances and his surrender of himself into God's hands, the new covenant he had made of selfless sacrifice, but he would face the struggle marching forward into the sun.

"I shall go now," Sarah said. "You need rest." She mixed a powder in a glass of mead and handed it to him. "Drink this," she said. "It will help you sleep." She left and Jack fell asleep soon after drinking the mix.

He woke to stabbing pain in his back and cold, clammy sweat covering his body. He shivered and turned to his side to reach down to the floor for the fallen blanket and gasped with surprise. Sitting in the darkness on the chair beside the bed was Frances.

"Frances! What are you doing here? You know Abraham said I am to be shunned for three weeks. If they find you here you will be punished and flogged too. You must leave!"

Frances leaned forward and took his hand. She was crying. "I will not leave you," she said. "I don't care what they do to me. It's all my fault that you were beaten and are here now."

"No, it's not your fault. The fault, this sickness in my heart lies with me. You did nothing but just be you, the most beautiful creature I've ever known, and that was all. Please go before they catch you and the wound in my heart equals the wounds in my back."

"No, I will not leave you," she said. "When you left I thought I would never see you again, and only then did I realize that I could not live without you – and not just as a brother of the community, but as a husband and father, as my other self."

"My heart has a wound as deep as yours and deeper still. I've struggled as much as you, have prayed for guidance as much as you, and have suffered in my heart as much. O, I cannot marry Emmanuel!" she cried and she buried her head on his shoulder and wept.

Jack pulled off her bonnet and smelled her long blonde hair. Flowers. He had only seen her without her bonnet a handful of times during the entire time that he knew her. He ran his fingers through her freed hair. "I wish you didn't have to keep your beautiful hair hidden underneath this bonnet all the time," he said. The gashes in his back didn't matter anymore. Nothing did, except that she loved him.

"Your cheek is so warm," she said. She felt his forehead. "Your brow is on fire. Here let me find a blanket." She pulled another blanket gingerly over Jack's torso as he lay on his side.

"Be still," she said. "I'll be right back."

"Where are you going?"

"I'll be right back," she said and she kissed his lips. She put her bonnet back on and rushed out the door. She came back fifteen minutes later with a bucket and a washcloth. She dipped the cloth in the bucket and wiped his forehead. Then she took the balm from Sarah's basket and rubbed it over Jack's wounds.

It stung, but she rubbed it so tenderly that Jack winced but didn't feel the agony he had when Sarah had applied it.

"I must go now," Frances said. "Vespers will begin soon and I must not be missed. I'll come back before bed if I can to check on you." Jack squeezed her hand.

"Thank you," he whispered. Sarah came after vespers and dressed his wounds. She stayed about an hour and read the Bible and Thomas Aquinas's Summa Theologica to him. Jack didn't hear half the words she spoke. He was thinking about Frances.

When Sarah left he waited a few hours for Frances, but she didn't come. He finally fell asleep. He woke at sunrise when he felt someone brushing the hair off his temple. It was Frances.

"Good morning," she said. "How are you feeling?"

Jack turned toward her and a jolt of pain shot down his back. "I'm good," he said. "Better now."

"I'm sorry about last night, but I could not come," she said. "After Sarah tended to you she sought me out to talk about my marriage preparations. When I finally was able to come see you, you were asleep. I didn't want to wake you."

She gazed toward the window. "Augustine, do you think fate is something to wait on, to sit idle until it plucks you by the collar, or is it something to pursue, something to fight for?"

"What do you mean? Why do you ask?"

"I asked Sarah why I was fated to marry Emmanuel and not you. She said because God willed it so. I asked her why and…" Frances stopped speaking.

"Why?" Jack asked. "What did she say? I have asked her the same question many times and she has only told me that it is God's will, nothing more. Did she tell you more?"

"No," Frances said, looking out the window. "She did not tell me." Her eyes returned their gaze to Jack. She stared at him.

"What, what is it?"

"Forgive me. That is not the truth…I do not want to hurt you. I asked her and she told me."

"What did she say? Tell me!"

"She said that you were not pure because you came from outside of the community. She said that is why you cannot marry. Only those who have not been tainted by the outside world can marry and have children. You are not meant to marry anyone from the community," Frances said.

"I can't believe it," Jack said. "Do you feel that way?" he asked.

"No Augustine. Of course not. But I prayed last night for God to reveal to me why He would will this and His ways remain a mystery and I don't understand. I find that I'm questioning the very things that once I was certain about."

"I have prayed for many years over these same questions Frances, and I also have not learned the answer," he said. He sat up on the bed and took her hands.

"The great theologians through the years – the ones we study – asked similar questions. How is the universe governed? Is it governed by chance? Blind fate, anonymous necessity? Or is it governed by the unseen benevolent hand of God – Divine Providence? Are our lives destined from birth, or do we shape our destiny as we go, with God's blessing?"

"We have been taught that our fates have been determined by God, who is the only one who knows our purpose here," Frances said. "We have been told that we must abide by the path determined for us and that to take a separate path is to bring eternal damnation upon us."

"I'm willing to risk eternal damnation if it means I get to spend the remainder of my earthly days with you," Jack said.

"You mustn't say such blasphemous things Augustine! I will pray God forgive thee for that." Something startled her and she jumped up and rushed to the window.

"What is it?" Jack asked.

"Nothing, I thought I heard someone," she said. "I must go soon but I had to see you." She clasped his hand in hers. "I pray and pray to our divine Father to guide us. I ask for His forgiveness and mercy. Oh Augustine! My soul has never been troubled as it is now. As much as I try to commit myself to God's will and to Emmanuel, I cannot do it! I curse my weakness and wickedness!"

Jack squeezed her hand. "You could never be wicked, and you've always been much stronger than I. You are the kindest, most pure and devoted servant of God and His children that I have ever known. God will answer us in His way and in His time," he said.

She smiled and kissed him on his forehead. "I'll come back when I can," she said, and she disappeared out the door.

For two and a half weeks Frances snuck in early in the morning before the others were awake and came again late at night when the others had retired to bed for the evening. Sometimes they talked for hours at night; sometimes she rubbed balm on his back with not a word passing between them, or she sat in the chair holding his hand as he rested. These evenings further cemented their bond, as they prayed together, meditated, and conducted unspoken symphonies that needed no words to convey the harmony their souls sang.

They talked often about their shared plight, their faith, and the dread they felt at the thought that they could not be together in the sunlight, only in shadow, and only for these few weeks when Jack was alone in the shed and prior to her marriage to Emmanuel.

Then one night when Frances was rubbing balm on his back, something happened that changed everything.

CHAPTER 50

A Man of Faith

They brought Gus back to the House of Correction that afternoon before dinner. He skipped dinner and crawled into his bed. It hurt to breathe. He fell asleep and didn't wake up until roll call the following morning. "What day is it?" he asked the guard.

"It's Sunday."

"I'd like to go to mass."

When Gus appeared at the chapel for mass that morning, Father Driscoll beamed. The opening hymn began – Amazing Grace – and Gus, who never sang in church, sang along. After mass and breakfast he went to the library to find a book. He saw Officer Daly.

"Hey Daly, still got that Fidelity account?" Gus asked.

"Yes, Sir."

"What type of account did you get? Retirement? Brokerage?"

"I got an IRA, but I want to open a non-retirement account too. It's been a little confusing though. There are so many options; I'm not sure what is best for me."

"That's okay I can help you," Gus said. "Can I make a deal with you?"

"Yeah?"

"I will help you with your account and teach you everything you need to know about investing and building your portfolio if you will teach me self-defense so I don't keep getting the crap kicked out of me."

Daly hesitated. The enthusiasm briefly reflected on his face disappeared. "I'm sorry Mr. Delaney. I don't think I can. We're not allowed to teach the inmates self defense."

Gus thought for a moment. "That's too bad because I could really use it." He laughed and Daly laughed nervously with him. He remembered Father Driscoll's kindness. "Listen, I'll still help you with your investing and maybe you can slip in a few suggestions on the sly once in awhile that will keep me alive in here. Would that be all right?"

Daly smiled, "I think that will be all right."

"Great. Well then, tell me, what do you have in your portfolio at the moment?"

"I have some IBM and Sears so far," Daly said.

"And what are your goals? You've got the retirement account. What do you want to do with the brokerage? Save for a house? Additional income? More retirement funds? What's your timeframe?"

"Well, I'd like to buy a house some day. I'm not sure what my timeframe is," Daly said

"Hmm," Gus said. He paced around the library, his mind whirring. He searched the library shelves. "Ah, here it is," he said, pulling out *Beating the Street*. "First, I want you to read this. I used to work with Peter. He's good and his book gives valuable advice."

"I read that already," Daly said. "But I'd love to get your advice. I'd love to know how you did it at the Elysium Fund."

"Well, for one, I was able to get out and visit companies, talk to their CEO's, look at their books, their products. Now I'm pretty certain I won't be able to do that for awhile, but you can help get me a lot of the information I'll need."

"I can't talk to CEO's or look at their books," Daly said.

"No, but these are publicly traded companies and you can get me annual reports and stuff like that. But even more basic, can you start by getting me the Wall Street Journal, Investors Business Daily, and other financial papers and trade magazines so I can catch up on trends and news about companies and industries? Like I said, I haven't really followed the market in ten years and I can't help you unless I know what's going on."

"One second, let me write these down," Daly said.

"Let's start with the newspapers, and I don't mean the Globe or the Herald."

"Which newspapers again?" Daly asked.

"The Wall Journal and Investors Business Daily. Can you arrange for those to be delivered each day?"

"I'm not sure, but I'll try. Where would I get those?"

"Any 7-11 or convenience store or newsstand should have them," Gus said. Officer Daly wrote down the newspapers and Gus told him to give him some time to read up on things and they would meet again to discuss Daly's portfolio. The next morning when Gus's cell door opened for breakfast, there was a copy of both newspapers at the foot of it.

The newspapers were dropped off at Gus's cell every morning. Gus asked for other information – company reports, industry reports, trade magazines, new tax law guidance. He spent a month reading everything to do with finance he could get his hands on. Then he began to tutor Daly and make recommendations on stocks, bonds, mutual funds, REIT's, spiders, options, commodities, emerging markets, short sales, P/E ratios, diversification, sector funds, large-cap, small-cap, taxes – the gamut.

Gus's lessons helped Officer Daly so much that he told some of the other guards about them. Soon Gus was conducting regular classes in the library each afternoon during recreation. He wrote information on a chalkboard they provided. He answered questions. All of the guards, including the warden, began asking him to help them with their portfolios.

The guards grew into a facsimile of Gus's old team at Fidelity. They did all the research and gathered the information and Gus told them what it all meant. With Gus's assistance they even managed to visit Massachusetts companies to collect information. Gus wrote down questions and they scheduled meetings with CEO's and COO's and wrote notes to take back to him.

Gus began to notice the other inmates become interested in Gus's little investment club with the guards. Not because they wanted to learn about investing, but because they thought it was bad form for him to be on such friendly terms with the guards.

Daly provided him with everything he asked for. He also taught him a few self-defense and hand-to-hand combat tactics at night. Gus soon realized that what Father Driscoll had told him was true: most of the guards were good guys – decent guys trying to do a difficult job in the midst of wise-ass punks and low-life scumbags.

When Gus listened to some of the verbal abuse and crap the guards put up with he marveled at their restraint. He would have wanted to slap the dirt-bag inmates silly. He wondered if he had acted the same way when he arrived. Had he immediately put them on the defensive with his shitty attitude?

For the remainder of his time at the Billerica House of Correction, Father Driscoll spoke to Gus about faith and listened to Gus talk about Jack; about Stacy; about Lilly and Victoria and his divorce.

He listened to anything Gus wanted to talk about. Then he'd teach him how faith could help him get through each day. "Gus, make peace with your past. Let go of the negative and hold onto the positive."

"But how, Father? How can I let go?"

"Through meaningful prayer. You must pray from a pure heart," he said. "Say real things to God – unveil yourself. To have a relationship with God we have to take off our masks and personas before Him."

"I'm still not sure what you mean."

"What I mean is to pray earnestly. Don't just go through the ritual. Feel God's presence. Be humble. Don't be afraid to open up. Talk to God like you would talk to a best friend. Say what is in your heart. Be vulnerable. God listens."

Gus began subconsciously nodding his head. "Yes, I think I understand," he said. "But I still struggle with what happened to Jack. I still think of him all the time – is he out there? Will I find him? Is he dead? Will I ever know or will I suffer for the rest of my life?"

"Only God knows the answers to many questions, but remember that failures and suffering move you in the direction of His will. *Fate* says: whatever will be, will be. *Faith* says with God's help and power, I can face anything that comes my way. Perhaps your fate was to end up here to finally find the faith to carry you through all the suffering in your life."

"Just take special care to not neglect the good things in your life each day – like you told me you did with Stacy," he continued. "There will be good things in your life in the days ahead and you must recognize them even though you may still grieve your losses. If you are going to reflect the glory of the Lord, you are going to have to open yourself to His grace."

For two and a half years, Father Driscoll met with Gus three mornings a week for breakfast to discuss faith – or the Red Sox – and to listen to Gus. For two and a half years, Gus attended mass every Sunday, read the Bible every night, and laid bare his heart to God. He asked for forgiveness, peace, and strength to get through each day. For two and a half years, he led the investment club and helped the guards with their finances.

Gus never had to use his self-defense lessons because none of the inmates ever touched him again. His fat-ass cellmate was transferred and Gus never got another one. He slept on the bottom bunk the remainder of his stay. He also quit smoking and lifted weights and played basketball every morning.

Father Driscoll told him he had to take care of himself because finding Jack would do him no good if he had a heart attack and died. "Corinthians says, 'Therefore glorify God in your body, and in your spirit, which are God's.' Gus, you must nourish your body just as you do your soul," Father Driscoll said. So he did. And of course Gus didn't drink in prison either. The result was he lost 40 pounds and found he had more energy than he'd had in ten years.

When the time came for him to leave, Gus looked around the library and chapel, the two places he had spent most of his time – praying, reflecting, reading, teaching

– and a tinge of nostalgia crept into his thoughts. He couldn't believe that he might actually miss the place; that he had found some peace there.

He said goodbye to Daly, the other guards with whom he had become close, and the warden. Father Driscoll walked him to the parking lot. "You've got a ride?"

"Yes, my mother is picking me up. I told her two o'clock, so I'm a little early. I'll wait for her here." They stood awkwardly in the parking lot for a minute, not speaking to each other and gazing at the passing cars. "Father Driscoll, will I still be able to see you?" Gus asked.

"Of course Gus. I was hoping you'd still want to have breakfast with me even though you're free."

"That would be great," Gus said, relieved. Father Driscoll was his one friend in the world right now and he didn't want to lose him.

"Good. Well now we can have breakfast in a nice place. There's a great diner on Treble Cove Road called Ma's Donut Shop. Why don't you meet me there on Monday?"

"Yes, I'd like that."

"Oh and Gus, I'll be saying the ten o'clock mass at Saint Andrews this Sunday. I'll expect to see you there."

Gus smiled. "Yes Father."

"All right. I'm going to go back in now. God bless you. As you go on from here, think on these things: whatever is noble, just, pure, lovely, and good. Remember everything we discussed; with God's help and power you can face anything that comes your way. Listen to your mother. She's right – God will never give you more than you can handle. I pray that you will find Jack. Never give up hope. Nothing is impossible with God."

CHAPTER 51

Seeing the Face of God

J ack's back had healed much in the two and a half weeks since his beating. Frances continued to visit him each morning and night. One evening as Frances applied balm, she moved her hands slowly across his back and continued to the edge of his sacred garment. She slipped her hand underneath the edge to follow a whip mark. Jack turned around suddenly.

"Oh! I'm sorry," she said, blushing, and she jerked her hand away. Jack grabbed her hand and put it at the edge of his sacred garment and began to move it down underneath the clothing.

"No," she said, and she pulled her hand back up.

"I'm sorry," Jack said. "I feel such urges with you. Forgive me."

"I feel them too but we must fight them."

"Will you lie with me here for a little while," Jack asked, "and take off your bonnet so I can run my fingers through your hair again?" She nodded and he pulled her on top of him, he on his back, she resting her head on his chest. He watched her head move along with his breathing. He moved his fingers along her neck through her hair. She shuddered. "That feels nice," she said. They remained that way for awhile. This moment, Jack thought, must be similar to how it felt to see God's face.

After about thirty minutes like that, Frances moved up until her cheek was touching his. He wrapped his arms around her. Slowly, their heads turned. Their cheeks brushed against each other until their lips met. They kept their lips pressed against each other for a long time.

It occurred to Jack that this was a compromising position and if anyone walked in they both would be punished severely. But nobody would, he assured himself. Everyone was asleep. They kissed, lips on sticky lips, and then he kissed her neck. Her back arched and then her body tensed. "What's wrong?" Jack asked.

"This is wrong," she said. "I have been living my whole life in pursuit of a godly life, pure and chaste, not to commit offenses against our Lord, and now I am doing just that. We're spitting in His face and ensuring our passages to hell."

She held his face in her hands. "This – being with you, surrendering myself to you – is in my heart. But I know it is wrong, and that I should only do so as your bride, our act sanctified by God's sacrament and blessed in heaven as well as here on Earth."

"Frances, my love for you is sanctified in my heart and if God would not bless our love then that is not a God I choose to serve anymore." Jack saw that these words shocked her. Her mouth hung open and her eyes were fearful.

"Augustine, please don't speak like that! You mustn't! Please repent them and ask for forgiveness."

"No. It's the truth. But Frances, what I'm trying to say is that I believe the God we love *would* bless our love – *has* blessed our love. I do believe in destiny. I believe God brought me here not only to find Him, but to find you too. I believe that Abraham has misinterpreted God's will."

"It is said that we are in a state of journeying – in statu viae – toward an ultimate perfection yet to be obtained," Jack continued. "I have found my perfection in your embrace tonight."

"But Abraham will never allow it," she said. "And whenever Abraham speaks on matters of faith or matters when God reveals Himself to him, he speaks ex cathedra and cannot be challenged or refuted. His word is God's word and we must obey or we offend God and risk banishment from His divine love forever."

"Why should Abraham have any special audience with God in matters that I've spoken to God about and thought about a thousand times more often than he?" Jack asked. "Who granted Abraham ex cathedra status except he himself?"

"Sarah has taught that God granted ex cathedra status to Abraham through a revelation," Frances said.

"Sarah speaks of God revealing Himself to Abraham many years ago, calling him to establish this community, but is he the first and last word on our destinies?" he said.

"The sacred books say that by humble listening God will show each of us our way," he continued. "When I was on that island, alone for a week, with only the woods and the birds and the ocean, I listened for the Lord to tell me the right word. Over and over again, He kept telling me in my heart that His will is for us to be together. I denied it and was determined to forget about you and devote my life to God, but that washed away like the sand the minute I saw you again."

"Please pass me the Bible," Jack said. He opened it and began to read: "Though I speak with the tongues of men and of angels, and have not charity, I am become as sounding brass, or a tinkling cymbal."

"And though I have the gift of prophecy, and understand all mysteries, and all knowledge; and though I have all faith, so that I could remove mountains, and have not charity, I am nothing."

"And though I bestow all my goods to feed the poor, and though I give my body to be burned, and have not charity, it profiteth me nothing."

He moved his finger down the page.

"Charity…Rejoiceth not in iniquity, but rejoiceth in the truth; beareth all things, believeth all things, hopeth all things, endureth all things."

He spoke now more deliberately, punctuating certain words, pausing to look at her and make sure she understood.

"Charity never faileth: but whether there be prophecies, they shall fail; whether there be tongues, they shall cease; whether there be knowledge, it shall vanish away. For we know in part, and we prophesy in part. But when that which is perfect is come, then that which is in part shall be done away." He spoke these words urgently.

"When I was a child, I spake as a child, I understood as a child, I thought as a child: but when I became a man, I put away childish things."

"And now abideth faith, hope, charity, these three; but the greatest of these is charity." Jack closed the Bible and took her hand.

"Don't you see? Charity – love – is the greatest of all our endeavors." He moved his face steadily toward hers. "It is the truth; prophesies cannot stand up to love, love is the truth, everything else must vanish." He looked into her eyes. Their faces were a foot apart. "When that which is perfect is come, then that which is in part shall be done away." He could feel her breath on his face. "My love for you is perfect, and true, and all prophesies fade next to it."

Jack closed his eyes and kissed her. He held her in his arms and could feel her trembling. "Marry me," he said.

Frances laughed a nervous laugh. "Marry you? Why do you talk like this when you know it is impossible?"

"Marry me tonight," Jack repeated. "Let us have one night as husband and wife before you marry Emmanuel next month. Can this be our wedding night and this our marriage bed?" He pulled her against him and kissed her. He was hard against her and his heart was beating like mad. She let out a soft sigh.

"Augustine, have you forgotten Timothy's beating for fornication? We can't." Jack kissed her neck lightly.

"I'd…risk…the worst whipping…that Abraham could give me…for one night…with you," he said. Frances became seized by some internal force as he continued to kiss her neck and mouth and she began to rub against his body, up and down, and lips and arms and bodies became tangled like a rosebush enmeshed around a lattice.

Jack remembered Ciara and that boy in the bedroom. This is how they were – like animals. He had been horrified and disgusted by them, but now he knew. And he knew he was sinning in the eyes of the community and God, but he didn't care.

He pulled up the hem of her long skirt and felt her. Her hands moved up and down his thighs. He was so excited. Her breaths and kisses and lips, heavy against his neck. Suddenly he was inside of her. "Oh!" she cried and her fingers pressed into his back. She was panting.

"Am I hurting you?" Jack asked.

"No!" she said breathlessly. Jack felt a tingle deep inside that built up, warm and – she moaned and he convulsed and the tingle burst and she convulsed and they were one, together and sweating, and then it stopped. She remained still on top of him, breathing hard. Then, suddenly, she pulled off of him and began to weep.

"What? Did I hurt you? What's wrong?" Jack asked, and he went over to comfort her but she turned away.

"We have sinned!" she cried. "We have committed blackest, foulest sin! I have brought shame upon myself and my family. I have acted no better than a whore or a dog. Oh God forgive me!"

"Frances, please be calm," Jack said. But she wasn't calm. She arranged her clothes and fixed her hair.

"I must go," she said. "I must go and confess my sins and ask for forgiveness and wait for God's judgment." She ran out of the shed. Jack called after her in a loud whisper.

"Wait Frances. No! Come back!" He went as far as the door. He couldn't risk confronting her in the open in her agitated state or they might wake someone up and be found. He watched her run down the path to her cottage until she disappeared in the darkness of the woods.

CHAPTER 52

A Horrible Secret

Jack's shunning ended late in the evening. Frances never came to see him again in the shed during his last week there. He returned to the basement room he shared with Emmanuel with whom, during ten years of rooming together, he had discussed many thoughts on faith, the community, and the daily happenings of its members. They had shared their hopes for the future and thoughts about the past. They helped each other in their moral accounting and discussed the works of the great theologians, from Augustine to Aquinas.

But ever since Jack had learned that Frances was to marry Emmanuel, they never talked about her. As Timothy had said to him, Jack and Frances's affection for each other had been interpreted by some members of the community. Jack and Frances had always been close – much fonder of each other's company, it seemed, than she and Emmanuel were.

Despite what Timothy said, in the past others could not be certain that this affection was nothing more than close friendship, or the bond of a brother and sister.

Now it was out in the open. Everyone knew his desire – romantic desire – for Frances, including Emmanuel. Jack looked over at him praying by his bed and felt both shame and anger. Emmanuel often told Jack his moral shortcomings – pointing them out, he said, so that Jack would recognize them and seek improvement.

Emmanuel had never been whipped, nor would he ever be. He was an example of pious duty for the entire community according to Abraham. He was such a stellar student of the Bible and catechism that Abraham gave him the great honor, only afforded to a few of the elder men in the community, of leading morning prayers and vespers.

During these moments, Emmanuel gave effective sermons on humble, obedient, godly living. He often could be found reading the sermons of Jonathan Edwards, and he modeled his sermons – with Abraham's approval – after Edwards's.

Emmanuel turned from his prayers to address him. "Augustine, I have prayed for you these past few weeks," he said kindly. "I have asked God to reveal

Himself to you so you can accept your fate. I have asked Him to forgive you for all of your sins and to welcome you back into His grace."

"Thank you brother Emmanuel," Jack said. "I am humbled by all of the community's prayers for me, and in my weakness I ask you to continue to pray and to help me live rightly."

"I shall help you," Emmanuel said. "You must continue to examine the faults in your character and seek redemption. Repent your sins and return to God's grace. I will continue to pray that you purge your greed and self-interest and keep our community pure. Fear not, Augustine, the Lord will show you the way."

Jack kneeled and prayed too. Then they turned out the lantern and went to bed. Emmanuel meant well and Jack tried to love him as he should. But he could not love him. He hated him. He hated him because he would possess the one thing Jack could not live without. "God forgive me," he muttered before falling asleep.

The next morning at prayers, Jack saw Frances for the first time since that night a week ago. He tried to catch her eye, but she never looked at him. She sang and his heart ached. At breakfast when she sat in her appointed seat next to him, he greeted her with a warm smile. She returned it with cold eyes that looked away from him quickly. She turned to Jacob and spoke with him.

Jack ate his oatmeal and eggs and surveyed everyone in conversation around the table. Towards the end of breakfast he tapped her on the arm. "Can we talk for a minute?" he asked.

"I do not think that is appropriate right now," she said.

"Why? What's wrong?"

"I am a sinner and I must repent my sins and seek redemption so I can return to God's grace," she said. "Repentance in Hebrew means to return or to feel sorrow. In Greek it means to see in a new way. I must see in a new way. I must return to my former self and surrender to the Lord. I must work to perfect what is lacking in my faith and I pray you will do the same."

She looked at her empty bowl of oatmeal while she spoke and never looked at his face. "I pray you will beseech our Divine Father to pardon us our transgressions." When she finished speaking she got up without looking at him and left the room.

During the next few weeks, the hot summer weeks when in years past they spent much time together walking the trails of the woods, she would not speak to him. Jack tried to ask her why they couldn't establish again their friendship, but her only answer was, "It cannot be."

For two months she did not speak more to him than to wish him good morning at breakfast. She avoided his path when she could, and when she couldn't, she walked by him with her head down and would answer his greeting with only a cool hello.

One day in early August, though, Jack sat down at the breakfast table and Frances leaned over and whispered to him. "I need to talk to you today. Can you meet me at the rock overlooking the pond after chores?" Jack heard a strain, a fear in her voice that he had never heard before.

"What's wrong Frances?" he asked.

"I cannot talk to you about it here. Please meet me at the pond."

Jack attended his studies after breakfast but he could not concentrate. The tone of her voice troubled him. Something was wrong. After chores he immediately started to walk down the path to the pond.

"Where are you going, Brother Augustine?" Moses called out. Why was he stopping him now? Jack wondered. Had he seen Frances whispering to him at breakfast? But how would he know what it was about? Had he overheard her talk about meeting at the pond?

"I'm just going for a walk in the woods," he said. "I'll be back for dinner."

"I was wondering if you could help me carry some bales of hay to the barn and spread it for the animals," Moses said.

"Right now?"

"Yes, I want to get it done before dinner." Jack panicked. What would he tell Moses? He couldn't help him, not right now.

"Moses, forgive me, but there has been something troubling me and I want to reflect on it. Can it wait until after dinner and I'll help you then?"

"Perhaps your reflection can wait until after dinner," he said. "Or perhaps you can unburden your troubles with me while we spread the hay and I will guide you."

Jack felt anger rising in him. "I'm sorry brother Moses. Thank you for your kindness, but I must do this now. Forgive me. Perhaps Emmanuel or Jacob will help you." Then he turned and began to walk.

"Augustine!" Moses yelled. "I will pray that God and Abraham forgive you for your selfishness today. I hope you will reflect, while in the woods, on becoming a better Christian and more conscientious brother!" Jack didn't answer but continued walking. He turned to see if Moses or anyone else was following him. He didn't see anyone. He began to jog down the path. By the time he got to the overhanging rock he was sprinting.

Frances was already there. She was pacing back and forth. Jack saw that her face was streaked with tears. He ran to her and embraced her. She clung to him as if she'd tumble down the ledge one-hundred feet below into the pond if she didn't.

"What is it? What's wrong?" he asked.

She let go of him and searched his face. She had such anguish in her eyes. "Augustine, I didn't know who else to turn to. I don't know what to do."

"Tell me what's wrong!" he said.

"I have a child growing inside of me…I have our child inside of me."

Jack staggered. His legs failed him and he had to grab onto a tree. "Wha…what? What are you saying?"

"I'm with child."

"How do you know?"

"I know."

"But how? How can you be sure?"

"Because the same things are happening to me that happened to Grace last year when she had a child inside of her."

"What things?"

"Womanly things. You would not know about them. But I am certain."

"How long have you known?"

"I have known for some weeks."

"Weeks! Does anyone else know? Have you told anyone else?"

"No, I have not told anyone except you here now, but before long I will not be able to conceal it. But God knows, Augustine. God knows and I cannot conceal it from Him."

"Why did you suffer with this alone before telling me?"

"I…I didn't know what to do. I did not want to burden you with my troubles."

"Burden me? Frances, your burdens are my burdens, always." He embraced her again. His mind reeled. *Frances had a child growing inside of her – his child.* Soon her belly would swell and everyone would know. Jack cringed when he thought about what Abraham would do to them.

"What are you going to do?" he asked.

"What do you mean?" She asked and began to cry.

"Oh no," he said. "I didn't mean it like that." He wiped her eyes and squeezed her tightly and rubbed her back tenderly. "I mean are you going to tell anybody else? I'm going to take care of you, I promise. But you'll need someone who knows about babies and about what to do."

"I'm scared," she said. Jack felt at this moment the strongest urge to protect her, this fragile, trembling creature. She was his; he didn't care what Abraham said, or the community or even God – he was not going to let anything happen to her. She had come to him – not Emmanuel or Sarah or Prudence – him.

"Frances, I promise I will never let anything bad happen to you. I will take care of you and protect you. I still love you." She grabbed hold of him and buried her head in his chest. He rubbed her hair. They remained in this silent embrace for a long time, each lost in their thoughts about what came next.

"What will we do?" Frances asked finally. "I've prayed to God to ask His mercy and to ask Him what to do, but I don't know the way."

"We'll find a way together," Jack said. "I will pray too and God will answer us. How long until you begin to show?"

"I don't know, but Faith began to show around five months. I'm nearly three months now, but I'm so tiny, I fear I may show sooner."

"Can you confide in any of the women as you have in me?"

Frances thought for a moment. "I'm not sure. I think anyone I tell will demand that I confess to the community in a public humiliation. I know I should confess and accept the shame and punishment of our brothers and sisters, but I'm scared about what will happen…to us."

"You do not have to confess to the community Frances," Jack said. "It is not for them to judge you—"

"But it is for them to judge me!" she cried. "And it is for me to confess and repent before them and beg for their mercy. For it is I who have stained the community's moral standing with the Lord. Because of our betrayal, I fear God will soon seek His divine vengeance on our family and something terrible will soon befall us if I don't repent and ask for forgiveness."

"Frances, do you really believe our love, and consummation of our love, justifies such horrible things to befall our family members? Do you believe we are damned to eternal hell for our love?"

"Augustine, we committed a carnal act and betrayed the fate the Lord had asked each of us to fulfill. I believe God must be deeply disappointed and angry with us."

"But can we not pray to Him intimately and ask Him to forgive any sins we may have committed? If we are truly sorry for our sins, for breaking our covenant with our Divine Father, can we not speak to Him directly and ask His forgiveness without the community's intercession?"

"No," she said. "We must also confess our sins publicly and ask our brothers and sisters to forgive us our trespass."

"Frances, I confess. I confess to you that I am not sorry for what has happened. I am not sorry for our love, and I'm not going to seek the community's forgiveness for something for which I am not sorry. Please don't do anything until I think upon it more," Jack said. "Let us think about what we are going to do."

"You mustn't say such things Augustine."

CHAPTER 53

The Discovery

The phone rang. Gus answered. His sister Lauren was on the other line. "Listen, Gus. I think you need to get away for a little while. You've been through a lot. We rented a cottage in Falmouth for the last two weeks of August. Tom and I and the kids are all going down. Why don't you come with us? I think it would do you good, and the kids would really like to see their uncle."

Gus thought about spending two weeks with the kids. Though he wanted to see them, he thought it might be too painful. They'd be doing all the things Jack and Lilly would have done. Whenever Gus saw James playing basketball or swimming or talking with girls at the beach, he thought about Jack.

Jack would be seventeen years old – a senior in high school. Gus thought about watching his baseball games, or watching Celtics games together. He would have loved watching Larry Bird. Gus thought about him, awkward and polite, asking some pretty girl to the prom.

Gus used to laugh when Jack would say, as all little boys do, that girls are gross. "Wait and see," Gus would tell him. "You'll change your mind someday."

Then Jack would make a face like he did when he had to eat broccoli and say, "No I won't! Never!"

Yes, it would be too hard. "No, I don't think I can," he said to Lauren.

"Why not," she asked.

"I'm not sure I'm up for it right now."

"Gus, you need to get out of the house and start doing things again. Get your mind off things."

"How will it help me to go with you to Falmouth?"

"Gus!" she shouted. "Since you got out all you do is sit around the house moping. Mom tells me. I'm worried about you. Please come with us. It will be fun. We'll go to Old Silver Beach, we'll walk to town in the morning for coffee, you can go to the movies with the kids at night, we'll dig for clams. We'll keep you busy, don't worry. Please!"

Gus thought. Maybe he'd just go for a few days. He always loved going to Falmouth and Old Silver Beach – the big wave beach – when he was a kid. Maybe she was right and it would be good for him to get away, spend some time with James and Tricia and Kelly.

"I don't spend my days moping! I've been fixing up the house because you guys let it go! I've been planting flowers and grass, fertilizing the lawn, painting the walls, cleaning the gutters, trimming the hedges. I don't think I can go; I have a lot of work to do still. I have to paint the ceilings."

"Gus!"

"Okay, okay! I'll go down for a couple of days and see how it goes."

"Oh good! We'll have fun, you'll see. I'm so glad you're coming and I hope you'll stay the whole two weeks."

"Me too. Thanks Lauren."

"You're welcome big brother. You take care of yourself and we'll see you in a couple of weeks."

Gus met with Father Driscoll at Ma's Donuts to talk to him about the anxiety he had about spending time with Lauren's kids when all he'd think about was Jack and Lilly. "Go Gus. It will be good for you. Remember, you can't neglect what is good in your life today worrying about what was in your life yesterday. You have a family that loves you and wants to spend time with you. So go enjoy yourself and live in the moment and not in the past."

"Okay Father, I'll try." Gus continued to work on the house, fixing it up to how it was in its prime, before Jack disappeared, when he was devoted to making sure it was blemish-less. The only times Gus left the house were to go to the hardware store, the grocery store, his mother's, and Sunday mass.

The day arrived to meet Lauren and Gus drove the familiar route that his parents had taken every summer when he was a child – down Route 24 to 495, past the Wareham water tank that jutted over the scrub pines next to the highway. The tank was a familiar landmark. His father used to play a game to see who would see the tank first.

Gus rolled down the Cranberry Highway, through Buzzards Bay, over the Bourne Bridge to Falmouth. Lauren's cottage was on a quiet little street a hundred feet from the beach and about a half mile from the town center.

"Mom, Uncle Gus is here," he heard Tricia yell when he parked in the driveway and got out of the car. Lauren came out smiling and hugged him. Then she shook his shoulders.

"I'm so glad you're here," she said. Gus walked into the cottage with his suitcase.

"Hi Uncle Gus," Tricia said. She kissed him on the cheek. She was going to be a senior at Boston College next year. She had gotten very pretty. Gus hadn't seen her much, maybe once, actually, in the past four years.

"Where should I put this?" Gus asked, lifting his suitcase in front of him.

"Oh there is a bedroom in the basement – that's where you're staying. You have to go outside, out back, to get to it. I'll show you in a few minutes. You can just put it right there for the moment."

Gus looked around. The cottage was plain, probably labeled 'rustic' in the rental listing. It had a big living room with three small bedrooms off the north-side wall – no hallway – with a small walk-in kitchen at the back. It was decorated in a nautical theme with a blue couch and chairs. A large lobster trap with a glass top served as the coffee table. Seashells and sea glass hung on the walls or rested on the two end tables as decorative incarnations. A four-foot high cast-iron lighthouse sat next to the TV stand, which was a large hope chest. The cottage was perfect.

"Where are James and Kelly and Tom?" he asked.

"Oh they walked to town for ice cream at the Emporium," Lauren said. "Do you want to try to catch up with them?"

"Sure that sounds good."

They walked down the street, past little weather-beaten Cape and Victorian houses, hydrangea flowers bursting from flower beds in front of wooden porches with rocking chairs on them, past kids on bikes and dogs barking in yards, past Burger Paradise and a Sour Grapes tee shirt shore, until they came to the town.

They found Tom, Kelly, and James sitting at a table in front of Ben & Bill's Chocolate Emporium, eating ice cream. The warm breeze brought the smell of cooking chocolate to his nose. James had grown eight inches since Gus last saw him four years ago. He was six feet, two inches – almost as tall as Gus. He stood up and shook Gus's hand. "Hi Uncle Gus, how ya doin'?" he asked.

Kelly hugged him limply. She forced a smile, an insincere smile. She had been best buddies with Lilly, even after the divorce. They were close in age. Lilly's hatred of her father, Gus guessed, must have rubbed off on Kelly. She had never been warm towards him like James and Tricia.

"I hope you guys haven't spoiled your appetite," Lauren said. "I'm going to cook the flounder James caught this morning for supper." They all walked back to the cottage. James, Tricia, and Kelly walked ahead; Lauren, Tom, and Gus lagged behind. Tom fidgeted with his hands as he listened to Lauren tell Gus all the things they could do in Falmouth in the next few days. She especially wanted to go for a drive to look for antique shops.

"So Gus, what are you going to do now?" Tom said finally.

"What do you mean?"

Tom kicked a pebble. "Well, now that you're out…it's been a long time since…what are your plans for work? Are you going to look for a job?" Gus saw Lauren elbow him.

"Tom!" she said. "He's here to enjoy himself, not get grilled on job prospects."

"What? I was just asking him what he wants to do. Maybe I can help."

"It's all right," Gus said. He had contacted dozens of brokerage firms and financial institutions – Putnam, Eaton Vance, Charles Schwab, Vanguard – but nobody wanted to touch him. He was toxic. His arrest had been splashed all over the papers: "High Profile Investor Arrested in Domestic Abuse Case," "Fidelity Fund Manager's Star Dimmed," "The Wonderboy's Fall From Grace."

Fidelity wouldn't take him back even before the arrest, telling him they had gone in a different direction, no doubt because of the suspicions, also printed in the paper, that cops had about him when Jack disappeared. Some people still thought that he was responsible for the disappearance of his son – ridiculous accusations that he might have killed Jack to get back at Victoria.

"I'm not sure," he said to Tom. "I've called all the brokerage firms and a bunch of other places already – I'm sure I've called at least 30 companies with no luck so far. I guess nobody wants to hire someone who just spent the last three years in jail."

"What about John Hancock? Have you called them?"

"No Tom, they are an insurance firm, not a brokerage firm."

"Well they invest in –

"No, its insurance, it's different."

"Well I don't see why you couldn't call them, if you haven't had luck anywhere else. I know a guy there. I could make a call."

Gus cringed. He began to think that coming down wasn't such a good idea after all. It grated on him to have Tom condescend to him. He hated to be the needy one. He used to be the one everyone came to for advice or money. Now Gus had to borrow money from his mother.

And now he had to listen to Tom, who never advanced beyond middle manager at Lechmere, give him career advice. He had to beg others to give him an opportunity to do something that he had once done better than anyone. That was a long time ago.

But he knew he could still do it. And he was sick of letting life dictate its terms to him. Three years locked in a 10 by 12 foot cell was enough dictation.

So nobody would hire him. Fine. He would start his own firm. Plenty of people still asked him for investment advice, and he always delivered superior returns. Even from jail. They may not ask his advice on marriage, but when they had questions about the stock market or how to make money, they turned to him for answers. Why not formalize it and start charging people for what he'd been giving away for free?.

"Thanks Tom, but I have a plan. I'll fill you in when it has percolated a little bit more." Tom looked at him funny.

"You do? Really? Good. Well let me know if I can help you percolate it at all."

"I don't think so, but thanks anyway," Gus said, and with that the subject was dropped and Tom remained silent for the rest of the walk while Lauren discussed a few antique shops that she wanted to visit the next day.

The following morning Tom and the kids walked to the beach while Lauren and Gus went for a drive.

"I think I'll leave tomorrow," Gus said once they were in the car.

"Oh, please don't let Tom get to you. He means well. Stay."

"It's not that. He's fine. It's just that I have a lot of work I have to do."

"On what? What is this plan you mentioned yesterday?"

"I'll tell you about it later," Gus said. They drove along and Lauren told him about the kids and what they were doing and who they were dating. They stopped in a few antique shops and then had lunch at a clam shack on the side of Rte 28A in North Falmouth.

After lunch, they drove down a road called Scraggy Neck and came to a small village. A sign at the side of the road said "Welcome to Van Winkle Village." A small store shaded by a large oak tree caught Lauren's eye. A sign on a post read, "The Mayflower." Vegetables and flowers and herbs filled tables set up in front of the shop and a man dressed in black with a long beard, wearing a hat, stood placidly watching customers in shorts, tee shirts, and flip flops rummage through the squash, potatoes, and daffodils.

"Oh, this is the place I was looking for," Lauren said. "One of the neighbors told me about it. It's run by some Puritans or Amish and she said they make incredible things."

"Look at the guy standing by the vegetables," Gus said. "He's wearing heavy black pants, and a black suit coat. It must be 90 degrees out. Weird."

"Yeah, Sheila – my neighbor – said they're some religious group and they live on a compound and don't come out in public except to run this store. They make furniture and quilts and sell fresh vegetables from their gardens. People come from all over to buy their stuff."

Lauren pulled to the side of the road and parked across the street from the store. "I want to see their quilts. Do you want to come in with me?" Gus looked over at the shop and then down the street. He saw an ice cream shop further down the road.

"Nah. It looks crowded. I've seen enough shops for one day. I think I'll take a walk and get an ice cream. Why don't you meet me there when you're done?"

"Okay. I won't be long," she said and she scampered across to the shop. Gus trudged down the road, past a bakery with pastries and tarts lined in the window, past a penny candy store and another antiques shop. He stopped in a pharmacy and bought a Boston Globe and then continued – past the fire station, a tee shirt shop, an inn, and a bookstore.

A warm breeze blew his hair and he could smell the ocean. The street was clean and hydrangea blossoms of blue and white bloomed in front of the shops. Daffodils popped out of flower boxes underneath windows and next to American flags flapping from the front of each building. This must be a nice place to live, Gus thought.

He waited in line outside of the ice cream shop then ordered a large pistachio ice cream on a sugar cone and sat at a picnic table in a small yard next to the shop. It reminded him of trips to Meadowlands Ice Cream with Lilly and Jack and the neighborhood kids so long ago.

He opened the Globe and flipped to the sports page. There was an article about Len Bias and how his mother was speaking at schools to warn kids about the dangers of drugs. Gus had read about Bias and how he died of a cocaine overdose two days after the Celtics drafted him with the second pick in the entire draft. What a waste. Bias had everything going for him and he blew it all to shove some shit up his nose to celebrate.

The Celtics could have used him too. It was unfortunate that fans would never get to see this guy that everyone said was athletic like Jordan but bigger and with a better jump shot. Larry Bird said it was the saddest thing he'd ever heard. The poor mother, Gus thought.

Gus finished his ice cream and the paper and meandered up the street, watching young lovers holding hands and grandparents with their grandkids. He didn't see Lauren, so he headed to the Mayflower. It was busy. Lots of tourists milled around, turning over trinkets in their hands.

He looked around. It was bigger than it looked from the outside. He searched for Lauren and saw her unfolding a white quilt with baby blue and sea-green flowers embroidered on it. He inspected a delicate-looking rocking chair and then eyed an ornate birdhouse. He checked the price tag. "Forty-three dollars!" he mouthed. "Some racket!"

He reached Lauren, who was still examining the quilt. "You've been here the whole time?" he asked.

"Oh, yes. Isn't this place great? What do you think of this quilt?"

"It's nice," he said. "How much?"

"Two hundred dollars."

"Two hundred dollars! Are you kidding me? That's crazy! You're not buying it are you?"

"Oh listen to you!" she said. "You never even used to look at prices. Now you're a bargain shopper?" She let out a little laugh and then caught herself when she saw Gus wasn't smiling.

"I'm sorry," she said. "I didn't think." She put the quilt down.

"No, that's okay," Gus said. "You're right. I never cared about the cost of anything before. I never had to. Funny how things change." His voice trailed off and his eyes fixed on the quilt.

"Gus, you'll get back on your feet. You're too talented not to."

Gus remained entranced by the quilt. "You should buy it," he said. "It's nice."

"You think?" she asked. She picked up the quilt and held it up, spread it out, examined it. "I really like it but it *is* expensive."

"Yes, you should. If you like it you should get it. And if you don't, I'm going to buy it for you because I'm back." The confidence with which Gus said this startled her.

"What are you talking about?"

"I'm going to start my own brokerage consulting firm. If companies' HR or PR offices are too scared to hire me then I'll hire myself." He saw she still had a curious look on her face – she furrowed her forehead. "I mean enough people still come to me for advice. All the guards had me do their finances. I can really help people."

Lauren put her hand on his arm. "Oh Gus! That's a great idea! You'd be wonderful. I'll be your first client. Tom doesn't have a clue about investing."

"Great, well you go buy that quilt and I'll help you make back your 200 dollars in no time. Hell, I can do that with a few options trades alone."

"Aren't options trades really risky?"

"Yes, they are risky, but I don't mind taking calculated risks because I know what I'm doing," Gus said. "I made a lot of money trading options and futures."

"Yes, I know," she said. "You do." She folded the quilt over her arm. "I'm going to buy it. I love it."

"Good," Gus said. They made their way to the front of the store, past a bin of fishing lures and a bunch of baskets, to the register and waited in line. Gus watched a young girl at the register. She wore a bonnet and heavy dress that brushed the floor when she moved.

When they got close to the register and he could hear her speak, he noticed she spoke in a strange dialect, like a British accent, but not really British. She was polite and said "bless ye ma'am" to a woman ahead in line who had purchased a basket and some herbs and told her how pretty she was. She was pretty, Gus thought. Her eyes were bright hazel and she had clear, pale skin with soft, high cheeks and petite features – at least the features that weren't covered by the dress – a button nose, small hands, and a long, thin neck.

Gus scanned the store. Just then one of the Puritan men came through the door. He wasn't a man really – still a boy. The young man took off a black derby hat when he entered the store. He had a long patchy, wispy beard – the kind of beard young men grow when their chins aren't ready to accommodate a thick one.

His outfit was the same as the man's Gus had seen outside the shop tending the vegetable and flower stands: long, black, thick pants, sandals, a white linen shirt, suspenders, and a black overcoat that looked like a frumpy, worn suit jacket that was much too big for his slender frame. His clothes hung off him like they were hanging from a tall skeleton. *What an interesting people*, Gus thought.

The young man looked around the shop nervously. Gus watched him scan the room until he saw the girl at the register. Gus's eyes followed him as he walked quickly to her. The girl's face changed when she saw him – from one of cheerfulness to one filled with anguish. She tried to turn her attention to the wares customers were handing her to ring up but she fumbled them. The woman she was helping asked her if everything was all right.

The boy walked up beside her and whispered something to her. She shook her head no. He continued saying things to her and she got an even more anguished look in her eyes and she again shook her head no. She looked at the floor and the customers and around the store, but at all times away from his pleading eyes.

Gus strained to hear what the boy was saying, but he spoke too softly. Gus was struck by his tender demeanor. His face and movements conveyed care, not anger or threat. Yet she was visibly upset by his presence. Her eyes welled and she laid on the counter the bowl she had held, said something to the boy, said "I'm sorry" to the customer she had been helping, and ran out the front door.

The boy stood there, distress etched in his eyes. A dark storm cloud seemed to pass over his face. He didn't run after the girl but just stood there. Then he rubbed his eyes.

"Oh my God," Gus said. Lauren looked at him. His face turned ashen.

"What? What's wrong?" she said.

"Look at that boy. Do you recognize him?"

Lauren looked around. "What boy? Who are you talking about?"

Gus tugged her sleeve and nodded in the direction of the cash register. "The kid dressed in the Amish clothes. It's him."

"It's who?"

"Jack!"

"Oh Gus, no," she said. "You can't keep doing this to yourself."

"Look at him closely. It's him. He just rubbed his eyes the exact way Jack used to and it hit me. I thought there was something about him but I couldn't figure it out until he rubbed his eyes. That's him!"

Lauren frowned. "Gus, you thought that boy in Kmart was Jack. You were certain of it, remember? You made a fool of yourself. It's not Jack!" She left the line and rushed back to where she had gotten the quilt and threw it down on the shelf. Gus ran after her.

"What are you doing?" he asked.

Her green eyes looked at him with a ferocity he hadn't seen in them before. "Come on, let's go. I'm not going to let you do this to yourself over and over again. Every month you see a boy that reminds you of Jack."

"That's not true."

"Yes it is!" she roared. "You spend all of your time looking at boys, wondering if they're Jack. I know it's impossible – no actually, I can't possibly know what you've gone through, what you go through every day. I hope I never do." She held his hands in hers. She squeezed them hard

"But it's been ten years," she continued. "Jack is gone. You've got to move on, live your life." Gus began to say something but she interrupted him. "I'm not saying to forget about him. That's not what I'm saying. And I'm not saying he's not alive. I'm just saying there's this whole life out there and for ten years you haven't seen any of it. Stacy was a beautiful girl and she was good to you. She cared about you, but you…nothing makes you happy and I hate to see you like this."

Gus, hurt, pulled away from her. "I need to talk to him. I need to know." He looked to the register. The boy wasn't there.

CHAPTER 54

A Fly Caught

Gus ran to the register, where another woman had taken over and was ringing up some fishing lures. She was older, probably in her early forties, and wore the same dress and bonnet as the other girl. "Excuse me, Miss," Gus said.

She smiled and greeted him cheerfully. "Good afternoon, Sir. How can I help you?" she said in a voice tinged with the same ancient English dialect. Gus thought they all sounded like the actors dressed in period costume portraying the Pilgrims at Plimouth Plantation. They looked like them too. Who the hell were these people?

"Can you tell me where the young man who was standing here went?" Her smile disappeared and she glanced around the store.

"There was a boy here, probably sixteen or seventeen years old," Gus said. "I think he works here. Do you know where he went?" He tried to mask the urgency – the anxiety – in his voice, but he was sure she could sense it. She hesitated.

"I'm sorry, Sir. I didn't see him," she answered finally in a soft voice.

"He was here a few seconds ago. You didn't see him?"

"No, Sir."

"Do you know the boy I'm talking about? About sixteen or seventeen years old, five feet eleven, really thin, brown, wispy beard, brown eyes, dressed in black, with an overcoat."

Gus noticed she had a nervous look in her eyes – she started looking over his shoulder around the shop. "No, I'm sorry, Sir, I don't know who you're talking about." Gus began to say something else, then he stopped, said, "Dammit" through gritted teeth and ran out the front door. Lauren ran after him.

"Gus, what are you doing?" she yelled. Gus looked up and down the street. He didn't see the boy or the girl. He sprinted toward the ice cream shop, looking along the sidewalk for either of them. He didn't see them. He ran inside the pharmacy and a few of the other stores. They weren't there either. He ran back to the Mayflower. Lauren stood outside.

"Gus," she called. "Stop! What are you doing?"

"I'm trying to find that kid. I need to talk to him." Lauren grabbed his arms.

"Gus, let it go. It's not Jack."

"How do you know it's not Jack, huh?" he broke from her grip.

"We've gone through this before," she said. "And every time you're wrong and you embarrass yourself."

"Well what if one of these times I'm right?" he spat. "Have you ever thought about that? I know he's out there, I just know it."

"Gus, 95 percent of missing children—" she stopped.

"Ninety-five percent of missing children are what, Lauren? Ninety-five percent are dead if they're not found in the first 24 hours? Is that what you're going to tell me?"

"No…" Her voice trailed off. "I'm sorry."

Gus rushed past her to go back into the store.

"What are you doing?" Lauren said.

"I told you. I've got to find him. I just have a feeling. I need to see him again. You wouldn't understand." He opened the door of the store.

"No I don't understand!" she shouted after him as he entered the building.

Gus scanned the store. He saw the woman with whom he had spoken a few minutes ago. She was now stacking quilts. "Excuse me, Ma'am. Sorry to bother you again. Do you know the girl who was working that register before you?"

The woman looked over to the register. "That's Prudence. Why do you want to know?"

"That's not the girl who was there before. There was another girl."

"I don't know who was there before," the woman said.

"She was petite, blond, a young girl."

"That must be Frances."

"Do you know where I could find her?" Gus asked.

The woman examined Gus. "No," she said. "Why do you want to find her?"

"Well, actually, I still want to find the boy. He came in to talk to her and then she ran out about ten minutes ago. I thought maybe the girl would know where he is." The woman's face twitched. She resumed folding the quilts briskly.

"The boy you described earlier came in to talk to the girl?" she asked as she folded and stacked.

"Yes. He came in and spoke to her and she seemed to be upset. She ran out the front door." The woman stopped stacking and looked around the store. Gus saw she was nervous. Then she looked at Gus again.

"And what do you want with this young man or lady? If you have a question about something we make or sell here I can help you or ask someone else here to help you."

Gus scratched his chin. "Well no. Not exactly."

"There are no questions that you need to ask any of us if it is not related to what we sell here," she said. "We are a private people." She again turned to folding quilts, at an even brisker pace than before. Gus thought for a moment.

"I think I know him," he said. The woman stopped midway through folding a quilt. The look on her face was as if she had just gotten caught stealing the quilt she was stacking. She read his face and dropped the quilt on the ground.

"What do you mean you know him? You couldn't possibly know him," she said.

"So you know the kid I'm talking about?" he asked. "You said before you didn't know anyone who fit the description I gave you." The woman's eyes searched frantically around the store. She began to walk, but Gus stepped in front of her. She was like a fly trying to get out of a closed window. Her way was blocked. She patted her dress and spoke in an agitated voice.

"No," she said. "I don't know this boy of whom you speak. What I meant is that there is no way you could know *anyone* from our community. We don't mix with others or see the outside world in any endeavor except this store. And only a few from the community are permitted to work here. And those who work here discuss only the products for sale, and nothing else. We go straight back to our home when we finish our work here. So you cannot know any of us, I'm afraid."

"Now I must finish my work here," she continued as she picked up the quilt she had dropped. "Please excuse me, Sir. May God bless you." With that she turned away from him and continued folding and stacking.

CHAPTER 55

The Meeting

G us walked up to the new girl at the counter. "Can you tell me how you get here?" he asked. "Do you drive?"

"No, Sir," she said. "We don't use cars."

"Well how do you all get to the store?"

"Why, we walk," she said.

"Wow, you walk? Do you live far from here?"

"No, only a couple miles." Just then the woman whom Gus spoke to earlier appeared.

"Sir, may I help you with anything?" she asked.

"No Ma'am, thank you." Gus ran out of the store. Lauren was sitting at a picnic table waiting.

"Come on!" Gus said.

"Where are we going?" she asked. "Gus, what are you doing?"

"They walk here. They live only a couple of miles from here. If we hurry we might catch him on the road."

"Gus, no!" Lauren yelled. "Stop this right now!"

"Lauren, I have to see. Please! Give me the keys! You can come if you want or I'll meet you back here. I won't be gone long."

She stood with her hands on her hips. "Lauren please! I'm not going to do anything crazy. I just want to talk to him, that's all."

"Go then!" she snapped and she threw the keys at him. "Go embarrass yourself again."

Gus ran to the car without answering. "I'll be at the pharmacy!" she said. Gus tore down the main road. He didn't know which direction the Puritan compound was; he should have asked the girl at the register before the older woman came.

He would drive a few miles in one direction and if he didn't see the boy he'd turn around and try the other direction. He drove down the road, slowing at side streets and looking to see the boy. He drove a couple of miles and didn't find him.

"Crap!" he yelled and he slapped the steering wheel. He spun the car around and raced back towards the Mayflower, driving past it in the opposite direction.

At this point he didn't hold much hope in finding the boy – so much time had elapsed.

He looked down the side streets. Nothing. Then he came to a narrow dirt road, tree-lined. The road intrigued him. If these people prized their privacy and lived on a secluded, hidden compound, this, he imagined, would be the type of street that would lead to it.

The car crawled down the dirt road, about two miles it seemed, the road winding like a snake cutting through the long grass. No houses lined it – just woods. It couldn't be down here, he thought. The girl said it was only a few miles from the Mayflower. This would be a helluva walk from there.

He decided to drive to the next cross road and then turn around and pick up Lauren and go back to the cottage. The road was too narrow to turn around otherwise. He came around a bend and saw up ahead, about a hundred yards, a gate. "Ugh," he said. He was going to have to drive in reverse awhile until he found a place wide enough to turn around.

He pulled closer to examine the gate. A sign posted to a tree said *No Trespassing*. Another one on another tree said *Beware of Dogs*. What was this place? Was this the Puritan's farm or whatever they called it?

He saw the road continued past the gate, but it veered to the right and he couldn't see where it led. Then suddenly the boy popped out of the woods on the other side of it. "Holy shit! I found him!" Gus said.

He wasn't sure what to do now. Shout out after him? He didn't want to scare him. He saw the boy look over at the car. Curious. Gus would be casual, friendly, let it play out and see what happened. He had learned his lesson with the Kmart kid. He'd be more subtle this time.

Gus hopped out of the car. "Hey!" he called. "Can you help me? I seem to be lost." The boy walked cautiously toward him. Gus studied his face and tried to imagine what Jack would look like at seventeen.

It was hard to do with the beard. What had made him so convinced that this boy was Jack? He had a familiar look about him, sure. Same big brown eyes; same shaped nose, high cheek bones. Yes, he recognized the features.

"Where are you trying to find?" the boy asked. He sure didn't sound like Jack, and not just because his voice had deepened with puberty. The way he spoke was different; he had that same archaic accent Gus had heard at the store.

"I'm visiting my cousin," Gus said. "He rented a place out here. I think I turned down the wrong street."

"You must've, Sir. Nobody lives on this street."

"Nobody?"

The boy looked behind him down the drive. "Well, Sir, I live here with my family." He looked behind him again, then towards the woods where he had popped out. "But nobody else lives here, Sir."

"Oh, I'm sorry to disturb you," Gus said.

"Tis no trouble at all, Sir," the boy said.

"Looks like beautiful country," Gus said. "I've never been down here before. I'm from a town north of Boston called Billerica. Ever hear of it?" The boy's eyes widened and he looked more intently at Gus. Gus watched his reaction closely in case he betrayed any emotion or recognition.

"I...I have heard of it, I think, Sir," he said. He kept looking behind him and around him as if he expected someone to sneak up and attack him. He also shifted his weight from foot to foot and rubbed his wisp-beard over and over.

"Did you grow up here?" Gus asked.

"Yes."

"Your whole life?"

"Yes," the boy said. He looked behind him. "Sir, forgive me but I must go now. I have errands to do before dinner." He tipped his hat and turned to walk away.

Think! Think! "Wait!" Gus shouted. "Sorry, before you go can you tell me how to get to Kingsbury Lane?"

A queer look entered the boy's face again. Did he recognize the name of his old street? "I'm sorry, Sir. I'm not sure where that is."

"Oh," Gus said. "It's around here somewhere. I'll find it."

"Good day and God speed, Sir," the boy said and he turned away and began walking down the drive. Gus watched for a few moments in anguish and tried to think of a way to re-engage him. He slapped the roof of the car.

"Jack!" he yelled. The boy stopped and whirled around.

"What did you say, Sir?"

"I said *Jack*. Isn't that what you said your name was?"

"My name?" the boy asked. "I didn't tell you my name. My name is Augustine." A scared look entered his eyes. "Why did you call me Jack?"

"I thought your name was Jack," Gus said.

"Why did you think my name was Jack? Who are you?" He had a wild, anguished look on his face, like a person watching his house and all his belongings burn to the ground.

"I'm sorry to startle you. Please listen to me for one moment and then I'll leave." Gus walked to the gate. "My name is Gus Delaney and I saw you at the store. I'm not crazy or anything. It's just that I had a little boy who disappeared ten years ago and I've been trying to find him ever since. His name was Jack and I know he's still out there somewhere." Gus was rambling, rushing to get all the words out before the boy, taking him for a lunatic, ran away.

"Something you did in the store – you rubbed your eyes a certain way – reminded me of Jack." Gus looked down at his feet. "It sounds crazy, but when I looked at you, I saw him." Gus had tears in his eyes now. "I can't explain it but I thought maybe…"

He looked up again at the boy and was surprised to see his face had turned ashen and his eyes were wide and his mouth hung open as if he was terrified of something.

Jack looked at this man standing before him crying. A stranger; yet he recognized his features. Could it be? He stood, paralyzed. He didn't know what to feel – joy, anger, hatred – but all he felt at the moment was numbness.

During the past ten years he had grown to despise the man whom he had been told abandoned him. The sinner who abused his mother physically and mentally and caused her to die because he made her stay at that hotel on Christmas Eve. The man who lived a life of rioting and drunkenness, wantonness and strife. Could this be that man standing before him?

"You shouldn't be here," he said. "I'm Augustine and I don't know anything about Jack. My father is Abraham."

"Why do you look at me like you're looking at a ghost?" Gus asked.

The boy turned away. "I'm…it is just that outsiders are not allowed here and I shall get in a lot of trouble if I'm caught talking to you. They'll be back soon."

"Why will you get in trouble? Who's coming back?"

"Because we are not supposed to speak with outsiders."

"What do you mean you're not supposed to talk to outsiders?" Gus asked. "What about the store? You talk to customers at the store all the time. I talked to a few of your…people today."

The boy hesitated. "*I'm* not supposed to talk to outsiders," he said. He continued to glance behind him. "It's not safe for you here. I beg you to please go and never come back."

"Why is it not safe for me here? And why are you not allowed to talk to people outside of your group?"

"Please," the boy pleaded. "Do not ask me any more questions. I cannot answer you. Please go now or I will be beaten."

"Whoa, whoa. Hold on a minute," Gus said. "You will be beaten just for talking to a guy who got lost and asked directions? Who will beat you?"

"Please leave, Sir. That would be best for both of us. I beg you."

"Are you sure that is what is best?" Gus asked. "Listen, I can help you."

"No, you cannot," the boy said. "I am not Jack and I ask you to leave." Gus stood for a moment, blinking in the summer sunlight. Something was wrong, but what could he do? He couldn't do what he did in Kmart. And he was on probation. If this boy was Jack, which he could not prove, then the boy might seek him out.

"Okay. I'll go. But I want you to know something. My name is Gus Delaney and I have been looking for my boy Jack for the last ten years. I've never stopped looking, and I never will. I'll be at 20 Puritan Lane down the road in Falmouth for another week." He wrote his name and the address on a piece of paper and handed it to the boy. "If you need anything – anything at all – or if you just want to talk, you come there and find me."

The boy looked at him for a moment, and without responding – not even a nod – he turned and ran down the driveway. Gus stood and watched him until he was out of sight. Then he got in the car and drove to pick up Lauren. She was standing outside the pharmacy.

"Where were you?" she asked as she got in the car. "Did you find the boy?"

"Yes, I found him," Gus said.

"And?"

"And I still think it might be him."

"You do? Did you talk to him?"

"Yes, and I can tell that something's wrong. He got really nervous about me talking to him."

"Well, yeah…a strange man coming up to him telling him he thinks he's his son who disappeared ten years ago. You'd make me nervous too."

"That's not it at all," Gus said. "When I told him who I was and why I was there and who I thought he was, he didn't deny it. He studied me – he was reading my face as if he was trying to remember what I looked like. I think he recognized me."

"Gus, I think you need help," she said. "I mean you've never seen anybody, a professional counselor – you've never really gotten help. You cannot do it alone, even though you've tried to for so many years."

"I talked to a priest in jail every week. A priest's a professional, is he not?" He paused. "What, you think I'm crazy? You think what I just told you is just some fantasy in my head?"

"No." She paused. "I just think the whole experience was so traumatic and you've never recovered. I don't know who this boy is, but I saw him too and I didn't see anything that made me think he was Jack."

"Well I did," Gus said.

"I think you try to find things because you hope so much that Jack is walking around out there and—"

"And what's wrong with that?" Gus yelled. "Is it a sin to hope that Jack is still alive out there somewhere? I mean we've never gotten any proof otherwise. Is it such a goddamn crime that I still hope I'll find him?" He slammed his fist on the dashboard.

"Gus," Lauren said gently. "It has been ten years. You know the percentages are—"

"I don't give a damn about the percentages!" he shouted. "Until someone shows me that Jack is dead, I'm going to believe that he is alive. And though you think I'm two steps from the funny farm, I'm telling you, that boy turned pale as a ghost when I told him I was Gus Delaney."

"Tell me what happened then. How did you leave it with him?"

"He said he would get in trouble for talking to me. He said he'd be beaten, that he wasn't allowed to talk to anybody outside of that crazy cult he belongs to. Don't you think that's odd?"

Lauren sighed. "Yes, that is odd. But that's how they operate. They are a weird group. They don't mix with people outside of their community. Except for that store, they don't do anything in public; they don't attend public schools, they don't walk in town or shop in the grocery store, they don't go to the hospital when they're sick. They keep themselves holed up in their compound."

"And you think it's odd that a young boy would act awkward talking to a strange man?" she continued. "I think you just frightened him because he's not used to talking to – or even seeing – outsiders."

Gus didn't answer. He drove down the winding road towards Falmouth and the cottage. He and Lauren did not speak for the rest of the drive, Lauren gazing out the window and Gus hardly seeing a thing beyond the fog of thoughts curling around his brain.

Gus pulled into the driveway of the cottage and turned off the engine. "Let's dig some clams and have steamers and lobster tonight," Lauren said. "Then we'll rent a movie – I think Lethal Weapon is out on video – and you forget about that boy, okay?"

"I don't want to forget about him," Gus said. "I want to go back there tomorrow to talk to him again."

Lauren sighed loudly. "Gus, why are you doing this? Why are you doing this to yourself? Don't go back there. Leave the kid alone and get some help."

Gus threw the door open. "Thanks for your support," he said and he slammed the door shut and walked down the road.

"Where are you going?" Lauren shouted after him.

"I'm just going for a walk," he said. "I'll be back."

"Stop putting yourself and all of us through this every day. Some day you'll have to move on with your life!" she yelled.

"That will be the day you bury me," Gus called over his shoulder.

CHAPTER 56

The Ghost

J ack ran toward the house and then veered off down the path. He sprinted to the pond – the place he always went to reflect. He paced back and forth from the jutting rock to the path and around in circles, stopping to look out over the water below.

His father had come for him. This man whom he had pushed from his memory had stood before him, flesh – not a ghost…a man he knew only as a cautionary tale of a sinful, wasted life destined for hell; a faded memory.

He was Augustine and had been for as long as he could remember. Jack? Who was Jack? He did not know this child Jack, nor did he want to. He had not heard that name in so long it jarred his ears just to hear it spoken. He did not want to see this stranger again.

He prayed that he would not come back looking for him. He had enough to worry about, not the least of which was Frances's soon-to-be swelling belly. It would be visible by the time she married Emmanuel. There was no way to hide the fact that the child was conceived four months before she ever consecrated her marriage bed with Emmanuel. Why had she rejected him in the store? Why did she say no to his plan? It was the only way.

He looked at the name written on the paper: Gus Delaney. A name long dead, now risen from the tomb. "Augustine!" said a breathless voice from behind the bend in the path. It was Frances. "Oh Augustine, I wish you wouldn't have done that today!" she cried.

"Done what?"

"Come into the store like that. You know you're forbidden to leave the compound. You will surely be punished."

"Why won't you run away with me?" he asked. "We will build our own life devoted to God together."

"I…I can't," she said. "I've prayed and listened for God's word; I still cannot hear it. But I don't believe He wants us to do what you ask – run away from the community, live in the outside world full of greed and evil. Full of sin. We must stay here where we belong and serve penance for our sin and regain the grace of the community and God." She glanced at the piece of paper Jack clutched in his hand. "What have you in your hand?"

"It's nothing."

"Please Augustine. Would you hide something from me?"

"A man saw me at the store today," Jack said.

"A man? What do you mean? What man?"

"My father."

Frances shook her head. The area between her eyebrows crinkled in confusion. "Abraham?"

"No, my real father. It is him. I'm certain of it. He followed me home from the store. This is his name." He showed her the paper.

"O Augustine. That is wondrous strange. What makes you certain?"

"I remember him." Frances stepped toward him and held his arm. Then she hugged him.

"I hate him!" Jack said suddenly. She stepped back, stunned. The anger with which he said those words surprised him too. Why did he have such strong feelings of anger toward this man he hardly remembered?

"God would not abide us hating any of His creatures," she said. "Augustine, why do you feel thus?"

"Because he is evil and he made me evil. I am impure from him and that is why Abraham will not let me marry you."

"Augustine!"

"It's true. My impure blood is why Abraham decreed I would never marry you. This blood has pumped lust into my heart and caused me to commit fornication with you, forever sealing our fate that we cannot be together in this community. My heritage has blackened my soul forever with no hope of ever seeing the face of God in Heaven."

"Augustine, that's not true. You mustn't say such things."

"It *is* true! I love you as I have never loved another, but this love brought about a passion, a heat that I could not control because of my black nature, inherited from that despicable man! Because I could not control myself, like a dog, I'll bring us both to the heat of hell, on Earth and in eternity. I am wicked, like my father, and I have infected you with this base poison!"

"Who is this person before me?" Frances said. She held his chin. "I do not recognize thee. Surely this is not the Augustine who once told me that our love was pure and good; that God must surely approve it and that Abraham is not the arbiter of God's desires. Who quoted me Corinthians? *Love never faileth: when that which is perfect is come, then that which is in part shall be done away. And now abideth faith, hope, charity, these three; but the greatest of these is charity.*"

She put her hand in his. "Do you not have faith in this anymore?"

"I don't know what I have faith in anymore Frances," Jack said, shrugging his shoulders. "Love is the greatest of faith and hope, but love for what? Love for God is greatest, not earthly love, as much as I do love thee." He held her temples in his hands. "Are you so sure in your faith?"

She had always been sure; he had always sought her guidance in moral matters. But she shook her head side to side. "I...I'm not sure of anything either," she said finally. "But what can we do? Soon I am not going to be able to conceal this child that grows inside of me and we are going to face the fruit of our action. O, I fear the consequence!"

"We must continue to pray," Jack said. "God will answer us in time." He paced back and forth on the rock ledge.

"But as for that man, I do not want to see him ever again. I do not want the help of a man who beat women, a man who staggered around in a blind drunk stupor all his days, aimless and useless to the world, who cursed God and all mankind, and whose home served as a brothel these last ten years." He crinkled up the paper with his father's name and threw it on the ground.

He noticed the slight change in the hue of the sky as the afternoon shadows lengthened. "We must go back now or we'll be missed. I must finish my afternoon chores and then get ready for dinner. Let us pray on it and meet together tomorrow eve after dinner. I'll go first and you soon follow. We must be careful not to be seen alone together."

Jack began to hurry down the path. He stopped suddenly and turned around and ran back to her. When he reached her he kissed her lips and her forehead. "No matter what happens I love you with everything I am and everything I may become in this world. God will guide us."

"Oh Augustine," she said and wrapped her arms around him in a burst that almost knocked him down. He squeezed her and smelled her hair.

"I must go now Frances. My heart and life are yours." He sprinted down the path. Behind a holly bush twenty feet away, two sets of eyes watched this whole scene. Then two figures darted through the woods; two shadows rushing toward the house with the gabled roof.

Jack ran to the barn to finish his chores. His mind was a blur of disconnected images of a long-ago childhood that he couldn't remember. He tried to grasp the memories but they slipped out like sand through his fingers. Why did his father come? He would get Jack in big trouble if anyone had seen him, and Jack had enough trouble as it was.

He yanked the pitchfork from its resting spot and just caught himself from uttering "Damn him." He asked God to forgive him for even thinking the words – words and thoughts that had never formed in his head before or issued from his lips.

He didn't know where his anger was coming from, but he felt such hatred for this man who had come and claimed to be his father, who claimed to be looking for him for the past ten years.

He began pitching hay. His shirt became drenched and sweat dripped into his eyes. He pitched more hay in an hour than he normally pitched in two. He worked himself to exhaustion; worked out the torment in his soul that Gus Delaney had brought to the surface like someone who had dug a hole and hit a geyser. Then Jack walked back to his room to bathe and pray before dinner. He had so many questions to ask God.

CHAPTER 57

The Answer

Gus looked out the front window of the cottage, up the driveway and down the road. Maybe Lauren was right. Maybe Father Driscoll was right. Maybe his mother and Stacy and everybody else in the world who told him to move on were right. This was Kmart all over again. He was certain that boy was Jack too, and he had only embarrassed himself and frightened a child. Why was he doing this to himself? Why couldn't he move on? It had been ten years after all and he had devoted just about every waking moment to finding Jack. Had he learned nothing from Father Driscoll?

This obsession had led to him losing his job, his daughter, a woman he loved, respect from his family, all his friends. He had nobody. "Dinner's ready Gus," Lauren said. "Are you going to join us?" Gus looked from the window to the dinner table where Tricia, Kelly, James, and Tom were all seated.

"Yes." He sat down and placed a bib over his shirt.

"I really think you should talk to someone when you get home," Lauren said. "You can't continue to carry this with you for the rest of your life."

"Yes, I know," he said, eyes staring at the table. "But can we not discuss this now? I just want to enjoy dinner and forget about today." Lauren didn't answer and everyone busied themselves with the task of cracking open their lobsters and eating. A knock at the door interrupted the silence.

"I'll get it," Lauren said. She opened the door and a young girl with a black eye and bloodied lip stood on the stoop. Her eyes darted around the room, scared. She wore what appeared to be a Colonial period dress and bonnet.

"Is there a Gus Delaney here?" she asked.

"Oh my God, what happened to your face?" Lauren asked.

"I have to find Mr. Delaney," she said. "It's important." Lauren turned to call him but Gus had gotten up from the table and was standing right behind her.

"I'm Gus Delaney," he said.

"Can I speak with you alone," she said, glancing at the table and Lauren's family.

"Yes, please. My God! What happened to you?" he said, noticing her bruises. She didn't say anything but looked toward the beach. "Okay, let's take a walk," Gus said. They took a few steps to the backyard before she spoke.

"Mr. Delaney, you have to help me. We're in trouble. They're going to hurt Augustine." A dozen questions flashed into Gus's head. Augustine – wasn't that the name the boy called himself whom Gus thought was Jack? Who was this girl?

"Who's going to hurt whom?" he asked.

"Abraham is going to hurt Augustine," she said.

"Augustine – is he the boy who came into the store today and said something to upset you?"

"Yes, Sir," she said and looked at the ground.

He looked at her bruised face. "Do you mind if I ask what happened to your face?" he asked.

"Please," she pleaded. "We don't have much time. Please come back with me and protect Augustine before it's too late."

"Why me?" Gus asked. "How did you find me and why do you think I can help?"

"Because," she said. "You are his father." Gus fell toward the post fence outlining the yard and grabbed it to hold himself up.

"What...what did you say?" he gasped.

"You are his father," she said in a clear, strong voice. "He told me. He dropped the paper with your name and address in the woods and I picked it up. Please hurry! I'm worried that they might beat him to death this time."

"H-h-how did you get here?" he stammered.

"I rode that bicycle," she said, pointing to an old bike that looked like it was from the 1940s lying at the end of the driveway.

"Wait here and I'll get the keys and drive us there," he said. He sprinted around the house and into his room in the basement, grabbing the keys from the night stand. "Get in the car," he yelled to the girl without going back into the house to tell Lauren where he was going. The car tires screeched as he pulled out of the driveway.

Tears flowed from his eyes in torrents. He couldn't stop crying. "What is your name?" he asked the girl.

"Frances."

"Okay Frances. Tell me everything. Who is Abraham?"

"He is our leader," she said. "He is the prophet."

"Is he the one who took Jack?"

"Took who?"

"Jack. His name is Jack, not Augustine."

"Oh, Augustine. I think Moses brought Augustine to us. Abraham asked him to do this, to save Augustine from a life of…wickedness."

"He took my son to save him from wickedness?" Gus pounded the steering wheel. "He kidnaps a seven-year-old boy from his family and destroys all our lives and he claims the moral high ground?"

"Sir," Frances said. "Abraham told us you spent your days and nights in drunkenness. That you were divorced and you and your wife said and did horrible things to each other. He said you cursed and took the Lord's name in vain, that your house was as a brothel, that you didn't go to church and many other horrible things. Abraham said he took Augustine so that he would have a chance to go to heaven. He said if he didn't pluck him from the wickedness of his old life he would have been banished to hell for eternity."

Gus thought for a moment. He had set a bad example in many ways. He knew that. He thought of Father Driscoll. But who was this Abraham? It was not for him to determine. "His name is Jack, not Augustine," Gus said softly. He gathered his thoughts. "Who is this man to judge me and my life and what was good for Jack? How did he determine any of this when I've never even met him or spoken to him?" He paused and looked at her. "Have I? Is it someone who knew me?"

"Forgive me, Sir, I have only known your son as Augustine and it is difficult to get used to calling him Jack. To answer your question: no, Abraham did not know you. But Moses and Elizabeth spoke with Augustine's mother – sorry, Jack's mother – at great length on Christmas Eve and she told him all of these things."

She studied Gus's face for a moment as he took all this in. Then she continued. "They were on their way home from a mission assigned by Abraham – I don't know what – and they were having car trouble so they spent the night at the same hotel as Aug— Jack's—mother and learned all these things…are they not true?"

Gus smacked the steering wheel again. "I knew it!" he yelled. His lips tightened and his teeth grinded. His eyes again became watery. He thought about how, only days after Jack disappeared, he had a gut feeling that those people with whom Victoria had spoken at the Holiday Inn had something to do with it. And he had helped them jump their car! He had facilitated them kidnapping his own son!"

He hit the steering wheel over and over again and the dam in his eyes burst. If only they – the police, the investigators – had been able to find these people…if only the hotel had done its job and gotten some real identification from them, he might have found his son ten years ago. He bit his fist. Why had he not found those people in ten years of searching? He had failed Jack; it should have been easy to figure out, but he hadn't. The car, already flying down the street, sped up and began lurching at a dangerous speed.

"What's wrong?" Frances asked as she braced herself by holding onto the dashboard.

"Do you know…do you have any idea how you people wrecked my life? Do you have any idea how I've suffered for ten years?"

"Abraham thought Aug—Jack—would not ever enter heaven if he didn't save him from the sinful world in which he was living," she said. "He received a vision – a revelation from God – telling him to do this."

Gus looked at her again. "Did it ever occur to you," he said, "that kidnapping another person's child is a sin? I don't think God condones kidnapping children, does He? Is that in the Bible?"

Frances stared blankly at him and then out her window at the trees whirring by. Then she turned to him again. She had tears in her eyes. "Abraham said that God told him to take Jack and save him from the evil life – he said it was evil – and teach him to reject and forget his old life. He said only by taking…Jack from the sin of his past would he gain entry into heaven and see the beatific vision. We all thought Augustine…sorry, Jack, was fortunate to have been chosen by Abraham to be saved from an eternity in Hell. He became our brother."

"Do you want to know what hell is like?" Gus said. "My life, because of this bastard, has been hell on Earth for ten years!" Tears streamed down his cheeks. "I'll kill him!"

Frances remained silent. She watched the tears dripping off his chin. "I'm sorry Mr. Delaney. I never realized what it did to you. I never knew."

"Were you taken away from your family? Were you kidnapped like Jack?" Gus asked.

"No," she said. "I was born into the community."

"Is this Abraham your father?"

She lowered her head. "Yes. He is my physical father as well as my spiritual father. Please, I beg you to not harm him. He may have wronged you, but his intentions were good, his instructions came directly from God. Please forgive him."

Gus looked at her, incredulous. "I'm sorry Frances, but I'm going to kill your father. Then he can ask God directly why he told him to kidnap someone else's child."

"Please Mr. Delaney, show forgiveness in your heart," she said.

"How can you expect me to forgive this man who stole my child, the child I've been looking for the past ten years, the man who you tell me is now going to beat him to death. You come and tell me all this and what do you expect? You expect me to forgive him? Turn the other cheek? I don't know what kind of religion you practice, but it's not mine. I will never forgive him. I will never forgive any of you for what you did to me. I'm going to kill him and I'm going to make him suffer."

Frances had a panicked look on her face. "Please, Sir, that is not what Augustine would want—"

"Jack! His name is Jack!" Gus yelled as the car tore down the street.

"I'm sorry, Sir," Frances whimpered. Tears streaked her cheeks. "Your son Jack would want you to forgive."

Gus looked at her, a scared child crying and cowering in the seat. He thought of Father Driscoll again, what he had told him, what he had taught him. What was he doing? He couldn't blame her. She came to him for help. "I'm sorry, I shouldn't have yelled at you. Tell me, why is Jack in danger? Why are they going to beat him? What about forgiveness?"

"It is not a matter of forgiving. When one sins, one must acknowledge and publicly confess his or her sin and face punishment. We know that we will be punished in order to gain God's grace. Abraham cannot spare the rod—"

"Spare the rod? You're telling me that beating the shit out of a kid gets you back in God's graces? This is what you believe?"

"This is what the Bible says. It is the word of God."

"And you believe this is how to get into heaven?"

"It's complicated."

"No, it's not. Why did you come to me then, if you believe that punishment by beating someone to death is appropriate behavior for people who profess to be pious?" He gripped the wheel hard.

"Why is Jack being punished?" he asked again. "You haven't told me what he did."

"It's what we did," she said.

"What do you mean *we*? Who's we?" Gus asked.

"Augustine and me."

"Jack—" He took a breath. "That's okay. You've only known him as Augustine. What did you do that is so awful? Is this why you have a black eye and a fat lip – you were punished? What did you do? Did you steal from this Abraham or something?"

"No," she said. Her cheeks flushed red and she looked away. Then she turned back. "I am with child," she said. She put her hand unconsciously on her belly.

"You're pregnant? You mean you're pregnant?"

"Yes." The tears flowed down her face.

"And Jack's the father?"

"Yes."

Jack's going to be a father? His Jack, his little boy, was going to be a father. His lip trembled a little and his eyes welled. This girl was only a child herself. He recovered himself. "Do you love each other?"

"We love each other very much. More than I can convey in words."

"And Abraham knows you are pregnant?"

"Yes, he found out today."

"How did he find out?"

"Jacob and Emmanuel overheard us talking about it in the woods today and they told Abraham. Moses had them follow us."

"Who are Jacob, Emmanuel, and Moses?"

"Emmanuel is the boy I am supposed to marry in October."

"Marry? But you love Jack?"

"With all my heart."

"I see now. How old are you, by the way?"

"I am sixteen."

"Sixteen and you're getting married?"

"Yes, I am required to marry Emmanuel."

"Required? Is that how you people operate? Arranged marriages?"

"Oh, Mr. Delaney, I don't love him!" Frances cried. "I love Augustine! Please help us!" Her jaw twitched and her eyes pleaded. "I don't want them to hurt him!"

Gus looked at this tiny, beautiful creature. She must have brought Jack happiness. Perhaps he wasn't as scared with her around. "How long have you known Jack?"

"Sir, I've known him since the day after he arrived."

"And he was afraid when he arrived?"

"Yes, he was afraid. I tried to provide him comfort and through the years we formed a bond that grew stronger each day until now I don't know how I'd live without him."

Gus stared blankly at the windshield. "Thank you," he said at last. She looked at him, not answering immediately.

"Thank you for what, Sir?"

"Thank you for bringing happiness to my boy and thank you for coming to get me." He smiled a crooked, pained smile at her. "Where is Jack now?" Gus asked. "Does he know he's in danger?"

"He's locked in the shed. Abraham called for everyone to gather in the barn after vespers tonight."

"What does that mean? What's in the barn?"

"That is where sins are confessed to the community and punishment is carried out. It is the location of public atonement."

"What will they do to him?" Gus asked.

"I don't know," she said. "I just fear they'll go too far this time."

"I'll kill that son of a bitch," Gus muttered. "I'll kill him."

CHAPTER 58

Atonement

They approached the gate by which Gus had seen Jack earlier that day. "You'll have to park here," Frances said.

"Where's Jack? Where's this shed?" Gus asked. Frances led him down a path through the woods. She told him they couldn't go up the driveway and risk being caught but would sneak to the shed from the back.

"So he's locked in there?" Gus asked.

"Yes, they locked him in the shed about an hour ago."

"Why aren't you locked up too? Why aren't you being punished and why don't you have to confess publicly in the barn?"

Tears trickled down Frances's cheeks. "I will be punished after Jack. They said they are going to take away my baby. Abraham called it a bastard child made with the devil, impure, and he said they cannot allow such a child to be amongst us." She wiped her cheeks.

"When I told Jack what they said he became angry and rushed to Abraham, I fear to commit some violence upon him. But Moses was with Abraham, and I heard Jack lunged at Abraham to strike him and Moses beat him and dragged him to the shed. This is why his punishment will come first and will be severe."

"Does he know you came to get me?" Gus asked.

"No, Sir," she said as they hurried along the wooded path. "I must tell you something." She hesitated.

"What? What? What do you want to tell me?"

"It's just that Aug—I'm sorry. I know him as Augustine and it is hard to remember to call him Jack."

"That's all right. What do you want to tell me?"

"Jack," she said softly, "talked about seeing you earlier today. He was confused and upset. He doesn't remember much about you...except what Abraham and Sarah told him."

"What do you mean?" Gus asked. "What did they tell him?"

"They told him what I told you in the car – that you were evil, a sinner. Aug—Jack...he has spoken vaguely about a past life and people who come into his dreams sometimes, but they are like ghosts to him. As far as he is concerned, he grew up here and has never known any different and what he knows about you is what Abraham has taught him. He has much misplaced anger towards you."

"But Sir," she continued. "I remember. I remember when he first arrived and he was so scared and he wanted to go back to his parents—" she began weeping. "And we all told him he must forget about you; to forget that life. And eventually, he did."

"It took a long time – many years – but finally you faded from his memory so completely that when you showed up and called him by his name, by Jack, he was…it was like he was in shock." Gus began walking faster, and Frances had trouble keeping up. He felt the vein throbbing in his neck.

"He told me what you said to him, how you haven't stopped looking for him for ten years and how much you've missed him. When I heard of your devotion a heaviness came over me and I was sorry that he was taken from you. No matter what you've done in your life, it was wrong to take your son."

"You didn't think that immediately?" Gus asked. "How could you ever think that stealing someone's child was not wrong?"

"I did not think it was wrong then. I thought we had saved Jack from great evil."

"Do I look evil to you?" Gus said, tears rolling down his cheeks.

"I'm so sorry."

"So why didn't Jack say anything when he saw me earlier today? Why didn't he come with me?"

"He…he didn't want to, Sir. He did not want to see you. He could not tell me why – I'm not certain he knows the reason himself. But I think he's scared. I think he is worried that by seeing you he would be rejecting God and would go to hell."

"So he was brainwashed," Gus said to himself. Frances heard him.

"It is what we believe," she said. "We live our faith and commit ourselves to God. The outside world holds many temptations and much evil, so we have always rejected that world."

"So he's locked in some dungeon, some shed and is repeatedly beaten and tortured, and you're telling me the evil is in the outside world? And you're telling me he doesn't want to leave?"

"I'm not sure he knows what he wants. He asked me to run away with him this morning at the store, to go out on our own, start our own community. Our faith is our life and we do not want to go out into a faithless world – please take no offense."

"So that's what he was asking you at the store that upset you," Gus said. "You're telling me you don't want to run away from this incomprehensible place where people torture and beat you?"

"It's all I know. I've never been outside, but the stories I've heard scare me."

"But why doesn't Jack want to come to me when they're about to beat him? I'm his father – I can help."

"I told you, he doesn't have any real memory of you, and what he learned about you has caused him to have ill thoughts."

"Tell me again. What exactly has he learned about me?"

"What he's learned about you from Abraham," she began. She took a deep breath. "What he knows about the outside world has made him…" She paused and thought. "Well, he's rejected all of that. He rejected that life soon after he arrived here. We all reject that life."

"Why did you come get me? What do you expect to happen now?"

"There…are things I can't abide anymore. There are things that trouble me – that trouble Jack and me both. I don't know what I expect to happen now, but I just want Aug—Jack to be safe." They came to a clearing. Across a mowed lawn Gus saw a large, wooden barn. To the left of the barn was a massive garden, and to the left of the garden was a huge gray house with large gables.

Down the slope of the lawn about fifty yards was the ocean. Gus inhaled the sea air. Nestled along the edge of the woods twenty feet away was a small, wooden shed. "That's where Jack is," Frances said. "That's strange. Nobody is guarding the door." Gus's heart began pounding.

"I don't know why someone isn't standing at the door guarding it," she said. "Moses and Timothy and Josiah were taking turns standing guard when I left." Her glance darted across the compound. She crept forward a few steps, looking back and forth across the lawn. "That's strange," she said again. "Where is everyone? What time is it?" Gus looked at his watch.

"Seven," he said.

"They must be getting ready for vespers. We can get Jack and leave and they won't notice until after." She glanced across the yard one more time and then turned to Gus. "We must hurry."

She sprinted toward the shed. Gus followed her. She swung the door open. "Hurry up! Get in!" she said. Gus stepped inside and she closed the door behind them.

Once inside she rushed over to the bed. Jack wasn't there. She flung the crumpled sheets and blankets to the floor. "Where is he?" she cried. "No! No!

Why isn't he here? He's supposed to be here!" She sat on the bed, buried her face in her hands and began weeping.

"What's wrong?" Gus asked. "Where is he?"

"I don't know. Maybe he is in his room."

"Where's his room?"

"In the basement of the main house." She wiped her face and stood. "Come on," she said and she opened the door. She peeked out, looked left to right, and then swung the door open and ran back to the woods near the path. She pulled Gus down behind some bushes 20 feet within the woods. "Wait for me here." She ran toward the house.

"Wait! Where are you going?" Gus yelled, but she didn't answer. He crouched behind the shrubs for ten minutes. There was no sign of Frances. "Dammit!" he said through his teeth. "Where is she?" He walked out from behind the bush to the edge of the woods. He stood behind a tree and looked out toward the house. He watched for a few minutes. Then the back door of the house opened. It was Frances!

A man led her out. She looked nervously in Gus's direction as the man pushed her forward. They walked past the garden and disappeared into the barn.

"Shit," Gus muttered. "What the hell is going on?" He remembered that Frances said punishments were carried out in the barn. He sprinted down to the ocean and jumped below the sea wall. He ran across to the other side of the lawn, climbed back up the wall, and scampered to the edge of the woods until he came to the side of the barn. He heard a lone voice, loud, angry.

He crept along the side of the barn to the entrance and peeked inside. He jerked his head back. There were about 40 people standing in a circle and a bunch were facing the entrance and could easily see him if he poked his head out. He hoped no one had seen him in that instant.

He looked up and along the side of the barn for a window or something where he might be able to see them all without being seen. There was none. He got as close to the entrance as he could without revealing himself and listened.

"Now brethren," the voice boomed, deep and tinged with the same ancient accent as the others. "Augustine has brought shame upon our community again. Past punishments for past sins have not taught young Augustine much it seems. He continues to defy God and put the fate of his brothers and sisters in peril."

Gus peeked into the barn entrance as discreetly as possible. He saw the group standing in a circle. A young teen-aged boy stood in the center, naked, his hands over his groin. It was Jack. Then he saw the man speaking. He stood within the circle as well, gesticulating as he spoke.

"As many of you have no doubt heard," the man continued, "Augustine fornicated with Frances and now a bastard child grows within her belly." The man gestured toward Frances. "Please step forward Frances." She took two steps forward and Gus saw her flash a scared look to Jack.

"These two sinners have committed sins punishable by death in the Bible. They have spat in the face of God and rejected every teaching of the Good Book. They would have been stoned to death in Biblical times, and rightly so."

"Who the hell does this guy think he is?" Gus muttered. He wondered why Jack was naked and what purpose this public humiliation served. They were barbarians, not Christians.

"He that spareth his rod hatesth his son: but he that loveth him chasteneth him betimes!" the man bellowed. Then he raised a switch in the air – Gus had not seen it in his hand – and brought it down with a loud snap against Jack's back.

"Get to your knees and beg for forgiveness!" the man yelled. He raised the switch and was about to bring it down again when a voice pierced the air.

"Don't you lay a hand on that boy again you piece of shit!" Gus yelled as he sprinted toward him. He didn't care if Jack wanted him to help or not; he didn't care if he didn't want him in his life or if he had been brainwashed to hate him. He was not going to let this man who had ruined his life harm his son anymore. He was not going to let this cult get away with what they did to him. No way.

He covered the distance from the entrance of the barn, past the circle, in a few seconds, barreling toward Abraham like an enraged animal. In a split-second Abraham turned to face him, whip held in striking position. The whip came down across Gus's neck just as he smashed into Abraham, knocking him ten feet and slamming him to the ground.

Gus began punching him in the face. He broke his nose and blood poured out. "Are you the son of a bitch who stole my child and ruined my life?" he yelled between punches. "Are you?"

Abraham screamed. "Get him off me! Get him off me! Moses! Josiah!"

Gus flailed away, yelling: "Is this what you call Christian living – beating children? You ruined my life you barbarian!" Suddenly hands grabbed his shoulders and pulled him off. Gus broke free and kicked Abraham in his ribs.

"Get him off me!" Abraham shrieked again. "Hold him!"

Two men ripped him off of Abraham again. Gus struggled to break free – and did, using one of the techniques Officer Daly taught him. He flailed like a wounded beast knocking the two men down until a third man came and hit him so hard in the gut he fell face forward on the ground and thought he was going to throw up.

"Punish him!" Abraham bellowed. Moses and Josiah stood still. "I said PUNISH HIM!" Moses stepped forward and started kicking him – in the head and in his stomach and back. Josiah stood frozen for a few seconds and then slowly backed away. Gus struggled to get to his feet but Moses's continuous kicks and punches kept him on the ground. He tasted blood in his mouth. It was a too-familiar taste. *So much for my self-defense classes*, he thought.

Abraham stood holding a handkerchief to his nose. It turned from white to blood-red. "So brothers and sisters, here today you can be witness to the evil of the outside world. Do you know who this sinner is?" Gus, crawling in the dirt, lurched at him and grabbed his ankles. Abraham stumbled but did not fall.

Moses pulled him away again and dragged him in the dust, then pulled him up and held him. "This is Satan's spawn, the man we saved Augustine from many years past." Everyone stood as they were in the circle, frozen, including Jack and Frances.

"This man, destined for the fiery pits of hell, has committed every sin you can imagine. Adultery, profanity, avarice, blasphemy. We took Augustine within our family and gave him the wondrous gift of God's grace and hope for salvation. Yet, as you have seen, he was infected with the strain of sin for which nothing can be done. Now he has brought that disease to all of us." Everyone continued to stand motionless as Abraham spoke.

"Now Augustine, whom I forbid to leave our Eden, whom I demanded never show his face in Van Winkle or our store, baldly disobeyed my decree and went to the store. Now you see why I did not allow him to go. For by doing so he hath brought evil back with him as I had feared and prophesied would happen."

Abraham walked closer to Gus, who struggled to break free from Moses. "I make rules and demand obedience for a reason. Always with a good reason," he said. "When you don't follow my commands – commands sent to me from God, as he reveals Himself to me – unspeakably tragic events result. Now, what must we do with this heathen who has come here uninvited and brought his infection to our people?" He picked up the whip lying on the ground.

Frances ran to Jack's side and helped him to his feet. He looked at her with a look he had never given her before. "Why?" he asked. "Why did you bring him here? Now this is going to be much worse than it would have been. I told you I did not want to see him and that I did not want his help."

Frances placed her hand in his. "Would it be worse? Would it be worse if you were beaten to death Augustine? We needed help. He was the only person I could think of that could help us. Something has gone terribly wrong with this community in which we live. Why does no one act to stop him? Why do they all stand paralyzed? Why do you do nothing to save your father?"

Jack didn't reply and only stared blankly in front of him as if in a trance. He glanced at Abraham pacing like a panther in a circle while he spoke, whip firmly in his right hand. "Take off this man's shirt," he commanded. Moses did as he said.

Abraham then walked up to Frances and Jack. "What must we do Master Augustine?" Jack didn't answer. "I can't hear you!" he said and he brought the whip down across his bare back. Jack cried out.

"We must ask for forgiveness," Jack said.

"No. He is beyond forgiveness." Abraham walked back to Gus. "We must punish those who sin and don't repent. This man who has corrupted young Augustine, a corruption of the soul that it is clear cannot be cured, must be punished according to the laws of God. *Woe unto the world because of offenses! For it must needs be that offenses come; but woe to that man by whom the offense cometh!*"

Jack knew this must mean death. Nobody had ever been put to death, though a few had been beaten near death. He still stood frozen, like all the others. Frances wept quietly beside him. "Augustine, you must do something," she said. Abraham lashed the whip across Gus's back. He winced in pain and moaned.

"What can I do?" Jack asked. But as he watched the whip crash again and again against his father's back, his contempt for the man subsided. He looked at him. His face was bashed in by Moses's boot. His eyes were nearly swollen shut. He stood there, held up by Moses, nearly unresponsive, while Abraham whipped him.

Jack's disdain directed at this broken-down man changed in the same manner it had changed ten years ago when as a child he wished Timothy would suffer for pulling him out of the tree and burning his feet in the fire. Then he had watched Timothy lashed with the whip in nearly the same way and felt sorry for ever wishing him harm.

A similar guilt washed over him now. Each crack of the whip and groan from this man, his father, elicited a sorrow and a sympathy he hadn't felt before;

sympathy for a man – whom he once called father – who had committed such acts that he would be banished from God's kingdom forever. Each crack of the whip, though, transferred gradually, viscerally, Jack's anger from the man he once called father to the man he currently knew as master.

Jack felt Frances's grip tighten around his hand. Every crack of the whip against the man's back caused her to jump and squeeze his hand harder. "Augustine, we must beg him to stop this…this is not God's way. This is wrong to me—"

She broke free from Jack's grip and rushed forward and stood between Abraham and Gus. "Stop this! I beg you! Please!" she cried.

"What do you know about God's way, when thou would sooner be a whore than gain God's kingdom!" Abraham said as he struck her face with the back of his hand. She fell to the ground and whimpered in the dust. Jack woke from his trance as if someone had struck him with a white-hot poker.

He seized a pitchfork leaning against a bale of hay behind him. Then he flew toward Abraham, pitchfork leading the way like a jousting rod. He slammed it into Abraham's chest, knocking him to the ground. "Don't you ever touch her again," he said. He stood over Abraham, glowering, fork impaled in Abraham's chest, pinning him on the ground.

"You have sealed your fate, *Jack*, and will never see the face of God," Abraham wheezed.

"Don't talk to me about God," Jack said. Moses rushed toward him. He held the whip in his hand and began to raise it in the air to bring it down on Jack's back. Jack jumped forward, yanked the whip out of Moses' hands, wrapped it around his neck, and pulled as hard as he could. Moses' face began to turn red and his hands reached desperately to try to pull the whip off his neck. "You'll never hurt me or my father again!" Jack cried.

Suddenly a gunshot echoed in the barn. "Freeze!" a voice yelled. Everyone stopped. Two cops stood at the entrance. Gus's sister Lauren stood with them. Gus lifted his head slightly from the dirt and tried to see what had happened. Lauren shouted to him.

"Gus! Oh my God, are you all right?" Gus couldn't speak. "That's her," Lauren said to the cops. She pointed to Frances.

"And who is the boy," one of them asked. Frances, and then the others, looked at Jack, who stood in the center of the barn, crying, holding the whip around Moses' neck. "Is this boy Jack Delaney?" the cop asked Frances. She nodded yes.

While the one cop handcuffed Abraham and Moses, the first cop walked over to Gus, who was still on the ground, woozy. "Well Mr. Delaney, you really did it this time. I thought you learned your lesson." Gus gazed up at him. "Don't you remember me?"

Gus tried to remember him. He looked familiar, but he couldn't place him. "It's Officer Batchelder. Remember? I was your friend in Kmart many years ago when that woman wanted to press charges. Looks like you got the right kid this time." Gus gazed in a semi-stupor, but he remembered him now.

"Here, let me help you up," Batchelder said and he extended his hand. He pulled Gus off the ground.

"But how did you…how did you find me?" Gus asked.

Batchelder looked at Lauren, who had walked over with him. "Your sister called the station. I transferred here to Van Winkle a few years ago. Never thought our paths would cross again."

"I'm sorry Gus. I overheard your conversation with the girl and I called the police," Lauren said. "I was worried." By this time Frances and Jack had walked over. Batchelder turned to Jack.

"You're a lucky kid. Your father never gave up. He never stopped looking and he never stopped believing that he would find you. He went through hell, but it looks like he finally found you."

Jack looked at Gus, bloodied and bruised, exhausted. He rushed to him and dropped to his knees and held his legs. Each of their bodies shook from sobbing as father and son embraced each other. Gus gazed into Jack's eyes. "You don't know how long I've wished and prayed for this moment. Every hour of every day for the past ten years. I'm so sorry I let you down son." He could hardly see Jack's face through his tears and swollen eyes.

"I'm sorry too," Jack wailed. He couldn't stop crying.

After some time they remembered that there were other people in the barn. Jack looked for Frances. She was standing with Lauren and Batchelder, crying as hard as Gus and Jack. Jack gestured for her to come to him. She rushed over and joined their embrace and cried with them.

"Come with me," Gus said to Jack. "You have a home…and Frances and your baby, when it comes, have a home. There is still good in the world outside. I know that now. We can begin a new life together – all of us. Teach me your faith and I'll introduce you to a real man of God, a good man. What do you say, Jack?"

Jack looked at Frances. "Will you come with me?" he asked. She nodded and took his hand in hers.

"Yes."

"Let's go home then," Gus said. They limped, arm in arm, out of the barn, past the gabled house, down the long driveway, and out the gate.

Finis

CPSIA information can be obtained at www.ICGtesting.com
Printed in the USA
LVOW11s0125271115

464317LV00002B/425/P